RAYMOND E. FEIST

TALON OF
THE SILVER HAWK

Conclave of Shadows
Book One

HarperCollins*Publishers*

Voyager
An Imprint of HarperCollins*Publishers*
77–85 Fulham Palace Road,
Hammersmith, London W6 8JB

www.voyager-books.com

Published by *Voyager* 2003

A catalogue record for this book
is available from the British Library

ISBN 978-0-00-779640-3

Set in Janson Text by
Palimpsest Book Production Limited,
Polmont, Stirlingshire

Printed and bound in Great Britain by
Clays Limited, St Ives plc

ACKNOWLEDGEMENTS

For many years I've started out my acknowledgement with the Mothers and Fathers of Midkemia, and this one is no different. Each time I get to play in the world you built, I'm blessed.

Again to all of those who have helped me survive a major change in my life over the last two years by making it better for their company, Andy, Rich, Ray and Kim, Jim and Karen, Rick and Audrey, Jim and Jenny, Mira, Leyla, Roseanna, and Rebecca, all of you, thank you. Your friendship has kept me sane, made my life richer, and returned fun to the equation.

I'd like to thank my collaborators, Janny Wurts, William R. Forstchen, Joel Rosenberg, and S. M. Stirling, for playing so nicely in my sandbox and leaving it in far better shape than they found it. It's been a learning experience every time, and I'm a better writer for having you teach me.

And a special thanks to my two editors, Jane and Jennifer, who for reasons well known, had to watch me burn the candle at both ends to get this one done and who kept me upright and moving forward.

For Jamie Ann
For teaching me things I didn't know I needed to learn

Contents

PART ONE

Orphan

'Death stands above me, whispering low
I know not what into in my ear . . .'

Walter Savage Landor

CHAPTER ONE

Passage

*H*E WAITED.

Shivering, the boy huddled close to the dying embers of his meagre fire, his pale blue eyes sunken and dark from lack of sleep. His mouth moved slowly as he repeated the chant he had learned from his father, his dry lips cracking painfully and his throat sore from intoning the holy words. His nearly black hair was matted with dust from sleeping in the dirt; despite his resolve to remain alert while awaiting his vision, exhaustion had overcome him on three occasions. His normally slender frame and high cheekbones were accentuated by his rapid weight loss, rendering him gaunt and pale. He wore only a vision seeker's loin cloth. After the first night he had sorely missed his leather tunic and trousers, his sturdy boots and his dark green cloak.

Above, the night sky surrendered to a pre-dawn grey and the

stars began to fade from view. The very air seemed to pause, as if waiting for a first intake of breath, the first stirring of a new day. The stillness was uncommon, both unnerving and fascinating, and the boy held his breath for a moment in concert with the world around him. Then a tiny gust, the softest breath of night sighing, touched him, and he let his own breathing resume.

As the sky to the east lightened, he reached over and picked up a gourd. He sipped at the water within, savouring it as much as possible, for it was all he was permitted until he experienced his vision and reached the creek which intersected with the trail a mile below as he made his way home.

For two days he had sat below the peak of Shatana Higo, in the place of manhood, waiting for his vision. Prior to that he had fasted, drinking only herb teas and water; then he had eaten the traditional meal of the warrior, dried meat, hard bread and water with bitter herbs, before spending half a day climbing the dusty path up the eastern face of the holy mountain to the tiny depression a dozen yards below the summit. The clearing would scarcely accommodate half a dozen men, but it seemed vast and empty to the boy as he entered the third day of the ceremony. A childhood spent in a large house with many relatives had ill prepared him for such isolation, for this was the first time in his existence he had been without companionship for more than a few hours.

As was customary among the Orosini, the boy had started the manhood ritual on the third day before the Midsummer celebration, which the lowlanders call Banapis. The boy would greet the new year, the end of his life as a child, in contemplating the lore of his family and clan, his tribe and nation, and

seeking the wisdom of his ancestors. It was a time of deep introspection and meditation, as the boy sought to understand his
place in the order of the universe, the role laid before him by
the gods. And on this day he was expected to gain his manhood
name. If events went as they should, he would rejoin his family
and clan in time for the evening Midsummer festival.

As a child he had been called Kieli, a diminution of
Kielianapuna, the red squirrel, the clever and nimble dweller in
the forests of home. Never seen, but always present, they were
considered lucky when glimpsed by the Orosini. And Kieli was
considered to be a lucky child.

The boy shivered almost uncontrollably, for his paltry stores
of body-fat hardly insulated him from the night's chill. Even in
the middle of the summer, the peaks of the mountains of the
Orosini were cold after the sun fled.

Kieli waited for the vision. He saw the sky lighten, a slow,
progressive shift from grey to pale grey-blue, then to a rose hue
as the sun approached. He saw the brilliance of the sun crest
the distant mountain, a whitish-golden orb that brought him
another day of loneliness. He averted his eyes when the disc of
the sun cleared the mountains, lest his sight flee from him. The
trembling in his body lessened as the sun finally rose sufficiently
to begin to relieve the chill. He waited, at first expectantly, then
with a deep fatigue-generated hopelessness.

Each Orosini boy endured this ritual upon the midsummer
day close to the time of his birth anniversary in one of the many
such holy places scattered throughout the region. For years
beyond numbering boys had climbed to these vantage points,
and men had returned.

He experienced a brief moment of envy, as he recalled that

the girls of his age in the village would be in the round house with the women at the moment, chatting and eating, singing and praying. Somehow the girls found their women's names without the privation and hardship endured by the boys. Kieli let the moment pass: dwelling on what you can't control was futile, as his grandfather would say.

He thought of his grandfather, Laughter In His Eyes, who had been the last to speak to him as he climbed the lonely trail from the valley where his people dwelt. The old man had smiled as he always had – he could hardly remember a time when he hadn't seen a smile on the old man's face. Grandfather's face was like brown leather from nearly eighty years of living in the mountains, his clan tattoos upon his left cheek still black despite years in the sun. The old man's keen eyes and strong features were always framed by steel grey hair down to his shoulders. Kieli resembled his grandfather more than his father, for they both shared the olive skin which turned nut-brown in the summer and never burned, and in his youth Grandfather also had hair the colour of a raven's wing. Others remarked that an outlander must have joined their family generations ago, for the Orosini were a fair race, and even brown hair was unusual.

Kieli's grandfather had whispered, 'When the gourd is empty, on Midsummer's day, remember this: if the gods haven't already provided you with a name, that means you're allowed to choose one you like.' And then the old chieftain had smothered him in a playful, but still-strong, hug that sent him stumbling along the path. The other men in the village of Kulaam looked on, smiling or laughing, for the festival would soon be upon them and the time of the naming vision was a joyous time.

Kieli remembered his grandfather's words and wondered if

any boy actually had his name bestowed upon him by the gods. Examining the gourd, he judged he would be out of water by midday. He knew he would find water at a brook halfway down the path to the village, but he also knew that meant he had to leave the ledge when the sun was at its zenith.

He sat silently for a while, thoughts of his village dancing through his mind like the splashing foam of the brook behind the long hall. Perhaps if he set his mind free, he thought, if he didn't try too hard to find his vision, it would come to him. He wanted to return soon, for he missed his family. His father, Elk's Call At Dawn, was everything the boy hoped to be, strong, friendly, kind, resolute, fearless in battle, and gentle with his children. He missed his mother, Whisper Of The Night Wind, and his younger sister, Miliana, and most of all, he missed his older brother, Hand Of The Sun, who had returned from his own vision but two years earlier, his skin burned red by the sun, except for a pale print of his own hand where it had rested all day upon his chest. Their grandfather had joked that Hand was not the first boy to have come to his vision while asleep. Hand had always been kind to his younger brother and sister, taking care to watch over them when their mother was out gleaning the field, or showing them the best places to find ripening berries. Memories of those berries, crushed with honey and served on hot bread made his mouth water.

The celebration would be joyous, and the thought of the food that waited below gave Kieli cramps of hunger. He would be permitted to sit in the long house with the men, rather than in the round house with his mother and the other women and children. He felt a pang of loss at that thought, for the singing of the women as they oversaw the domestic chores of the day, their laughter and chatter, the gossip and the jokes, had been a part of his daily life for as long as he could remember. But he also looked forward with pride to being allowed to sit with the men of the clan.

His body shivered uncontrollably for a moment, then he sighed and relaxed as the sun warmed him further. He let his stiff muscles loosen, then moved to his knees and attended to the fire. He placed a few fresh twigs upon the glowing coals, then blew upon them, and in a few minutes it was done. He would let the flames die down after the mountain air warmed up, but for now he was thankful for the nearby heat.

He sat back against the rocks, which were warming with the sunlight despite the lingering chill in the air, and took another drink. Letting out a long sigh, he glanced at the sky. Why no vision? he wondered. Why had he received no message from the gods granting him his man's name?

His name would be the key to his *na'ha'tah*, the secret nature of his being, that thing which only he and the gods would know. Other people would know his name, for he would proclaim it with pride, but no one would know the nature of his vision and what his name said to him, about his place in the universe, mission from the gods, or his destiny. His grandfather had once told him that few men truly understood their *na'ha'tah*, even if they thought they did. The vision was only the first hint from the gods as to their plans for a man. Sometimes, his grandfather had said, the plan was a simple one, to be a good husband and father, a provider for the well-being of the village and the nation, an example for others to emulate, for it might be that his role was to be a father to someone chosen, a special one, a *na'rif*, and that plan would unfold long after a man's death.

Kieli knew what his grandfather would say at this moment, that he worried too much, and that he should simply put aside worry and let the gods bring to him their will. Kieli knew his father would say the same, adding that to hunt or give counsel in the long house, or to be a good husband, first one must learn to be patient and to listen.

He closed his eyes and listened to the sounds of the breeze in the mountains. It spoke to him as leaves rustled in the cedars and pines. At times the wind could be a cruel companion, cutting through the heaviest of furs with a bitter, freezing edge. At other times it was blessed relief, cooling the hottest days of summer. His father had taught him of its voices and taught him that to learn the language of the wind was to be one with it, as were the hawks and eagles who built their nests among the craggy peaks. A screech split the morning air and Kieli's head turned with a snap as a silver hawk struck at a rabbit less than a dozen yards from where he rested. The rarest of the hawks of the high mountains, its feathers were actually grey, with a mottling of near black around the head and shoulders, but an oily sheen upon the wings caused the bird to glisten with silver highlights when it sped through the clear sky. With a single beat of its wings, the hawk gripped the struggling rabbit tightly and launched itself into the air. Like a kitten carried by its mother, the rabbit hung limply from the bird's talons, as if resigned to its fate. Kieli knew the animal had gone into shock – nature's kindness as pain and thought were dulled. He had once seen a stag lying motionless on the ground, awaiting the hunter's final mercy with a knife, felled by an arrow that hadn't killed it.

In the distance he saw other birds wheeling lazily in the morning air, catching thermals off the rapidly heating rocks so that they could glide in search of a meal. Turkey buzzards, he knew. Their large wingspan allowed them to drift on the rising hot air while they scanned below for the dead and dying. Ungainly and ugly on the ground as they hopped to the carcass of a fallen animal, on the wing they were majestic.

To the south he saw a black-tailed kite balanced in mid-air, tail pointed downward while its wings beat quickly for two or three strokes, then halted to allow it to fall slightly, then beat again, to hold the kite in place above its intended kill. Then with stunning swiftness, it stooped, talons extended downward, and with precision bordering on the supernatural, struck the ground in a tight arc, lifting off without even a moment's hesitation, a squealing vole clutched in its claws.

From the distance, forest sounds reached him. The rhythms of the day and night were different, and now the diurnal residents of the forests below were making their presence felt as their nocturnal neighbours sought out shelters in which to sleep. A woodpecker industriously sought out insects in the bark of a nearby tree. From the pattern of the sound, Kieli knew it was the large red-topped who was digging out his meal; his tapping was slow, thunderous and persistent, unlike the more dainty staccato of his smaller, blue-winged cousin.

The sun rose higher in the morning sky and soon the fire died, unneeded as the heat of day returned to the rocks. Kieli resisted the temptation to finish drinking the last of his water, for he knew that he must harbour it until he was ready to descend the trail. He could drink his fill at the creek below, but he had to get there first, and should he waste his water now, there was no guarantee he would safely reach the creek.

It was rare that a boy perished upon the peaks, but it had

happened. The tribe prepared each boy as fully as possible, but those who had failed to survive the naming ordeal were considered to have been judged by the gods as lacking and their families' mourning was a bitter counterpoint to the celebration of Midsummer.

The heat increased and the air dried, and suddenly Kieli realized a *sa'tata* was upon them. The wind from the north blew cold year round, but the summer western wind would grow hotter and dryer by the minute. The boy had seen grass turn brown and brittle in less than three days and fruit dry upon the branch from this wind. Men grew restless and women irritable when the *sa'tata* lingered more than a few days, and the skin itched. Kieli and his brother had swam in lakes and rivers on such days, only to be dry by the time they had returned to the village, as if they had not felt the cooling touch of water at all.

Kieli also knew he was now in danger, for the *sa'tata* would suck the moisture from his body if he remained. He glanced at the sky and realized he had only two more hours before midday. He glanced at the sun, now more than half-way along its climb to the mid-heaven, and he blinked as tears gathered in his eyes.

Kieli let his mind wander a few moments, as he wondered who would be chosen to sit at his side. For while Kieli lingered on the mountain, waiting for his vision from the gods, his father would be meeting with the father of one of the young girls of the local villages. There were three possible mates for Kieli from his own village: Rapanuana, Smoke In The Forest's daughter; Janatua, Many Broken Spears' daughter, and Eye of the Blue-Winged Teal, daughter of Sings To The Wind.

Eye of the Blue-Winged Teal was a year older, and had gained her woman's name the year before, but there had been no boy of the right age in the local villages to pledge her to. This year there were six, including Kieli. She possessed a strange sense of humour that made Kieli wonder what she found funny most of the time. She often seemed amused by him and he felt awkward when she was near. Though he hid it well, he was more than a little scared of her. But Rapanuana was fat and ill-tempered, and Janatua was pinched-faced and shy to the point of being speechless around boys. Eye of the Blue-Winged Teal had a strong, tall body, and fierce, honey-coloured eyes that narrowed when she laughed. Her skin was lighter than the other girls' and scattered with freckles, and her heart-shaped face was surrounded by a mane of hair the colour of summer's wheat. He prayed to the gods that his father had met with her father the night before Midsummer, and not with one of the other girls' fathers. Then with a surge of panic, he realized his father might have met with the father of one of the girls from close-by villages, the slow-witted Pialua or the pretty but always complaining Nandia!

He sighed. It was out of his hands. Stories were told of men and women who longed for one another, sagas told by the story-tellers around the fire, many of them borrowed from singers from the lowlands as they passed through the mountains of the Orosini. Yet it was his people's way that a father would choose a bride for his son, or a husband for his daughter. Occasionally a boy – no, he corrected himself, a man – would return from his god's vision and discover that no bride waited to sit next to him at his manhood festival and he would have to wait another year for a bride. Rarely, a man would discover that no father wished his daughter wed to him and he would have to depart the village to find himself a wife, or resign himself to live alone.

He had heard of a widow once whose father had died before her husband and she had taken one such man to her hut, but no one considered that a proper marriage.

He sighed again. He longed for this to be over. He wanted food and to rest in his own bed, and he wanted Eye of the Blue-Winged Teal, even though she made him uncomfortable.

Upwind he caught a sound he knew to be a sow bear with cubs. She sounded alarmed and Kieli knew her cubs would be scampering up a tree at her warning. Kieli sat up. What would alarm a black bear this close to the mountain? A big cat might, if a leopard or cougar were ranging nearby. They were too high up for the big cave lions. Maybe a wyvern was hunting, he thought, feeling suddenly small and vulnerable out on the face of the rocks.

A small cousin to a dragon, a wyvern could hold off half a dozen or more skilled warriors, so a boy with only a ceremonial dagger and a gourd of water would make a very satisfying break of fast for such a beast.

Hunting packs might frighten the sow bear; wild dogs and wolves usually avoided bears, but a cub was a manageable meal if they could draw the sow away from one of her babies.

Or it could be men.

In the distance the circle of buzzards grew and the boy got to his feet to gain a better view and was suddenly gripped with a light-headedness, for he had stood up too quickly. Steadying himself with one hand upon the rocks, he gazed into the distance. The sun was now high enough that the haze of morning had burned off and he could clearly see the buzzards and kites wheeling in the distance. Kieli's sight was legendary in his village, for few could see as far as he, and none in the memory of his clan could see better. His grandfather joked that whatever else he lacked, he had a hawk's eyes.

For a long moment Kieli's eyes saw without him comprehending, then suddenly he realized the birds were circling over Kapoma village! Alarm shot up through him like a spark and without hesitation he started down the trail. Kapoma was the village nearest to his own.

There was only one possible explanation for so many carrion-eaters above Kapoma: a battle. He felt the panic rise up in him. Moreover, no one was clearing away the dead. If marauders were ranging through the valleys, Kulaam would be the next village they raided!

His mind reeled at the thought of his family fighting without him. Twice as a boy he had stayed in the round house with the women while the men had defended their village from attack. Once it had been a clan fight with the men from the village of Kahanama, and another time a goblin raiding-party had sought children for their unholy sacrifices, but the stout stockade had proven sufficient to repulse the invaders. Who could it be, he wondered as he stumbled down the path toward the trees below.

The moredhel – those the lowlanders called the Brotherhood of the Dark Path – had not been seen in these regions since his grandfather's boyhood, and the trolls usually gave the villages of the Orosini a wide berth. There were no clan feuds currently being fought. The people who lived in the High Reaches to the north-east were currently peaceful and Latagore and the Duchy of Farinda to the south had no issues with the Orosini.

Raiders, then. Slavers from the City of Inaska or Watcher's Point down in Miskalon would sometimes venture into the mountains. The tall, strong, red and blond-haired Orosini fetched high value on the slavers' blocks down in the Empire of Great Kesh. Fear overtook Kieli: he felt it start to freeze his mind.

He drank what little water and herbs he had left, secured the gourd around his waist with a cord, then took half a dozen wobbly steps down the trail and lost his footing. Attempting to catch himself with his outstretched right hand, the youth fell and twisted, falling hard into a large rock. Pain shot through him and his head swam as he realized he had injured his left arm. It didn't feel broken, but there was already a massive red mark running from his shoulder down to the elbow which would turn to a deep bruise. It hurt when he moved it. He tried to stand and his stomach heaved from the pain, and he sat down and vomited.

Kieli's vision swam and the landscape turned a vivid yellow, and he fell back upon the road. The sky above turned brilliant white and the heat seared his face as he gazed upwards, his eyes gradually losing focus. The ground beneath him spun until everything was swept away as he fell through a tunnel into darkness.

Pain woke him. He opened his eyes as it seared through his left arm. His field of vision narrowed, contracting and expanding for a moment as dizziness washed through him. Then he saw it.

On his arm, flexing slightly, rested what looked like a spread talon. Kieli didn't move his head, just shifted his eyes. Barely inches from his nose stood a silver hawk, one leg bent as it rested its talon upon his arm, its claws digging into the skin but not piercing it. Almost as if seeking to awake the stunned youth, the hawk flexed its claws again, dug deeper.

Kieli found himself looking into the bird's black eyes. The bird's claws tightened again and pain shot through his arm again. Kieli's eyes locked on the birds, and then the words came. *Rise, little brother. Rise and be a talon for your people. As you feel my talon upon your arm, remember you can hold and protect, or you can rend and revenge.* Kieli heard the words in his mind. Suddenly he pushed himself upright and stood bearing the hawk on his arm. The bird's wings flared as it kept its balance.

Pain was forgotten for a moment as Kieli stood facing the bird. The hawk stared back; then bobbed its head, as if nodding agreement. Their eyes locked once more and then with a screech the bird leapt upwards, a single snap of its wings taking it right past the young man's ear. Kieli felt another slight pain and reached up to touch his right shoulder. His eyes saw upon his arm the pinprick marks of the bird's claws.

Was this my vision? he wondered silently. No hawk had ever behaved so in the history of his people. Then, with a dull shock, he remembered his reason for hurrying down the mountain.

The heat of the day still baked the rocks around him. He felt weak and his left arm throbbed, but his mind was clear and he knew he would reach the creek. He picked his way carefully among the rocks, seeking good footing lest he fall again and suffer further injury. If there was a fight coming to his people, injured arm or not, he was now a man and would stand with his father, uncles and grandfather to defend his home.

Kieli stumbled down the dusty trail, his left arm sending jolts of agony up into his shoulder with every movement. He summoned up a chant, a mind-numbing exercise that would reduce the pain, and softly intoned it in rhythm. Soon he felt less pain, though the chant didn't work as well as his grandfather had told him it would; his arm still hurt, but at least wasn't making him dizzy from pain.

He reached the creek and fell forwards into it, his arm suddenly exploding in hot agony at that foolish choice. He gasped and was rewarded with a choking mouthful of water. Then he rolled over on his back and spat out water, clearing his nose as he sat up, coughing for a moment. At last he rolled over onto his knees and drank. He filled his gourd quickly, tied it again around his waist then resumed his journey.

He was starving, but the water had settled down his thinking. It was a two-hour walk to his village. If he ran at a steady pace, he would be there in a third of that time. But with his injured arm and in his weakened condition, he couldn't sustain any sort of steady run. Below the creek he entered the heavy woodlands where he felt the day's heat lessen and then settled for a fast walk, jogging over open stretches of trail, moving as quietly as he could, his mind focused on the coming struggle.

As he neared his village, Kieli heard the sounds of fighting. He smelled smoke. A woman's scream pierced his heart as sharply as if a blade had struck. Could that be his own mother? No matter, he knew that whoever it was, it was a woman he had known all his life.

He took the ceremonial dagger and held it tightly in his right hand. How he wished he had two good arms and a sword or spear. In the heat of the day he had not felt the need for his usual clothing, though he had missed his cloak and tunic at night, but now he felt particularly vulnerable. Even so, he hurried along, the anticipation of the combat to come dulling the pain in his arm and forcing his fatigue aside.

Choking clouds of smoke accompanied by the sound of flames warned him of the devastation that greeted him a moment later. He reached the point in the trail where it left the woodlands and passed between the village's large vegetable gardens before reaching the stockade. The gate was open, as it was during peaceful times. No enemy had ever attacked on Midsummer's Day, which was a day of almost universal truce, even during time of war. The condition of the wooden walls and the surrounding earthen foundations below told the boy that the enemy had rushed through the gate before the alarm had sounded. Most of the villagers would have been in the central square, preparing the feast.

Everywhere was flame and smoke. He could see figures in the smoke, many on horse, and the outlines of bodies on the ground. Kieli paused. To run down the trail would make him a target. Better to circle along the line of the wood until reaching the point closest to the village, behind Many Fine Horses' home.

As he moved to his right, he found the smoke blowing away from him. Now he could see the carnage in the village. Many of his friends lay motionless upon the ground. It was hard to make sense of the tableau before him.

Men on horseback, wearing various styles of clothing and armour rode through the village, several who were bearing torches firing the houses. Mercenaries or slavers, Kieli knew. Then he saw footmen wearing the tabard of the Duke of Olasko, ruler of the powerful duchy to the south-east. But why would they be aiding raiders in the mountains of the Orosini?

Reaching the back of Many Fine Horses' home, Kieli crept along. He saw an Olaskan soldier lying motionless just beyond the edge of the building. Casting aside his dagger, Kieli decided to make a run for the man's sword. If no one noticed, he would attempt to remove the round shield on the man's left arm as well. It would hurt to carry the shield on his injured arm, but it could also mean the difference between life and death.

The sound of fighting was coming from the other side of the village, so he thought it possible he might be able to fall upon the invaders from behind. Creeping forwards, he retrieved the shield and sword and paused for a moment.

In the smoke, he could faintly discern figures moving in the distance, cries of outrage and pain drifted towards him, as his people struggled to repel the invaders.

His eyes smarted from the acrid smoke and he blinked back tears as he reached the fallen soldier. He turned over the body to retrieve the sword and as his hand fell upon the hilt, the soldier's eyes snapped open. Kieli froze, and as he yanked back the sword the soldier lashed out with his shield, bashing him in the face.

Kieli fell back, his vision swimming and the world seemingly tilting under his feet. Only his natural quickness saved him, for just as the soldier was on his feet, dagger drawn and slashed at him, Kieli dodged.

For a second he thought he had avoided the blade, then pain erupted across his chest and he felt blood flowing. It was a shallow wound, but a long one, running from just under his left collarbone down to his right nipple and there to the bottom of his ribs.

Kieli slashed with his own blade and felt shock run up his

arm as the soldier deftly took the blow on his shield.

Another attack and the boy knew that he was overmatched, for he only narrowly avoided death from a dagger-slash to the stomach. Had the soldier attacked with his sword instead of with a short blade, Kieli knew he'd be lying gutted upon the ground.

Fear threatened to rise up and overwhelm him then, but the thought of his family fighting for their lives only yards beyond the masking smoke forced it aside.

Seeing the boy's hesitation, the soldier grinned wickedly and closed in. Kieli knew that his only advantage was the length of his blade, so he offered his already-wounded chest as a target and clumsily raised the sword with both hands as if to bring it crashing down upon the soldier's head. As Kieli had hoped, the soldier reflexively raised his shield to take the blow and drew back his dagger for the killing thrust.

Kieli, however, dropped to his knees with a spin, bringing his sword down and around in a powerful arc which sliced through the soldier's leg, knocking him backwards screaming. Blood sprayed from the severed arteries just below his knee. Leaping to his feet, Kieli stepped upon the man's dagger-hand, and struck straight down with the sword's point into the man's throat, ending his agony.

He tried to wipe his sword-hand dry, but discovered that blood was flowing freely from the long cut on his chest and knew he'd soon be weakening if he didn't bind it, though he thought it probably looked a great deal worse than it was.

As he hurried toward the sounds of battle a gust of wind cleared his vision for a moment so that he had a clean line of sight and could see the village's central square. The tables that had been heavily laden with food and ale were overturned, the ground around them littered with the feast for the day's celebration. The flower garlands were crushed into mud made up of soil and blood. For a panic-stricken second, Kieli faltered, horror causing his gorge to rise. He blinked back tears – though whether they were caused by smoke or rage he didn't know. A short distance away lay the bodies of three children, obviously cut down from behind as they raced for shelter. Beyond them, he could see the men of his village making a stand before the round house. Kieli knew the women and surviving children would be inside, the women armed with knives and daggers to defend the children should the men fall.

Men he had known all his life were being slaughtered, despite fighting with desperation to protect their families. The soldiers had set up a shield wall and were pressing in with spears levelled, while behind them sat mounted soldiers, calmly loading and firing crossbows into the villagers.

The Orosini bowmen responded, but the battle's outcome was obvious, even to a boy like Kieli. He knew he would not survive this day but even so, he could not stand behind the invaders and not do whatever was in his power.

On wobbly legs he started forwards, his target a man upon a black horse, obviously the leader of these murderers. Next to him sat another horseman wearing a black tunic and trousers. His hair was as dark as his clothing, pulled back behind his ears and falling to his shoulders.

The man somehow sensed something was behind him, for he turned just as Kieli started to run. Kieli saw the man's face clearly; a dark beard trimmed close to his jaw-line, a long nose which gave him a harsh appearance, and pursed lips as if he had been lost in thought before he heard Kieli's charge. The rider's eyes widened slightly at the sight of the armed and bloody boy then he calmly said something to the officer, who turned. The man in black carefully lifted his arm. There was a small crossbow in his hand. He calmly took aim.

Kieli knew he had to strike before the man's finger tightened on the release. But two strides away from the horseman the boy's knees weakened. Kieli's newly acquired sword felt as if it had been fashioned of lead and stone and his arm refused to obey his command to deliver a killing blow to the invader.

The boy was one stride away when the black clad man fired the crossbow. Then his knees buckled. The bolt had taken him in the chest, high up in the muscle below his first wound.

The bolt spun him around completely and his blood splattered both men as it fountained from the wound. The sword flew backwards from fingers that could no longer grip. His knees struck the ground and he fell over backwards, his eyes losing focus as pain and shock swept over him.

Voices shouted, but the sound was muted and he could not understand what they were saying. For a brief instant, he saw something: high in the sky above him a silver hawk flew in a circle, and to Kieli it seemed to be looking directly down at him. In his mind he heard the voice once again. *Linger, little brother, for your time is not yet. Be my talon and rend our enemies.*

His last thought was of the bird.

• CHAPTER TWO •

Kendrick's

*K*IELI'S PAIN pierced the darkness.

He couldn't will his eyes open, yet he knew he was alive. He felt hands upon him and as if from a great distance heard a voice mutter, 'This one's still alive.'

Another voice said, 'Let's get him in the wagon. He's lost a lot of blood.'

Part of Kieli's mind registered he was hearing words in the traders' language, what was called the Common Tongue, not the language of the Orosini.

He felt another pair of hands upon him. As they began to move him, he groaned and lapsed back into unconsciousness.

Pain coursed though Kieli's body as he came awake. He forced his eyes open and tried to lift his head. The effort brought forth a wave of agony and his stomach churned, yet there was nothing in it for him to vomit up. The wracking pain that swept through him made him gasp aloud and moan.

His eyes couldn't focus so he could not see the owner of the gentle hands that pushed him back and said, 'Lie still, lad. Breathe slowly.'

Kieli saw shapes before him: heads in shadow, lightning in the sky above them. He blinked and tried to clear his eyes. 'Here,' said another voice from above him, and a gourd of water touched his lips.

'Drink slowly,' said the first voice. 'You've lost a lot of blood. We didn't think you'd make it.'

The first swallow of water caused the spasms to return, and he vomited up the tiny bit of water. 'Sip, then,' said the voice.

He did as he was instructed and the mouthful of water stayed down. Suddenly he was thirsty beyond memory. He tried to swallow, but the gourd was removed from his lips. He attempted to lift his hand to grasp it, but his arm would not obey his command.

'Sip, I said,' demanded the voice. The gourd was pressed against his lips again and he sipped, and the cool water trickled down his throat.

He focused his meagre strength on getting the water down and keeping it down. Then he lifted his eyes above the rim of the gourd and attempted to discern the features of his benefactor. All he could see was a vague lump of features topped by a thatch of grey. Then he fell back into darkness.

At some point they stopped for a few days. He recognized a structure around him, a barn or shed, he couldn't be sure which.

And he knew it was raining for a time, because the air was heavy with the scent of wet soil and the mustiness of mould on wood.

After that images came and fled. He was in a wagon, and for a brief time one afternoon he sensed he was in the woodlands, but not those near his home. He didn't know how he knew – some glimpse of trees that didn't match the lofty balsams, cedars and aspens of his own forest. There were oaks, and elms and trees he didn't recognize. He lapsed back into his troubled slumber.

He remembered bits of food being pressed to his mouth and how he swallowed them, his throat constricting and his chest burning. He remembered feverish dreams and awoke several times drenched in sweat, his heart pounding. He remembered calling out his father's name.

One night he dreamed he was warm, at home, in the round house with his mother and the other women. He felt awash with their love. Then he awoke on the hard ground with the smell of wet soil in his nostrils, the smoke from a recently-banked campfire cutting through the air, and two men asleep on either side of him and he fell back, wondering how he had come to this place. Then memory returned to him and he recalled the attack on his village. Tears came unbidden to his eyes and he wept as he felt all the hope and joy die in his chest.

He could not count the days he travelled. He knew there were two men caring for him, but he could not recall if they had given him their names. He knew they had asked him questions and that he had answered, but he could not recall the subject of those discussions.

Then one morning, clarity returned to him.

Kieli opened his eyes and although he was weak, he found he could understand his surroundings. He was in a large barn, with doors at either end. In a close-by stall, he could hear horses eating. He was lying upon a pallet of straw covered by a double blanket, and had two more blankets over him. The air was hazy with smoke from a small camp stove, a rectangle of beaten iron sheeting within which coals were allowed to burn. Safer in a barn full of hay than an open fire. Kieli elbowed himself up and gazed around. The smoke stung his eyes a little, but much of it escaped through an open door in the hayloft. It was quiet, so Kieli judged it was not raining.

His body ached and he felt stiff, but his slight movement didn't bring on waves of pain as it had before.

There was a man sitting upon a wooden stool, regarding him with dark eyes. The man's hair was mostly grey, though bits of black still remained. His droopy moustache hung down on either side of a mouth that was tightly pursed as if he were concentrating. A heavy fringe hid most of his forehead, and his hair hung to his shoulders.

Blinking an accumulation of gunk from the corners of his eyes, Kieli asked, 'Where am I?'

The man looked at him inquisitively. 'So, you're back with us?' he asked rhetorically. He paused for a moment. 'Robert!' he shouted over his shoulder towards the barn doors.

A moment later the doors swung open and another man entered the barn and came to kneel beside Kieli.

This man was older still, his hair grey without colour, but his eyes were powerful and his gaze held the boy's. 'Well, Talon, how do you feel?' he asked softly.

'Talon?'

'You said your name was Talon of the Silver Hawk,' supplied the older man.

The lad blinked and tried to gather his thoughts, struggling to understand why he might have said such a thing. Then he recalled the vision, and he realized that it had, indeed, been his naming vision. A distant voice echoed in his mind, *rise and be a talon for your people.*

'What do you remember?'

'I remember the battle . . .' A dark pit opened inside his stomach and he felt tears begin to gather. Forcing the sadness aside, he said, 'They're all dead, aren't they?'

'Yes,' answered the man named Robert. 'What do you recall after the battle?'

'A wagon . . .' Kieli, who now had to think of himself as 'Talon', closed his eyes for a while, then said, 'You carried me away.'

'Yes,' agreed Robert. 'We couldn't very well leave you to die from your wounds.' Softly he added, 'Besides, there are some things we would know of you and the battle.'

'What?' asked Talon.

'That can wait until later.'

'Where am I?' Talon repeated.

'You are in the barn at Kendrick's Steading.'

Talon tried to remember. He had heard of this place, but could not recall any details. 'Why am I here?'

The man with the droopy moustache laughed. 'Because we rescued your sorry carcass and this is where we were bound.'

'And,' continued Robert, 'this is a very good place to rest and heal.' He stood and moved away, stooping to avoid the low ceiling. 'This is a forester's hut, not used for years. Kendrick is allowing us to use his barn without charge. His inn has warmer rooms, cleaner bedding, and better food –'

'But it also has too many eyes and ears,' offered the first man.

Robert threw him a glance and shook his head slightly.

The first man said, 'You bear a man's name, yet I see no tattoos upon your face.'

'The battle was on my naming day,' Talon answered weakly.

The second man, the one called Robert, looked back at his companion, then returned his attention to the boy. 'That was over two weeks ago, lad. You've been travelling with us since Pasko found you in your village.'

'Did anyone else survive?' Talon asked, his voice choking with emotion.

Robert returned to the boy's side, knelt and put his hand gently on his shoulders and said, 'Gone. All of them.'

Pasko said, 'The bastards were thorough, I'll give them that.'

'Who?' asked Talon.

Robert's hand gently pushed the boy back onto the pallet. 'Rest. Pasko will have some hot soup for you soon. You've been at death's door. We didn't think you'd survive for a long while. We've seen you through with sips of water and cold broth. It's time to put some strength back in you.' He paused. 'There are many things to talk about, but we have time. We have a great deal of time, Talon of the Silver Hawk.'

Talon did not want to rest: he wanted answers, but his weakened body betrayed him and he lay back and found sleep welcoming him again.

The song of birds greeted him as he awoke ravenous. Pasko brought over a large earthen mug of hot broth and urged him to drink slowly. The other man, Robert, was nowhere to be seen.

After stinging his mouth with the hot liquid, Talon asked, 'What is this place?'

'Kendrick's? It's an . . . inn, buried somewhere in the forests of Latagore.'

'Why?'

'Why what? Why are we here, or why are you alive?'

'Both, I suppose,' said Talon.

'The second, first,' answered Pasko, as he sat down on the little stool and hefted his own mug of broth. 'We found you amidst carnage unlike any I've seen since my youth – when I was a soldier in the service of the Duke of Dungarren, down in Far Loren. We'd have left you for crow bait with the others, save I heard you moan . . . well, wasn't even a proper moan, more like a loud sigh. It was only by the hand of fate you survived. You had so much blood on you and such a jagged wound across your chest, we both took you for dead to start with. Anyway, you were breathing, so my master said to fetch you along. He's a soft-hearted sort, I can tell you.'

'I should thank him,' said Talon, though he felt so miserable for being alive while the rest of his family had perished that he didn't feel remotely thankful.

'I suspect he'll find a way for you to repay him,' said Pasko. He stood up. 'Feel like stretching your legs?'

Talon nodded. He started to rise and found that his head swam and his body ached. He had no strength.

'Gently, my lad,' said Pasko, hurrying to give Talon a helping hand. 'You're weaker than a day-old kitten. You'll need more rest, and food, before you're close to being fit, but right now you need to move around a bit.'

Pasko helped Talon to the door of the barn and they went

outside. It was a crisp morning, and Talon could tell they were in a lowland valley. The air smelled and felt different from the air in his highland meadows. Talon's legs were shaky and he was forced to take small steps. Pasko stopped and let the boy take in his surroundings.

They were in a large stabling yard, surrounded by a high wall of fitted stones. The boy instantly recognized the construction as a fortification by its design, for stone steps flush with the walls rose up at several locations a short distance from the large building which he took to be the inn. The top of the wall had crenels and merlons, and a walkway broad enough for two men to pass one another as they defended the grounds.

The inn was as large a building as Talon had ever seen, dwarfing the round house and long house of his village. It rose three storeys into the air, and the roof was covered with stone tiles rather than thatch or wood. It was painted white, with wooden trim around the doors and windows, the shutters and doors having been painted a cheery green. Several chimneys belched grey smoke into the sky.

A wagon had been pushed to the side of the barn, and Talon assumed it was the one that had carried him here. He could see the tops of trees some distance off, so he assumed the forest around the inn had been cleared.

'What do you see?' asked Pasko, unexpectedly.

Talon glanced at the man, who was studying him closely. He started to speak, then remembered his grandfather telling him to look beyond the obvious, so he didn't answer, but instead motioned to Pasko to help him to the nearest steps. He climbed up them slowly until he was on top of the wall and able to look over.

The inn sat in the centre of a natural clearing, but the stumps of a fair number of trees revealed that it had been enlarged years before. The stumps were covered with grasses and brambles, but the road into the woods had been kept clear.

'What do you see?' Pasko repeated.

Talon still didn't answer, but began walking toward the inn. As he did so, the layout of the inn called Kendrick's unfolded in his mind's eye. He hesitated. He had as much fluency with the Common Tongue as any boy in the village, but he rarely spoke it, save when traders came to . . . He thought of his village and the cold hopelessness returned. He pushed down the ache and considered the words he wanted. Finally, he said, 'This is a fortress, not an inn.'

Pasko grinned. 'Both, actually. Kendrick has no fondness for some of his neighbours.'

Talon nodded. The walls were stout, and the forest on all sides had been cleared sufficiently to give archers on the wall a clear field of fire. The road from the woods turned abruptly halfway to the inn and circled around to gates he assumed were on the other side of the inn. No ram or burning wagon could easily be run along to destroy the gates and gain entrance.

He glanced at the placement of the building. Archers in the upper windows would provide a second rank of defenders to support anyone on the wall. He returned his gaze to the doors and saw they were also heavy with iron bands. He imagined they could be barred from the inside. It would take stout men with heavy axes to break those down. He glanced up, and saw the murder-holes above each door. Hot oil or water, or arrows could be directed down at anyone in front of the door.

At last he said, 'They must be difficult neighbours.'

Pasko chuckled. 'Indeed.'

While they stood upon the parapet looking at the inn, a door opened and a young girl appeared carrying a large bucket. She glanced up and saw them and waved. 'Hello, Pasko!'

'Hello, Lela!'

'Who's your friend?' she asked playfully. She appeared to be a few years older than Talon, but unlike the girls he had known among his people, she was dark. Her skin was dark with a touch of olive colour, and her hair was as black as night. Her large brown eyes sparkled as she laughed.

'A lad we picked up along the way. Leave him alone. You've enough admirers already.'

'Never enough!' she shouted playfully, swinging the bucket around as she twirled a step, then continued on her path. 'I could do with some help fetching water,' she said with a flirtatious grin.

'You're a healthy enough lass, and the boy's injured.' Pasko paused, then asked, 'Where are Lars and Gibbs?'

'Kendrick's got them out,' Lela said, disappearing behind the other side of the barn.

Talon stood silent for a moment after she vanished from view, then asked, 'What am I to do?' Inside he felt a profound hopelessness, a lack of volition and will he had never known in his young life. Without his family . . . Memories of his village made tears gather in his eyes. The Orosini could be an emotional people, given to loud celebration in times of joy and tears in times of sorrow. But they tended to be reserved in the presence of strangers. All that seemed without purpose now and Talon let the tears run down his face.

Ignoring them, Pasko said, 'You'll have to ask Robert about

that when he returns. I just do as I'm bid. You do owe him your life, so that debt must be settled. Now, let's walk you around a little more, then get you back inside to rest.'

Talon felt a desire to explore, to go inside the inn and investigate its wonders, for a building this large must contain many, he judged. But Pasko took him back to the barn, and by the time they reached his pallet Talon was glad to be there, for he felt exhausted deep into his bones. The wounds on his body ached and stung and he knew that even that little bit of exercise had torn some new scar tissue and that he would need time to heal. He remembered when Bear Who Stands had been gored by a boar. He had limped for almost a half year before regaining full mobility in his leg.

Talon lay back on his pallet and closed his eyes while Pasko puttered around in the barn with some items he had brought in from the wagon. Despite having felt alert when he had awoken just a scant half-hour before, the boy drifted back off to sleep.

Patient by nature, Talon let the days go by without pestering Pasko with questions. It was obvious to him that the servant was by nature taciturn, and by instruction not very forthcoming. Whatever he discovered would be through his own powers of observation.

The pain caused by his people's destruction was never far from his thoughts. He had shed tears nightly for a week, but as the days passed, he turned away from his grief and began to court anger. He knew that somewhere out there were the men responsible for his people's obliteration. Eventually he would hunt them down and take retribution; such was the Orosini way.

But he was also enough of a realist to understand that one young man on his own had little chance of extracting full vengeance. He would need to gain strength, power, knowledge of weapons, many things. He knew that his ancestors would guide him. Silver Hawk was his totem: the boy once known as Kielianapuna would be a talon for his people.

The days became routine. Each morning he would awake and eat. Pasko and he would walk, at first just around the compound surrounding the huge inn, then later into the nearby woods. His strength returned and he started helping Pasko with chores, hauling water, chopping wood, and mending reins, halters and traces for the horses. He was a clever lad and had to be shown a thing only once or twice to grasp it. He had a fierce passion for excellence.

Occasionally, Talon would catch a glimpse of Robert as he hurried about the inn, often in the company of any of three men. Talon didn't ask Pasko to name them, but he marked them. The first Talon guessed to be Kendrick. A tall man with grey hair and a full beard, he moved around the property as if he owned it. He wore a fine tunic and a single ring of some dark stone set in gold, but otherwise serviceable trousers and boots. He often paused to give instructions to the servants – the girl Lela, and the two younger men, Lars and Gibbs. Lars and Gibbs had also been regular visitors to the barn when travellers called at the inn, for they cared for the horses.

The second man Talon saw he thought of as Snowcap, for his hair was as white as snow, yet he looked to be no more than thirty or so years of age. He was not quite as tall as Kendrick or Robert, but somehow seemed to look down at them. He carried himself like a chieftain or shaman, thought Talon, and there was an aura of power about him. His eyes were pale blue, and his face was coloured by the sun. He wore a robe of dark grey, with an intricate pattern woven at the sleeves and hem, which was just high enough for Talon to glimpse beneath it very finely crafted boots. He carried a wooden staff upon occasion, while at other times he affected a slouch hat that matched his robes in colour.

The last man bore a faint resemblance to the second, as if they were kin, but his hair was dark brown, almost the same colour as Talon's. His eyes were a deep brown as well, and his manner and movement suggested a warrior or hunter. Talon called him the Blade in his mind, for his left hand never seemed to venture far from the hilt of a sword, a slender blade unlike any Talon had seen. He wore blue breeches tucked into knee-high boots and a dark grey shirt over which he wore a tied vest. He also wore a hat all the time, a twin to Snowcap's slouch hat, though this one was black. Once Talon had seen him leave the inn at sunrise carrying a longbow and that night he had returned carrying a gutted deer across his shoulders. Instantly the young man had felt a stab of admiration; hunting was considered a great skill among the Orosini.

Robert, Pasko and Talon were treated much as if they were part of the surroundings. Only Lela took a moment now and again to call out a greeting to Pasko and Talon, or to nod or wave. Lars, a stocky red-headed lad, and Gibbs, a slender older man, would occasionally speak to them, asking for a piece of tack, or assistance in holding a horse that was being tended. But both avoided any casual conversation. Most of the time, Talon felt as if he and Pasko didn't exist in the minds of those inside the inn.

After a full month had passed, Talon awoke one morning to find Robert deep in conversation with Pasko. The young man arose quietly, and dressed, then made his presence known.

'Ah, young Talon,' said Robert, smiling at him. 'Pasko tells me you're recovering nicely.'

Talon nodded, 'My wounds are healed, and most of the stiffness is gone.'

'Are you fit enough to hunt?'

'Yes,' he answered without hesitation.

'Good; come with me.'

He left the barn and Talon fell into step beside him. As they walked to the inn, Talon said, 'Sir, I am in your debt, am I not?'

'Agreed,' replied Robert.

'How shall I discharge my debt?'

Robert stopped. 'I have saved your life, true?'

'Yes,' replied the boy.

'If I understand the ways of your people, you have a life-debt to me, correct?'

'Yes,' Talon said calmly. A life-debt was a complex concept, one that involved years of service, directly or indirectly. When a man of the Orosini saved the life of another, the man who was saved was considered to be at the call of the other. It was as if he became a member of that family, but without the privileges of that membership. He was honour bound to ensure that his saviour's family ate, even should his own go hungry. He was obliged to help bring in his saviour's crops before his own. In every way, the rescued man was in debt to the other. What Robert was telling Talon was that he must now consider Robert his master until such time as Robert released him from service.

'This is a heavy debt, is it not?'

'Yes,' Talon replied evenly.

The wind blew slightly, rustling the leaves in the distant trees and Robert was silent, as if thinking. Then he said, 'I shall test you, young Talon. I will judge your mettle and see if you will do.'

'Do for what, sir?'

'For many things. And I shall not tell you half of them for years to come. Should you prove lacking, I will bind you over to Kendrick's service for a number of years so that you may learn to care for yourself in a world other than the highlands of the Orosini, for that life is now denied you forever.'

Talon heard those words and felt as if he had been struck a blow, but he kept his expression blank. What Robert said was true. Unless others had somehow survived the attack and crept away into the mountains, he was now the last of the Orosini and no man could live alone in those mountains.

Finally Talon said, 'And if I am not lacking?'

'Then you shall see things and learn things no Orosini could imagine, my young friend.' He turned as another man approached. It was the Blade, and he had a longbow across his back, and carried another in his hand, with a hip-quiver of shafts. 'Ah, here he is.' To Talon, Robert said, 'This man you have seen, I am sure, for you do well in observing things; that I have already noticed. Talon, this is Caleb. He and his brother Magnus are associates of mine.'

Talon nodded at the man, who remained silent, studying him. Up close, Talon decided that Caleb was younger than he had at first thought – perhaps no more than ten years his senior, but he stood with the confidence of a proven warrior.

Caleb handed the bow and hip-quiver to Talon, who tied the quiver-belt around his waist, and inspected the bow. It was longer than the one he had learned with, and as he tested the draw, he felt Caleb's eyes observing his every move. There was wear at one end of the string, but he didn't judge it frayed enough to be a problem yet. Even so, he asked, 'Extra bowstring?'

Caleb nodded.

Talon set the bow across his back and said, 'Let us hunt.'

Caleb turned and led the way, and soon they were trotting down the path into the woods.

They moved silently through the trees. Caleb had not spoken a word to Talon yet. Half an hour into the hunt, Caleb led Talon off the path and down a game trail. The younger man looked around, marking signs in his mind to guide him back to the road should there be a need.

Caleb had led the way at a steady trot, a pace that would have been no problem for Talon when he was fit. But his injuries had weakened him and he found the pace difficult after the first hour. He was considering asking for a rest, when Caleb slowed. He had a water skin on his left hip, where his sword usually rested, and he unslung it and handed it to Talon. Talon nodded and drank sparingly, just enough to wet his throat and mouth. Feeling revived, he passed the skin back to Caleb. The silent man motioned as if asking if Talon wished to have another drink, and Talon shook his head. Looking at the rich woodlands around him, Talon reckoned he could not be far from any number of sources of water – streams, pools and brooks – but being from the high mountains where water was far more difficult to find, drinking sparingly while on a hunt was an inborn habit.

They resumed their hunt, but now Caleb led them at a walk rather than at a trot, looking at the ground for game sign. They entered a meadow after a few minutes, and Talon paused. The grass was nearly waist-high, pale yellow-green from the summer sun and ample rain.

He quickly unslung his bow and tapped Caleb on the shoulder with it. He motioned with his left hand, and Caleb looked to where he indicated. They made their way into the meadow, noting how the grass had been parted and some of it broken and crushed. Talon knelt and looked for prints. In a depression in the damp soil, he found one.

Softly he said, 'Bear.' He reached out and tested the broken blades. They were still moist at the break. 'Close.'

Caleb nodded. 'Good eyes,' he said softly.

They began to follow the bear's trail, until they had crossed nearly half the meadow. Caleb held up his hand and they halted. Then Talon heard it. In the distance, the snuffling sounds of a bear, and a dull thump.

They crept along until they reached a small brook. On the other side stood a large brown bear, busily rocking a dead tree trunk and ripping at it with its claws in an effort to expose a hive of bees, which were swarming futilely around the animal. The bear tore open the dried wood and revealed the rich comb inside while the bees stung ineffectually at its thick hide, one occasionally finding the only exposed part of the animal, its tender nose. Then the bear would hoot in outrage, but after a moment it would return to its task of getting to the honey.

Talon tapped Caleb on the shoulder and motioned towards

the bear, but the older man shook his head and motioned back the way they had come.

They moved silently away from the scene and after a short distance, Caleb picked up the pace and led them back towards the road.

Nightfall found the two hunters returning to the inn, a deer across Caleb's shoulders and Talon carrying a pair of wild turkeys tied together at the feet.

Robert waited at the gate. When they got there, Gibbs appeared and took the turkeys from Talon. Robert looked at Caleb.

Caleb said, 'The boy can hunt.'

Talon watched Robert's face and saw a flicker of satisfaction. He wasn't sure what had been said, but he was certain it had to do with more than merely hunting game in the woods.

Caleb followed Gibbs around the side of the inn, towards the kitchen door.

Robert put his hand on Talon's shoulder. 'So, it begins.'

• CHAPTER THREE •

Servant

*T*ALON STRUGGLED.

He followed Lela up the hill from the stream that ran through the woods, carrying a large basket of dripping-wet laundry. For the previous week, he had been put in her charge, essentially providing an extra pair of arms and legs for her.

The one oddity had been Robert's insistence that she speak only the language of Roldem to him, answering him only when he asked a question correctly. A few of the words in that language were used in the Common Tongue, but Common was mainly the hybrid of Low Keshian and the King's Tongue, developed by years of trading along the border of those two vast nations.

Still, Talon discovered he had an ear for language and quickly picked up the language from the constantly cheerful girl.

She was five years his senior, and had come to Kendrick's by a circuitous manner, if her story was to be believed. She claimed to have been a serving girl to a Princess of Roldem, who had been en route to a state arranged marriage with a noble in the court of the Prince of Aranor. Depending on his ability to understand her language and the frequency with which her story changed, she had either been abducted by pirates or bandits and sold into slavery, from which she had been freed by a kind benefactor or had escaped. In any event, the girl from the distant island nation across the Sea of Kingdoms had found her way to Kendrick's where she had been a serving girl for the last two years.

She was constantly happy, always quick with a joke, and very pretty. Talon was becoming quickly infatuated with her.

He still ached inside at the thought of Eye of the Blue-Winged Teal, lying dead somewhere with the rest of her family. Left unburied for the carrion-eaters. He shoved the image aside and concentrated on lugging the huge wicker basket he carried on his back.

Lela seemed to think that because he was assigned to her she was freed from the need to make several trips to the stream to clean the clothing. So she had found a basket four feet high and had rigged a harness so he could haul it up the hill on his back. Taking the clothing down to the stream was the easy part of the morning; carrying the sopping-wet garments back up to the inn was the difficult part.

'Caleb says you're a good hunter.'

Talon hesitated for a moment. He had to think about the words before he answered. 'I've hunted my life for all.'

She corrected his sentence structure and he repeated what she had said. 'I've hunted all my life.'

Talon felt considerable frustration as Lela prattled on; half of what she said was lost on him even though he listened hard, and the other half was mostly gossip from the kitchens, about people he had barely glimpsed.

He felt lost in a lot of ways. He was still sleeping in the barn, though alone now that Pasko had vanished on some errand for Robert. He saw Robert only rarely, glimpsed him through a window of the inn, or as he was crossing from the rear of the inn to the privy. Occasionally, the man who had saved his life would pause and exchange a few idle pleasantries with Talon, speaking in either the Common Tongue, or in Roldemish. When he spoke the latter, he also would only reply if Talon spoke in that language.

Talon was still not allowed inside the inn. He didn't think that strange; an outsider wouldn't have expected to be admitted to an Orosini lodge, and these were not the Orosini. Since he was a servant now, he assumed his sleeping in the barn to be a servant's lot. There was so much about these people he didn't understand.

He found himself tired a great deal. He didn't understand why; he was a young man, usually energetic and happy, but since he had come to Kendrick's, he found himself battling black moods and almost overwhelming sadness on a daily basis. If he was set to a task by Robert or Pasko, or when he was in the company of Caleb or Lela, he was distracted from the darker musing he was prey to when he was left alone. He wished for his grandfather's wisdom on this, yet thinking about his family plunged him deeper into the morbid introspection which caused him to feel trapped within a black place from which there seemed to be no escape.

The Orosini were open amongst themselves, talking about their thoughts and feelings easily, even with those not of the immediate family, yet they appeared stolid, even taciturn to outsiders. Gregarious even by the standards of his people, Talon appeared almost mute to those around him. Inside he ached for the free expression he had known in his childhood, and though the edge of that childhood was only weeks earlier in his life, it felt ages past.

Pasko and Lela were open enough, if he asked a question, but Lela was as likely to answer with a prevarication or misinformation as Pasko was likely to dismiss the question as being irrelevant to whatever task lay at hand. The frustration Talon experienced as a result only added to his bleak moods. The only respite from this crushing darkness was to be found in hunting with Caleb. The young man was even more reticent than Talon, and often a day of hunting would go by with less than a dozen words spoken between them.

Reaching the stabling yard, Lela said, 'Oh, we have guests.'

A coach, ornate with gilded trim on black lacquered wood and with all its metal fittings polished to a silvery gleam sat near the barn and Gibbs and Lars were quickly unhitching from the traces as handsome a matching set of black geldings as Talon had ever seen. Horses were not as central to the mountain tribes of the Orosini as they were to other cultures in the region, but he could still appreciate a fine mount. The coachman oversaw the two servants, ensuring that his master's team was treated with due respect.

'Looks as if the Count DeBarges is visiting, again,' said Lela.

Talon wondered who he might be, but remained silent.

'Put the basket down in the back porch,' Lela instructed.

Talon did so and the girl smiled as she vanished through the rear door to the kitchen.

He waited a moment, unsure what to do, then turned and headed back towards the barn. Inside, he found Pasko seeing to one of the many constant repairs the old wagon required, humming a meaningless tune to himself. He glanced up for an instant, then returned his attention to the work at hand. After a few moments of silence, he said, 'Hand me that awl there, boy.'

Talon gave him the tool and watched as Pasko worked on the new leather for the harnesses. 'When you live in a big city, boy,' Pasko commented, 'you can find craftsmen aplenty to do such as this, but when you're out on the road miles from anywhere and a harness breaks, you have to know how to do it for yourself.' He paused for a moment, then handed the awl back to Talon. 'Let me see you punch some holes.'

The boy had watched Pasko work on this new harness for a few days and had a fair notion of what to do. He began working the straps where he knew the tongue of the buckles would go. When he felt unsure, he'd glance up at Pasko who would either nod in approval, or shake his head indicating an error.

Finally, the strap was finished, and Pasko said, 'Ever stitch leather?'

'I helped my mother stitch hides . . .' he let the words trail away. Any discussion of his family brought back his deep despair.

'Good enough,' said Pasko, handing him a length of leather with the holes already punched. 'Take this buckle—' he indicated a large iron buckle used to harness the horses into the traces of the wagon '—and sew it on the end of that strap.'

Talon studied the strap for a moment and saw that it had

been fashioned from two pieces of leather sewn together for extra strength. He noticed there was a flatter side. He picked up the buckle and slid it over the long strap, the metal roller opposite the tongue he placed against the flat side. He glanced up.

Pasko nodded and smiled faintly. Talon picked up the heavy leatherworker's needle and started sewing the buckle in place. When he had finished, Pasko said, 'Fair enough, lad, but you made a mistake.'

Talon's eyes widened slightly.

'Look at that one over there,' Pasko said, pointing to another finished strap. Talon did as Pasko instructed and saw that he had made the loop where he had sewn the end together too short; this belt had triple stitching below the buckle for added strength.

Talon nodded, picked up a heavy knife and began to cut the stitches. He pulled them loose, careful not to damage the leather and then adjusted the strap so that the holes on one side would be where the first line would be stitched and the holes on the other piece would match up with the third. He carefully stitched those two lines, then added a third halfway between.

'That's right,' said Pasko when Talon was done. 'If you need to do something for the first time and there's an example of the work close to hand, take a moment and study what you're attempting. It makes for less mistakes, and mistakes can cost a man his life.'

Talon nodded, though he thought the remark odd. After a while he said, 'Pasko, may I talk with you.'

'About what?'

'About my life.'

'That's something you need to take up with Robert,' said the servant. 'He'll let you know what it is he expects as things move along, I'm certain.'

'Among my people, when a youth becomes a man, another man is always ready to guide him, to help him make wise choices.' Talon stopped and stared into the imagined distance for a moment, as if seeing something through the walls of the barn. 'I have . . .'

Pasko said nothing, merely watching him closely.

Talon remained quiet for a long time, then he went back to working on the harness leathers. After more time passed, he said, 'I was to be wed. I was to have joined the men in the long house, and I was to have joined in the hunt, planted crops, fathered children. I know what it was I was born to be, Pasko.' He stopped and looked at the servant. 'A man was to guide me in those things. But none of those things matter now. I'm here, in this barn, with you, and I do not know my lot in life. What is to become of me?'

Pasko sighed and put down the leather he was working on. He looked Talon in the eyes and put a hand upon the boy's shoulder. 'Things change in an instant, lad. Nothing is forever. Remember that. For some reason the gods spared you among all those of your race. You were given the gift of life for a reason. I do not presume to know that reason.' He paused as if thinking about what to say next, then he added, 'It may be that your first task is to learn that reason. I think you should speak with Robert tonight.' He put down the harness and started to walk out of the barn. Over his shoulder he said, 'I'll have a word with him and see if he's of a mind to speak with you.'

Talon was left alone in the barn. He regarded the work before him and remembered something his grandfather had once said to him: tend to the work at hand and set aside worrying about the work to come. So he turned his mind to the leather in his hand and concentrated on making the stitches as tight and even as he possibly could.

Weeks passed and summer became autumn. Talon sensed the change in the air as might any wild creature who had lived his entire life in the mountains. The lowland meadows around Kendrick's were different in many ways from the highlands of his home, but there were enough similarities that he felt one with the rhythm of the seasons' changes.

When he hunted with Caleb he noticed the coats on rabbits and other creatures was thickening, anticipating winter's approach. Many of the trees were losing leaves. Soon a cold snap would turn them red, gold, and pale yellow.

Birds were migrating south and those beasts that spawned in the autumn were in rut. One afternoon he heard the roar of a male wyvern, bellowing a challenge to any other male that might trespass on his range. With the shortening days a melancholy came upon Talon. Autumn meant the harvest, and putting up salted meats and fish for the winter, gathering nuts and mending cloaks, blankets, and getting ready for the harsh weather to follow.

Winter would bring a greater sense of loss, for while the harsh mountain snows could isolate a village until the first thaw, it was that time when the villagers drew close, huddling in the long house or round house telling stories. Families would often crowd together, two, three or even four to a house, comforted by closeness and conversations, old stories being retold and listened to with delight no matter how familiar they had become.

He recalled the songs of the women as they combed their daughters' hair or prepared a meal, the scent of cooking, the sound of the men telling jokes in low voices. Talon knew this winter would be the harshest so far.

One day upon returning from hunting, the coach of Count Ramon DeBarges was again visible in the courtyard. Caleb took the brace of fat rabbits they had trapped while Talon deposited the carcass of a fresh-killed deer on the back porch of the kitchen.

Caleb paused for a moment, then said, 'Good hunting, Talon.'

Talon nodded. As usual they had hardly spoken throughout the day, depending on hand gestures and a shared sense of the environment. Caleb was as good a hunter as Talon had seen among his own people, though there were a dozen or so in the village who could . . . who *had* matched his skill.

Caleb said, 'Take the deer into the kitchen.'

Talon hesitated. He had never set foot inside the inn, and wasn't sure if he should. But Caleb would not ask him to do something forbidden, so he reshouldered the deer and mounted the broad steps to the rear door. The door was of solid oak with iron bands, more the sort of door one might expect on a fortification than a residence. Talon was certain that Kendrick's had been designed as much for defence as it had for comfort.

He lifted the heavy iron handle and pushed inwards, and the door swung open. He followed its arc into the kitchen and discovered a world unlike anything he had seen before.

Orosini cooking was done over open fires or in large communal ovens, but never in a central location. Talon's first sense was one of chaos, and as he paused a moment, surveying the scene before him order emerged.

Lela looked up and saw him, greeting him with a quick flash

of a smile before returning her attention to a large pot hanging before one of three huge hearths. A stout woman saw Lela's glance and followed it to the rawboned boy holding the carcass.

'Is it dressed?' she demanded.

Talon nodded. Then he thought to add, 'But not skinned.'

She pointed to a large meat hook in the corner, above a large metal pan he assumed was used to catch blood and offal. He took the deer over and hung it by the strap holding together its hind legs. Once it was in place, he turned and waited.

After a few minutes, the older woman looked over and saw that he was motionless. 'Do you know how to skin a deer, boy?' she demanded.

He nodded.

'Then get to it!'

Talon didn't hesitate, but set to skinning the deer in an efficient, practised fashion. He also didn't think for a moment about who this woman was and why she should order him about; among his people, women were in charge of all food preparation and men did as they were told around the hearth, fire pits, and ovens.

He was finished quickly, and as he turned around to find a rag upon which to clean his belt knife, someone threw him one. He caught it in mid-air. A grinning Gibbs was standing before a large block upon which rested a heap of vegetables, which he was cutting with a large knife.

Behind Gibbs, Talon could see other servants cooking meats at one hearth, while others saw to the baking of fresh bread in the ovens. Suddenly Talon was at once overwhelmed by the aroma of the kitchen and by a fierce hunger which stabbed through his chest. For a moment the warm smells shocked him back into memories of his mother and the other women preparing meals.

As his eyes threatened to well up with tears, Talon saw a large door swing aside, through which strode a man. He was of middle years, heavy set with a large belly protruding over his belt – which looked more a horse's girth than a belt to Talon – breeches tucked into mid-calf boots, and a voluminous white shirt, covered with spatters of food and wine. His face was almost perfectly round, his hair black but shot through with grey and was tied back in a horse's tail. His long sideburns almost met at the point of his chin. He glanced around with a critical eye and found nothing lacking until his gaze fell upon Talon.

'You, there, boy,' he said pointing an accusatory finger at Talon, though his eyes were merry and he had a slight smile on his lips. 'What is it that you're doing?'

'I've skinned this deer, sir,' Talon said, haltingly, for the man was speaking Roldemish. The question snapped him out of his sadness.

The man walked purposely towards the boy. 'That is something which you have done,' he said in an overly loud voice. 'What is it you are currently doing?'

Talon paused, then said, 'Waiting for someone to tell me what to do next.'

The man's face split into a grin. 'Well said, lad. You're the boy from the barn – Talon – is that correct?'

'Yes, sir.'

'I am Leo, and this is my kingdom,' said the man, spreading his arms in an expansive gesture. 'I've served as cook to nobility and commoners alike, from Roldem to Krondor, and no man living has a complaint of my cooking.'

Someone in the busy kitchen muttered, 'Because they died before they had the chance.' This brought a moments laughter before the workers stifled the outburst. Leo turned with unexpected swiftness, a black look crossing his visage. 'You, there, Gibbs! I recognize that smart mouth. See to the slops.'

Gibbs stood very stiff and said, 'But the new boy should do that, Leo. I'm for the serving table.'

'Not tonight, my glib Gibbs. The boy will stand at the table, and you can see to the pigs!'

As a dejected-looking Gibbs departed the kitchen, Leo winked at Talon. 'That'll sort him out.' He glanced over the boy's rough appearance. 'Come with me.'

Without waiting to see if he was being followed, Leo turned and pushed aside the large door through which he had entered. Talon was a step behind.

The room was obviously some sort of servant's area, with another door in the opposite wall. Large side tables ran along the left and right walls. Upon one table sat a variety of dishes, bowls, goblets, and other table service. 'This is where we keep our dishes,' said Leo, pointing out the obvious. 'If we have a reason, we'll show you how to set the table for guests.' He pointed to the other table, which now sat empty. 'That is where the hot dishes will be at supper time. Lela and Meggie will serve.'

He pushed through the second door and Talon followed him into the centre of a long hallway. The wall facing them was ranged with shelves upon which a variety of items rested: lamps, candles, mugs, goblets, an entire inventory of supplies for a busy inn. 'Here's where Kendrick keeps the knick-knacks we need,' said Leo. Pointing to the door at the lefthand end of the hall. 'That's the common room. If we have a caravan stopping by, or a patrol from one of the local castles, it'll be full of loud, drunken fools.' He pointed to the door at the right end of the hall and said, 'That is the dining room, where the nobles and guests of stature eat. Tonight you'll serve in there.' He paused and rummaged through the shelves until he came away with a long, white tunic. 'Put this on,' he said to Talon.

Talon did so and found the tunic came to the midpoint between his hip and knee. There were drawstrings at the cuff of the puffy sleeves and he tied them.

'Let me see your hands, boy,' Leo demanded.

Talon held out his hands.

'I'm not the fanatic for washing up some are, but you can't be serving nobility with blood from a skinning under your nails,' Leo said. He pointed back into the kitchen. 'Go back and wash. Use the brush to get the blood out.'

Talon moved back through the serving room into the kitchen and found a large bucket of soapy water used to clean the pots and dishes. He saw Lela standing before the wooden table Gibbs had vacated, finishing up the vegetables. He started to wash his hands and she glanced over and smiled. 'Serving tonight?'

'I suppose so,' Talon answered. 'I haven't been told.'

'You're wearing a server's tunic,' she informed him. 'So you're serving.'

'What do I do?' asked Talon, trying to suppress a sudden nervousness in his stomach.

'Leo will tell you,' Lela said with a bright smile. 'It's easy.'

Talon inspected his hands and saw the blood was gone from his nails. He returned to the hall where Leo waited.

'Took you long enough,' said the cook, raising an eyebrow. Talon was beginning to think that this cook was a lot like his grandfather had been, playful with his scolding, never truly meaning a word of it.

'Come along,' Leo said.

Talon followed him into the dining room. It was a long room with a huge table, the biggest the Orosini boy had ever seen. At each end was placed a pair of high-backed chairs, and eight ran along each side. The wood was oak and ancient, polished by years of wear and oil and rags, and it shone with a dark gold, and the stain of a thousand spilled wine goblets and ale mugs mottled the hue from one end to the other. Noting the boy's expression, Leo said, 'Kendrick's table. It's legendary. Cut from the bole of an ancient oak in a single piece. Took a score of men and two mules to haul it here.' He glanced up and waved his hand. 'Kendrick built this room around it.' He smiled. 'Don't know what he'd ever do if he had to replace it. We could cut this one up with axes for firewood, but how'd we ever get another in?'

Talon ran his hand over the surface and found it extraordinarily smooth.

'A thousand rags in the hands of hundreds of boys like yourself have given it this finish. You'll have your turn at it.' Leo turned and surveyed the room. 'Now, here's what you'll be doing.' He pointed to a long side-table. 'In a few minutes some pitchers of ale will be fetched in here as well as some decanters of wine, and then you'll have your work to do. See those goblets?' He pointed to those already upon the table.

Talon nodded.

'Some of them will be filled with ale. Others will be filled with wine. Do you know the difference?'

Talon suddenly found himself wanting to smile. He kept his face straight as he said, 'I've tasted both.'

Leo feigned a frown. 'In front of the guests you will call me "Master Cook", is that clear?'

'Yes, Master Cook.'

'Well, then, where was I?' He looked puzzled for a moment. 'Oh, yes, your task is to stand upon this side of the table. This side only, is that clear?'

Talon nodded.

'Observe the guests before you. There will be six on this side, seven upon the other, and two guests will be seated over there.' He pointed to the pair of chairs at the end of the table on Talon's right. 'No one will sit at the other end.'

'Six on this side, Master Cook,' Talon repeated.

'You will be responsible for keeping goblets filled. Should a guest have to ask for more ale or wine, Kendrick's honour will be besmirched and I will view that as a personal affront. I will most likely ask Robert de Lyis to have Pasko beat you.'

'Yes, Master Cook.'

'Make certain you pour ale into those goblets containing ale, and wine only into those containing wine. I have heard that some barbarous people down in Kesh actually mix them, but I find that difficult to believe. In any event, mix them and I will ask Robert de Lyis to have Pasko beat you.'

'Yes, Master Cook.'

He gave the back of Talon's head a slight slap. 'I may ask Robert de Lyis to have Pasko beat you just because you are a boy, and boys are annoying. Stay here.'

With that, the Master Cook departed, leaving Talon alone in the room.

Talon let his eyes wander. There were tapestries above the sideboard behind him, and in the right corner of the room as he faced the table was one small hearth. Another lay at the far lefthand corner opposite him. Between the two they would provide ample heat for the long dining hall on any but the coldest nights.

Against the far wall another sidetable waited, and a moment later, Lars entered carrying a huge platter with dressed mutton heaped upon it. In what appeared to be controlled frenzy Meggie and Lela, along with several others he had seen in the kitchen whose names were unknown to him, came hurrying into the room bearing platters of steaming vegetables, hot breads, pots of condiments and honey, tubs of freshly churned butter and trays bearing roasted duck, rabbit and chicken. They ran back and forth bringing new platters until the sideboard was filled with food, including many items unlike anything Talon had seen before. Fruits of strange colours and textures were placed alongside familiar apples, pears, and plums.

Then the ale and wine was fetched in, and Lars remained standing opposite Talon on the other side of the table as Meggie went to the left end of the far table, and Lela went to the right end of the sideboard behind Talon.

There seemed to be but the merest pause, a moment in which to catch one's breath, to compose oneself, then the doors opened and a parade of well-dressed men and women filed in, each taking a place at the table, based upon some system of rank, Talon assumed, for a man and a woman stood behind the chairs at the end of the table and those who came in after them each took their appointed place. It seemed to Talon that this was much like the seating in the men's long house in his village. The senior chieftain would sit upon the high seat, the most prominent in the building, with the second most senior chieftain on his right, the third on his left, and so forth until every man in the village was in his place. A change in the order only occurred when someone died, so any man in the village might expect to sit in the same place for years.

Last through the door was Kendrick, dressed much as he had been the first time Talon had seen him. His hair and beard looked freshly washed and combed, but his tunic was much the same colour, and his trousers and boots were still workaday. He stepped to the chair before the man at the head of the table and pulled it out.

Talon saw Lars moving to the chair closest to the head of the table and begin to pull it out. Talon hesitated only for a moment, then moved to his right to the chair closest to the head of the table and mimicked the others, pulling out the chair with a slight turn and allowing the dinner guest – a striking woman of middle years with a lavish necklace of emeralds around her neck – to move in and be seated, then pushing the chair in slightly as the guest sat. Talon was only a beat behind the others, but he managed the task without a flaw.

He anticipated the need to move down to the next chair and repeat the action, and quickly all the guests were seated. As Talon returned to his station, he saw Kendrick watching him and Lars move back to stand by the sideboard.

The girls began serving food, and then Lars took up a pitcher of ale and a decanter of wine and moved to the head of the table. Talon hesitated and looked across at Kendrick. Kendrick glanced first from Talon to the sideboard, then back to the young man.

Talon duplicated what Lars was doing. He moved to the side of the man at the head of the table and offered him a choice of wine or ale. The man spoke in a heavily accented speech, but the words were Roldemish, and it was clear that amidst the flurry of witticism and observations he was instructing Talon to pour the wine. Talon did so, attempting not to drip upon the table or the guest.

He then moved down the row of other guests quickly filling goblets as they instructed him.

Once that had been accomplished, the rest of the evening passed without event. Throughout the course of the meal he refilled goblet after goblet and when his own pitchers and decanters were nearly empty, one of the girls took them to the kitchen for a refill.

From Talon's inexperienced point of view things seemed to be progressing smoothly. Near the end of the meal he sought to refill the goblet of the man at the head of the table, but the man indicated he wished no more by putting his hand briefly over the goblet before him. Talon had no idea what to say, so he bowed slightly and backed away.

Kendrick stood discreetly behind the head of the table, watching his staff's every move, looking for any need that was going unmet.

When the meal was over, the guests indicated they were ready to leave. Talon hurried to a place behind the first guest he had seated as he saw Kendrick and Lars do, and was only half a beat behind them in gently pulling out the chair so the guest could rise gracefully.

When the last guest had left, Kendrick followed. As the door into the common room swung shut, the door from the serving room swung open and Leo strode through, shouting, 'All right then! What are you about! Get this mess cleaned up!'

Suddenly Meggie, Lela, and Lars were grabbing platters and dishes off the tables, and Talon did likewise. They hurried back and forth between the dining room and kitchen and the task of cleaning began.

Talon quickly sensed a rhythm in this business, a matching of task to person, and he found it easy to anticipate what to do next. By the end of the night's work, he felt comfortable in the tasks asked of him, and knew that he would be even better able to execute them the next time he was asked.

As the kitchen staff prepared for the morning meal, several staying to prepare the morning's bread, Lela came to him and said, 'Before you sleep, Kendrick wants to see you.'

He looked around. 'Where?'

'In the Common Room,' she replied.

He found Kendrick sitting at one of the long tables before the bar with Robert de Lyis, both of them enjoying a mug of ale.

Kendrick said, 'Boy, you are called Talon?'

'Sir,' said Talon in agreement.

'Talon of the Silver Hawk,' supplied Robert.

'That is an Orosini name,' said Kendrick.

'Yes, sir.'

'We have seen a few of your people here from time to time over the years, but usually you tend to stay up in your mountains.'

Talon nodded, uncertain whether an answer was required.

Kendrick studied him a moment in silence, then said, 'You hold your tongue. That is a good quality.' He rose and came to stand before Talon as if seeking to see something in his face up close that he could not see from a distance. After a brief inspection, he asked, 'What did Leo say you were to do?'

'I was to pour wine into wine goblets and ale into ale goblets.'

'That was all?'

'Yes, sir.'

Kendrick smiled. 'Leo thinks it amusing to toss a boy into service without much preparation. I shall have to have words with him again. You did well enough, and none of the guests realized you were not experienced.' He turned to Robert. 'I will leave him to you. Good night.'

Robert rose and nodded in farewell, then motioned for Talon to come sit.

Talon did so and Robert studied him. Finally, he said, 'Do you know the name of the man who sat at the head of the table?'

Talon said, 'Yes.'

'Who is he?'

'Count Ramon DeBarges.'

'How do you know that?'

'I saw him, the last time he visited the inn. Lela told me his name.'

'How many rings did he wear on his left hand?'

Talon was surprised by the question, but said nothing as he tried to remember. After calling up an image of the count holding his wine goblet for more wine, he answered, 'Three. A large red stone in a silver setting upon his smallest finger. A carved gold ring upon his next finger, and a gold ring with two green stones upon his pointing finger.'

'Good,' said Robert. 'The green stones are emeralds. The red stone is a ruby.'

Talon wondered what the purpose of these questions was, but said nothing.

'How many emeralds in the necklace worn by the lady to the Count's left?'

Talon paused, then said, 'Seven, I think.'

'You think or you know?'

Talon hesitated, then said, 'I think.'

'Nine.' Robert studied the young man's face, as if expecting him to say something, but Talon remained silent. After a long pause, he asked, 'Do you remember what the Count and the man two places down on his right were speaking of when you were serving ale to the lady between them?'

Talon remained quiet for a minute as he searched his memory. 'Something about dogs, I think.'

'Think or know?'

'Know,' said Talon. 'They were speaking of dogs.'

'What about dogs?'

'Something about hunting dogs.' He paused, then added, 'I still do not speak the Roldemish tongue well, Robert.'

De Lyis was motionless for a few seconds, then nodded. 'Fair enough.' Next, he launched into a series of questions, ranging from who ate what, what was discussed at various times, what manner of clothing and accessories the ladies wore, and how many drinks each man consumed, until it seemed to Talon he would be there all night.

Suddenly, Robert said, 'That's all. Return to the barn and sleep there until you are called. Then you will be moving into the servants' quarters here; you will share a room with Gibbs and Lars.'

'Am I then to be a servant in Kendrick's household?'

Robert smiled slightly. 'For a time, young Talon. For a time.'

Talon rose and made his way through the kitchen, where loaves were rising before the hearth, waiting to be baked first thing in the morning. Realizing he had not eaten for hours,

Talon paused to snatch an apple from a large bowl and bit into it. He thought they were to be used for pies, but was content that the loss of one would be no great hardship to Leo.

Making his way outside, he saw that the eastern sky was lightening. Soon it would be the time before dawn his people knew as the Wolf's Tail, that grey-upon-grey time in which a man can steal an early march upon the hunt or a long journey, before the dawn breaks.

Entering the barn and seeking out his pallet, Talon threw himself down, fatigue overwhelming him. The half-eaten apple fell from his hand. As he wondered what fate had in store for him and the reason behind Robert's many and seemingly pointless questions, Talon fell quickly into an exhausted sleep.

• CHAPTER FOUR •

Games

*T*ALON FROWNED.

He looked at the cards laid out upon the table and attempted to discern any choice that might create a solution. After examining the four cards he had just turned over, he realized there was no possible way he could continue the game.

Sighing, half in frustration, half out of boredom, he swept up the cards and began reshuffling them. He resisted the temptation to turn and see if the two men watching him were showing any reaction.

The white-haired man he had thought of as 'Snowcap', but who was actually named Magnus, stood beside Robert, who was sitting on a stool, brought into the dining room from the common room. Robert had introduced the concept of cards to Talon a week earlier.

The deck consisted of fifty-two cards, in four suits: cups, wands, swords and diamonds, each a different colour, the cups being blue, wands green, swords black, and diamonds yellow. They were used primarily for games likel-in-land, pashawa, and poker, or po-kir as it was called in Kesh. Robert had demonstrated several games and had Talon play a few hands of each to get familiar with the ordering of the suits, from the card known as the 'ace', which Robert explained came from a Bas-Tyran word for 'unit', to the lord. The lower cards were numbered from two to ten, but Talon saw no logic as to why the unit, or the one as he thought of it, was the most valuable card, more so than the lord, lady, or captain.

Talon smiled slightly to himself. He didn't know why that little fact, that the lowest number, the single unit, was the most valuable card, irritated him. Still, he did well enough with the games Robert had taught him. Then Robert had introduced him to the concept of solitary play, using the deck for idle amusement when lacking opposing players. The games were roughly a variation on a theme, different 'layouts', as Robert called them, with different ways in which to draw cards from the deck. Some games required the player to build cards in rows based on rank, in alternating colours of light and dark, or in order of number, or a combination.

Earlier in the previous day Robert had taken Talon from the kitchen – there were no guests so duty was light – and had brought him into the dining hall. There he had introduced the game of 'four lord's.

It was a perplexing game. Four lords were laid out from right to left, and four cards were dealt face up. The object of the game was to place the cards by suit next to the lords, the only prohibition being that cards must be placed next to cards of the same number or suit. The next goal was to create 'packs' of four identical number cards, in a square. This continued until all four aces were together, at which point they were retired from the game. Then the twos, and so fourth until only the lords remained.

Talon had discovered early on that it was a very difficult game to win, relying far too much on the random luck of cards coming out in a certain order, rather than skill. But some skill was required in anticipating situations in which cards would be isolated from others of like value.

For half a day Talon had eagerly played the game, determined to become a master at it. Then he realized just how much random luck was involved and became disenchanted with it. Yet Robert still insisted that he play, and sat behind silently to observe.

As Talon laid out the next game, he wondered not for the first time exactly why Robert was doing this.

Magnus whispered, 'Robert, why are you doing this?'

Robert whispered, 'The boy's people have little abstract logic in their daily lives. They were hunters, farmers, poets and warriors, but their mathematics were basic and all the disciplines based upon advanced logic were lacking to them. They had builders, yes, but no engineers and far fewer magic-users than any other people I'm aware of, perhaps one or two throughout the entire land of the Orosini.'

They spoke in the King's Tongue, the language of the Kingdom of the Isles, to prevent Talon from understanding them – and Robert judged his hearing very sharp.

'So the games are to teach him logic?'

Robert nodded. 'They are a start. This is very basic problem-solving.'

Magnus's pale blue eyes were fixed upon the cards on the table. 'I've played four lords, Robert. You taught it to me, remember? It is a difficult game. He won't win many.'

Robert smiled. 'It's not about winning. It's about recognizing a no-win situation. See, he's recognized that those four cards ensure that he can't win.' They watched as Talon gathered up the cards, leaving the lords in place, and started a new game. 'At first, he went through the entire deck to reach the point of realizing he had no chance of winning. Now, less than two days later he's recognizing the more subtle combinations that show he can't win.'

'Very well. So he's got potential, talent even. That doesn't address the question of what it is you plan to do with the boy.'

'Patience, my impetuous friend.' He glanced at Magnus, who watched Talon with a fixed gaze. 'It would have been better had you more of your father's temperament than your mother's temper.'

The white-haired man didn't shift his gaze, but he did smile. 'I've heard that from you more than once, old friend.' He then looked at Robert. 'I'm getting better at reining in my temper, you know.'

'Haven't destroyed a city in the last few weeks, have you?'

Magnus grinned. 'Not that I noticed.' Then the stern expression returned. 'I chafe at these games within games.'

'Ah,' said Robert. 'Again your mother's son. Your father has taught me over my entire adult lifetime that we can only deal with our enemies when they present themselves. Over the last thirty years we've seen so many different assaults upon the tranquillity of our lives that it defies imagining. And there's only been one constant.'

'Which is?' Magnus turned his attention again to Talon's game.

'That no two ploys of the enemy have been alike. The servants of the Nameless One are cunning and they learn from their mistakes. Raw power failed, so now they achieve their goals through stealth. We must respond in kind.'

'But this boy . . . ?'

'Fate spared him for a reason, I believe,' said Robert. 'Or at least, I'm trying to take advantage of an unexpected opportunity. He's got . . . something. I think had this tragedy not befallen his people, he would have grown up to be simply another young Orosini man, a husband and father, warrior when the need arose, farmer, hunter and fisherman. He would have taught his sons the ways of his ancestors and died in old age satisfied at his lot.

'But take that same lad and forge him in the crucible of misfortune and heartbreak, and who knows what will occur? Like fired iron, will he become brittle and easily broken, or can he be turned to steel?'

Magnus remained silent as Talon began another game. 'A dagger, no matter how well forged, has two edges, Robert. It can cut both ways.'

'Don't teach your grandmother to suck eggs, Magnus.'

Magnus grinned. 'My father never knew his mother, so the only grandmother I'm aware of did a fair job of conquering half the world; I wouldn't have dreamed of teaching her anything.'

'And you have your mother's nasty sense of humour, too.' He turned from the King's Tongue to Roldemish to say, 'Talon, that's enough. It's time for you to return to the kitchen. Leo will tell you what needs to be done.'

Talon put the cards away in a small box and handed the box to Robert, then hurried to the kitchen.

Magnus said, 'I'm still uncertain what you think this boy will contribute to our cause.'

Robert shrugged. 'Your father showed me many things when I was young, but the most important lesson of all was simply the very nature of your home. Your island provided refuge and school to all manner of beings I couldn't have imagined in my most youthful dreams.' He pointed towards the kitchen. 'That boy may prove to be nothing more than a valuable servant, or perhaps a well-crafted tool.' His eyes narrowed. 'But he also could be something far more important, an independent mind loyal to our cause.'

Magnus was silent for a long moment. Then he said, 'I doubt it.'

Robert smiled warmly. 'We had doubts about you when you were younger. I remember a certain incident when you had to be confined to your room for . . . what was it? A week?'

Magnus returned a faint smile. 'It wasn't my fault, remember?'

Robert nodded indulgently. 'It never was.'

Magnus looked toward the kitchen. 'But the boy?'

'He has many things to learn,' said Robert. 'Logic is only a start. He must come to understand that even the most important issues in life can often be seen to be games, with a sense of risk and reward and how to calculate them. He must learn when to walk away from a conflict, and when to press his luck.

Much of his nature, what he was taught as a child among his people, must be taken from him. He must learn about the game of men and women – did you know his future wife was being arranged for him while he waited upon a mountain-top for his manhood vision?'

'I know little of the ways of the Orosini,' confessed Magnus.

'He knows nothing of the most common knowledge in the city; he has no sense of duplicity and deceit, so he has almost no instinct for when someone is lying to him. Yet he has a sense in the wild that would rival that of a Natalese Ranger.'

'Caleb told me he hunted like no city-born man,' agreed Magnus.

'Your brother spent years with the elves; he should know.'

'Agreed.'

'No, our young friend Talon is an opportunity. He is, perhaps, unique. And he is young enough that we may be able to educate him to be something few of us can be.'

'Which is what?' asked Magnus, clearly interested.

'Unlimited by our heritage. He's still able to learn, while most of us at his age are already convinced we know everything.'

'He does seem a ready student,' Magnus conceded.

'And, he has a sense of honour that would serve a LaMutian Captain of Tsurani descent.'

Magnus raised an eyebrow. Those of Tsurani descent were as hidebound where honour was concerned as any men living. They would die to discharge a debt of honour. He looked for a moment to see if Robert was exaggerating and realized that he wasn't. 'Honour is useful, at times.'

'He has a mission already, even if it has yet to come to the surface of his mind.'

69

'Mission?'

'He is Orosini. He must hunt down and kill the men responsible for the obliteration of his people.'

Magnus let out a long sigh. 'Raven and his band of cutthroats. No mean feat, that.'

'The boy's already a hunter. When he is ready, he'll seek them out. I would rather have him do so with better weapons than his bare hands and native wit. So, there is much we must teach him, both of us.'

'He has no skill for magic, I imagine, or else you would have sent him back to Father instead of bringing him up here.'

'True, but you have other skills besides magic, Magnus. I am not jesting; he has a nimble mind and there are far more complex tasks to discipline thought than playing games with cards. If he is to serve us, he must be as tough in spirit and intellect as he already is in body. He may not have any skill in magic, but he will face it, and he will face minds far more adept in backstabbing, double-dealing and deception than he could possibly imagine.'

'If it's double-dealing you're worried about, you should have brought in Nakor to tutor him.'

'I might still, but not yet. Besides, your father has Nakor down in Kesh on some errand or another.'

Magnus stood up. 'Ah, then the prospect for war between the Kingdom of the Isles and the Empire of Great Kesh is now excellent.'

Robert laughed. 'Nakor doesn't wreak havoc *everywhere* he visits.'

'No, just most places. Well, if you think you can ready the boy to chase down Raven and kill him, good luck.'

'Oh, it's not Raven and his murderers I'm concerned with. Hunting them is only part of Talon's training, albeit his journeyman's piece. If he should fail, then he would lack the true test of his skills.'

'I'm intrigued. What lies beyond?'

'Talon will avenge his people when he kills everyone responsible for the obliteration of the Orosini. Which means he may not rest until he faces down and destroys the man *behind* that genocide.'

Magnus's eyes narrowed, the pale blue becoming icy. 'You're going to turn him into a weapon?'

Robert nodded. 'He will need to kill the most dangerous man living today.'

Magnus sat back on the seat again and folded his arms across his chest. He looked towards the kitchen as if trying to see through walls. 'You're sending a mouse to beard a dragon.'

'Perhaps. If so, let's ensure the mouse has teeth.'

Magnus shook his head slowly and said nothing.

Talon hauled water up the hill and saw that Meggie waited for him and that she was frowning. She was the antithesis of Lela, tiny where Lela was voluptuous, fair to the point of pallor where Lela was dark, plain where Lela was exotic, dour where Lela was exuberant. In short, at not even twenty years old, she was more than halfway to being a middle-aged scold.

'Took you long enough,' she said.

'I didn't realize there was a rush on,' said Talon, now comfortable with the idiomatic Roldemish he was being told to use almost exclusively.

'There's always a rush on,' she snapped.

Following her up the hill, Talon asked, 'Why did you come down to meet me?'

'Kendrick said I was to find you and tell you you'd be serving again tonight in the dining room.' She wore a shawl of drab green which she gathered tightly around her shoulders as she walked before him. The days were growing cold and the nights colder; autumn was turning to winter and soon snow would come. 'There's a caravan from Orodon to Farinda staying over tonight, and it seems there's someone important travelling with it. So, Lela and I are assigned to the common room with Lars, and you and Gibbs to the dining room.'

'You could have waited until I got back to the kitchen to tell me that,' Talon observed.

'When I'm told to do something, I do it at once,' she snapped. She picked up her pace, hurrying on ahead. Talon watched her stiff back as she walked in front of him. Something struck him oddly for a moment, then he realized what it was; he liked the way her hips moved as she climbed the hill. He felt that same strange stirring in his stomach he often felt when he was alone with Lela and wondered about that. He didn't particularly like Meggie, but suddenly he found himself thinking of the way her nose turned up at the tip, and how on those very rare occasions she smiled at something, she got tiny lines – crinkles Lela called them – at the corners of her eyes.

He knew that something had passed between Meggie and Lars for a while, but that for some reason they were barely speaking to one another now, while everyone spoke with Lela. He pushed away his discomfort. He knew what passed between men and women – his people were open enough about sex and he had seen many women naked at the bathing pool when he was still a child – yet the actual fact of being close to a young women caused him much distress. And these people were not Orosini – they were outlandish – though after an instant's further thought he has to concede that now he was the outlander. He did not know their rituals, but they seemed to make free with their bodies before they were pledged. Then he realized that he didn't even know if they did pledge. Perhaps they didn't have marriage like the Orosini at all.

Kendrick had no wife as far as Talon was aware. Leo was married to the heavy woman, Martha, who oversaw the baking, but they were from some distant place called Ylith. Perhaps here in Langadore men and women lived apart, only . . . he shook his head as they reached the outer gate to the stabling yard. He didn't know what to think. He resolved to speak of this with Robert should the opportunity arise.

He noticed that Meggie was standing in the porch, waiting for him. 'Fill the barrels,' she instructed.

Softly he said, 'I know what to do.'

'Oh, do you?' she returned, her meaning obscure.

As she turned to hold the door open, he waited, then moved past her. As she closed the door behind him, he put down the large buckets of water and said, 'Meggie?'

'What?' she said, turning to face him, her face set in a half-frown.

'Why do you dislike me?'

The openness of the question took her aback. She stood speechless for a moment, then she brushed past him, her voice soft as she said, 'Who said I didn't like you?'

Before he could answer, she was gone from the kitchen. He

picked up the buckets and carried them to the water barrels. He really didn't understand these people.

After dinner that night, Talon sought out Robert, who stayed in a room at the back of the inn, on the first floor. He knew he had a life-debt to this man. He knew that until he was released from that debt, he would serve Robert de Lyis for the rest of his life, or until such time as he saved Robert's life. But he was uncertain as to the plans Robert had for him. He had been numb with grief and overwhelmed by the changes in his life since Midsummer, but now with winter fast approaching, he had come to think about the future more and wonder what his fate would be after the spring came, and the next summer was upon him.

He hesitated before the door; he had never intruded upon Robert's privacy before, and did not even know if such an approach was permitted. He took a breath, then knocked lightly.

'Come in.'

He slowly opened the door and leaned in. 'Sir, may I speak with you?'

Robert's room contained only four items of furnishings, a bed, a chest for his clothing, a small table and a stool. He sat upon the stool in front of the table, consulting a large object, which appeared to Talon to be many parchments bound together. Next to it rested a candle, the room's only illumination. A water basin and a pitcher indicated the table's other function when Robert was not using it for his work.

'Come in and close the door.'

Talon did so and stood awkwardly before Robert. 'Is it permitted?' he asked at last.

'Is what permitted?'

'For me to ask you a question.'

Robert smiled. 'Finally. It is not only permitted, it is encouraged. What is on your mind?'

'Many things, master.'

Robert's eyebrows went up. 'Master?'

'I do not know what else to call you, and everyone says you're my master.'

Robert waved to the bed. 'Sit down.'

Talon sat, awkwardly.

'To begin with, it's appropriate for you to call me "master" in front of anyone well known to us, but when we are alone, or with Pasko, you may address me as "Robert". Understood?'

'I understand that is what I am to do. I do not understand why.'

Robert smiled. 'You have as keen a wit as you do an eye, Talon of the Silver Hawk. Now, what is it you wished to see me about?'

Talon composed his thoughts, taking a few moments to weigh his words. Then he asked, 'What are your plans for me?'

'This concerns you?'

Talon lowered his eyes for a moment, then remembered his father's words, that he should always meet another man's gaze and always face a problem directly. 'It concerns me.'

'Yet you have waited for months to ask.'

Talon again fell silent. Then he said, 'I have had to consider much. I am without a people. Everything I know is gone. I do not know who I am any more.'

Robert sat back. He drummed his fingers lightly upon the table and said after a while, 'Do you know what this is?' He touched the large bound sheaf of parchment.

75

'It is writing, I think.'

'This is called a book. In it is knowledge. There are many books with many different kinds of knowledge in them, just as each man is a different kind of man.

'Some men live their lives, Talon, without having to make many decisions. They are born to a place, grow up in that place, marry and father children in that place, grow old and die in that place. This is how it was to have been for you, is it not?'

Talon nodded.

'Other men are cast adrift by fate and must choose their own lives. That is how it is with you now.'

'But I am in your debt.'

'And you shall replay that debt. Then what?'

'I don't know.'

'Then we have a common purpose, for in discovering how you may best serve me, we shall also discover what your destiny is.'

'I don't understand.'

Robert smiled. 'That's not necessary, yet. You will in time. Now, let me tell you some things you should know.

'You will spend the next year here, at Kendrick's. You will do many things, serving in the kitchen as you have, and in the stable, and in other capacities as Kendrick sees best. You will also, from time to time, serve Caleb or Magnus, should they need you while they are staying here. And from time to time you will travel with me.' He turned, putting his hand upon the book once more. 'And we shall start tomorrow by teaching you to read.'

'To read, Robert?'

'You have a bright mind, Talon of the Silver Hawk, but it is untutored. You were educated in the ways of your people to be a good and true man of the Orosini. Now you must be educated in the ways of the world.'

'I still don't understand, Robert.'

Robert motioned for Talon to stand. When he had, Robert said, 'Go away and go to sleep. You will understand over time. I sense a potential for greatness in you, Talon. I may be wrong, but if you fail to develop that potential, it will not be for a lack of effort.'

Not knowing what to say, Talon merely nodded, turned and left. He paused outside Robert's door and thought to himself, *Potential for what?*

Talon waited, sword ready. Magnus stood a short distance away, observing. The boy was already drenched with perspiration and was sporting several red welts on his shoulders and back from the blows he had taken.

Kendrick stood before him, a wooden training sword in his hand, motioning for the boy to attack one more time. He had allowed Talon to use a real blade, claiming that if the boy could cut him he deserved to bleed, and so far he had proven his ability to avoid being touched. But Talon was fast and learned quickly, and he was getting closer and closer to reaching Kendrick.

Magnus had said nothing during the training exercise, but he watched every move closely.

Talon attacked, this time holding his blade back as if readying for a downward strike. He suddenly spun away from Kendrick's right side – his sword side – and slashed down and sideways with the blade, a vicious swing at Kendrick's unprotected left side. Kendrick sensed the move only at the last instant, and barely got his own blade in place for a block, but suddenly Talon reversed himself and slashed in a backhand at Kendrick's right side, which was now unprotected since he had over-extended himself for the block.

With a satisfying 'thunk' the flat of Talon's blade slapped into the innkeeper's back, eliciting a grunt of pain and Kendrick shouted, 'Hold!'

Talon turned, his chest heaving as he tried to catch his breath and watched as the innkeeper studied him. 'Who taught you that move, boy?'

'No one, sir. I just . . . thought of it a moment ago.'

The innkeeper reached back and rubbed where Talon had struck him. 'Fancy move, and beyond most swordsmen's imagination, let alone their capacity, yet you pulled it off the first time.'

Talon didn't know what to say. He wasn't sure if he was being praised or not. He was getting to be almost fluent in Roldemish, but some of the nuances and idioms were still lost on him.

Kendrick handed his practice blade to Talon and said, 'We're done for today. Put these away and see what Leo has for you do to in the kitchen.'

Talon wiped his forehead with the sleeve of his tunic, took the weapon and hurried off towards the kitchen. When he was out of hearing, Magnus said, 'Well, what do you think?'

'He's a cat, that one,' said Kendrick. 'I would have wagered a bag of gold he couldn't touch me for at least two more lessons. At first I could whack him at will. Then he started anticipating my blows. Defence first, instinctually, knowing that survival comes before victory. He's a smart one, too, as well as fast.'

'How good can he be?'

Kendrick shrugged. 'If you want a battle-butcher, I can have him ready to storm a wall in a month. If you want a swordsman, he'll need better masters than I.'

'And where would I find such?'

'Give him to me for the year, then he'll be ready for the Masters' Court in Roldem. One or two years there and he'll be one of the finest swordsmen I've ever seen.'

'That good?'

Kendrick nodded. 'More. He may be the best if something doesn't ruin him along the way.'

Magnus held his iron-shod staff and leaned against it, staring at where Talon had last been visible, as if maintaining the image of the fatigued youth, dripping with his own perspiration, his hair lank and plastered to his head, hurrying to the kitchen. 'What sort of something?'

'Drink. Drugs. Gambling. Women. The usual.'

Kendrick looked at Magnus. 'Or whatever plots and intrigues your father has lying in wait for him.'

Magnus nodded. 'Father's left the boy's fate up to Robert. Talon is not part of our plans . . . yet, but father heard Robert's report on him and counts him a fortuitous opportunity.'

'Fortuitous for whom?' asked Kendrick. 'Come, I need to bathe. That lad worked me more than I expected.'

Magnus said, 'Had Robert and Pasko not found him, Talon would be dead with the rest of his tribe. It's Robert's judgment that every minute from that moment on is borrowed time. The boy's got a second chance.'

'Ah, but who is going to use that chance?' asked Kendrick. 'That's the question, isn't it?'

Magnus said, 'We're all used, in one fashion or another. Do you think for a moment my life could be any different?'

'No, you were fated by nothing more basic than who your parents were. Your brother, however, had choices.'

'Not that many, really,' said Magnus. 'Caleb had no gift for magic, but he could have been something more than a soldier.'

Kendrick said, 'Your brother is more than a soldier. Elven-trained as a hunter, master of more languages than I know of, and as skilled a student of men as lived. I wish I'd had him with me back when we put down the rebellion in Bardac's Holdfast; trying to get information out of the prisoners at Traitors' Cove was no spring fair, I can tell you. Caleb can tell when a man is lying just by looking at him.' Kendrick shook his head, 'No, there is nothing about any member of your family that I'd count as begging. And I think it's much the same with the boy. I think he could be many things.' He slapped Magnus lightly upon the shoulder. 'Just don't ruin him by trying to make him too many things, my friend.'

Magnus said nothing. He stopped to let Kendrick move ahead of him, then turned and looked into the sky as if trying to read something in the air. He listened to the sound of the woodlands, and then cast his senses outwards. Everything was as it should be. He turned and looked back. What had briefly troubled him? Perhaps it was Kendrick's warning about the boy. Still, a sword was not forged until the metal was heated, and if a flaw existed in the steel, that was when you found it, in the crucible. And every blade would be needed for the war to come if his father's plan wasn't successful.

* * *

Talon heaved the last of the flour sacks onto the pile he had been constructing. A wagon-load of provisions had arrived from Latagore and he had spent the afternoon unloading it, hauling them down the steps into the basement below the kitchen. Besides enough flour for the winter, there were baskets of vegetables and fruits imported from other lands, preserved by some fey art that Talon didn't understand, though he had overheard enough in the kitchen to know that such magic preservation was costly beyond the means of any but the noble and wealthy.

Leo and Martha had taken command of a variety of small boxes, containing spices, herbs and condiments that the cook counted more valuable than their weight in gold. All their provisions for the winter, with what they could grow in the garden and harvest in the autumn, and what Talon and Caleb could hunt, meant a winter of good food, far beyond what the boy was used to.

'Talon!' came Lela's voice from above. He hurried up the broad wooden steps, and saw her standing next to the wagon, a rapt expression on her face. 'Look!' She pointed skyward.

Snow was falling, tiny flakes blown about by a gentle but persistent breeze, most of them melting upon reaching the ground. 'It's just snow,' Talon said.

Lela threw him a pout, one of her many expressions which caused his stomach to go hollow. 'It's wonderful,' she said. 'Don't you think it's beautiful?'

Talon watched the flakes falling for a moment, then said, 'I never thought of it. In my village, snow means months inside our houses or hunting in drifts as high as your chest.' For some reason, just mentioning the word 'chest' caused his eyes to drift to Lela's ample bosom, though after an instant he averted his eyes. 'My toes always hurt after a hunt.'

'Oh,' she said in mock disapproval. 'You have no sense of beauty. I come from a land that never sees snow. It's wonderful!'

Talon smiled. 'If you say so.' He looked into the rear of the wagon and saw that it was empty. 'I need to go tell the driver I've finished.' He closed the large wooden doors down into the cellar, then moved around to the kitchen door. Once inside, he realized how cold the air outside had become, for the kitchen seemed hot and close to him.

The wagon driver and an apprentice teamster sat at a small table in the corner of the kitchen, eating the meal Martha had prepared for them. They looked up as Talon approached. 'Wagon's unloaded,' he said.

The teamster, a gaunt man whose nose looked like a buzzard's beak grinned, showing that he was missing two front teeth. 'Be a good lad and unhitch the horses, will you? We're not done quite yet and it wouldn't do to leave them shivering out in the cold. We'll be staying the night and heading back north first thing in the morning.'

Talon nodded, and turned back towards the door. Lars intercepted him. 'You shouldn't have to see to his team. That's his job.'

Talon shrugged. 'I don't mind. No guests to worry about and it's either see to horses or scrub pots in here. Not much to choose from.'

Lars said, 'Suit yourself,' and returned to his duties.

Talon went back outside. The few moments in the kitchen had turned the air outside from brisk to uncomfortable. He hurried to the wagon and led the horses to the mouth of the barn. He had developed a fair hand in dealing with the fractious animals, and while his few attempts at riding had been less than pleasant, he found stable-work easy and mostly enjoyable. The heavy wagon had been drawn by a team of four, and it took a bit of convincing to get the animals to back up enough to put the wagon neatly out of the way. He quickly unhitched each animal, took it inside and got it into a stall. Then he set to brushing each of them. Even after having stood motionless for nearly a half-hour while he unloaded, the horses were still damp from their long pull to the inn that afternoon. Steam rose from their backs as he brushed, as the air turned bitterly cold.

By the time water and fodder had been placed in the stalls, Talon knew that the weather was turning serious. He went out into the stabling yard and looked up at the sky. The sun was setting, but he could see that the clouds were growing darker and thicker and the snow more insistent. He thought the teamster and his apprentice needed to be quick on the road to Latagore or else they would find themselves in snow up to their hubs in the next few days. If they were lucky. If a big storm was heading their way, they could find themselves snowed in for the winter at Kendrick's.

Supper passed uneventfully. After the kitchen had been cleaned and the bread readied for baking in the morning, Talon was about to retire to the room he shared with Lars and Gibbs, when Lela approached him. 'Don't go to your room, yet,' she said in a whisper. She put her hand upon his arm and led him to the pantry between the common room and the dining room. She pushed the door to the common room slightly ajar.

Gibbs was sitting quietly before the hearth, staring into the dying embers as he nursed a mug of ale. Lela closed the door, a mischievous smile in place. 'Lars needs the room for a while.'

'For what?' asked Talon.

Her eyes widened and she giggled. 'For what? You don't know?'

He frowned. 'If I knew, would I ask?'

She playfully put her hand on his stomach and gave him a gentle push. 'He and Meggie are there.'

Talon said, 'Why?' Then before she could answer, he realized. 'They need to be alone?' he asked.

'Of course, you fool!' she said playfully.

'With my people it is different,' he explained. 'We live in community buildings during the winter, and often a man and woman will lie together under bearskins. Everyone else pretends not to notice.'

'Around here we notice,' she said. Looking at him with a glimmer in her eye, she said, 'You look troubled. What is it?'

Talon's mind returned to Meggie's quirky smile and upturned nose, and the way her thin frame swayed slightly when she walked. At last he said, 'I don't know.'

Suddenly, Lela's eyes widened. 'You're jealous!'

Talon said, 'I don't know that word.'

'You want Meggie for yourself!' she said with a merry laugh.

Suddenly Talon's face was flushed and he wanted to be just about anywhere else. 'I don't know what you mean,' he stammered.

Lela gave the boy an appraising look for a long minute. Then she said, 'You're turning into a handsome young man, Talon.' She put her arms around his waist and pressed closer, her face just in front of his. 'Have you known a woman before?'

Talon felt his pulse race and he found himself speechless. Eventually, he shook his head.

Lela laughed and thrust herself away from him. 'You are *such* a boy.'

Abruptly, Talon found himself angry. For some reason the remark stung and he almost shouted, 'No, I am a man of the Orosini! I went upon my vision quest and . . .' He paused. 'I would have had my manhood tattoos upon my face had my family not been killed.'

Lela's expression softened, and she stepped back towards him. 'I'm sorry. I forgot.'

His anger soon fled as she pressed herself against him and kissed him, her soft, warm lips causing stirrings that threatened to overpower him. He grabbed her hard, and pulled her into him, eliciting a squeak of protest. She pushed him back slightly and said, 'Gently.'

Talon blinked in confusion, his mind swimming in feelings he could put no name to; he ached to pull her back into an embrace.

She grinned. 'You know nothing of the game of women and men.'

'Game?'

She took him by the hand. 'I've seen those games Robert and Magnus have taught you. Now I think it's time to teach you the best game of all.'

Feeling fearful and flushed with anticipation, Talon clung to Lela's hand as she led him through the common room towards the room she shared with Meggie.

Seeing what was transpiring, Gibbs grinned and hoisted his ale-jack in salute. As they climbed the stairs to the now-empty guests rooms, he said, 'Got to get another girl working here; that's all there is for it.'

Lacking any other comfort, he elected for one more ale before finding a place for himself for the night.

• CHAPTER FIVE •

Journey

*T*ALON SNEEZED.

'Too much pepper,' said Leo.

Talon wiped away the tears in his eyes with the hem of his apron and nodded. He had been working in the kitchen for a year now and over the last four months had come to feel at home there. He still served elsewhere at Kendrick's discretion, but most of his time recently had been spent with the cook.

Four months earlier Leo had walked in one day and beckoned Talon to his side, showing him how to prepare dishes for baking pies, a simple task involving lard and wheat flour. From there he had moved on to washing vegetables and fruits. He then worked his way up to preparing simple dishes. In the last few weeks, Talon had learned the basics of baking, cooking meats, and was now being trained how to make sauces.

Talon smiled.

'What's amusing you, young fellow?' asked Leo.

'I was just thinking how much more there is to getting food ready to eat than what I learned as a boy. My father and the other men of my village would sit around a large spit upon which a deer turned, talking about the hunt or crops or which son was the fastest runner, and the women baked bread or cooked stews or soup.

'My mother would have gawked in wonder at the spices in your cupboard, Leo.'

'Simple fare can be challenging, too, Talon. A spit of beef must be dusted lightly with salt and pepper at the right moment, then graced, perhaps, with a kiss of garlic just before presentation.'

Talon grinned. 'My mother would never have understood presentation.'

'You've only seen the barest glimpse of it, boy,' said Leo. 'What we do here is wasted upon commoners for the most part, and even those lords and ladies who stop by on their travels would count our fare rustic compared to the tables at which they've dined in the great cities.

'The noble tables of Rillanon and Roldem are each night piled high with the efforts of dozens of cooks and hundreds of kitchen whelps such as yourself. Each plate is graced with just such a portion of this dish, just such a portion of that delicacy. There is an art in this, boy.'

Talon said, 'If you say so, Leo. Though I'm not sure what you mean by "art". We have no such word in my language.'

Leo stopped stirring his own reduction sauce and said, 'You don't?'

Talon was fluent in Roldemish and now found himself being

corrected only on pronunciation and occasionally on his delight in profanity, which seemed to amuse Leo, irritate Robert, and outrage Martha. The Orosini were comfortable with sex and other natural body functions, and Talon found it oddly amusing that describing defecation or the sex act was considered 'bad' in Roldemish society.

'No,' said Talon. 'The closest the Orosini tongue can get is "graceful" or "beauty", but the idea of doing something just to do it is . . . not something I grew up with.' Talon had come to terms with the destruction of his family over the last year. Rather than the terrible pain it had given him, now it had become more of a dark memory which haunted him from time to time. The desperate anguish was gone, for the most part. Learning to do new things was part of the reason; and Lela was the rest.

'Well, then,' said Leo. 'You learn something new every day.'

Talon agreed. 'We have –' he corrected himself, '– *had* art in some of the crafts the women practise. My grandmother made patterned blankets that were prized by everyone in the village. Our shaman and his acolytes would make prayer . . . you don't have a word for it, circles of patterns of coloured sand. They would chant and pray while they worked, sometimes for days, in a special tent that they would put up and work inside. When they were finished, the entire village would gather to see the work and to chant as the wind took the prayer to the gods. Some of them were beautiful.' Talon paused. 'Those paintings Kendrick hangs in the dining room . . .'

'Yes?' asked Leo.

'I wish some of my grandmother's blankets or the sand prayer-circles could be remembered like that, hung on a wall for people to see. They were beautiful.'

'An eye for beauty, young Talon, is a gift.' Leo said.

Just then, Lela walked into the kitchen.

'And speaking of beauty . . .' muttered Leo with a grin.

Talon glanced at the girl and smiled slightly. His people could mask their feelings around strangers, but he felt now that the kitchen-staff were his family and everyone knew of his relationship with Lela. He had slept in her bed almost every night for the better part of the last year. Close to sixteen years of age, a man by the standards of his people, he would have been wed and a father by now had his village survived.

Lela returned his gesture with a smile.

'To what do I owe this pleasure?' asked Leo. 'Is the washing done?'

'Yes,' she said pertly. 'Meggie and Martha are folding the last of the dyed bedding and I came to see what needed to be done here.'

'Of course you did,' said the cook with a chuckle. He moved Talon gently aside, dipped a spoon into the sauce the young man was preparing and tasted it. He stared off into space reflectively for a long moment, then said, 'Simple, yet . . . bland.' His fingers danced across the small jars of spices before him, picking up a pinch of this, a dash of that, which he added to the sauce. 'This is for chicken, lad, and slowly roasted chicken. It is a bland meat, not full of flavour like those lovely partridges and turkeys you bring home from the hunt. Those require a simple sauce to bring out the bird's taste. This sauce needs to *give* the bird flavour. Here!' He poked the spoon at Talon's lips. 'Taste!'

Talon did so and nodded. It was exactly the sauce he had been trying to make. 'So I should have used more spices, Leo?'

'By twice, my boy, by twice.' The cook put down the spoon

and wiped his hands on his apron. 'Now, be a good lad and go and help Lela wash vegetables.'

Talon nodded and went over to the large wooden sink attached to the rear wall of the kitchen. It had a drain that cleverly went out through the wall and emptied into a small culvert that ran along the base of the building, then into a pipe under the ground and eventually into the cess pit Kendrick had dug beyond the outer wall of the courtyard. He hefted a bucket of cold water and stood there, pouring slowly while Lela washed the freshly-dug vegetables. It was the first of the spring crop and the thought of fresh carrots, radishes, and turnips made Talon's mouth water.

'Why the sauce?' asked Lela. 'We don't have any guests tonight.'

'That's why,' said Talon. 'Leo decided that since we had no one to complain about the sauce, he'd let me try another one.'

'You must be making progress,' Lela observed. 'He didn't throw this one across the kitchen.'

'True,' said Talon. 'You people can be strange at times.'

'*We're* strange?' She flicked water from her fingers at him as he put down the bucket. 'From what you've said about your people, *you're* the strange one.'

Talon's features darkened. 'It hardly matters. I'm the only one left.'

She tried not to look amused. 'Ah, I've hurt your feelings.' Playfully, she kissed his cheek. 'I'll have to make it up to you.'

Instantly his mood lightened. 'How?'

She spun away from him. 'Clean up the sink for me, and if you come to my room tonight, I'll show you.'

Lars entered the kitchen carrying a large quarter of beef. 'This is the last of the winter's storage,' he announced. 'Cold room is empty.' The cold room was an underground storage area Kendrick had built. It was frozen solid like everything else during the winter, and any provisions put in it were also frozen quickly. But in the spring it was slow to thaw, keeping anything inside frozen until spring was past and into summer and keeping things very cold from then to the next snowfall.

Leo said, 'We'll have to plan a trip to Latagore. We need to buy cattle as well as provisions.'

Talon said to Leo, 'May I go?'

Leo scratched his chin for a moment. 'Don't know, boy. That would be up to Robert, I assume. I'd be glad for the company, but usually I go with Kendrick or one of the lads.'

Lars hung the beef on the hook, pulled out a large knife and began to cut the meat. 'Why do you want to go, Talon?'

'I've never been to a city,' said Talon. 'I'd like to see one.'

'Well, then,' said Leo. 'I'll ask Robert what he thinks about it.'

As Talon finished cleaning up the vegetable waste left in the sink by Lela, he considered which was making him feel the most anticipation, visiting Lela after supper or visiting a city.

Talon watched as the lake appeared as if by magic once they crested the rise. They had come down out of the higher reaches of the sprawling forest of Latagore, known as the Greatwoods, into rolling hills and through half a dozen small valleys until they had entered a deep ravine, cut through by a small, but fast-running river. The landscape to their left was blocked from their view by a rising cliff face of stone and hard-packed earth, from which rose stubborn brush gripping for all it was worth. Off to the right, the land fell away rapidly, revealing the river gap, and in the distance there was a hint of blue which must surely be the Great Lake of Latagore.

Talon was fascinated by everything he saw and was content to ride in silence. Which was a good thing, given that Caleb had been selected to go to market by Kendrick, for reasons not given to Talon.

Talon had lived at Kendrick's long enough to have puzzled out a few things about the odd relationships between those who worked at the inn and those who stayed there. Kendrick owned and ran the inn, of that there was no doubt. Robert held some position of authority, relative to Kendrick, but Talon wasn't quite sure what it was. Robert and Pasko would leave the inn, for weeks at a time – once for two months – then return and reside there for a while. They were currently leaving on another journey and would be gone from the inn by the time Talon returned.

Talon had tried to understand the relationships at the inn in terms of his own people for quite a while, until he decided that trying to do this was proving to be an impediment to understanding. He knew Kendrick had a son somewhere, who was rarely mentioned. He knew Leo and Martha were man and wife, but without children of their own. He also knew that Lars and Meggie were occasionally lovers, though they seemed to be going though one of their many periods of barely talking to one another. And he knew that although everyone else considered him Lela's man, he was still unsure what Lela thought about it. He had puzzled out other relationships among the servants at the inn – those who resided either at the inn itself or on one of the nearby farms Kendrick owned in order to supply the inn with vegetables. But much of it still seemed alien to him; despite feeling some kinship with the kitchen staff at Kendrick's, he felt isolated, deprived of the traditional ties of family and clan.

He turned his mind away from that; dwelling on his lost past only led to despair and he knew he must make the best out of what life offered him. He watched the lake grow in size as they approached; then, as they crested another rise, he saw the city of Latagore.

The midday sun threw the city into sharp contrast: edges and lines, shapes and contours. Talon's eye almost refused to define the chaos of it; then order began to emerge. Kendrick's had been the largest man-made structure he had seen so far, and the sheer scope of the city nearly overwhelmed his senses. The city rested upon the shore of an inlet, miles across, which gave it the appearance of having been set down by some giant hand in a crook of the shoreline.

Caleb glanced over and saw Talon agape. 'What do you see?'

Talon knew that question. Robert asked it all the time, as did Marcus when he was tutoring Talon. It wasn't about his impressions or feelings, but rather the detail of what he observed: *facts* as Robert put it.

Talon instantly became analytical. 'The city has a wall around it, extending into the water . . . I'd judge a hundred yards or more into the water.' He narrowed his eyes. 'There's a large building in the middle of the city that rises high enough to over-look everything for miles. I don't know what it's called.'

'It's called a citadel. It was once a castle erected to defend this lake shore. The city grew up around it.'

'There are five large . . . things that stick out into the water.'

'Docks.'

Talon's eyes wandered for a moment and then he was struck by the size of the lake. Surely this couldn't be just a lake. It must be a sea.

Caleb's voice jerked him out of his reverie. 'What else?'

Talon began to list the details that appeared to his almost supernatural sight. Each time he encountered something alien he would struggle to describe it, Caleb would supply the word and he would move on.

As they passed down the road, heading towards the plain upon which the city rested, Talon lost his vantage point and was forced to rely upon memory. When they reached a stand of trees which cut off all sight of the city, Caleb said, 'You did well. You missed things, but you're new to this business of paying attention.'

'Paying attention to what?' asked Talon.

Caleb smiled – a rare occurrence – and he said, 'Why to everything. You pay attention to everything.'

'Why?'

They worked their way along the road, through the woods and past a meadow as Talon waited for his answer. At last Caleb said, 'When you hunt, to what do you pay attention to?'

'To everything,' answered Talon. 'The direction of the wind, the scents upon the air, the sounds of the woods, to anything that has left tracks.'

Caleb nodded. 'Always think of yourself as being on the hunt.'

'Always?' asked Talon.

'Always.'

'Why?'

'Because it'll keep you alive,' said Caleb.

They rode in silence for another hour before reaching a crossroads and an inn. It was an hour after midday and Caleb said, 'We'll rest the horses and eat here. Then we'll be in the city by supper.'

Talon had no argument. They had spent two days on the

road, and while sleeping under the wagon had been no burden, he welcomed the idea of a hot meal.

The inn was a tiny place, a way-stop for those few people who either found themselves just a little too late in the day to reach Latagore or who, like Caleb and Talon, were stopping for a midday meal. The sign above the door showed a man holding a pitchfork in one hand and a large mug in the other. The paint on the sign was faded, but Talon could see that the man's expression was one of sublime happiness.

'What is this place?' he asked Caleb quietly as the wagon ground to a halt.

'It is called the Happy Farmer Inn.'

Hearing the wagon, a boy appeared from out the back and listened as Caleb instructed him on how to take care of the two horses. As the wagon was empty, the horses were still fit and required only water and some hay. They would need more rest and grain on the long climb back up into the hills with the wagon loaded.

Caleb led Talon into the inn and crossed to an empty table in the corner. He removed his black slouch hat and adjusted the sword at his side so that he could sit comfortably at the table, and then motioned for Talon to sit down opposite him.

A middle-aged woman with an agreeable manner approached and asked their pleasure. Caleb ordered a meal and ale for both of them and then sat back to observe the other customers.

The common room was quiet, with only four other men taking their midday ease. Two were obviously traders of some fashion, portly men in sturdy but finely-fashioned travel clothing. The other two sat at the next table, heads together, speaking quietly. They appeared to be fighting men of some stripe; both wore simple clothing – tunics, trousers and over-jackets – but no jewellery was evident to Talon. However, their boots and weapons were well cared for, which Talon took to mean they spent a lot of time walking and fighting.

Food was brought and Talon and Caleb ate in silence. The meal wasn't as good as what was served at Kendrick's, but it was filling and the young man found the ale satisfactory.

Before they had finished, Talon saw all four other men rise and leave together. After they had gone, Caleb asked, 'Who do you judge them to be?'

'Two merchants on their way to Latagore, with two guards to accompany them.'

'A fair assumption. Though I wager something more was in the wind.'

'What do you mean?'

'I mean it's not unusual for guards to eat near their employers, at a separate table, as those two did, but they seemed intent upon a topic they wished their employers not to overhear. They spent the entire meal in deep conversation.'

Talon shrugged. 'I'm not sure what this means,' he said.

'It means nothing, except that it was not "business as usual" for the guards. One didn't touch his meal.' He indicated the table where the two guards had sat, and Talon saw that one plate was indeed untouched.

Talon had served enough guards and mercenaries during the year at Kendrick's to know that most of them ate whatever was in front of them as if it might be their last meal. 'All right, Caleb. What do *you* think this means?'

'There was no wagon in sight either in the stableyard behind the inn as we approached, or on either side of the building, but there were four horses being looked after by the boy who came to take our wagon.'

Talon reflected upon what he had seen and what he knew of travelling merchants. 'So, this would mean that those two merchants were travelling to buy goods in Latagore?'

'Or to arrange for transport somewhere else, but they are not selling wares in the city.'

'Which means they are carrying gold.'

'Perhaps, but the two mercenaries they hired are likely to assume as much.'

Talon hurried to finish his meal.

'What are you doing?' asked Caleb.

'We're going to hurry after them and help, aren't we?'

'We are not,' said Caleb. 'You'll find enough trouble on the road without volunteering to take up someone else's.'

'But those two guards will kill those men for sure,' said Talon, draining his mug and standing up. 'We can stop black murder.'

Caleb shook his head. 'Most likely they will take whatever gold the merchants have, and the horses, and leave them to walk to Latagore. By the time they reach the city, the two mercenaries will already have left on a boat for the far shore and be on their way to High Reaches or Coastal Watch.'

'Or they could simply slit their throats and linger in Latagore. The nervous one might get panicked and act rashly.'

Caleb stood up and signalled to the woman who had served them. 'Tell the boy to ready our wagon.' Looking at Talon he said, 'We will have to whip the horses to a froth to overtake them.'

'Not necessarily,' said Talon. 'The mercenaries do not look like the type to ride in haste. They will attempt to keep the merchants deceived until they attack them. You've travelled this road before; where would you judge the most likely place for the murders to take place?'

'There's a deep ravine five miles along from here, and it abuts the road. If I were to carry out an attack, that is where I would do it, for it would be easy enough work to drag the bodies up into the ravine for half a mile or so, then quickly return to the road without anyone noticing. It might take months for anyone to stumble on the bodies should that be the case.'

Talon said, 'Then we need to hurry. They must already be a mile or more down the road.'

Caleb fixed Talon with a curious look for a moment, then said, 'Let us go, then.'

They had to wait a few minutes for the wagon to be fetched around from the back. The boy had brushed the horses while they had rested and Caleb gave him a copper piece for doing the extra work.

Caleb set the horses to a fast walk, causing them to snort in protest at the faster than average pace. 'If you're right, we'll overtake the merchant and guards just as they reach the ravine cut-off.' He glanced over and saw that Talon's face was set in a mask of determination. 'Why are you so anxious to intervene, my young friend?'

Talon's expression turned dark. 'I don't approve of murder.'

Caleb nodded. After a moment he said, 'If you're going to act the hero, it would be well for you to go armed.'

Talon nodded. He turned and fetched out a sword and belt-knife from behind the wagon's seat. He had seen no reason to don them prior to this moment.

Caleb kept the horses moving and after a few minutes of silence, asked, 'How are the two mercenaries armed?'

Without hesitation, Talon answered, 'The taller one, the calm one, wore a long sword on his right hip – he's left-handed. He wore a long dagger on his left hip, and I glimpsed the hilt of a throwing knife inside the top of his right boot.

'The nervous fellow wore a short sword on his left hip and had two daggers in the right side of his belt. He had several knives inside that black sleeveless over-jacket he wore and another small blade in the sweatband inside his slouch hat, on the side with the black crow's feather.'

Caleb laughed, an even more rare occurrence than smiling. 'I missed that last one.'

'It deformed the hat slightly.'

'You've taken to your lessons at Kendrick's well. All you missed was the blade behind the buckle of the nervous man's belt. I only noticed it because he took care standing up and put his thumb behind it for a moment, as if preventing getting cut by it.'

'Sounds like a bad place to keep a blade.'

Caleb said, 'If done right, it's a good place, really. If done poorly . . .' He shrugged.

They rode along at a good clip as the sun travelled across the sky. As they crested a hill, Caleb said, 'There.'

In the distance, Talon could see the road rise up on the left and fall away on the right. The city was now clearly in view in the distance: they would easily have reached it before nightfall if things had gone as planned.

At the far end of the road, Talon saw movement. 'Four riders.'

Caleb snapped the reins and set the horses to a faster trot. 'They're going to reach the ravine sooner than I thought!'

The wagon picked up speed and Talon hung on to the seat with both hands as the heavy axles sent every bump from the wheel straight up into his back. This wagon was built to haul heavy loads, not provide comfort for those riding it.

The sound of the wagon flying down the road should have alerted the riders, but by the time Talon and Caleb drew near they could see the four men had squared off, the two merchants arguing with the two guards. The mercenary Talon thought of as 'the nervous one', drew his sword, just as his companion turned to see the wagon approaching. He yelled and the first man turned to see what the problem was.

The two merchants turned their horses and attempted to ride away, causing the nervous mercenary to swing his sword at the nearest merchant, cutting him on the left shoulder. The man shrieked and fell from his mount.

Caleb steered the now-galloping horses to the left of the three who were milling around. The merchant who had fallen scuttled like a crab, scrambling backwards away from the two riders. The other merchant was now charging down the road, arms flapping as if he was attempting to fly off the back of the horse.

Talon stood and launched himself off the wagon as it sped past, knocking the nervous rider from his horse, sending his sword flying. Caleb did his best to keep the wagon from overturning as it slowed down. The other mercenary quickly evaluated the situation and spurred his own mount to a gallop up the road, back the way they had come.

Talon landed on top of the nervous one who grunted as the breath was knocked out of him, then thrashed as Talon rolled off him. Talon came to his feet, sword in hand, expecting the man to be rising.

Instead the man lay on the ground clutching at his stomach. Blood fountained through his fingers and he looked at Talon.

'Look what you've done to me! You've killed me!'

Talon kept his sword in his hand as he went and knelt next to the man. 'That blade behind the buckle?' he asked.

'Damn thing never worked,' said the injured man. 'Now I'm bleeding like a stuck pig.'

Caleb had turned the wagon around and driven back to where Talon and the other two men waited. Talon pushed aside the wounded man's hands and disengaged the buckle. He pulled out the blade, a three-inch-long piece of sharp steel with a 't' cross handle; it was designed to slip out of the buckle and sit between the two middle fingers of the hand, the handle resting on the palm. It would be a dangerous jabbing weapon.

Caleb said to the merchant, 'Are you hurt?'

The man held his hand over his bleeding shoulder. 'I'll live, no thanks to that blackheart.' He was a stocky man with a balding pate, a fringe of grey hair circling the back of his head. His eyes were dark and his chin sported a tiny beard.

Caleb got down from the wagon and came to stand beside Talon. He looked down at the mercenary on the ground, at the knife and the wound and said, 'You'll live to hang. That little blade didn't cut too deep.'

He took the palm-knife from Talon, cut off some cloth from the mercenary's shirt and wadded it up. 'Press it hard against the wound with both your hands.' To Talon he said, 'Help me get him in the back of the wagon.'

Between them they got the wounded would-be robber in the back of the wagon. Then Caleb took a look at the merchant's shoulder. After a moment he said, 'You'll be fine.'

'Why are you helping?' he asked. 'I mean, thank you for saving me, but why?'

Caleb nodded towards Talon, who had taken up a position in the back of the wagon next to the wounded man. 'My young friend there has a streak of decency in him, I fear. He objects to murder, it seems.'

'Well, then thanks to the gods you both came along.'

'Let's get on to Latagore,' said Caleb. 'You ride up front with me.'

'I'm Dustin Webanks, merchant from Olasko. I was travelling to Latagore with my partner to purchase lumber.'

'And those two you hired sought to rob you of your gold.'

'Foolishly, yes. We carry no gold. We have letters of credit from the Royal Bursar in Opardum to make purchase on account.'

'So, you represent the Duke, then?'

Climbing gingerly up to the wagon, he said, 'Yes. Duke Kaspar is building a new hunting lodge, and he likes some wood carvings he's seen somewhere or another. Must have a particular wood for them, a wood that appears only to be harvested from the forests up here in Latagore. Hence, the journey.'

Caleb shrugged, as if it was of no matter to him. 'Your friend will send back the city guard for you, I expect.'

'Most likely,' said Dustin.

'Then they can escort us to the city, friend merchant.'

They all fell silent, each considering the events of the last few minutes. Talon looked at the prisoner, who appeared to be lost in some dark reflection on his plan going bad and wondered what had possessed the man to attempt to rob the merchant. Then he decided it might better serve him to discover what had caused him to act in such a rash fashion to aid a stranger.

CHAPTER SIX

Latagore

*T*ALON GAWKED.

He had remained silent as they had approached the city, reaching one of the western gates an hour before nightfall. He had been astonished at the size of Latagore as they had drawn near, but as they reached the outer boundaries of the city, he was dumbfounded.

Nothing in his experience had prepared him for the sight of so many people living so close to one another. The bustle and noise threatened to overwhelm him at first, then he began to drink in the sights and sounds.

Peddlers hovered near the gates of the city, hawking a variety of wares to any within the sound of their voices – trinkets, good luck tokens, items whose nature was unknown to Talon. Many who approached were ragged beggars, offering blessings to those who would aide them and curses to those who ignored them.

Caleb glanced over at the speechless lad and said, 'Better close your mouth before a bird builds a nest in it.'

'So many people,' Talon gasped.

Dustin Webanks looked over his shoulder at the boy. 'Never been to a city before?'

'No, sir.'

The prisoner, who'd been content to ride along in sullen silence, except for an occasional grunt of pain when the wagon bounced especially hard, said, 'This is nothing, boy. If you ever get down to Opardum or Kalesh'kaar, then you'd be seeing something. Latagore here is hardly big enough to rightly be called a city. More like an oversized town.'

Caleb grunted. 'Big enough city to have a guard and plenty of rope.' To Talon he said, 'This gate's the one you want when coming into the city. Most of the locals use it, because the other gates are used by travellers and caravans, so getting through takes time. That's why it's called the Locals' Gate.'

'How many gates are there?' asked Talon, thinking of the simple stockade around his village with its single gate.

'I believe this city has twenty . . . four? Yes, twenty-four gates.'

They pulled into a queue of people waiting to be admitted to the city before night fell and the gates were closed. Only two wagons and a band of men on horseback were in front of them, so they quickly reached the portal.

'Ho, Roderick!' shouted Caleb as he reined in.

'Caleb!' cried a soldier in the deep forest green uniform of the city. 'You here to sell or buy?'

'Buying,' said Caleb. 'We're empty coming in.'

The soldier motioned him through.

Caleb said, 'Can we drop off a bandit?'

A quick discussion with the soldier resulted in their prisoner being taken away. Dustin Webanks left them as well, to press charges with the magistrate, promising them a reward should they seek him out the next day at the Sign of the Running Footman.

Caleb drove the wagon through the city, heading to an inn where those from Kendrick's stayed when they were in the city. As darkness fell, they reached a cheery-looking building with a large stabling yard on the right. The sign hung outside it showed a man throwing balls into the air while blindfolded. A young man of roughly the same age as Talon appeared at the sound of the wagon's arrival.

'Ho, Caleb!' he shouted, upon seeing who was driving the wagon.

'Jacob!' Caleb returned.

The young man had sandy hair and a raw-boned, rangy look. He wore a simple cotton shirt and leather trousers, with heavy work boots. He took the horses in hand and said, 'Who's your friend?'

'Talon, this is Jacob.'

Talon nodded and jumped down from the wagon.

'Father will be glad to see you,' said Jacob. 'He's got some more hunting stories for you.'

'He found time to go hunting?' asked Caleb.

With a grin, Jacob answered, 'No, but he's got some new stories.'

Caleb smiled. ''Tis ever thus.'

They left the wagon to Jacob's care and entered the inn. A plump woman brightened as she saw Caleb. She hurried around from behind the long bar and threw her arms around him. 'Caleb, you rascal! It's been too long between visits! We haven't seen you since last summer!'

If the usually taciturn hunter was discomfited by the overwhelming embrace, he bore up with good grace, and when at last she released him, he said, 'Hello, Angelica.' Then he indicated his companion. 'Talon here is helping me on this trip.'

Suddenly, the boy found himself engulfed in a fragrant bearhug.

'Welcome to the Blind Juggler, Talon.' To Caleb she said with a wink, 'Ella's in the kitchen.'

Caleb said nothing, just smiled slightly. 'We'll need a room for two, perhaps three, days.'

'You have it,' said the woman. 'Now, get yourselves a good table by the fireplace. The porters and teamsters will be filling the place up as soon as it's dark, and then it'll be every man for himself.'

Caleb pointed to a small table in the corner near the fireplace, and Talon went over and sat down. 'We'll wash one at a time,' Caleb said. 'She's right. In a few minutes there'll hardly be room to turn around in here.'

Angelica appeared a moment later with two large mugs of ale. Handing a key to Caleb, she said, 'First room, top of the stairs. It's the best.'

'Thanks,' said Caleb.

Talon sipped at the brew and found it strong and flavourful.

'Watch how you drink that, Talon. It'll sneak up on you if you're not careful.' Leaning forward he continued, 'Learn to sip and look as if you're drinking more than you are.'

'How do I do that?'

Caleb demonstrated. He picked up the mug and appeared to take a hearty draught, but when he put the mug under Talon's chin for inspection, the boy saw only a drop of the ale was gone. 'You spill some on the floor or let it drip down your chin if you're with rough company. If you're dining with quality folk, you motion for the server to bring you a fresh goblet from time to time. No one except the servant, will notice he's carrying away a half-filled cup, and he'll not speak to anyone – most likely he'll drink it himself before he reaches the pantry.'

'Why?'

'Why will he drink it?'

Talon shook his head and grinned. 'No, I get that part of it. No, why do I want to appear to be drinking more than I am?'

'Make it a habit. Men in their cups are fools, more often than not. And it can be wise to look the fool at times.' Caleb stood. 'I'm going to have a wash.'

Talon nodded and sat back. Caleb headed out through a door next to the bar, which Talon assumed led to the kitchen. Like most of his people, Talon had swum in the rivers and lakes in the mountains in all but the coldest months. He had cleaned his skin in the sweat lodge of his village; sitting with the men and women as they scraped the day's dirt off their skins with gracefully curved sticks, then rinsed off with a bucket of tepid water kept next to the stones to make steam. Using soap and water – cold most of the time – had seemed a strange ritual, but Talon had learned to make it a habit. Most people, he noticed, including the nobility, seemed to bathe or wash their hands and face at whim, yet those at Kendrick's spent a signifi-cant amount of time bathing and washing. Talon had asked Lela about that, and she had said that it had been the habit there when she arrived and she didn't mind too much.

Talon thought of Lela now and his stomach tightened. He missed her, despite the excitement of the journey. He had never known a woman before her; as was the custom of his people, he would have remained untouched by a woman until the night of his wedding. The practice was not always observed, especially among those who had no mate chosen during the year they reached manhood or womanhood, but it was a tradition, and most Orosini followed tradition. Talon's thoughts occasionally wandered to Eye of the Blue-Winged Teal and the other girls of his village; he wondered if they would have been as joyous in their lovemaking as Lela, who laughed and was playful as often as she was ardent. He pushed aside thoughts of his village and the girls he had grown up with, for it was still a painful subject for him if he dwelt upon it; Robert had taught him to keep his thoughts in the presence or near future, for as Robert had told him, 'To dwell in the past is to live in regret'.

As was becoming his habit, Talon studied his environment. The room hosted a dozen tables, so perhaps as many as fifty guests could comfortably fit in; more, if they didn't mind standing at the bar. Talon recalled the exterior of the building, compared it to Kendrick's and decided there must be six or eight rooms upstairs. Like most inns of the region, some guests would sleep here in the common room, under the tables for a few copper coins. While the floor might seem unwelcoming, with a heavy cloak to lay upon it, it was definitely better than trying to sleep in the open. The banked fire in the hearth would provide warmth throughout the night and there would be a hot meal available upon waking.

After a minute of quiet reflection, Talon saw the front door open and half a dozen burly men enter. They were all dusty and wore rough homespun. From the heavy boots (many with double reinforced toes) and uniformly massive builds, Talon assumed these men to be porters, those who unloaded the trading wagons and carried crates to shops and warehouses throughout the city. They all walked quickly to the bar and one shouted, 'Angelica! Ella! Someone! We perish from thirst!'

A couple of the men chuckled but they all waited quietly for a moment, until Angelica appeared through the kitchen door. She greeted the porters by name and drew their drinks without asking their pleasure; obviously they were regular customers.

Over the next few minutes another dozen or so men entered the inn, all of them workers, either porters like the first group or wagon drivers and teamsters.

Caleb returned and sat down. 'What have you learned?'

Talon glanced at his companion. For a moment he didn't understand the question, as he had been sitting alone, then he realized that Caleb was asking him what he had deduced from his observations. He told him about his guess as to the size of the inn, then added, 'The stabling yard to the rear must be spacious, because it took our wagon with ease, and we will use only one of the rooms. I assume it can house as many as a dozen horses, perhaps more.'

'More,' said Caleb as a pretty girl entered from the kitchen and brought over a tray of food. 'Talon, this is Ella.'

Talon glanced at the girl, who was slender as a reed, yet he instantly saw the resemblance to Angelica. She was perhaps a few years older than Talon, with blue eyes and very dark hair, made dramatic by a very pale complexion and pinkly rosy cheeks. She wore a plain dress of blue linen and a white apron, but the belt around her waist revealed a pleasing proportion and ample curves despite her being so slender.

'Hello,' he said.

She smiled and instantly Talon was struck by how pretty she was. She put down the tray and glanced at Caleb with an open warmth and then said, 'I'll be back if you need anything.'

As she hurried back to the kitchen, more workers entered the inn. When she reached the bar, one of the arriving porters called out, 'Ella!'

She paused for a moment and her expression darkened. 'Hello, Forney,' she said, then without another word she walked quickly into the kitchen.

Talon studied the newcomer. He was a young man, perhaps Caleb's age, sturdily built with a thick thatch of black hair. His clothing was rough, but relatively clean. He moved to the bar with his companions.

Jacob came into the bar from the kitchen, greeted a few of the regular patrons of the inn and came over to the table. Caleb pushed out a chair for him and the young man sat down. 'Your horses are bedded and fed. The bay mare was favouring her left front hoof, so I had a look at it. Picked up a small stone. Could be forming an abscess.'

Talon had picked out the hooves every night and when resting at noon, so the animal must have picked up the stone along the last leg of the journey.

Jacob continued. 'I'll keep an eye on it.' He leaned forward and lowered his voice. With an evil grin, he said, 'So, has Forney seen Ella talking to you yet?' Caleb didn't look amused. Jacob turned to Talon. 'My sister has set her cap at our friend here, but young Forney over there is determined to marry her.'

Talon was still vague as to the marriage customs of these people, but he was beginning to sense things were nowhere near as formal among the city people – as he thought of everyone who wasn't Orosini – as they had been at home. Not quite knowing what to say, Talon said nothing.

Caleb glanced over at Forney then said to Jacob, 'I've told your sister I like her, but you know as well as I do I'm a long way from marriage.' He got a distant look, then added softly, 'If I ever do wed.' He gave them a slight smile. 'Besides, if I read things right, Forney would have his work cut out for him even if I'd never set foot in Latagore.'

Jacob laughed. 'He does get on Ella's bad side more than most, for some reason. But then it's all of a piece, isn't it? You want what you can't have.'

Talon looked puzzled. Jacob noticed and said, 'Ella wants Caleb here, but can't have him, and Forney wants Ella, and can't have her. It's the same, see?'

Talon didn't, entirely, but he nodded as if he did. After a moment, he said, 'Who is he?'

'Forney?' asked Jacob with a shrug. 'He's a good enough sort, but nothing special.'

Caleb raised an eyebrow and gave Jacob a sardonic half-smile.

'All right, so his father is the wealthiest shipper in the region.'

Talon didn't know much about people of wealth, save those who visited Kendrick's, so he said, 'He dresses much like the others.'

'That's his father's doing. The old man wants the son to learn the business from the wagon-hubs up. As I said, he's not a bad sort.' Then he added, 'Nothing like our mysterious travelling man, here.' He patted Caleb on the shoulder. 'Ella's had her cap set at him since she was . . . what? Fifteen?'

'That was four years ago, Jacob.'

Jacob nodded. 'I keep telling her that if she got to know you, she'd change her mind, but you know how sisters are.'

'Not really,' said Caleb. 'I have a brother, remember?'

A strange expression passed over Jacob's face. It was only for a bare instant, but Talon noticed it. Then, forcing lightness into his voice, Jacob said, 'Magnus is hard to forget.' He pushed his chair back noisily and stood up. 'Well, I have other duties to attend to. If you need anything, just ask.'

'We'll be fine,' said Caleb.

Talon waited for a moment for Jacob to leave, then said to Caleb, 'There are so many things I don't understand about you people.'

'You people?' repeated Caleb.

'You and Jacob, and those back at Kendrick's.' He struggled with the concept. 'People who are not Orosini.'

Caleb glanced around the room. 'It's better that you forget you're Orosini, at least when you're within hearing range of strangers.'

'Why?'

'Someone went to a lot of trouble to see the Orosini dead, Talon. While you, alone, pose no threat to those people, the fact that you witnessed the calculated genocide of an entire nation makes you a potential . . . embarrassment.' He raised his voice. 'Now, back to what you said; you don't understand what?'

Talon looked away as if unwilling to meet Caleb's gaze. When he spoke again, his voice was quiet and flat. 'The . . . banter, I think is the word. The . . . joking, but not joking speech.'

'The teasing.'

'Yes, that's the word. Lela does it with me sometimes, and there are moments when I don't know if she's serious about what she's saying or not.'

Caleb shrugged. 'That hardly makes you unique among young men, Talon.'

'Perhaps, but you're older than I am and I thought—'

Caleb cut him off with a rare laugh. 'I can be of no help to you, my young friend.' He leaned forward and looked into his mug of ale. 'Some day, perhaps, you'll meet the rest of my family and see where I was raised. But even if you never do, you should know that my upbringing was anything but ordinary.' He glanced up and smiled. 'I grew up as a blind man would among the sighted.'

'What do you mean?'

'One day I'll explain that, but suffice it to say I was not a happy child. My parents are exceptional people, talented beyond imagining, but they had no means to heal what I saw as a flaw in my nature.'

Talon sat back, his expression one of open astonishment. 'I perceive no flaw in you, Caleb. I judge you to be the best hunter I have known, and my people are renowned for hunting. I have studied enough with Kendrick with the sword to see you're as gifted with the blade as with the bow. You're plain speaking, yet thoughtful. You have patience and look deeply into things. What is lacking?'

Caleb smiled and sat back. 'Becoming a student of human nature, aren't you? Robert will do that to a man, given enough time. It's one of his gifts. What is lacking,' he said softly, 'is magic. My brother is not the only practitioner of magic in my family; rather I am the only one who does not have the gift. I grew up on an island where I was virtually alone in this.'

Talon said, 'So Robert and your brother are both magicians?' He kept his voice low.

'You didn't know?'

'I never saw either of them practice, although . . .' He paused. 'The lessons your brother teaches are all about using the mind, more . . .' He groped for a concept. 'Stranger than the lessons in logic which Robert gives me. Magnus shows me how to do things –' he tapped his head, '– in here, that I didn't imagine were possible. Yet I have no talent for magic.'

'You know this for certain?' asked Caleb, as if making light of the subject.

'Among my people we have very few who are called to be . . . *shaman*, a magic priest. Each baby is tested, and those who have the talent leave their villages as children to study with the shamans. Among my people, there are a handful, and they . . .' Suddenly feeling overwhelmed, Talon said, 'It doesn't matter. They are all dead.' He felt moisture gathering in his eyes and blinked. 'It's been a while since I've felt that.'

Caleb nodded. 'It never goes away, completely. But you'll discover other things in life.' His manner brightened. 'My point was that while I've long since recovered from the imagined slights of my birth and upbringing, one thing I was *never* good at was understanding women. And like you, I was an "outsider" when I first came to this part of the world, with no bearings to go on.' He took a drink of ale then said, 'On the other hand, learning can be very pleasant at times.'

Talon grinned. 'It can be. Lela is . . .'

Caleb finished for him. 'Lela. She's a lively lass, I'll grant you that.'

'How do I . . .'

'What?'

Talon attempted to frame his thoughts. After a long silence, in which the two young men sat looking at one another while the porters engaged in a loud discussion in the background, Talon leaned forward and said, 'Among the Orosini our mates are selected for us by our parents. I have no parents, and I do not know about Lela's parents—'

Caleb interrupted. 'You're thinking about marriage?'

Talon blinked as if surprised to hear it put that way, but at last he nodded. 'I don't know what to do.'

Caleb said softly, 'Talk to Robert.'

Talon nodded.

Caleb then said, 'But I must warn you, I don't think it's going to happen, even should Lela be willing, which I don't think she is.'

'But she loves me!' Talon said, just loud enough to cause two of the porters to turn and regard him. With a laugh and a rude remark, they returned to their own conversation.

'As I said, I am no expert on women, Talon. But this you must know. You are not the first lad to warm Lela's bed.'

'I knew that,' said Talon.

Caleb sat back as if considering his words. After a moment, he said, 'What passes between a man and a woman is their own business. But I will tell you this. You know men who have been in Lela's arms.'

Talon blinked, as if he hadn't considered this. 'Gibbs?' Caleb nodded. 'Lars?' Again Caleb nodded.

Talon said, 'But Lars is with Meggie.'

'Now, but they fall out as often as not; Meggie is no one's

idea of a summer festival. She has qualities, but she can be a difficult woman.'

'But that's not right,' said Talon.

'Talon, it's not a question of right or wrong. It's the way it is. Among your people, your mates are selected and you can go through life knowing only one woman, but here . . .' He sighed. 'It's different.'

Talon appeared distressed.

Caleb said, 'You should know that I have been with Lela.'

Talon looked shocked. 'You!'

'Last Midsummer, on the day Pasko and Robert found you, she and I drank too much ale and ended up spending the night together. And she has done the same with a few handsome travellers, as well.'

Talon looked as if his world was falling in on him. 'Is she . . . what is that word?'

'What word?'

'A woman who lies with men for money.'

'A whore,' supplied Caleb. 'No, my young friend, she is not. But she is a healthy girl who likes men, and she's from a land where people don't think twice about lying with one another for amusement.'

Talon felt an empty pit form in his stomach. 'It's not right,' he muttered.

Caleb said, 'Go and wash your hands.' He waved towards the door into the kitchen. 'The food will be here in a moment. Just remember that in most things, right or wrong depends on where you're standing at the moment. My father's people would have thought having your life's mate picked out for you by your parents to be . . . well, barbaric.' As Talon's expression started to darken, Caleb added, 'No offence intended, but I'm pointing out that things look the way they do because that is how you were taught as a child. And the rest of the world is vastly different to what a child can imagine. Now, go and wash.'

Talon stood up and made his way past the bar and into the kitchen. There he discovered familiar sights. Angelica and Ella were working alongside two others: a man who must be Jacob's father, given their resemblance, and another man, who was obviously the cook. Talon found a bucket and soap and had a wash. When he looked up, he found that Ella was giving him a sidelong glance of appraisal.

He ventured a tentative smile and wiped his hands upon a cloth hung next to the bucket. Although she had affection for Caleb, she seemed to be looking at him in a disquieting way. He left the kitchen and returned to where Caleb was waiting. He sat down and looked at the man he had considered to be a friend; yet he had been with the woman Talon loved! How was he supposed to feel now?

Finally, Talon let out a long sigh and said, 'I will never understand women.'

Caleb laughed and said, 'Welcome to the brotherhood, my friend.'

Early the next day, Caleb started his rounds of the city. Five or six times a year, Kendrick had specific goods shipped out to the steading, including wheat flour, rice, sugar and honey, and seasonal items. But twice a year a special list was prepared and someone had to go into the city to purchase those particular items. Often it was Kendrick himself, but this time Caleb had elected to go.

After the third shop had been visited, Talon was beginning to understand why. Caleb seemed to possess a knack for negotiations. He could sense when a merchant was ready to accept a lower price, or when he was at his limit. As they walked down the street to the next shop, Talon asked, 'How do you know?'

'How do I know what?'

'When to stop arguing over the price?'

Caleb dodged aside as a small band of urchins came racing down the street towards them, followed a moment later by an angry merchant. 'There are things to watch for. It's the same when you gamble or if you're trying to see if a man is lying.'

'What things?'

Caleb said, 'Many things, but let's start with the more obvious ones. The expression. The spice trader, this morning, for example, was pleased to see a customer. His face mirrored genuine delight at our arrival.'

'How could you tell?'

'The moment you enter a shop, watch the man's face. Most merchants will pause for a brief instant to see who calls upon them. In that moment, you'll see a truth. It takes a while to learn, but you'll soon discover for yourself the difference between a man who's genuinely pleased to see a customer and one who is feigning pleasure. The first needs to sell you something, while the second may or may not.

'There are many other truths buried behind a false smile, a proffered wish for good health or a claim that a price is too low or too high. For the time being, just watch the men with whom I deal, not me, and see what you see.'

Talon watched throughout the day and after each bargaining session, he would ask questions. Slowly, he began to understand a little of what Caleb meant, that there were telltale signs to be seen if one had the patience to look for them.

A little after midday they reached a small market near the eastern wall of the city and wended their way through the stalls of merchants offering food, clothing, live poultry, jewellery, tools, weapons, even a broker for mercenary guards. The shoppers looked different to the people who populated the rest of the city and Talon felt a stab of recognition. For a brief instant he thought he was among his own people! The men wore tattoos upon their faces, although the markings were unfamiliar. They wore fur over-jackets, not unlike those worn by the Orosini, and they travelled in groups that included children and the elderly.

He heard speech that was tantalizingly familiar, peppered here and there with words that he recognized. He put out his hand and halted Caleb, who turned to see what was wrong. Noting the expression of concentration upon Talon's face, Caleb said nothing but waited as Talon strained to make sense of what he heard.

After a few moments of listening to a man speaking with a woman whom Talon took to be his wife, he realized he understood the speech, even though it was heavily accented and contained several strange words and phrases. Leaning close to Caleb he asked in low tones, 'Who are these people?'

Caleb motioned for Talon to follow him and as he moved away from the couple of strangers, he replied, 'These are the Orodon. They live on the other side of a mountain range to the north. They are distant kin to the Orosini, though they are plainsmen and fishermen of the deep oceans, not mountain people. They have villages, but no cities, so each winter many of them journey south and in the early spring come here to the market in Latagore. There are traders who also put in at coastal villages up and down the land of the Orodon regularly.'

'Why have I not heard of them?'

Caleb shrugged. 'You would have to ask someone who is now dead – your father or grandfather. Once all these lands belonged to your ancestors, Talon. Men from the south, city men, moved northwards and pushed your people up into the mountains, and the Orodon to the north. The nations to the south are all related to the nation of Roldem, which is why that language is spoken throughout these kingdoms.'

Talon glanced over his shoulder as they left the open market and walked down another street. 'I would like to know more of these people.'

'Magnus will be thrilled,' Caleb said. 'He has a particular bent for history and will be happy to teach you. It bores me, I'm afraid.'

They reached an inn, the sign of which showed a man in footman's livery running after a departing coach. 'The Running Footman,' said Caleb. 'In which we'll find our friend Dustin Webanks.'

They entered the relative darkness of the common room of the inn and stood blinking for a moment as their eyes adjusted to the darkness. Then with an inarticulate shout of rage, Talon drew the sword at his side and charged straight at a man who was standing at the bar.

· CHAPTER SEVEN ·

Education

*C*ALEB MOVED SWIFTLY.

He saw Talon draw his sword, shout in rage and charge at a man standing at the bar. The man – a mercenary, judging by his garb and weapons, was a seasoned veteran who reacted with shock only for a moment before recognizing a threat. But as his hand moved to his sword, Caleb reached out with his left leg and caught Talon's right ankle, tripping him.

A second later Caleb had his own sword in his hand and had moved to stand between Talon, who was scrambling to his feet, and the man at the bar. He lowered his swordpoint in the general direction of the stranger and with his left hand pushed Talon back to his knees as he attempted to rise.

'Hold on!' Caleb shouted. 'Wait a minute!'

The mercenary assumed a defensive position rather than

attacking either of the two men he faced. 'I'm holding,' he replied. 'But not for long.'

Talon attempted to get up again and Caleb grabbed his tunic by the fabric at the shoulder and hauled at him. Instead of the resistance he had anticipated, Talon found his upward motion aided so that suddenly he was standing upright on his toes. Caleb let him hang there for a moment before releasing him. Talon crashed to the floor, landing on his backside.

'Wait, damnit!' shouted Caleb.

Talon waited.

'What is this about?' yelled the mercenary.

'He's a murderer!' Talon shouted, trying to rise once more, his face full of rage. In his anger, he had reverted to his native language.

Caleb let him get halfway to his feet, then kicked his left heel, sending him back to the floor again. In the language of the Orosini, Caleb said, 'No one here but me understood what you just said. Who do you think this man is?'

'One of the men who killed my people!'

Caleb did not take his eyes off the mercenary for more than a second. 'Your name?' he asked the man in Roldemish.

'Who wants to know?'

'Someone trying to keep the bloodshed to a minimum,' answered Caleb.

'My name is John Creed, from Inaska.'

Glancing at Talon, to make sure he was still behaving, Caleb asked, 'Have you ever served with Raven?'

Creed nearly spat. 'I wouldn't piss on Raven if his arse was on fire. I'm a mercenary, not a child killer.'

Caleb said to Talon, 'Slowly,' and let him rise.

Sensing the crisis had past, the mercenary asked, 'Who's your hot tempered friend?'

'This is Talon, and I'm Caleb.'

Putting his sword away, John Creed said, 'If that lad's looking for Raven's bunch and he acts like that you'd better make sure he has enough silver on him to pay for his funeral pyre. They'll cut him up for dog meat without spilling a drop of ale and laugh while they're doing it.'

Turning to Talon, Caleb said, 'What were you thinking?'

Talon slowly put his sword away, not taking his eyes from Creed. 'He looks . . .'

'He looks like someone else, so you just go witless and forget everything you've been taught, is that it?'

Talon studied the man, attempting to fit him into the images that still were vivid in his memory and gradually realized how foolish he had been. Creed was a brawny man with black hair which hung to his shoulders. His nose had obviously been broken more than once and was little more than a distorted lump in the centre of his face. His mouth was topped by a drooping moustache. His face was unremarkable, except for his eyes, which were narrowed as he studied his erstwhile attacker. Talon recognized his eyes; they were like Caleb's, dark and intense, and they didn't miss a detail of what they saw. This man resembled one of the men who had destroyed his village, one of the men Talon had surprised before he was shot with the crossbow bolt, but he wasn't the same man.

'I'm sorry,' he said to Caleb.

'Don't tell me. Tell him.'

Talon moved past Caleb and stood before John Creed. 'I was wrong. I am sorry.' He looked the mercenary straight in the eyes.

Creed was silent for a moment, then the left corner of his mouth moved upward and with a crooked smile he said, 'No harm done, lad. A hot temper is a sign of youth. You'll outgrow it . . . if you're lucky to live long enough.'

Talon nodded. 'I acted rashly.'

Creed continued to appraise the boy. Finally he said, 'Raven's men must have done you quite an injury for you to go flying off the handle like some loose axe-head.'

'They did,' was all Talon said.

'Well, if you're looking for Raven and his bunch, word is he's been working for the Duke of Olasko for the last few years. Young Kaspar has them involved in some difficulty down in the Disputed Lands, bumping heads with the Duke of Maladon and Simrik's men. So you're in the wrong end of the world if you're trying to find Raven.'

Caleb said, 'Let us buy you a drink, to make amends.'

'Thanks,' said Creed.

Caleb looked around the crowded inn, which was returning to a semblance of normalcy now that the potential confrontation was halted. Caleb instructed the innkeeper to provide Creed with a drink, then took Talon by the elbow and moved him through the crowd. At a corner table he half-pushed the lad down into a chair. He looked at the boy for a long while. After a few minutes of silence between them, Caleb said, 'For someone who is normally thoughtful and reflective before acting, you were as rash as a man can be.'

Struggling with the frustration and rage that were bringing him to the edge of tears, Talon nodded. 'I saw that man . . . and something inside just rose up and overwhelmed me. I was certain he was . . . one of the men I fought when my village was destroyed.'

Caleb signalled for a serving girl to bring them drink and food, then removed his gauntlets, and threw them on the table. 'You're young. As Creed said, you'll outgrow the rashness if you live long enough.'

Talon remained silent. The drinks and food appeared and they ate without discussion. Talon brooded upon what had occurred and as they finished eating, he said, 'Caleb, why didn't you tell me?'

Caleb said, 'What?'

'That you knew who it was that raided my village?'

Caleb's eyes flickered only for an instant, but Talon knew he had caught him out. 'You told me about the raid, many times,' he replied.

'But you never told me their leader was called Raven. You knew who they were!'

Caleb let out a long sigh. 'Very well, Raven and his company are well enough known. I guess it never occurred to me that you needed his name.'

'There's something else. What is it?'

'Nothing.' Caleb spoke softly, but his eyes warned Talon not to press the matter.

Calmly, Talon said, 'You know. Tell me.'

Caleb regarded the young man for a while, then he said, 'Not today.'

'When?'

'When you're able to understand.'

'Among my people I have been a man for nearly two years, Caleb. If . . . my village still existed, I would almost certainly be a father. What is so difficult to understand here?'

Caleb sipped at his ale. Finally he said, 'There are many more things involved in such a choice than I can reveal to you. I judge you able in many things, Talon. More able than most your age, and even than some twice your years, but the decision wasn't mine alone.'

'Whose, then? Robert's?'

Caleb nodded. 'He is responsible for your training.'

Talon turned his head slightly, one eye fixed upon Caleb. 'Training for what?'

'Many things, Talon,' said Caleb. 'Many things.'

'Such as?'

'That is most certainly a topic for you to take up with Robert. But this much I will tell you, Talon of the Silver Hawk. Should you learn all that is given you to master, you will become an unusual and dangerous man. And you will need to be such should you choose to avenge your people.'

'I have no choice in the matter,' said Talon in even tones. 'Once free of my debt to Robert, I must find the men who destroyed my people.'

Caleb knew what he intended once he found those men. Finally he said, 'Then be diligent in your work, and learn your lessons well, Talon, for those you seek have powerful and deadly friends and masters.'

Talon sat quietly, contemplating what Caleb had said, while around him the bustle in the room increased as more men came in to drink. Among them was Dustin Webanks and his companion from the day before.

'Hello!' Dustin called out as he spied them in the corner. 'I feared you wouldn't appear, but I'm glad you have for I feel strongly in your debt.'

He crossed the room to them and Caleb indicated that he

and his companion should take the remaining two chairs, but Webanks declined. 'We have much to do so we will be on our way shortly.' He removed a pouch of coins from his belt. 'There is no value I can place on my life, but please accept this gold as a reward for your actions on my behalf.'

His companion looked away, as if embarrassed by the fact that he had fled while Webanks was in peril. The pouch hit the table with a loud clinking sound and Caleb looked at Talon. When the boy didn't move, Caleb said, 'It was your idea to take a hand; you leapt from the wagon to knock the assassin off his horse. You deserve the reward.'

Talon looked at the pouch. He had served long enough at the inn to have some idea of how many coins filled a pouch of that size, and calculated that the gold in it amounted to more than he could rightly expect to earn in ten years of toil. Yet he hesitated. At last he reached out and pushed the bag back towards Webanks.

'You refuse it?' asked the merchant in astonishment.

Talon said, 'As you said, your life is without price. Instead of gold, however, I would ask you a favour.'

'Name it.'

'Should I come to Opardum in the future, I will ask it of you then.'

Webanks seemed confused by the request, but said, 'Very well then, I am in your debt.' He picked up the gold, then glanced at his companion who seemed likewise bemused by the young man's refusal of the gold. They exchanged perplexed expressions and, bowing slightly, withdrew from the men.

Caleb waited until they had left and then said, 'Why?'

Talon said, 'Gold will buy things I don't need. I have food, clothing and friends at Kendrick's. But if what you say is true, that my enemies have dangerous friends and powerful masters, I need more friends. Merchant Webanks may prove to be such a friend in the future.'

Caleb sat back and considered what Talon said. After a moment, he smiled. 'You learn quickly, my young friend.'

Instead of acknowledging this remark, Talon's face whitened and his hand flew to the hilt of his sword. But rather than leap to his feet, he sat there as taut as a bowstring. Caleb slowly turned to see what he was looking at. 'What is it?'

'That man,' said Talon.

Caleb saw that a man had entered the inn and was now over by the bar speaking with Webanks and his companion. Caleb's own hand drifted to the hilt of his sword. He turned and looked at Talon. 'What of him?'

'He *is* one of those who destroyed my village.'

'Are you certain?'

'Yes,' said Talon, his voice the hiss of a coiled serpent. 'He wore the tabard of the Duke of Olasko, but he sat upon a black horse, commanding the murderers who killed my people.'

Caleb looked around and saw that four other men had come in behind the man. They were glancing around the room, as if seeking any sign of trouble. Caleb returned his attention to Talon and said, 'What do you propose to do?'

'Watch.'

Caleb said, 'Well done. You do learn quickly.'

For fifteen minutes they sat there, sipping at half-empty mugs of ale, until the five men left. Talon got up instantly and crossed to Webanks. With a calm voice he asked, 'Master Webanks, a question.'

'Certainly, young Talon.'

As Caleb joined them, Talon said, 'I noticed just a moment ago you were deep in conversation with a man, one who looked passingly familiar to me. I believe he may have visited the inn where Caleb and I are employed. But I can't recall his name.'

Webanks looked disturbed and said, 'He is just a guard, one I've hired for the return trip to Opardum. He and his four men are waiting for us to finish our business on behalf of the Duke and then depart.' With a nervous laugh he added, 'I can't recall his name at the moment. Ah . . . Stark. Yes, I believe it's Stark.'

'Thank you,' said Talon. 'I must have been mistaken.'

Talon then left the inn at such speed that Caleb had to hurry to keep up. Outside, he glanced left and right and caught sight of the men rounding a corner.

'What are you doing?' asked Caleb.

'Tracking.'

Caleb nodded and they followed the men. Talon's exceptional vision kept him from losing the five men, even though they moved quickly through the press of the bustling market and down streets thronged with wagons, carts and travellers. Finally they saw the men halt, look around to see if they were being followed, clearly decide that they weren't, and enter a nondescript building.

'What now?' asked Caleb.

'We wait.'

'For what?'

'To see what happens next,' said Talon, hunkering down with his back against a wall, so that he looked like a rustic hunter in the city taking his ease.

Caleb said, 'You're certain you recognized that man?'

'Yes, the man called Stark.'

Caleb leaned against the wall, his eyes upon the door. Time passed slowly, then a pair of men walked up to the door and entered without knocking. 'Well, then,' said Caleb.

'What?'

'Let's go back to our rooms,' he said.

'I want to see what happens next.'

Caleb reached down and gripped Talon's upper arm, pulling him to his feet. 'What happens next, my young friend, is war.'

'What?'

Not waiting to answer, Caleb turned and walked back towards the Blind Juggler. 'I'll tell you when we're out of the city.'

Talon followed him quickly.

The wagon lumbered out of the gate, and Talon looked over his shoulder. It was unusual for a wagon of trade goods to be leaving the city so late in the day, and as a result there was no other wagon ahead of them for inspection and they left quickly. They would spend the night at the Inn of the Happy Farmer and leave at first light the next day for Kendrick's.

Caleb had finished his shopping with unnatural speed, and had arranged for a variety of goods to be shipped to Kendrick's rather than wait for them to be loaded into the wagon. It would cost more, but Caleb seemed to think nothing of the added expense.

When they were free of any chance of being overheard, Talon said, 'Tell me.'

'That man Webanks called "Stark" is no mercenary.'

'I assumed that much, since he was wearing the tabard of the Duke of Olasko when he raided our village.'

'His name is Quentin Havrevulen, and he is the fourth son of a minor noble from Roldem, now serving as Special Captain in the service of Kaspar, Duke of Olasko. Captain Quint, as he's called, is as tough a man as they come and an exceptional soldier. He gets all of Duke Kaspar's difficult assignments.'

'What is one of the Duke of Olasko's captains doing in Latagore, disguised as a guard for some merchants?'

'Meeting two officers of the Latagore Army.'

'The two men you saw enter the building?'

'The same. One of them I recognize by sight, but the other I know by name and have spoken with. He's Captain Janoish, and for him to be speaking with Quint means that Latagore has been betrayed.'

'Why?

Moving the horses along the road at the best rate he could manage, Caleb said, 'Because Janoish is in charge of city defence, and for him to speak to an officer of another nation's army is treason.'

'So war is coming?'

'It has arrived, my young friend. I'll wager every coin Webanks offered you that Olasko's army is on the march.'

Talon said, 'Why would the Duke of Olasko want to attack Latagore?'

Caleb replied, 'Ask Robert.'

Talon glanced at his companion and saw a firmness to his jaw that indicated that further questions would be pointless.

The return journey took longer, for the wagon was now loaded with provisions and the horses required more rest. The sense of urgency mounted as each day passed.

Eventually, they came within sight of the steading and as soon as Caleb was inside the gates he told Talon to care for the horses and get Gibbs and Lars to unload provisions while he went to find Kendrick. Talon did as he was instructed and when the wagon and horses were put away he hurried into the inn.

He passed through the kitchen with only a perfunctory greeting for Leo, Martha and Meggie. Leo started to speak to Talon, but his words were lost as the young man pushed his way through the door into the common room.

There Robert and Pasko sat with Kendrick. There appeared to have been a lull in the conversation, for when Talon appeared, all were silent. Robert motioned Talon to sit down. Then he turned to Caleb and said, 'I'll send word at once to your father and ask him to have your brother return as quickly as possible.'

With a wry smile Caleb replied, 'Which means Magnus will be here a minute after your message arrives at the island.'

Robert then turned to Talon. 'It is clear from what Caleb has told me that you have become aware of issues that might have better remained unknown to you.'

Talon shrugged. 'I cannot claim the wisdom to know whether that is true or not. I do know that you've hidden things from me, and that you know more about the destruction of my people than you have thus far admitted. I also know that some of the men responsible for this horror are now in Latagore plotting to overthrow the Dominar and his council.'

Kendrick glanced at Robert, as if seeking permission to speak. Robert shook his head slightly and turned back to Talon. 'We know all this, and more.' He looked at Talon for a long time, then asked, 'What do you think of all this?'

Talon was torn between his natural frustration at seemingly pointless questions and the suspicion that Robert's questions tended never to be pointless. He stopped and considered. Finally, he spoke: 'There are several ways to look at the situation, Robert. Politically, I know from what I overheard when Count DeBarges was visiting that there's a royalist movement in Latagore.'

Caleb smiled slightly.

'So it may be that the Duke of Olasko thinks it to his advantage to help them overthrow the Dominar and restore the old King's grandson. But then the question arises as to why Duke Kaspar of Olasko would care who sat at the head of the Council of Latagore.'

'Care to wager a guess?' Robert asked.

'I can guess at reasons, but I do not know for sure.' Then Talon leaned forward, 'Unless it's a military reason.'

'And that would be?' asked Kendrick.

Talon said, 'Until this week I could not begin to imagine why the Duke of Olasko's men would help an army of murderers to obliterate my people. But now I realize I had it backwards. Raven and his company were working for the Duke. Their only reward was gold and perhaps slaves. The Duke, however, obviously wanted the Orosini out of their mountains.' He paused, as if considering what to say next. 'I could not imagine the reason, until now.'

'This military reason?' Kendrick asked.

'Yes. With the Orosini out of the mountains, and Latagore in the hands of a friendly ruler, or at least in the throes of civil war, then there is only one conclusion I can draw. He wants Latagore neutralized on his flank, so that he can attack the Duchy of Farinda.'

Kendrick said, 'Where did you learn about military strategy?'

Talon looked embarrassed. 'I didn't, or I mean I haven't. But you talk a lot about your battles and things like keeping your flanks protected seem to be very important.'

'He's a bright one, yes?' Kendrick said to Robert.

Robert smiled. To Talon he said, 'Your deductions are clever, but incorrect.'

Talon said, 'They are?'

'Yes. There's far more in play than you understand, but your ability to deduce as much as you have is very unusual. The Duke of Olasko does wish to have a friendly regime in Latagore, and eventually he will invade Farinda, but probably not for a few years yet. You've done well to spy out even a few pieces of the puzzle.'

Talon looked a little embarrassed. 'Then what is going to happen?'

Kendrick stood up. 'What's going to happen is that a lot of soldiers from Olasko will be marching through the woods around here soon, so I'd better make sure we're ready for them.'

He left and Talon asked, 'Will they attack?'

'Probably not,' answered Caleb. 'They don't consider us a big enough threat to leave behind them, and they can't spare time to dig us out.'

Robert said, 'It's known we have resources beyond the modest ones apparent to casual observation. I suspect that Kaspar will leave us alone while he commits his next act of bloodshed against innocents.'

'What are we going to do?' asked Talon.

'Why, we're going to sit tight,' said Robert. 'Latagore can fend for itself. It's not that important whether Kaspar's friends rule or the Dominar stays in power. What's important is that we move ahead with our own . . .' He caught himself just in time and said to Talon, 'You may leave us now. Go and see if Leo needs help.'

Talon hesitated, then rose and went into the kitchen.

As he returned, Meggie said, 'What was all that about?'

Feeling that he was included in a select group and not wishing to share the information, Talon said, 'I can't tell you.' He had expected some sort of reaction from the slight girl, but all he got was a shrug, as if secrets were nothing new to her, so instead he asked, 'What can I do to help?'

'Everything is just about finished,' she replied. 'You can carry that bucket out and dump it.'

Talon picked up the indicated bucket then said, 'I haven't seen Lela. Where is she?'

Meggie's expression turned troubled. 'That's what I was trying to tell you when you came rushing through a while ago. Lela's not here.'

'Where is she?'

Meggie looked down, as if not wanting to look him in the face. 'Gone. She left yesterday with Count Ramon DeBarges's entourage. They turned up two days earlier, and when they left to go back south, Lela went with them.'

Talon didn't know what to say. He carried the bucket outside and dumped the contents in a trench near the wall. He paused for a moment to listen to the shift of sounds in the surrounding woods as day gave way to night. He savoured the noise of night creatures awakening, sounds so familiar to him and so different to the sounds he had experienced in the city. He let the familiarity of the woodlands flood over him, then headed back to the kitchen. When he returned, 'And Lars and Gibbs?'

'They went, too.' With a shy smile, she said, 'I guess for a while it's just the two of us, Talon.'

Talon looked at the slender girl and felt a sudden stab of

confusion. She was flirting with him the way she had with Lars when they weren't fighting. But Lela was gone! He had thought himself in love with her, until Caleb had told him that he had been with her, as had both Lars and Gibbs. Now the girl he thought of as Lars's woman was turning her attention to him.

Suddenly he was very tired. The tension of the trip, the simmering rage of seeing the men who had been responsible for the death of his family, the knowledge that they were returning north; and his confusion at the strange games in which Robert and the others were involved were all taking their toll.

Just then an odd popping sound came from outside, followed by a sizzling sound like ball lightning rolling across a distant meadow.

Meggie exclaimed, 'Magnus is here!'

Before Talon could ask how she knew, the kitchen door opened wide and the white-haired man entered. He glanced around the kitchen then, without saying a word, passed into the common room.

'I thought he was on some journey to visit his family,' said Talon.

Meggie leaned forwards. 'Haven't you understood it yet? Magnus and Robert can do magic! They can come and go in the blink of an eye if they wish it.'

Talon remembered the conversation with Caleb which had confirmed his suspicions. It made him feel uncomfortable. It was another thing Robert had neglected to tell him, another thing he had had to find out for himself.

Leo and Martha prepared a small meal for the four of them; then Leo took food into the commons for the others. They dined in relative silence, with Leo or Martha occasionally asking

Talon about something he might have noticed in the city. More often than not it was a question about some feature of the city he had neglected to notice. Halfway through the meal the conversation fell off into an awkward silence.

After the kitchen had been cleaned and preparations made for the morning meal, everyone turned in, leaving Talon alone in the kitchen. He ventured to peer into the common room and there he saw Robert, Caleb, Pasko and Magnus deep in conversation. Robert glanced up and seeing him standing there, said, 'Good night, Talon.'

Talon closed the door and stood outside for a moment, uncertain of what to do. He had no room of his own to go to, having left the barn for Lela's room. After some consideration he decided that if she was gone, he might as well use the room for himself.

He mounted the back stairs and opened the door. The room was empty. The simple chest stood open, and the bed was made up, but there were none of Lela's personal belongings left behind. Her brush was missing from the small table, as were the tiny boxes in which she kept the few belongings she had acquired over the years.

He fell hard upon the straw-filled mattress, causing the rope-and-wood frame to groan, and lay thinking. What was to become of him? He had stumbled upon some insights, but he knew there was far more going on than he imagined. Robert was obviously involved with people a great deal more important than Kendrick. Caleb had mentioned his father in passing, but Talon had no idea of his name or what his stake in these things might be.

The conversations downstairs appeared to be much more earnest than they would have been if they'd simply been gossiping about the coming war, or concerned over the defence of the steading.

No, there was far more here than Talon had yet comprehended, and it frustrated him not to understand the full picture.

He was so lost in thought he barely heard the door open behind him. He rolled over and saw Meggie slip through the door. She smiled at him and whispered, 'I thought I might find you here.'

He was about to ask her what she wanted, when he saw her reach up and unfasten the ties at the shoulders of her shift. The simple dress fell away and she came over and knelt upon the pallet next to him. 'Move,' she snapped, as if he was too slow to understand, and when he did, she slipped under the blanket.

He stood in mute amazement, until she said, 'It's chilly and you didn't seem inclined to offer me the blanket.' When he continued to stand mute, she said, 'Well, don't be addled. Get in here!'

Pushing aside his momentary confusion, he obeyed the girl. She pushed him back out of the bed and he landed on the floor. 'What?'

She giggled. 'It's easier if you get undressed before you get into bed, stupid.'

He quickly did as instructed, and slipped into the bed next to her. She put her arms around his neck and said, 'Obviously, Lela didn't teach you very well. We'll have to do something about that.'

Then she kissed him and all concerns for what was occurring in the common room below were forgotten.

• CHAPTER EIGHT •

Magic

*T*ALON SAT UP.

His heart raced as he heard footsteps pounding up the stairs and for a moment he was disoriented. Meggie stirred next to him and he glanced over and felt more disorientation, though this time it was emotional. How easy it had been to let Lela become a dim memory while he was in Meggie's arms.

The door opened to reveal Magnus standing there. He was wearing his slouch hat and holding his staff, and across one shoulder hung a large black belt, supporting a leather bag at his hip.

Meggie stirred and her eyes came open. Suddenly they went wide as she spied the magician and she pulled the blanket up to her chin.

Magnus ignored her, 'Talon, get dressed and gather whatever personal belongings you have. We leave at once.'

'Huh?'

But the door had already slammed shut behind the departing magician.

Talon stumbled out of bed and looked around. He didn't have many personal belongings. He had two clean tunics and another pair of trousers, the boots beside the bed, and a small pouch with a few coins he had earned doing extra work for guests. Even the sword and dagger he used were not his, but belonged to Caleb.

He looked down at Meggie who smiled shyly up at him. Not knowing what else to say, he said, 'I've got to go.'

She nodded. He dressed, gathered up his meagre pile of possessions and hurried down to the common room, where Magnus was waiting with Robert.

Robert said, 'Talon, you're to go with Magnus. Do as he bids as if he was speaking for me. I will see you again, but not for a while.'

'Where am I going?' Talon asked as all vestiges of sleep fell away from him.

'Everything will be explained to you after you arrive.' Robert's manner precluded any more questions.

Magnus moved towards the kitchen saying, 'Follow me.'

Talon did so, passing through the kitchen where Leo and Martha were preparing the day's food. He followed Magnus into the courtyard, where the magic-user said, 'Stand next to me and hold onto my staff.'

Talon stood next to Magnus, shifting his pouch and clean clothing into the crook of his left arm so that he could grip the staff with his right hand.

Without a word, the magician withdrew a device from the folds of his robe, a sphere made from a metal that had a sheen of bronze or, perhaps, even gold. Talon saw Magnus depress a lever in the side with his thumb and the sound of a hive of angry bees engulfed them.

Talon felt as if the world had dropped away from his feet. His heart leapt into his throat. For a moment he thought he had gone blind, but rather than blackness, he found he could see a profound grey, a void of absolute nothingness. Then the ground was back below his feet, but felt as if it was shifting. He gripped Magnus's staff hard to keep himself from falling. Suddenly he had the distinct feeling that he was far from the inn. It was still night. And he could smell a strange tang in the air, a pungency he had never encountered before, and in the distance there was an odd sound, like thunder, but low and rolling, repeating itself regularly as he listened.

The magician watched him for a moment then said, 'You're hearing the breakers.'

Talon looked at him in the darkness. Magnus's features were hidden in the shadow of the brim of his slouch hat and the only light upon him was from the small moon which was setting. 'Breakers?'

'Waves breaking upon the rocks.'

'We are near the sea?' Talon asked, realizing as he spoke that it was a stupid question.

But Magnus did not chide him for his disorientation. 'Come,' he said.

They walked down a path and up a rise, and found themselves before a small hut. For some reason the sound of waves upon the rocks here was louder. 'At sunrise, you'll be able to see the north shore of the island from here,' Magnus said and entered the hut.

Talon followed and found himself in a small room inside a daub and wattle building, a thatched roof above his head. The floor was earth, but it had been hard packed. As he moved forward, he saw a faint shimmer of light reflected from the low fire in the stone hearth. He knelt and touched it.

Magnus put his staff in the corner, removed his hat, and took off his travel pack. Glancing back at Talon, he smiled. 'Noticed the floor,' he observed.

'What is it?'

'Rock. It was mud, but a very clever spell turned it to rock. I was trying for something a little closer to marble, but somewhere in the cantrip I neglected a phrase.' He shrugged. 'It is a bit of vanity on my part, really.' He motioned with his hand towards the walls and roof. 'The walls will never need to be reworked or the thatch replaced.'

In the room were four items: a huge chest, a table with two chairs, and a pallet on the floor. 'That is my pallet,' said Magnus. 'You will sleep in front of the hearth.'

Talon nodded. He held out his belongings and asked, 'Where shall I put these?'

The magician raised an eyebrow as he inspected the young man's scant possessions. 'Use the clothing as a pillow. Put the belt-purse anywhere out of the way.'

Talon nodded and looked around. One corner next to the hearth housed tongs, a kettle and a broom, but the other was empty. He placed his little bundle of clothing in a pile in this empty corner.

'Come outside,' said Magnus.

When they were standing under the night sky, he said, 'You are not a stupid boy. Look at the stars and tell me where you think we are.'

Talon gazed up and compared the sky to the one he had known as a child in his homeland mountains. He took in the small retreating moon and glanced to the east, where a glow heralded the rising large moon. 'It is four hours until dawn,' he observed. 'It was dawn at Kendrick's when you woke me.' He knew the barest geography, having seen only a few maps at Kendrick's as Robert studied them. But using what little knowledge he had, he said at last, 'We are upon an island in the Bitter Sea.'

'Good. How did you deduce this?'

'We are west of Kendrick's, or else it would have been daylight, or if we were far to the east, it would be late in the day, or early in the night and Little Moon would be low in the eastern sky, rather than setting in the west. But we are not far enough west to be beyond the Straits of Darkness and in the Endless Sea. We are . . . south of Kendrick's.'

'Good,' repeated Magnus.

'May I know why I'm here?' asked Talon.

Magnus said, 'Grip the staff again, and do not let go for any reason.'

Talon gripped the staff, and suddenly felt himself shoot into the air, as if carried aloft by a giant's hand. The ground fell away with dizzying swiftness and they soared up through the clouds.

Then they stopped and Talon knew without looking that his knuckles were white, for he was holding onto the staff with all his strength.

'Behold the world, Talon of the Silver Hawk.'

In the east, the rising Large Moon bathed the distant landscape in silvery relief. The air blew briskly, but Talon shivered for other reasons. He was terrified.

Yet he maintained his poise and glanced around him. The island below was hidden in clouds and darkness, yet he had a sense of size as they had shot upward. The hut was on the north shore of the island, and the land had dropped away to the south, perhaps into a valley. Talon knew little of oceans and islands, save what he had glimpsed on Robert's maps, but he judged it to be a fair-sized place – more land than the woodlands around Kendrick's if he could judge such things.

After a moment, his fear abated and he looked in all directions. The rising moonlight played upon the clouds below them, and the sparkling of the sea to the north showed him the curve of the planet.

'So big,' he said at last.

'Good,' said Magnus as they started to descend. 'You're learning perspective.' When they were safely on the ground again, he went on, 'The reason you're here, Talon of the Silver Hawk, is to learn.'

Talon said, 'Learn what, Magnus?'

The magician put a hand on Talon's shoulder and gave it a gentle squeeze. 'As much as I can possibly teach you.' Then, without another word, he turned and entered the hut, and after hesitating for a moment, Talon followed him into what was obviously going to be his new home for a while.

Talon read the passage aloud for the fifth time, with Magnus listening closely. When Talon had finished the magician said, 'That is satisfactory.'

For the first month since arriving on the island, Talon had been forced to read aloud, with Magnus correcting his grammar and his pronunciation, his inflection and tone. Talon knew from having heard Count Ramon of Roldem speaking that Magnus was attempting to make him sound as much like a noble of Roldem as possible.

'This is something new,' said Magnus, holding out a book.

It was written in a script unknown to Talon. 'What is it?'

'It is a rather dull book on the life of a minor king of the Isles, Henry the Third. But it is simply written and shall be your introduction into reading and writing the King's Tongue.'

'Magnus, can I take a break from this?'

'Break?'

'My mind is swimming and the words on the page are just a blur. I have been inside this hut for a week. My last venture outside was a walk to the beach for an afternoon while you were gone.'

There was a peevish quality to Talon's voice that was unusual for him. The magician smiled thinly. 'Restless, are you?'

'Very. Perhaps I could go hunting?' He paused. 'If you had a bow . . .'

Magnus said, 'I do not. But do you fish?'

Talon sat upright, his face alive with enthusiasm. 'I've fished the lakes and rivers of my homeland ever since I could walk.'

Magnus regarded him silently for a moment, then said, 'Very well. Let me show you how to fish in the ocean.'

With a wave of his hand, he caused a black void to appear in the air. Then he reached through it and appeared to be feeling around for something. 'Ah!' he said with satisfaction. When he withdrew his arm, there was a pole in his hand. He pulled it through and handed it to Talon.

Talon saw that it was a fishing pole, but unlike any he had

seen before. It was long – a foot longer than his own six feet in height – and it had an odd device affixed to it, a cylinder with a ratchet and crank, around which a prodigious amount of line was wrapped. The line was threaded through a series of loops – looking to be fashioned out of cane or bamboo – to a metal loop at the tip. On top of the reel lay a metal bar.

Magnus fetched out another of these poles and then a wicker basket on a belt, which Talon recognized as a fisherman's creel.

'Come then, let us fish, but while we do, we shall also study.'

With a sigh, Talon picked up the creel and the two poles and followed. Even if his lessons continued, at least he would be outside for the afternoon.

He followed the magician down the rocky path from the bluff to the beach below. The wind whipped up small whitecaps and blew spindrift off the top of the breakers. Talon had come to find the sound of the waves upon the rocks soothing and the smell of sea air as invigorating as the scent of the pines and aspens of his home.

When they reached the beach, Magnus hiked up his robes and tucked them into his belt. On another man, it might have been a comic sight, but there was nothing comical about Magnus. Talon noticed his powerful legs and decided that despite being a user of magic rather than a hunter or warrior, Magnus was as powerfully built a man as his younger brother.

The magician showed Talon how to hold the rod. He pointed out the items on the 'reel', as he called the device attached to the pole, and explained that the bar was a 'brake' which would slow down the reel if a large fish struck it and tried to run. The ratchet allowed the fisherman to reel in the fish, keeping it from pulling away unless the fisherman released the brake.

Talon was fascinated: his entire experience of fishing had involved nets and a line tied to the end of a long stick. He watched as Magnus pulled out some dried meat from the creel and threaded it onto a large metal hook. With two steps and a half-trot half-leap, he whipped the end of the pole towards the waves, casting the hook far out beyond the breakers.

'Make sure you know where the hook is before you cast,' he warned Talon. 'It's no fun to catch yourself with it. You have to push the damn thing through the skin and cut it off to get the hook out of your flesh.'

Talon sensed he spoke from bitter experience. Moving a short distance away from Magnus, Talon put the dried beef on the hook. Then he let the line rest on the sand as he stepped forwards a pace, then with a whip of the pole cast the line farther out than Magnus had.

'Well done,' the magician said.

They stood there in silence for nearly half an hour. Neither man feared silence. Then Magnus said, 'What do your people believe about this world?'

Talon asked, 'I'm not sure what you mean.'

'What stories do they tell regarding the nature of the world?'

Talon thought about the stories told by the old men around the fire during the summer, and when the shaman would come and speak of the history of the race. 'The Orosini believe the world is a dream, fashioned by the gods, living in the mind of the Sleeper.'

'And what about the people?'

'We are part of that dream,' Talon responded. 'But to us everything is real, because who can know what is real to a god?'

Magnus said nothing for a while. Then he said, 'Your people

may be right, because nothing in that concept of this world is in conflict with what we know of it. But for the moment, put aside your people's beliefs and listen to me. Here is what I know to be true.

'The world is a large ball of earth, mud, rock and water, with air surrounding it. As vast as it is, it is but a tiny part of a universe which is large beyond imagining, and full of other worlds, many with life on them.

'There are billions of worlds in the universe.'

'Billions?'

'What has Robert taught you of numbers?' Magnus asked.

'I can add and subtract, multiply and divide, if I am careful.'

'Better than most men. How many figures can you manage?'

'I can multiply four numbers by four other numbers.'

'Then you know what a thousand is.'

'Ten hundreds,' answered Talon.

'And ten thousands by ten is a hundred thousand.'

'Yes, I understand.'

'And ten such is a million.'

'Ah,' said Talon, sounding uncertain.

Magnus cast him a sidelong glance and saw that Talon was now lost. 'Look, let me explain it this way. Should I give you grains of sand, one each second, in one minute you would have sixty in your hand.'

'And if you did so for one thousand seconds, I would have a thousand. Yes I see,' Talon said, anticipating where the lesson was going.

'It would take more than thirteen days for me to hand you a million grains of sand, if I continued at one a second without stopping.'

Talon looked amazed. 'That long?'

'A billion would take me more than thirty years.'

Talon looked at Magnus in complete disbelief. 'Can there be a number that big?'

'Bigger,' said Magnus. With a slight smile he said, 'Two billion.'

Talon could only laugh. 'And then three billion and four: yes, I see.'

'There are many billions of worlds in the universe Talon, perhaps even too many for our gods to know them all.'

Talon showed no emotion, but it was clear that he found the idea fascinating. Magnus went on, describing a universe of endless variety and possibility.

'What of the life on these other worlds?' Talon asked at one point.

'You've heard the stories of the Riftwar?'

'Yes, told me by my grandfather. He said to the west . . .' Talon paused, then glanced at the sea and said, '. . . the west of our homeland – I guess it might be to the east of here.'

'No, it is still to the west of here, off in the Far Coast. Continue.'

'He said that men from another world came by magic to wage war on our world, but that the Kingdom repulsed them.'

'That's one version,' said Magnus with a wry expression. 'I'll tell you what really happened some other time.'

'Are these people like us?'

'As much as the Orosini are like the men of Roldem.'

'Not very much, then,' said Talon.

'Enough like us that eventually we found common ground and ended the war. You can meet some of their descendants some day.'

'Where?'

'In Yabon Province of the Kingdom of Isles. Many settled in the city of LaMut.'

'Ah,' said Talon as if he understood.

They stood there in silence for another half an hour, then Talon said, 'We don't seem to be doing very well.'

'At catching fish?'

'Yes.'

'That's because we're using the wrong bait.'

Talon looked at his teacher in surprise. 'The wrong bait?'

'We might hook a bottom feeder or a shark with dried meat, but if we wanted something lively, we should have put a fresh mackerel on the hook.'

'Then why are we doing this?'

'Because fishing isn't about catching fish.' The magician looked into the water and Talon felt the hair on his arms rise, which meant Magnus was about to use magic. 'There,' he said pointing. He motioned upward with his right hand and something large seemed to leap out of the sea. It was about the size of a small horse, and covered in red scales and had a lethal-looking array of teeth. Once out of the water it thrashed about in mid-air, attempting to bite at whatever unseen foe held it aloft.

With a flick of his wrist, Magnus let the fish fall back into the waves. 'If I want fish, I take fish.'

'Then why do we stand here with these poles?'

'For the pleasure of it,' said Magnus. 'It's a way to relax, to think, to ponder.'

Despite feeling completely silly holding the pole, Talon nevertheless found himself reverting to the lessons he had learned about the process of dragging a hook through the surf.

As the day grew late, he said, 'Magnus, may I ask you something?'

'How am I to teach you if you don't?'

'Well . . .'

'Out with it,' said Magnus, making another cast into the surf. The wind was picking up, blowing the magician's white hair back from his face.

'I'm confused about something.'

'What?'

'Women.'

Magnus turned to stare at Talon. 'Something specific about women, or just women in general?'

'In general, I suppose.'

'You're hardly the first man to say that.'

'So I've come to understand,' said Talon. 'It's just that among my people, things between men and women were . . . predictable. Your bride was selected before you returned from your vision quest, and you married shortly afterwards. You stayed with one woman . . .' He lowered his voice. 'I've already known two women, and I'm wed to neither.'

'This bothers you?'

'Yes . . . no . . . I don't know.'

Magnus planted his pole in the sand and walked over to Talon. 'I can tell you little, my young friend. My experience in this area is very limited.'

Talon looked at the magician. 'You don't like women?'

Magnus smiled. 'No, it's not that . . . I had some experience when I was young . . . about your age. It's just that some of us who practise the magic arts prefer to stay aloof. Matters of the heart confound things.' He looked out at the sea. 'I like to think I gain clarity by avoiding such things.' He looked back at Talon. 'But you and I are set upon different paths. What is your question?'

'I was . . . with Lela, for a while. I thought perhaps we might . . .' Talon looked down at the sand, feeling very self-conscious. 'I thought we might even wed.'

Glancing at Magnus he saw the magic-user betray an instant of amusement, but then his face became once again an immobile mask.

Talon continued. 'But when I returned from Latagore with Caleb, she was gone. I barely had time to think about not seeing her again when Meggie . . .'

'Ah,' said Magnus. 'You were with her when I woke you that morning, that's right.'

'Well, how can I feel so strongly for Lela, yet so easily find myself with Meggie? And I didn't even think about Lela the whole time we were together.'

Magnus nodded. 'Let me ask you, if I could bring either girl here this instant, who would you wish to see?'

Talon stood silently, holding his fishing pole. 'I don't know,' he answered at last. 'I thought I loved Lela . . . I do love her. But there's something about the way Meggie . . . moves. She's . . . ardent. That's the word isn't it?'

Magnus fell silent for a moment, then he said, 'The ways of the heart are complex.' He looked out at the ocean again. 'The waves churn and break upon the rocks, Talon. So do human feelings. Passion can be a man's undoing. With passion must come wisdom, otherwise your enemies have a weapon to use against you.'

'I don't understand.'

'Most men are passionate about something, at some time in their lives. It may be about a woman he loves, or his calling or craft, or it may be about an ideal.'

'An ideal?'

Magnus nodded. 'There are men who would willingly give their lives for an ideal. Men who put the greater good ahead of their own personal gain.' He looked at Talon. 'Then there are the dark passions: ambition, greed, lust, a hunger for power.

'What you feel for Lela and Meggie is somewhere between those extremes, between the ideal and the dark. At its worst, what you feel is blind lust, without regard for the complexities of the women you pursue. At its most ideal, you will fall under the spell of women too easily, thinking each worthy of selfless adoration.

'Either extreme is a mistake.'

Talon nodded his understanding.

'You are young. There will be many women in your life if you want them. But circumstances may place you in such a position where you must discern the truth quickly, as to whether it is mere lust or if there is some deeper love involved.

'Both young women you have known are good women, for the most part. At least they had no evil designs upon you. They cared for you in their way, and you for them. But I also remember what it was like to be your age, to gaze into a pair of green eyes and be swept away by feelings so intense I thought my heart would stop, only to have the feelings repeated just a few short days later when gazing into brown eyes.

'That is the heart of a young man, Talon. It must be tamed and reined in, like a fractious colt. It must be made to follow the mind, for you will learn that love is a difficult thing.'

'I don't know if you've answered my question.'

'I don't know if you've understood what it was you were asking.' Magnus picked up his pole, reeled in the line and cast it out in the surf again. 'We'll speak more about this, soon. And before too long there will be others you can ask about such things. Others who are more able than me to address your concerns.'

'Thank you, Magnus.'

'Think nothing of it. You will have many more questions for me before our time on this island is over.'

'How much longer will I be staying here?'

'As long as it takes.'

'As long as what takes?'

'Whatever it is we are to accomplish,' answered Magnus.

Talon started to ask another question, then thought better of it.

The afternoon wore on and Talon grew hungry. 'Are we likely to catch any dinner here?'

'Getting hungry?'

'Yes, actually.'

'Do you know how to cook fish?'

Talon had prepared a number of fish dishes with Leo. 'I do, but you have only the kettle and spit to cook upon. I suppose I could fashion a chowder . . .'

'No,' said Magnus. 'I was thinking about something a bit more refined. We've been eating soups and roasts for a month or more. Let us have some fine dining tonight.'

'How shall I prepare such a meal?'

'Don't worry,' said Magnus. 'First we must find you a proper main course.' He closed his eyes and then opened them again, and Talon thought he saw a faint sheen of light upon them. Magnus held out his hand, palm up, then slowly rasied it. From out of the sea came a fish, something close to four foot long. Magnus motioned and the creature floated through the air and dropped at Talon's feet. The fish flopped and writhed upon the sand.

'Be careful, those fins can actually cut you if you grab it too firmly.'

Talon looked at Magnus. 'I'm to carry it up to the hut?'

'How else will you get it there?' asked the magician.

Talon attempted to pick up the thrashing creature, but found it both slippery and heavy. 'Is there something I can hit it with, to stun it?' he asked after several exasperating attempts to subdue the fish.

'Oh.' said Magnus. With a flick of his hand, the fish fell quiet. 'It's still alive, so it will be fresh when you fillet it. This creature is called a tuna, and you can grill it lightly, with a variety of different spices. A lightly seasoned rice and an assortment of steamed vegetables would complement it nicely. And some chilled white wine – perhaps an off-dry from Ravensburgh.'

Talon picked up the huge fish and looked at the steep path up to the bluff. 'Anything else?'

'If I think of anything, I'll let you know.'

Talon trekked slowly back up the trail, and by the time he reached the hut he was in considerable pain. His arms and shoulders were in knots and his knees shook. The fish must weigh almost as much as he did, he was certain. He wondered what he was supposed to do with it. He could gut it on the table, but it would be messy. Perhaps on the ground outside, then he could wash way the offal with well water. That should get the dirt off it. And if the fillets were large enough, he could spit and roast them.

But where was he going to find rice, or spices? The food so far at Magnus's hut had been plain, to put it kindly.

He put the fish down, relieved to do so, and stood up, his back rewarding him with a spasm of pain to remind him not to attempt such a foolish thing again. He rubbed at it with the knuckles of his left hand while opening the door with his right.

He stepped inside the hut and almost fell over in shock. Instead of the small interior he had come to know so well, he was standing in a large kitchen. Larger than the hut. He glanced backwards out of the door, and saw the familiar landscape in front of the hut, but the inside of the hut was still quite different.

He took in a large preparation table with a pump where he could clean the fish, and beyond it a stone stove. Next to the stove, a fire burned beneath a metal grill. He saw shelves on the distant back wall and had no doubt there would be spices and rice there. And he was certain that the door would lead to a wine cellar where he'd find just the right chilled white wine to serve with dinner.

'How did he do this?' Talon murmured softly to himself.

- **CHAPTER NINE** -

Confusion

TALON BLINKED.

He was reading another Kingdom language book, this one a chronicle of the life and times of a merchant of Krondor, named Rupert Avery. The merchant before his death had commissioned the tale and had it published, a paean to his own vanity, from Talon's point of view. The story was badly written and improbable to say the least, for if the tale as told by Avery was to be believed, he was instrumental in Kingdom history, almost single-handedly defeating the agents of chaos attempting to conquer his nation.

Talon judged it a story fit for a talker around the campfire, but only if more attention was paid to the warriors and magicians in the tale and less to a boy who grew rich. He tilted the chair he was sitting on back against the wall. He was beginning to understand the concept of wealth. Other people seemed to delight in amassing it. He was Orosini, and from his point of view anything you couldn't eat, wear, or use was a luxury. And collecting luxuries after a certain point was a waste of time and energy.

Yet with his understanding of the concept of wealth, he was beginning to understand the concept of power. For reasons alien to him, there were those who lusted after power as much as this Avery had lusted after wealth. Men like the Duke of Olasko who wanted nothing so much as to wear a crown and be called King, though from what Caleb and Magnus had told him, he might just as well be called King in the lands of Olasko and Aranor right now.

Talon rocked his chair forward again and put the book on the table. He had been alone for three days because Magnus was off on one of his mysterious journeys. Talon had been given a set of tasks by the magician, some reading – which Talon enjoyed now that he had been reading for over a year – practising a strange series of moves, almost like dance, which the magician had taught him. Magnus claimed that the dance was a form of open-handed fighting, called Isalani, if Talon had it right, and that years of studying it would make him more proficient in other areas of combat. He also had to keep the hut clean and feed himself.

It filled most of his day, but what time he had left he used to explore, though Magnus had instructed him to stay on the north shore of the island. To the south a ridge of hills rose up, perhaps half a day's easy walk, and Magnus had instructed him not to climb those hills or pass along the beach south of them. Magnus didn't explain why he should not go south, or what would happen if he ignored the instruction, but Talon was not inclined to challenge the magician.

A great deal of Talon's life was now centred around waiting. He was waiting to discover what he was being trained to do, for now he was certain Robert and the others had a purpose for him.

His education was proceeding at a fast pace: languages – he was now almost fluent in the King's Tongue, (as the main language of the Kingdom of the Isles was known), spoke almost flawless Roldemish, and was starting to learn dialects from the Empire of Great Kesh – geography, history and he had studied music.

Music was what he enjoyed the most. Magnus had a spell he used to conjure up performances by musicians whom he had encountered over the years. Some of the simpler music sounded almost familiar to Talon; but more sophisticated music, played for nobles by accomplished musicians, was just as compelling. To aid in his understanding of music, Magnus had told Talon he would learn to play instruments, and had started him off with a simple pipe, which now lay on the table – a long wooden tube, with six holes cut in it. It was very much like one his father had played and Talon had quickly mastered playing some simple melodies on it.

Talon rubbed his face with one hand. His eyes felt gritty and his back hurt. He stood up and glanced out of the window. The afternoon sun was setting. Talon realized he had been studying the book all afternoon.

He glanced at the hearth where a large cauldron sat half-filled with a stew he had prepared two days before. It was still edible, but he had tired of the same fare. He judged that he had maybe an hour in which to hunt or hurry to the shore and fish.

Sundown was a good time for either activity. The island had a large pond a short distance away from the hut where game would gather to drink at sunrise and sunset, and the fish beyond the breakers seemed to be more active at sundown.

He wrestled with the choice for just a moment, then decided that fishing was more to his liking. The stalking of game required too much concentration and right now he was in the mood to stand upon the sand, with the wind in his face and his eyes focused on something farther away than the end of his arms.

Talon grabbed his pole and creel and headed out of the door.

The sun had set by the time Talon started back up the hill. In a few short minutes he had managed to catch two large jack smelts, more than enough for his supper. He would cook them over the wood fire in the hearth, upon a metal grill, and add some spices Magnus kept in a small chest. He wished he had some rice to cook with it, and realized how much luxury he had been exposed to by Leo in the kitchen at Kendrick's. His mother often prepared fish, and served it with whatever roots or berries the women had gathered. Sometimes a corncake, hand-rolled and cooked by the fire, made with honey, berries or nuts, would be served along with the game. But Talon now appreciated food far more than his mother would ever have imagined. It was amusing to think he was probably the best cook in the history of his people.

As he rounded a small bend in the trail near the summit of the bluff, he stopped. The sky was still light with the just-set sun, but darkness was quickly descending. He sensed something.

He listened. The woods near the hut were silent. There

should have been noises, the scurrying of the day animals seeking out their lairs as the night predators made their presence known. Night birds should have been flitting about, seeking insects.

Instead, there was a stillness that could only mean one thing: men were nearby.

For an instant Talon wondered if Magnus had returned, but somehow he knew this wasn't the case. It just felt wrong.

Talon suspected there might be others on this island, people living south of the ridge whom Magnus didn't want him to meet, at least not right now, but Talon didn't think it likely they'd come calling unexpectedly. He put down the fishing rod and creel, then realized he had left his weapons in the hut.

He pulled a scaling knife out of the creel, a poor weapon, but better than nothing, and advanced slowly towards the hut, his every sense extended. He listened, he looked, he sniffed the air.

There seemed to be a presence near the hut, something unfamiliar, outside his experience. He had thought it might be *someone* at or in the hut, but now he considered it to be some *thing*.

A figure stepped out of the door, almost too quickly for his eye to have caught the motion, but in that instant he recognized a human-like form, but one devoid of features. Detailless black from head to toe it was a silhouette that flickered past his consciousness into the darkness of night.

He halted, keeping his breath as shallow as possible, using every sense to determine where the creature had gone. A slight shift in the air behind him alerted him to someone moving rapidly and silently at his back, and he dropped to his knees. Without hesitation, he struck backwards with the scaling knife, a slash that would have taken any man somewhere between knee and groin.

An inhuman warbling cry erupted through the night as the blade struck something, and Talon was knocked over by a tremendous blow to the right shoulder, as if a large body had fallen into him.

Talon used the momentum of his fall to tuck and roll back up to his feet, and as a gust of air went past him, he knew he had somehow dodged a blow from another unseen assailant. By instinct alone, he sensed that two attackers were behind him, and he leapt forward, towards the hut. If he had any hope of surviving this attack, he had to reach his sword.

The hair on the back of his neck rose up as he neared the door of the hut, and without looking back he dived through the door, landing hard upon the floor as something invisible cut through the air where his chest should have been.

He slid on his stomach under the table and turned, coming up quickly with his sword. He cast aside the scabbard and kicked the table towards the door, to slow whoever might be coming through.

The table struck something just inside the door and Talon saw the darkness in the doorway move. A figure appeared framed in the door, one he could see only because of what it blocked out behind, for light from the early evening sky still illuminated the branches and leaves, but the silhouetted form blotted out all detail.

Then the thing was in the hut. Talon saw only a man-shape of featureless black as if light was not reflected off its surface. He knew there was another, still outside, so he retreated to the hearth and impulsively grabbed a burning brand from out of the fire, holding it aloft in his left hand.

The creature's hand lashed towards him and Talon ducked to

his right. Pain erupted across his left shoulder. The creature's hand retracted and for a brief instant Talon thought he saw a faint movement in the air, as if a lash was being drawn back. Talon didn't have to look to know he had been cut by some invisible weapon. He could feel burning on his shoulder and feel dampness spreading as blood seeped from the wound.

There came a flicker near the door and Talon knew that another of his unseen assassins had entered the room. Another flicker out of the corner of his eye warned him and he fell to the right. More pain shot down his arm, but he knew that had he not moved, it would have been his throat bleeding instead of his arm.

He fell hard against the wing-arm holding the kettle as he hit the floor, rolling away from where he assumed the assassin to be. The kettle swung back hard into the fireplace and overturned, dumping the remaining stew upon the blazing fire, and the room erupted in steam and soot.

Suddenly Talon could see a leg before him, outlined in the air. Without hesitation, he lashed out with his sword at the creature's leg, and the same warble of pain he had heard outside was repeated inside, at greater volume.

The hut filled with smoke and now Talon could see three figures clearly outlined. They were man-shaped, and they seemed unarmed, yet he knew that to be a false impression. Talon scooted back against the wall.

The others seemed to be casting about, as if unable to see him. Talon gripped his sword, ignoring the fire in his left shoulder, and pushed himself upright, his back against the wall. He was partially hidden by a floor-to-ceiling shelf that Magnus had made him install in which to house the books he studied.

The two creatures who had come in through the door stepped forward, one blocking the door, the other coming towards him. The one nearest the door was limping visibly, and Talon knew instinctively that was the one he had cut with the scaling knife.

Now that he had his sword, Talon felt too confined to fight. He needed to be outside, but only just outside, blocking the door so the creatures could come at him only one at a time. The figure nearest him reached back, as if about to attack with its flail again, and he leapt out, striking with his sword, seeking to drive the thing back. He jumped the fallen table, lowering his uninjured shoulder and slamming into the midsection of the one waiting before the door.

Pain exploded along his back and ran down his left hip. He gasped in agony. The creature to his left had managed to get in a strike, and Talon felt his knees go weak.

As he fell to the ground, he lashed down with his sword and was rewarded with a deep, meaty bite and an inhuman shriek that ended abruptly.

Rolling away, he tried to come to his feet as something flickered through the door. There was a third assailant! He swiped backhanded with his sword in the general direction of the door, and had made it almost to an upright position when pain seared down his left cheek, shoulder and chest.

Shortness of breath, a soaking tunic, and shaking knees meant he was losing too much blood, too fast. His heart pounded and Talon knew that unless he somehow killed the remaining two creatures he was doomed.

There was another flicker at the door and Talon knew that both of them were now outside with him. He blinked and turned his head this way and that, trying to see something of their dark shapes in the night, but to all intents and purposes, they were invisible.

He had a sense of motion to his right and so fell to his left. He had meant to catch himself and come upright, but his left leg failed to obey him, and he crashed to the ground. A searing pain ripped down his right leg. He lost his grip on his sword; and as much as his mind willed his body to roll away, to put distance between himself and the two creatures, he could not force it to do so.

There was another searing line of fire across his right shoulder and Talon screamed out. He was about to die.

His people would go unavenged, and he would never know who his murderers were or why he had been chosen to die.

His final thoughts were of dark despair and deep regret as a blinding white light exploded around him, and he fell into oblivion.

Talon was adrift in a sea of pain. Fire burned his skin and he was bathed in torment. Yet he couldn't move. Voices and images came and went, a few familiar, most alien.

'. . . too much blood. I don't know . . .'

Blackness folded over him and then more pain.

'. . . survived is beyond my understanding . . .'

A strange sound rang in his ear for what seemed to be the longest time, then suddenly it resolved itself into music. Someone nearby was playing a flute.

Then more darkness.

Time passed in fits and starts, vaguely remembered images, sounds, smells, and textures. A woman's face appeared before him repeatedly. Her features were lovely, but her expression was stern, even harsh. She spoke to others nearby, but often he couldn't hear or understand the words.

Fever dreams gripped him in which creatures of nightmare appeared. A blue being with silver horns hovered over him for a time, speaking in a language of hoots and whistles. Other faces came and went, some clearly human, others with subtle differences, an ear too long, an eyebrow of feathers, or a nose with a small thorn at the end.

Other dreams came, dreams of his childhood at the village of Kulaam. He saw the face of Eye of the Blue-Winged Teal, her honey-coloured eyes looking down on him with sadness. He saw his grandfather, Laughter in his Eyes, living up to his name, smiling at him with amusement. He saw his mother and sister, and the other women going about their chores.

He saw himself coming down the mountain, exhausted yet running as fast as he had ever run.

He saw smoke, and death, and fire. And he saw a man on a black horse.

'Raven!' he shouted as he sat up.

A woman gripped his shoulders and said, 'Calmly. Relax. You're going to be fine.'

Talon realized that he was drenched with perspiration. He felt light-headed. His bandaged body shook with a sudden chill as bumps rose on his arms. He looked around the room.

The room he was in was white with several finely made pieces of furniture, and through a large window he could see a blue sky, a warm day. A scented breeze blew through the window and he could hear voices in the distance.

'Where am I?'

The woman stood up. 'You're among friends. I will get Magnus.'

Talon fell back against a trio of heavy pillows stuffed with soft down. He rested naked between sheets of fine white cloth, unlike anything he had seen before. The sheets were drenched, and he knew he had just broken a fever. Bandages covered his shoulder, back, his ribs on the left side, both thighs, and his right calf.

A few minutes later, Magnus appeared with the woman a step behind him. 'How are you feeling?' asked the white-haired magician.

Lying back on the pillows, Talon said, 'I couldn't fight a kitten.'

Magnus sat on the side of the bed and put his hand on Talon's forehead. 'Fever's gone.' He put his thumb on the top of Talon's left eyelid and lifted it slightly. 'So is the jaundice.'

'What happened?' Talon asked.

Magnus said, 'It's a long tale. The short version is that someone sent three death-dancers to kill me. They found you instead.'

'Death-dancers?'

'I'll explain it all, at length, but for now you need to rest. Are you hungry?'

Talon nodded. 'I could eat.'

The woman said, 'I'll get some broth,' and left the room.

'How long have I been like this?' asked Talon.

'Ten days.'

'I've been here ten days?'

Magnus nodded. 'You almost died, Talon. Had you been just about anywhere other than this island, you almost certainly would have done. Perhaps a powerful temple priest might have saved you, but few apart from those living here would have possessed the skills to keep you alive.

'The death-dancer's touch is poison, so even if the kill isn't clean, the victim rarely survives.'

'How did I get here?'

'When the death-dancers set foot upon the shore, some of us knew instantly something was amiss. We hurried back to the hut once it was clear no attack was mounted here. The death-dancers expected to find a magician, alone in the hut, and instead they found a swordsman.

'Had they been hunting you, you would have died without knowing who struck you down. But they were prepared for magical resistance rather than cold steel and that bought you enough time for us to rescue you.'

'Thank you,' said Talon. 'Who is "us"?'

'Myself, and others,' said Magnus. He stood up as the woman returned with a large bowl of broth and a slice of bread on a tray.

Talon elbowed himself up so that he could eat, but the exertion made his head swim. The woman sat down next to him and picked up the spoon and rather than object, he allowed her to feed him. She was a beautiful woman, possibly in her middle thirties, with dark hair, striking blue eyes and a firm set to her mouth that made her appear stern.

He glanced from her face to Magnus's and between spoonfuls of steaming broth, said, 'I can see a resemblance. You never said you had a sister.'

The woman smiled and Magnus did as well, and the resemblance became even more pronounced. The woman said, 'You flatter me.'

'Talon, meet Miranda, my mother.'

Talon swallowed and said, 'I find that difficult to believe.' If anything, she looked younger than her son.

'Believe it,' said Miranda. 'This is a very remarkable place.'

Talon said nothing and continued to eat. When he was finished, Miranda set aside the bowl. At once he started, 'What—'

'Not now,' she interrupted. 'You will have time to ask questions, later, but for now you must rest.'

Talon's curiosity was overwhelmed by his fatigue, and even before she had left the room, his eyes were closed and his breathing was slow and rhythmic.

Two days after he had regained consciousness, Talon was allowed to get up and walk about. Magnus lent him a staff, which Talon leaned on, since both his legs were weak and sore from his injuries, and he hobbled along next to the magician, who said: 'Welcome to Villa Beata.'

'That's the name of this place?'

'Yes, it means "Beautiful home" in an ancient tongue.'

They were in a large courtyard, surrounded by a low wall. The buildings around them were all white plastered, with red tile roofs.

'I've never imagined a place like this.'

'Those who built it were less worried about defending this place than they were about comfort. There are many stories about how it came to be.'

'Do you know the truth?'

Magnus smiled. 'I don't. My father claimed to have heard the truth on the subject, but the man who told him the story was known to make inventions when it suited him, so we may never know how this place came to exist.'

'Is this your home?'

'This is where I grew up, yes,' said Magnus.

Talon looked around and his eyes grew wide as he saw a creature with blue skin and silver horns carrying a large basket of wet laundry around the corner and into a building. 'What was that?' he asked.

'That was Regar, a C'ahlozian. You will find many people here who look nothing like you or me, Talon. Just remember they are still people. You would be as out of place in his homeland as you think him to be here.'

Talon said, 'Before I met you, Magnus, I would have thought him a thing of campfire tales, and when I saw him during my illness, I thought him part of a fever dream. Now, I begin to think little can surprise me.'

'Oh, just wait a bit, my young friend. There are surprises aplenty waiting for you. But for now, just enjoy the warm afternoon and walk around these grounds for a while. You need to rebuild your strength.'

As they walked slowly around the compound, Talon caught a glimpse of people scurrying here and there upon errands, most looking very normal, but one or two decidedly not. The walk caused him some shortness of breath, so he saved his questions for later, but he did manage to pause long enough to ask, 'Magnus, who was trying to kill you?'

'That, my young friend,' replied the magician, 'is a very long story.'

Talon smiled; it hurt too much to laugh. 'I don't seem to be going anywhere for a long while.'

From behind him, a voice said, 'A sense of humour. That's good.'

Talon turned and saw a small, frail looking man standing behind them. He was bald-headed and wore a simple tunic that closed over his left shoulder, leaving the right bare. Upon his feet were cross-gartered sandals, and he held a staff in his left hand. Across his shoulder hung a bag, and his face appeared ancient, yet possessed an almost childlike quality. Dark eyes studied Talon, eyes with a strange, almond-shaped cast to them.

Magnus said, 'Talon, this is Nakor.' With a slight change in tone that Talon didn't quite understand, Magnus added, 'He's one of my . . . teachers.'

Nakor nodded and said, 'Some of the time. At other times I felt more like a cell guard. Magnus when young was quite a troublemaker.'

Talon glanced at Magnus, who frowned, but didn't dispute the claim. Magnus appeared about to say something, but it was Nakor who spoke.

'As for your question, young fellow, it's quite a tale, and one that you'll need to hear, but not right now.'

Talon looked from face to face, saw a silent exchange between the two men, and realized that somehow Nakor was telling Magnus not to speak any more on the subject of the attack.

Nakor said, 'Magnus, I believe your father wanted to speak to you.'

Lifting an eyebrow slightly, Magnus replied, 'No doubt.' Turning to Talon, he said, 'I'll leave you to Nakor's tender mercies and advise you not to wear yourself out. You've been badly injured and need rest and food more than anything.'

Nakor said, 'I'll see him back to his room.'

Talon bid Magnus good day and turned back towards his own

quarters. His legs were trembling by the time he got back to his bed, and Nakor helped him get in.

There was something about the seemingly frail little man that intrigued Talon. He was certain there was a great deal of strength to him, and more. Yet Magnus's former teacher had said nothing as they walked back.

'Nakor?'

'Yes, Talon?'

'When will I know?'

Nakor studied the young man's face, and saw how he fought to keep his eyes open. When fatigue finally overwhelmed Talon, and his eyes closed, Nakor answered. 'Soon, Talon, soon.'

A week went by and Talon's strength returned. He watched with interest as his bandages finally came off and discovered a set of scars which would have done any senior member of his clan proud. Not yet twenty years of age, he looked like a veteran of many battles, a man twice his age. For a moment he felt a profound sadness, for he realized there was no one among his people to whom he could reveal these marks of a warrior. And as his hand strayed absently to his face, he realized that even if any such survivor existed, he had no tattoos upon his face to reveal that he was of the Orosini.

Miranda removed the last bandage and noticed the gesture. 'Thinking of something?'

'My people,' said Talon.

Miranda nodded. 'Many of us come from hardship, Talon. The stories you might hear on this island alone would teach you that you are not alone.' She sat on the edge of the bed and took his hand in hers. 'Some here are refugees, fleeing from murder and bloodshed, much as you have, and others are survivors, as you are, who have also lost everything of their homes.'

'What is this place, Miranda? Magnus avoids my questions, and Nakor always turns the conversation to something . . .'

'Frivolous?'

Talon smiled. 'He can be funny at times.'

'Don't let that grin fool you, boy,' Miranda said as she patted his hand. 'He may be the most dangerous man I've met.'

'Nakor?'

'Nakor,' she echoed, standing up. 'Now, wait here and rest a bit longer, and someone will be along shortly.'

'For what?' he asked, feeling very restless and wanting to get out of the room.

'To take you somewhere.'

'Where?'

As she left his quarters, she said, 'You'll see.'

Talon lay back upon his bed. His body was stiff and aching, and he felt the need to be out doing something, if only for a little while, to stretch his muscles and force air deep into his lungs. He wanted to run, or climb, or stalk a deer in the woods. Even fishing would be welcome, for the hike down to the beach and back would work up a sweat.

Talon closed his eyes and drifted off into his memories – of the men sitting around telling stories before a bright fire in the long house. He thought of the cleansing rituals, for which special buildings were constructed as the snows receded from the slopes of the mountains, where billowing steam from heated rocks would engulf the gathered groups of ten or more men and women, boys and girls who would chant a welcome to the spring and then remove the winter's accumulated dirt and grime.

He thought of his father and mother and sadness rose up in him. The harsh bitterness he had felt for the first year after the destruction of his people had been replaced by a quiet wistfulness, a resignation to the fact that he was the last of the Orosini and that to him fell the burden of revenge, but beyond that point, his future was unknown to him.

He was drifting, half in a doze, when suddenly he felt someone enter the room.

His eyes snapped open and his heart raced, then he looked up into the face of a young woman he had never seen before. Her face was dominated by the most startling blue eyes he had ever seen, large and the colour of cornflowers. Her face was delicate, with a fine chin, full mouth, and almost perfectly straight nose. Her hair was the colour of pale honey, with lighter streaks from the sun. She wore a simple blue dress, with bare arms and a scooped neckline, one he had seen many of the women at this place wearing, but on her it looked magnificent, for she had a tall, slender body and moved like a hunter.

'You are Talon?'

'Yes,' he said, having to force that single word through his teeth, for she took his breath away.

'Follow me,' she said.

He rose and followed her as she left the room. Outside, he managed to catch up enough to walk next to her and asked, 'What is your name?'

She turned and regarded him with a serious expression, dipping her chin slightly as if to see him better. Then she smiled and suddenly her face seemed alight. She spoke in soft tones, her voice almost musical, as she answered, 'I am Alysandra.'

He could not think of anything to say. She robbed him of words. Any memory he had of Lela or Meggie vanished before the beauty of this young woman and suddenly an ache sprung up in his stomach.

They crossed a large courtyard and moved towards part of the main house that Talon had never visited before.

All too quickly, she turned and said, 'In there,' pointing to a doorway. Then, without waiting, she departed, leaving him standing open-mouthed as he watched her retreat across the court-yard, everything about her tightening the knot in his stomach. He watched for what seemed only an instant and then she vanished through a doorway and he was left alone before the door.

After a moment he gathered himself and regarded the door. It was a simple thing of wood with a single handle. He gripped the handle and entered.

Three men stood in an empty room. Two of them Talon recognized: Nakor and Robert.

'Master!' Talon said in surprise.

Robert nodded and said, 'Stand there, Talon.' He pointed to a spot in the middle of the room.

The third man was short, with a beard and dark hair, and he regarded the young man with a gaze that caused Talon some discomfort. There was no mistaking that this man had power. His bearing alone showed that, but there was more to it than that. In the time spent with Magnus and Robert before him, Talon had come to sense something of the magic arts in a man, and this man fairly reeked of them.

He spoke. 'My name is Pug. I am also called the Black Sorcerer.'

Talon nodded, saying nothing.

Pug continued. 'This is my island and all who dwell upon it are my friends and students.'

Robert said, 'Pug was my teacher, as was Nakor, Talon.'

Talon remained silent.

Nakor said, 'The attack of the death-dancers has changed things, boy. We had been evaluating your progress and were waiting to judge you.'

Talon again remained silent, but his eyes spoke questions.

Robert went on, 'You were being judged to see if you were going to stay in my service, until such time as I discharged you from your blood debt, Talon; or to see if you were perhaps gifted enough that you might be invited to join this company, here upon the island.'

Finally Talon asked, 'What company, Master?'

The three men exchanged glances, and Robert said, 'We are called the Conclave of Shadows, Talon. Who we are you shall learn in time, if you are accepted into our ranks. What we do will also be made clear to you.'

'But before you can be told these and many other things,' said Pug, 'you must choose to join us. Your debt to Robert will be considered discharged, and you will be a free man, free to do as your conscience bids you – though you will also have obligations to the Conclave.

'But with those obligations come benefits. We have wealth, enough to provide you with whatever you need for the rest of your life. We have powerful allies, so that you may move easily among nobles and men of power should there be a need.'

Nakor continued, 'But we also have powerful enemies. The death-dancers represented a single attempt among many to remove one of our more important members. Had they succeeded in killing Magnus, our cause would have suffered for years to come.'

'What am I being asked to do?'

Robert said, 'You are being asked to swear an oath of loyalty, not to me, but to the Conclave, Talon. You will leave this room as a member of our society, and with that oath will come benefits and responsibilities we have as yet only hinted at.'

Talon said, 'It sounds as if I am being given a choice in the matter.'

Nakor said, 'You are.'

'What is my other option?'

Pug glanced at Robert and Nakor, then replied, 'Death.'

CHAPTER TEN

Decision

*T*ALON STOOD IN SILENCE.

His eyes moved from face to face as he studied the three men and sought to glean some clue from their expressions as to what was expected of him.

All three of them waited motionlessly, their faces revealing nothing of their thoughts. Pug seemed to be watching him as if trying to read his mind. Robert appeared simply to be waiting to see what he would say. Nakor was clearly attempting to interpret something from Talon's posture, his expression, or any other physical sign of a reaction to the choice just put before him.

After a long silence, Talon said, 'There is apparently no choice.'

Robert said, 'No, there is always a choice. What we have come to, however, is a very difficult choice.' He paused, then said, 'Pug here is my teacher, and the leader of our community.'

Pug studied Talon for a moment, then smiled. When his features relaxed, he suddenly looked years younger than Robert, his student. 'You were never meant to come here, Talon. My son brought you to the north shore of the island to isolate you and concentrate on your studies, and to evaluate you more.' The magician waved his hand and candles set in a metal ring suspended from the ceiling sprang to life so that the room was fully illuminated. Robert and Nakor moved to the corners of the room and returned with four stools. Robert placed one behind Talon and then the other next to Pug and the three interrogators sat down. Pug indicated that Talon should do likewise.

Talon did so and then said, 'You'd really kill me if I say no?'

'No,' said Pug, 'but you would "die" in a sense. We would be forced to remove your memories. We would not be unkind in the process. You would simply fall asleep and when you awoke, you'd be someone else. A young man who suffered an injury in a war, perhaps, or from falling off the roof of his home.

'People who would claim to have known you all your life would welcome your return to lucidity and would quickly remind you of the knowledge you lack. We can arrange for it to be very persuasive and in time, you would come to believe that is who you are.'

Talon said, 'But in a way you are right: Talon of the Silver Hawk would be dead.'

Robert nodded.

Nakor said, 'The last of the Orosini would be lost.'

Talon remained silent for a long while, pondering this. At last he said, 'Tell me more, so that I can choose wisely. I have

no desire to lose my knowledge of who I am – though forget-
ting the death of my people might seem a blessing at times –
but I have debts I must repay, and I can not ignore those.'

Robert spoke. 'Should you choose to serve, your debt to me
would be considered discharged.'

'There is another,' said Talon.

Pug nodded. 'You have a blood-debt.'

'To my people. Had it been only one member of my family
or clan, I would still have hunted them down until each had
been repaid in kind for his deeds. But these men destroyed my
race, for unless anyone has managed to elude death without my
knowing of it, I am the last of the Orosini.' He nodded in
Nakor's direction. 'I cannot die, in either sense of the word –
in body or memory – until they are avenged.'

Nakor said, 'We are not necessarily at cross-purposes here.'
He glanced at Pug and said, 'May I?'

Pug nodded.

Nakor sat back on his stool, reached into a pack he carried
on his hip and pulled out an orange. Then he dug a thick thumb-
nail into it. He glanced at the other two men and raised an
eyebrow. Both of them shook their heads, just a little, and Nakor
returned his attention to Talon.

'You see before you the leaders of a group of people,' Nakor
began. 'This place, this island home, was once the refuge of a
nation fleeing a war, or so the story goes. Later it was home to
the first Black Sorcerer, a man named Macros. Miranda is his
daughter. Pug is Miranda's husband. They are mistress and
master of this island, Talon. You've met both their sons.

'Over the years many people have come to stay with us on
this island. Students from . . . well, from many places, some

never even imagined by most men.' He grinned. 'Some I couldn't have imagined, and I've got quite a good imagination.'

Pug interrupted, 'We can dispense with the history until later, Nakor. Tell him about what faces him.'

Nakor lost the grin. He bit down on the orange and chewed for a moment, deep in thought. 'As I said, we are the leaders of a group of people. Many have come here to train and serve.'

'Serve?' asked Talon.

Nakor grinned. 'You know, I've never had to explain to anyone in one sitting what it is we do, Pug.'

Pug nodded. 'And you will not now. Just give him a general sense of who we are and if he agrees to serve, we shall educate him incrementally along the way.'

Robert held up a hand. 'If I may?'

Pug nodded.

'Talon, we three belong to the Conclave of Shadows. The Conclave consists of men and women who have banded together for a reason. That reason will become clearer to you as time passes, but for the moment, there are things you are not ready to understand.

'I can tell you this much. We serve a purpose which opposes much of the evil abroad in the world today, including the forces that conspired to destroy your homeland. If your current goal is to avenge your people, your best opportunity to do so rests in serving us.'

Talon looked Robert in the eye. 'I owe you my life, Master, and will honour my debt, but you ask me to take at face value a very serious claim. I have seen nothing at Kendrick's or here to make me question that claim, and nothing that would make me think you or these other men might be evil. But my grandfather once told me that men who do evil often do so in the name of a great good, and that the Orosini had history with shamans and chieftains who misled the people, claiming they were doing right.

'I saw evil with my own eyes the day my people died. I do not know the reason for the destruction of my nation. I only know that those men who killed the women and children of my clan did evil.'

Robert held up his hand. 'This much I can attest to: the men who destroyed your home were not acting out of any misplaced sense of a greater good. They were hired mercenaries who kill for gold, aided and abetted by soldiers from the Duchy of Olasko. We will talk in the future about that. For the moment, consider that we have common cause against those whom you seek for revenge.'

'Robert, you saved my life when others might have simply left me for the crows and vultures,' Talon said. 'I have seen nothing in you or your friends that I find to be dishonourable. Caleb and Magnus –' he nodded at Pug '– have taught me much and while I lingered here healing I heard laughter . . .' He thought about Alysandra. 'There is much here that brings joy.' He took a deep breath and went on, 'The gods have placed my feet upon a path, to what purpose and what ends I can only guess. But since the day I awoke in your wagon, Robert, I have been in your care. Tell me what to do.'

'I cannot, Talon. You must know this. Any oath made to the Conclave of Shadows must be made freely and without doubt. For once you enter our ranks, you may not turn back. To renounce that oath will bring you death.'

Pug added, 'And not merely the death of the memory. For

once you become one with us, you will begin to learn things that may not be shared with outsiders. Things that you must be willing to die to keep secret.'

Nakor grinned. 'But there is good in taking that oath, too. We have many marvels to show you, and wonders to behold. You will learn more in a year here than you would in a dozen lifetimes in the mountains you knew as home.'

'Already I have learned a great deal,' Talon said.

Nakor continued, 'When you seek your revenge, you will need resources, and allies. We can provide you with both.'

'What must I do?'

Pug got off his stool and went to stand before Talon, while Nakor and Robert moved so that one of them stood on each side of him.

'Do you swear to give first fealty to the Conclave of Shadows, Talon of the Silver Hawk? Do you enter our ranks freely and of your own will? Do you swear to obey those given dominion over you and to protect with your life those given to your care? Do you swear to keep those secrets entrusted to you? Answer to all with affirmation, or be silent. All or nothing, Talon. What do you say?'

Talon was silent for a moment, then he took another deep breath and said, 'Yes, I will serve.'

'Good. That is good,' Nakor said. He placed a hand on the boy's shoulder and produced another orange. 'Want one?'

Talon took it. 'Thank you.'

Robert said, 'Well, then, I suppose I should tell Magnus to close down that little hut of his and join us here. Talon's education is about to begin in earnest.'

And with that, he left the room.

'Nakor,' said Pug. 'Show Talon where he will be staying. Put him in with Rondar and Demetrius.'

Nakor nodded. 'Come along, boy.'

After they had gone, Pug stood alone for a long minute, then he said as if into the air, 'What do you think?'

From the shadows in the farthest corner of the room there came a voice: 'I think you gave the boy no choice.' Miranda stepped out into the light.

'What else could I do?'

'Heal him, and let me take his memories and put him back in Magnus's hut. Magnus could have told him some story about a fall from the bluffs or a wild animal. With the right suggestion, the boy would have accepted it.'

Pug nodded. 'You're right.'

With a wry smile she came and slipped her arm around her husband's waist. 'I'm always right.'

'Of course, my love,' said Pug, returning the smile.

'So, the question remains, why did you give him no choice?'

Pug was silent for a moment. Then he said, 'I don't know. A sense of something in him. I think he's going to be important to us.'

'Why?'

'I don't know. I only know that lately our enemy has grown subtle. Those death-dancers were unexpected. They remind me of years gone by.'

'They fear Magnus's growing power.'

'Well they should. He may eventually be the most powerful magic-user to have set foot on this world.'

'If we can keep him alive,' Miranda said with a mother's worry in her tone.

'Those death-dancers are more in keeping with the days when we were attacked with armies or demons.'

'Something's got them annoyed.'

Pug laughed. 'Magnus destroying that death cult's temple down in southern Kesh might have irritated them enough to try something like this.'

'Death-dancers are not trivial magic, my love. If I had the inclination to practise that sort of foul art, and three humans willing to give their souls to create them, it would still take me months to do so.' She regarded her husband quizzically. 'And I am better at that sort of thing than you.'

Pug smiled. 'I know. But that's why I think Talon may prove important.'

'Why?'

'Because while wolves fight over the carcass of a deer, a mouse may slip in and grab scraps.'

'Wolves eat mice,' she reminded him.

'Only if they know they're there. But while our enemies are attempting to destroy our son, they won't see Talon coming.'

Miranda snuggled closer to her husband as if suddenly cold. 'For the boy's sake, I hope you're right.'

'Which boy? Talon or Magnus?'

Miranda sighed. 'Both.'

Talon followed Nakor down the corridor, his small bundle of belongings clutched to his chest. His body still felt weak, but the stiffness was leaving him. They passed a series of doors, most of which were closed, but through a couple of open ones Talon saw beds set up, four to a room.

As he passed one room, he could see Alysandra sitting on a bed, engaged in a low conversation with a dark-haired girl who was giggling, her hand covering her mouth. Both girls glanced up as Talon went by, and Talon heard both girls start to laugh.

An irritated feeling rose up in him, a feeling Talon couldn't quite place, save that the giggling seemed somehow inappropriate given that he had just made a solemn vow placing his life in the service of an organization whose purpose he hardly understood.

Eventually they reached a door which gave access to a slightly larger room than the others. As in the other rooms, four beds had been placed in it. Nakor waved for Talon to sit on a bed farthest from the door on the left, while he sat on the bed opposite it. 'Well, here's where your new life begins.'

Talon shrugged. 'My new life began when Robert found me, I guess.'

Nakor shook his head. 'No, your old life ended that day. What you've been living these last two years has been an existence. You were healing and learning, but you had no purpose.'

'Now I have a purpose?'

'A far greater purpose than you suppose,' said Nakor. 'There is much to learn, but you have time. I remember the impatience of youth,' he added with a grin. 'You appear to me to be more patient than most boys your age, yet I know you still want questions answered, positions made clear, and motives revealed. But all in good time.'

'Since coming under Robert's care I have felt as if I were moving in a direction unknown to me,' Talon said. 'I have grown, I think—'

'Much, according to your teachers.'

'Are you now one of my teachers?'

Nakor shrugged and stood up. 'We'll see. Now, I hear your new companions returning, so I'll leave you to get to know one another.'

As he reached the door, two young men of roughly Talon's age entered the room. Seeing Nakor, they stepped back to let him pass, bowing their heads slightly in respect. 'You have a new boy to share your quarters with,' Nakor said as he passed.

'Yes, Master Nakor,' said one of the two boys, a fair-haired, broad-shouldered boy with green eyes and a dusting of freckles across his nose.

The other young man had dark hair, but was fair-skinned, and Talon couldn't tell if he was attempting to grow a man's beard of if he had just done a poor job of shaving the day before. He had almost black eyes which narrowed slightly at the sight of Talon. He threw himself down on the bed against the same wall as Talon's, while the lighter-haired boy took the bed opposite.

'I'm Demetrius,' he said. He pointed to the dark lad and said, 'That's Rondar. He doesn't talk much.' They spoke the King's Tongue, which seemed to be the preferred language on the island.

Rondar nodded, but kept silent.

'I'm Talon,' said Talon.

Demetrius returned the nod. 'Heard of you. You managed to avoid being killed by three death-dancers. Impressive.'

Talon sat back on the bed, leaning against the wall. 'I don't even know what a death-dancer is.'

Rondar said, 'Bad.'

'Very bad,' agreed Demetrius. 'Conjured beings, using the souls of the damned. One mission, to kill a specific person. Very hard to avoid one, but three . . .'

'Impressive,' said Rondar.

Talon said, 'Have you been here a long time?'

'Five years,' Demetrius replied. 'My father used to make potions and poultices in a village down in the south of Kesh, near a city called Anticostinas. Well, it was hardly a city – a big town, really. Some priests of Guis-Wa denounced him as a "heretic" because he was "using magic", even though I didn't see much magic involved, just a lot of herbs, plants and common sense. But one night some drunks from the city came out and burned the house to the ground, killing my family. I wandered around for a while until I ran across Nakor, who showed me some tricks.

'Turns out my father wasn't a magician, but maybe I am. So I'm here to learn.'

'I lost my family, too,' Talon said. He looked at Rondar, who looked at Demetrius and nodded once.

'His father is the chief of a band of Ashunta horsemen down in northern Kesh. Very good horsemen—'

'Best,' added Rondar.

'—good hunters—'

'Best,' repeated Rondar.

Talon grinned. 'We'll see about that!'

'—and otherwise a bunch of opinionated, unwashed barbarians who treat women like cattle and cattle like pets.'

Rondar shrugged. 'True.'

Talon's grin widened. 'How does he get along with Miranda?'

Demetrius laughed. 'She's educating him as to the proper respect to show to women.'

Rondar's expression darkened. With a sigh of resignation, he rested his chin on his arms and said, 'Painfully true.'

Talon said, 'How'd you get here?'

Rondar rolled over. He was quiet for a moment, and then spoke as if talking at all was a trial to him. 'My people are horsemen. If you can't ride and hunt, no women. No women, no children.' He put his arm across his eyes as if remembering was fatiguing. 'Men who can't ride are . . . less. Less than men. They gather firewood, help with the cooking, raise the boys.'

Talon glanced at Demetrius. 'What do the women do?'

Demetrius grimaced and said, 'They're property.'

'They make babies. Men raise boys.'

Demetrius said, 'It's a close thing as to what's worth more to an Ashunta horseman, a good horse or a woman.'

Rondar said, 'Depends on if there are more horses or women around.' He rolled over again and leaned on his elbows. His dark eyes looked hard at Talon. 'We have our ways,' he said. 'I'm not a good rider, but the shaman says I have talent. So, I go live with the shaman.' He looked as if he had reached the limit of his patience and said to Demetrius, 'You tell him.'

Demetrius made a wry expression and said, 'The home of the Ashunta is in the west of the Empire, rolling grasslands no one else wants, but a good way for slavers and renegades to move around without running foul of the Imperial army. Our friend and his master were off gathering herbs for some sort of ritual when a band of slavers happened on them. The shaman was too old to be worth anything, but our strapping young friend here was a prize for the auction blocks.'

'Nakor bought me,' Rondar offered. 'He talks too much.'

Talon smiled. 'Who, Nakor or Demetrius?'

Rondar said, 'Yes.'

Demetrius reached over and gave Rondar a playful slap to

the back of the head. 'Our taciturn friend here is actually a very good fellow, despite his pretence of being a man of few words – he's glib enough when one of the girls is in the mood to listen to his nonsense.'

Rondar lifted his head and grinned. 'True.'

Talon said, 'About the girls . . .'

Rondar and Demetrius exchanged glances, then with one voice said, 'Alysandra!' and burst into laughter.

Talon felt himself flush, but kept his smile fixed on his face. 'What about her?'

Demetrius said, 'I heard she'd been in to tend you from time to time.'

Rondar said, 'Every boy wants her.'

'You two as well?' asked Talon.

Demetrius said, 'Everyone has a try when they meet her. She's different. But she has a way of making you a friend and feeling like an idiot for trying to get her off alone somewhere.'

Rondar sighed. 'She's worth a lot of horses.'

Talon laughed. 'You sound like you're in love.'

Rondar said, 'True. Everyone's in love with her.'

'Who is she?'

'No one knows,' said Demetrius. 'Or at least, no one who knows is talking. She's been here longer than either of us, and she's obviously someone special. I've heard her talking to a lot of outlanders in their languages, and she spends a lot of time alone with Miranda.'

'Why is that special?' asked Talon.

Demetrius rose as a bell sounded. 'Supper,' he announced. 'We'll talk on the way.'

They left through the door with Rondar a step behind. Talon

moved carefully, but could keep up as long as Demetrius kept to a casual walk.

'You know Miranda is Pug's wife?' asked Demetrius.

Talon nodded. 'I know their sons.'

'Pug is the . . . "ruler" for lack of a better word of this place. But Miranda is his equal in just about every way. And some say she's a more powerful magician. All I know is she spends a little time with every student here, but a lot of time with Alysandra.'

Talon said, 'So, that's why she's special.'

Rondar said, 'Took a lot of words for you to get it, Talon.'

Talon laughed. 'I know.'

'So, if you want to take your chance with Alysandra, no one is going to blame you.'

'True,' said Rondar.

'But don't expect to get anywhere.'

Talon caught sight of Alysandra ahead, talking to two other girls. To his two new friends he said, 'One thing my father taught me: there is no reward without risk, and you can only fail if you don't try.'

'Hug,' said Rondar.

'What?' asked Talon.

Demetrius shook his head. 'No, kiss on the cheek.'

'What are you talking about?'

'Alysandra will let you court her, my friend,' supplied Demetrius. 'I think she's secretly amused by the attention. And she's very sweet. I don't think she has a mean thought in her, but by the end of the first evening you court her, she'll have you swearing that you'll be just like a brother to her, and you'll know that you're never going to get your arms around that slender waist, and just before she turns you around and points you back to your own quarters, you'll either get a tiny hug, one so brief you'll barely feel her next to you, or a fluttering kiss on the cheek, with her lips hardly touching your face. A kiss on the cheek is considered a badge of achievement among the lads here.'

As if sensing she was the object of this conversation, Alysandra looked back over her shoulder. When she saw Talon and the others, she smiled.

Talon glanced at his friends, both of whom were avoiding eye contact with the young woman. So he returned his gaze to her and gave her the broadest smile he could. She held his gaze for a step longer, then dropped her eyes and turned back to her companions.

Rondar said, 'I'll wager a copper it's a hug.'

Demetrius said, 'Done. I wager a kiss on the cheek.'

Talon lowered his voice. 'I'll take both those wagers, for I'll have more than a kiss on the cheek from her.'

'Determination,' said Demetrius. 'I like it!'

'Humph,' was Rondar's inarticulate comment.

Talon watched the slender girl as she entered the common building where the students ate their meals. 'I'll have much more,' he said quietly, to no one but himself.

CHAPTER ELEVEN

Purpose

*T*HE HORSES RACED ACROSS the meadow.

Nakor and Magnus watched as Talon kept low against the neck of his mare, pushing her as much with will as with any skill as a rider. Rondar's gelding pulled slowly away as he stayed fluidly poised on two stirrups, his back straight and his hands light upon the reins.

Nakor said, 'For someone who was counted a bad rider by his people, Rondar seems to know his way around a horse.'

Magnus nodded as he said, 'You know more about the Ashunta than I do, but aren't they counted as the finest horsemen in the world?'

'Best light cavalry, certainly. The Empire had to bring fifteen legions into their lands to subdue them in the end. They were key to Kesh's conquest of the western Empire two centuries ago, but a revolt by Ashunta chieftains ended that.' Nakor studied the riders, while Demetrius stood whooping and cheering a short distance away. 'Talon will be a very good horseman soon.'

'This I understand, Nakor –' Magnus waved his hand slightly in the direction of the two riders '– Talon learning languages, riding, swordsmanship, the rest – but why are you including him in the classes on magic with the others?'

Nakor grinned at his former student. 'Magic? There is no magic.'

Magnus tried not to laugh, and failed. 'You can debate that with Father until the universe ends, but we both know your "stuff" is just another way of looking at the process of using magic.'

'It's more than that, and you know it,' said Nakor. 'It's a way to free the mind of preconceived notions.' He paused, 'Besides,' he added with a chuckle, 'it was your father who first said "there is no magic".'

'Are you or Father ever going to tell me how he knew to send that message to you with James on his first trip to Kesh? You two hadn't even met.'

'He's never told me how he knew.' Nakor replied. 'There are things your father trusts to no one, not even to your mother.'

'The Black Sorcerer,' said Magnus with a sigh. 'It's too easy to forget it's not just a role to terrorize sailors who get too close to this island.'

'No, it's far more than that, as your grandfather knew.'

Magnus's grandfather, Macros, had been the first magic-user to employ a Black Sorcerer to secure the island's privacy. He also had been an agent for Sarig, the lost god of magic, and had given Sorcerer's Island to Pug and Miranda.

Nakor and Magnus were as highly placed as one could be within the Conclave of Shadows, yet neither fully understood the deepest mysteries of the organization. Magnus had once asked his father who should take control if anything happened to him, and Pug had replied cryptically that everyone would know what to do if that should happen.

Magnus turned his thoughts back to the matter at hand. 'Still, magic or stuff, you've not told me why Talon is studying the mystic arts.'

'True, I haven't.'

'Nakor, are you planning to irritate me all day?'

Nakor laughed. 'No, I just forget sometimes you have a problem with the concept of humour.' He pointed towards the other end of the meadow, where the race had ended and the three boys were standing, awaiting instruction. 'Talon needs to know as much as he can about any potential enemy. Our enemies have relied on the black arts for years, and Talon's ability to survive the attack of those three death-dancers gave me an idea.'

Magnus was silent. He knew that had he been alone in the hut, those death-dancers most likely would have killed him. He had speculated late into the night with his father why the enemy had taken such a bold step and why he had been selected as the target, but in the end all they were left with was speculation.

Magnus said, 'You want him able to recognize magic?'

'If possible. Years ago, Lord James, Duke of Krondor, told me he could always feel the hair on the back of his neck rise when someone was using magic. He also talked about his "bump of trouble", his ability to sense something was about to happen that was bad. It was a special intuition that saved James on several occasions.'

'You think Talon might have that ability?'

'I don't know yet, but it might prove useful to have someone who is not obviously a magic-user, but who has some sense of it, who can enter places that will have wards set against magicians, and yet be able to act with some knowledge.'

'Seems a vague enough motive for subjecting the boy to extra hours of study, especially since it will only be in the abstract and he will never be able to put that knowledge into practise.'

'You never know,' said Nakor. 'In any event, it will make him a far more educated person than he is, and that is to everyone's benefit.' He watched as the boys switched roles, so that Demetrius and Talon were to ride the next race, while Rondar observed.

'I'm thinking we must also see to another phase of Talon's education. I read with interest your notes on his encounters with those two girls at Kendrick's. I think we need to further those lessons.'

'Alysandra?'

'Yes. I think it's time for her to start using the skills we've taught her.'

'Why?'

'Because Talon will face things far more dangerous than steel and spell.'

Magnus turned to look back at the large buildings of his father's estate. 'How did we become such men, Nakor? How did we become capable of doing such evil things?'

'The irony of the gods,' Nakor replied. 'We do evil in the name of good, and our enemies have at times done good, in the name of evil.'

'Do you think the gods are laughing at us?'

Nakor chuckled. 'Constantly.'

'You didn't . . .'

'What?'

'When I was your student. You didn't . . . Helena . . . she wasn't one of yours, was she?'

'No,' said Nakor, his features softening. He put his hand on Magnus's arm and added, 'That harsh lesson was of your own devising. Life is like that sometimes.' Then he turned his attention back to the three boys as the new race began, with Demetrius and Talon riding with all the skill they could muster, while Rondar shouted insults at both of them.

When Nakor looked back at Magnus, he found the magician lost in thought. Having some idea of where those thoughts led, Nakor said, 'You should have found another, Magnus.'

Magnus looked down at his former teacher. 'Some wounds never heal. You just bind them up and go on with life.'

Nakor nodded. 'I know, Magnus.'

Magnus smiled. He knew that Nakor understood, for he had once been wed to Magnus's grandmother and had loved her up to the very moment he had been forced to kill her.

Magnus took a deep breath. 'Very well. When shall we start?'

'Might as well be tonight,' said Nakor.

Magnus started walking. 'Then I had better go and tell the girl.'

Nakor called after him: 'Just tell her what to do. She'll know exactly how to do it.'

When he turned back it was in time to see Talon finish slightly ahead of Demetrius, both boys exulting loudly as they reined in before Rondar. Nakor reflected that youth often understood without having to be taught about seizing the joy of the moment, about not thinking too much of tomorrow and the worries and concerns it would bring, or too much about yesterday, with all its regrets and guilt. Softly, Nakor said, 'Enjoy this moment, Talon. Savour it.'

Then with a sigh of regret, he turned his back upon the three students and started walking towards Pug's quarters. They had a lot to discuss, and much of that would be unpleasant.

Talon dried his hair with a coarse towel. He enjoyed bathing, though it had not been a regular part of his childhood. The Orosini had to heat water in which to bathe, since all the rivers ran with snowmelt year round and only in the hot months of summer could one swim in the lakes and rivers of the mountains. In winter you sweated in the lodges and scraped off dirt with a stick.

He had been introduced to bathing at Kendrick's, but there he had to use a tub, often after others had used it, so it seemed that all he was doing was trading his own dirt for someone else's. But the Villa Beata had a wonderful set of rooms in which to bathe. It had three connecting baths with cold, warm and hot water which were enjoyed by many folk in the community on a daily basis. And smaller tubs were available in each wing of the estate buildings.

After working or riding, he was glad to get the grime off and don fresh clothing. And every day there was fresh apparel in his clothes-chest. He knew that other students were assigned work in the laundry, but it still seemed like magic to him. He would leave his dirty clothing in a hamper outside the door to the room, and when he returned from his studies or exercises, clean garments awaited him.

As he wiped his face dry, he felt the stubble along his jaw.

He had started shaving the year before, in the same manner as Magnus, although the Orosini's preferred method was to pluck each hair out of the chin one by one. Talon decided he much preferred a sharp razor.

Talon stropped the razor while Rondar and Demetrius came in from their baths. 'What are you doing after supper?' he asked, lathering his face.

Rondar threw himself upon his bed, a coarse towel his only garment, and grunted something noncommittal. Demetrius said, 'I've got kitchen duty tonight, so I'll be serving, and cleaning up. You?'

'I'm free,' said Talon as he started shaving. 'I thought we might build a fire in the pit down by the lake and see who turns up.'

'It helps if you spread the word during supper that you're doing so.'

Rondar said, 'Girls.'

'An impromptu gathering is often the best.'

'Well, tomorrow's Sixthday, so no matter how tired you are in the morning, by midday you can rest.'

'I can,' said Demetrius. 'And he can,' he pointed to Rondar, 'but you can't. Didn't you check the roster?'

'No.'

'You've got kitchen duty all day, sunrise until after last meal.'

Talon sighed. 'So much for a revel tonight.'

'Well, it's a good idea, even if you're not going to be there,' said Demetrius.

'Yes,' Rondar agreed.

'Thanks. I think of it, and I can't go.'

'You can go,' said Demetrius. 'Just don't stay up too late.'

'Wine,' said Rondar, as he sat up and began dressing.

'Yes, we'll need wine.'

Demetrius looked at Talon who grinned at him. 'You're the one in the kitchen tonight.'

'If Besalamo catches me in the cellar again, he'll cook and eat me.'

'Taldaren,' observed Rondar with a nod.

Talon laughed. Besalamo was a magician from another world – a fact that had taken Talon some time to fully assimilate – and looked almost human, save for two fins of white bone that ran fore and aft along his skull in place of hair. And he had bright red eyes. 'I think he started that rumour about Taldaren eating boys to keep us in line.'

'You want to find out?' asked Demetrius.

'No, but I'm not the one who needs to get us some wine. Without the wine the girls won't come down to the lake.'

'They might, if you asked them,' suggested Demetrius.

Talon flushed at the suggestion. It was becoming clear that as the new boy he was the object of much curiosity among the girls on the island.

In total, there seemed to be about fifty students on the island, and after taking away those who weren't human, there were sixteen young men, from Talon's age up to their mid-twenties, and fourteen girls, aged fourteen to twenty-two.

'Alysandra,' said Rondar.

'Yes,' Demetrius agreed. 'Invite her. If she says yes, all the boys will come, and if all the boys are down by the lake, then all the girls will come as well.'

Talon's face and neck turned deep crimson.

'Blushing,' said Rondar with a laugh, as he pulled on his trousers.

'Leave him alone, you useless barbarian. If we're going to get the girls to the lake tonight, we need Talon to ask Alysandra.'

Talon gave Demetrius a dubious look but said nothing. He had no problem talking to Alysandra, as some of the other boys seem to have, yet he had come to the conclusion that she was totally uninterested in him. Between her polite but unenthused responses to him over the last few weeks whenever circumstances brought them together, and the near awe with which the boys regarded her, he had decided early on that any pursuit of her was a waste of time.

Still, if Demetrius was willing to risk the cook's wrath by pilfering some wine, and even Rondar was excited at the prospect of the gathering, Talon felt he'd best do his part.

He finished dressing and set out to find Alysandra.

The fire burned brightly as the young men and women of the island sat in pairs or threes talking quietly. Except Rondar, who sat slightly away from Demetrius and a girl whose name Talon didn't know.

Talon was surprised to see nearly fifty people around the fire. The two bottles of wine Demetrius had produced were augmented by a large cask of ale someone else had purloined from the storage shed, and a few of the boys were already showing the effects of too much to drink. He helped himself to a goblet, and walked a little away from the group.

Talon enjoyed wine, but ale held little interest for him. The honeyed drinks of his childhood were but a dim memory and he had been denied the fermented honey the men drank. He stood there, on his own, swilling the pungent liquid around his mouth, savouring its taste.

'Why are you alone?'

Talon looked up and found a slender dark-haired girl named Gabrielle standing next to him, a light shawl around her shoulders. She had startling blue eyes and a warm smile.

'Hardly alone.' Talon said.

She nodded. 'Yet you always seem . . . apart, Talon.'

Talon glanced around and said nothing.

'Are you waiting for Alysandra?'

It was as if the girl had read his mind; and on *this* island, that was a distinct possibility! Gabrielle's smile broadened. 'No . . . yes, I suppose so. I mentioned this gathering to her before supper and –' he waved his hand at the other girls '– apparently she mentioned it to a number of the girls.'

Gabrielle studied his face then said, 'Are you yet another of those who have fallen under her spell?'

'Spell?' asked Talon. 'What do you mean?'

'She's my friend. We share a room and I love her, but she's different.' Gabrielle looked at the fire as if seeing something within the flames. 'It's easy to forget that each of us is different.'

Talon didn't quite know where Gabrielle was taking the conversation, so he was content to remain silent.

After a long pause, Gabrielle said, 'I have visions. Sometimes they are flashes, images that are with me only for a brief instant. At other times they are long, detailed things, as if I were in a room watching others, hearing them speak.

'I was abandoned as a child by my family. They were fearful of me because I had foretold the death of a nearby farmer, and the villagers named me a witch-child.' Her eyes grew dark. 'I was four years old.'

When Talon reached out to touch her, she pulled back and

turned towards him with a pained smile. 'I don't like to be touched.'

'Sorry,' he said, withdrawing his hand. 'I only—'

'I know you meant well. Despite your own pain you have a generous spirit and an open heart. That's why I see only pain for you.'

'What do you mean?'

'Alysandra.' Gabrielle rose. 'I love her like a sister, but she's dangerous, Talon. She will not come tonight. But you will find her, soon. And you will fall in love with her and she will break your heart.'

Before he could ask any more questions, she turned and walked off into the dark, leaving Talon staring after her bemusedly. He weighed her words and found himself feeling a mixture of confusion and anger. Hadn't he had enough pain already in his life? He had lost everything dear to him, nearly been killed, been taken to strange places, and asked to learn things that were still alien and disturbing to him at times.

And now he was being told that he had no choice in how his heart was to be engaged. He stood up and turned his back on the revellers and slowly started to head back towards his quarters. His mind spun this way and that, and before he knew it he was in his quarters, lying upon his bed, staring at the ceiling. It seemed to him then that two faces hovered above him, changing places: Alysandra, whose brilliant smile seemed to make a lie of Gabrielle's words – for how could someone so gentle and beautiful be dangerous? But then he'd recall the pain he saw in Gabrielle's eyes and knew that she was not giving him false counsel. She had perceived danger, and Talon knew he must heed that warning.

He was dozing when Rondar and Demetrius returned from the gathering, both of them a little drunk. They were chattering. Or rather, thought Talon, Demetrius was chattering for both of them.

'You left,' said Rondar.

'Yes,' said Talon. 'As you recall, I have a long day in the kitchen tomorrow, so do us all a favour and stop talking.'

Demetrius looked at Talon then at Rondar, and started to laugh. 'That's our Rondar, talk, talk, talk.'

Rondar pulled off his boots, grunted, and fell upon the bed.

Talon turned his face to the wall and closed his eyes, but sleep was a long time in coming.

Weeks passed, and the events of the night in which Gabrielle shared her vision with him faded. Talon found much of the work that was given to him routine and predictable, but there were always enough new lessons to maintain his interest. As Magnus had predicted, Rondar turned Talon into a fine horseman, and over the next few months the Orosini emerged as the most able swordsman on the island. It felt, however, something of a hollow honour, as most of the students on Sorcerer's Isle spent little or no time studying weapons and their uses.

The magic classes were strange. He barely understood half the things under discussion, and seemed to have no natural aptitude for the subject at all. Once or twice he would get an odd feeling just before a spell was executed, and when he told Magnus and Nakor about this, they spent over an hour asking him to describe that feeling in great detail.

The most amusing situation to arise during those weeks was

Rondar's infatuation with a newly-arrived girl named Selena, a hot-tempered, slender Keshian girl who despised Ashunta horsemen on general principle, for she had seen them on the edge of her town many times as a child. Her outrage at his culture's treatment of women seemed focused upon Rondar as if he was the sole architect of his cultures values and beliefs. At first, Rondar had been silent in the face of her anger, ignoring the barbs and insults. Then he had returned the anger, speaking in rare, complete sentences, much to Talon and Demetrius's amusement. Then against any reasonable expectation, he became enamoured of her.

His determination to win her over resulted in Talon sitting quietly, biting his tongue to keep from laughing, as Demetrius tutored Rondar in how properly to pay court. Talon knew himself to be no expert in such things, and judged that the girl had a great deal more to say in these matters than the boy, but his experience with Lela and Meggie at least had made him a little more comfortable around girls than Rondar and Demetrius. Around all girls, that is, except Alysandra.

His initial attraction to her had been supplemented by his reaction to Gabrielle's warning. He now found her both appealing and daunting in the extreme. There was a sense of danger about her, and he wondered if it was of his own imagining, or if there was something truly risky in having any contact with her.

He decided that the best answer was avoidance, and when a situation arose which threw them together he was polite, but distant. He also found as many excuses as possible to keep away from her until he puzzled out how he felt about all this.

Nakor and Magnus provided new things for him to do all the

time, and one afternoon he found himself undertaking the strangest task so far. Nakor had taken him to the top of a hillock, upon which sat a stunted birch tree, nearly dead from some pest, with gnarled branches and few leaves. Nakor had handed Talon a large piece of parchment stretched over a wooden frame, then a fire hardened stick, with a charcoal point. 'Draw that tree,' he said, walking away without waiting to hear Talon's questions or remarks.

Talon looked at the tree for a long time. Then he walked around it twice, and then stared for nearly half an hour at the blank parchment.

Then he noticed a curve below one branch, where a shadow formed a shape like a fish. He tried to draw that.

Three hours later he looked at his drawing and then up at the tree. Frustration rose up in him and he threw the parchment down. He lay back and looked up at the clouds racing overhead, letting his mind wander. Large white clouds formed shapes and in those shapes he saw faces, animals, a castle wall.

His mind drifted away, and before long he realized he had dozed off. He was not sure how long he had slept for – only a few minutes, he judged – but suddenly he understood something. He sat up and looked at his parchment; then the tree, and frantically began another drawing, to the left of the original sketch. This time he stopped looking for details and just tried to capture the sense of the tree, the lines and shadows which his hunter's eye had revealed. The details weren't important he realized: rather, it was the overall sense of the object that mattered.

Just as he was completing the drawing, Nakor returned and peered over his shoulder. 'Have you finished?'

'Yes,' said Talon.

Nakor looked at the two trees. 'You did this one first?' He pointed to the one on the right.

'Yes.'

'This one is better,' he said, indicating the drawing on the left.

'Yes.'

'Why?'

'I don't know. I just stopped trying to do everything.'

'That's not bad,' said Nakor, handing back the drawing. 'You have a good eye. Now you must learn how to record what is important and not what is unnecessary. Tomorrow you will start to learn to paint.'

'Paint?'

'Yes,' said Nakor. Turning back towards the estate, he said, 'Come along.'

Talon fell in alongside his instructor and wondered what Nakor meant by 'learning to paint'.

Maceus scowled as he watched Talon. The man had appeared as if by magic outside Nakor's quarters the day after Talon had sketched the tree. He was a Quegan with an upturned nose, a fussy little moustache and a penchant for clucking his tongue while he reviewed Talon's work. He had been teaching the young man about painting for a month now, working from dawn to dusk.

Talon was a quick study. Maceus proclaimed him without gifts and lacking grace, but grudgingly admitted he had some basic skill and a good eye.

Nakor would come in and observe from time to time as Talon struggled to master the concepts of light, shape, texture and colour. Talon also learned to mix his colours and oils to create what he needed and to prepare wooden boards or stretched canvas to take the paint.

Talon used every skill he had learned in every other discipline he had been taught, for as much as anything he had ever tried to master, painting caused him seemingly unending frustration. Nothing ever looked the way he had imagined it would when he started. Maceus had started him off painting simple things – four pieces of fruit upon a table, a single leather gauntlet, a sword and shield; but even these objects seemed determined to escape his efforts.

Talon studied and applied himself, failing more often than not, but slowly he began to understand how to approach the task of rendering.

One morning he arose and after finishing his duties in the kitchen – painting made him long for the relatively simple joy of cooking – he found himself looking at his latest attempt, a painting of a porcelain pitcher and bowl. Off-white in colour and with a decorative scroll of blue knotwork along the rim of the bowl and around the middle of the pitcher, the items required a subtle approach.

Maceus appeared as if sensing he had finished, and Talon stood aside. Maceus looked down his nose at the painting and said nothing for a moment. Then he prounounced: 'This is acceptable.'

'You like it?' asked Talon.

'I didn't say I *liked* it; I said it was acceptable. You made correct choices, young Talon. You understood the need for representation rather than exact delineation in the painted knot-work. Your pallet was correct in rendering the white.'

Talon was gratified to earn even this guarded praise. 'What next?'

'Next, you start painting portraits.'

'Portraits?'

'You'll paint pictures of people.'

'Oh.'

Maceus said, 'Go and do something else. Go outside and use your eyes to look at the horizon. You've been taxing them with close work for too long.'

Talon nodded and left the room. Everyone else was doing their assigned work, and he didn't want to ride alone, or walk down to the lake and swim on his own. So he wandered across the meadow north of the estate and at last came across a group of students working in the small apple grove that bordered the deeper woods.

A familiar figure called out to him and he felt his pulse race. 'Talon!' Alysandra cried. 'Come and help!'

She stood at the top of a ladder which was leaning against a tree. The ladder was being held by a boy named Jom. Talon saw that there were twelve students in all; six pairs.

Talon came to stand at the foot of the ladder and called up, 'What do I do?'

She leaned over and handed down a large bag of apples. 'Put that with the others and fetch me another bag. That way I don't have to climb up and down.'

Talon did as she asked and carried the apples to a large pile of full bags. In the distance he saw another student driving a wagon slowly in their direction, so he assumed it was close to finishing time. He took an empty bag back to the ladder, climbed up a little way and handed the bag to Alysandra.

Her hair was tied back and tucked up under a white cap, accentuating the slenderness of her neck and how graceful her shoulders were. Talon saw that her ears stuck out a little and found that endearing.

'Why don't you go and help the others?' She said after a moment. 'We're almost done.'

Talon jumped down and grabbed up an armful of bags. He exchanged empty bags for full ones, and by the time the wagon pulled up, the harvest was complete.

The students quickly loaded the wagon and started the trek back to the estate. When they were almost there, Alysandra fell in beside Talon and said, 'Where have you been keeping yourself? I hardly see you any more.'

'Painting,' said Talon. 'Master Maceus has been teaching me to paint.'

'Wonderful!' she exclaimed and her eyes seemed enormous as she looked up at Talon. She slipped her arm through his and he felt the softness of her breast against his elbow. He could smell the faint scent of her mixed in with the overwhelming scent of the apples. 'What do you paint?'

'Mainly what the master calls "still life" – things he arranges on a table, or pictures of the land. Tomorrow I start painting portraits.'

'Wonderful!' she repeated. 'Will you paint a portrait of me?'

Talon almost stuttered. 'Ah . . . certainly, if Master Maceus allows it.'

She rose up on her tiptoes for a brief instant with the grace of a dancer, and kissed him lightly on the cheek. 'It's a promise,' she said. 'I'll hold you to it.'

And with that she hurried ahead, leaving Talon standing as if thunderstruck, while several other boys laughed at his obvious state of confusion.

Talon reached up slowly and touched the cheek she had kissed and for a long time thought of nothing else.

• CHAPTER TWELVE •

Love

*T*ALON FROWNED.

'Hold still, please,' he pleaded.

Demetrius and Rondar both attempted to hold their poses for a moment longer, but at last Demetrius burst out, 'I can't do this!'

Talon threw his brush down in disgust. 'All right. Let's take a minute to relax.'

Rondar came around to where Talon had set up his easel with a treated piece of wood resting on it. He examined the portrait Talon was painting of the two young men and grunted. 'Pretty good.'

Demetrius picked up an apple off the small table by the door and bit into it. Around a mouthful of fruit, he said, 'Do you have any idea why they're doing this?'

'Doing what?' asked Talon.

'Making you learn to paint.'

Talon shrugged. 'They have had me learning all manner of things over the last few years that don't make a lot of sense to me. But I owe Robert de Lyis my life and he's bound me over to Master Pug's service, so I do what they tell me.'

'But aren't you the least bit curious?' asked Demetrius.

'Of course, but they'll tell me what I need to know when I need to know it.'

Rondar sat down on a bed and said, 'It's simple.'

'What?' asked Demetrius, his freckled face resolving into a frown.

'Why he paints,' replied Rondar.

'Well be so kind as to explain it to us, then, why don't you?' Demetrius looked at Talon who smiled.

Rondar shook his head as if it was obvious to any but a fool. Then he stood up, crossed the room and put his hand on Talon's shoulder. 'Talon: Mountain boy.'

'Right,' said Demetrius, his expression showing he wasn't following so far.

'Talon: Roldemish gentleman.' With that, Rondar sat down.

Demetrius nodded as if understanding.

'What?' asked Talon, puzzled.

'How many languages do you speak now?'

'Six, including Orosini. I speak fluent Roldemish, King's Tongue, the Common Tongue, pretty good Keshian; and I'm getting decent with Quegan – which is pretty close to ancient Keshian. Next I'm supposed to learn Yabonese.'

'And you're the best on the island with a sword.'

'Yes,' said Talon without modesty.

'Do you play an instrument?'

'A flute. Nakor showed me how to make one.'

'Well?'

'Well enough.'

'You play chess, cards, dice, right?'

'Yes.'

'And you're good at them, right?'

'Yes,' Talon repeated.

Demetrius grinned. 'Rondar's right. They're going to pass you off as a gentleman of Roldem.'

'Cook?' asked Rondar.

Talon grinned. 'Better than Besalamo, if I'm honest.'

'That's not saying much,' observed Demetrius. 'Look, if they start teaching you how to play more instruments and everything you need to know about wine and other such niceties, then Rondar's right. The masters of this island are transforming you into a gentleman of Roldem.'

'But why?' asked Talon.

'You'll know when they tell you,' Demetrius replied.

Talon pondered the possibility for a moment, then said, 'All right. Back to your places. I told Master Maceus I'd have something to show him before supper.'

The two young men resumed their positions and Talon turned his mind away from the question of what he was being trained to do and back to the task at hand.

Master Maceus considered the portrait. After a while he said, 'Passable.'

'Thank you,' Talon replied without much conviction. He was

frustrated by the shortcomings he recognized in his work; the figures were stiff, unnatural, and showed little of the nature of his two friends.

'You need work on the structure of the body,' said his instructor.

'Yes, sir.'

'I think your next study should be a nude.'

Talon raised an eyebrow. He had grown up in a culture in which the sight of the human body was no cause for notice, yet he had learned since coming away from the mountains of the Orosini that many other people viewed nakedness in a very different fashion. Some students swam nude in the lake, while others avoided those gatherings, preferring to swim and bathe alone, or wearing clothing designed for wear in the water. Others, like Rondar, avoided swimming altogether.

Talon had even discussed the matter with Nakor, which probably had been a poor choice, since his instructor had left him with more questions than answers. Even so, Talon felt compelled to ask, 'Master Maceus?'

'Yes?'

'Are such paintings common?'

'Common enough,' said Maceus, though he added a self-conscious cough and remarked, 'Though not often for public viewing. Private collections and the like. Still, statuary, that's another story. Great heroes are often depicted in various stages of undress, their bodies showing magnificent wounds. But I'm not concerned about your ability to create something to titillate a bored noble; nor do I think you have the makings of a sculptor. It's a matter of seeing below the surface, Talon.' He pointed to the work on the easel and went on, 'You've captured the surface of the boys, the overall sense of the planes and angles of their faces and clothing, but the muscles underneath, the curves of their shoulders, arms, chest – all that is missing. When you paint a portrait you must think of the body beneath, the spirit within: then you clothe the subject with your brushes and knives. When you look at the naked body, see the bone, sinew and muscle within, and clothe them in skin and hair. You'll learn to understand this.' With a rare smile, he added, 'We may make a painter of you yet.'

Thinking of trying to persuade Rondar to stand in the room with no clothing, Talon said, 'Should I seek another subject?'

'Do not concern yourself. I'll send someone along tomorrow.'

Talon nodded, thinking about what his instructor had said, and slowly began to clear away his brushes and paints.

Talon hurried from the kitchen. He had been assigned break-fast duty and had been up for two hours before the rest of the community had arisen. He had spent the entire time in the kitchen, until the afternoon crew had come aboard. He was to have returned to his quarters to meet the model for his new painting, but Nakor had found him and sent him off on an errand, telling him he'd meet the model later.

It had taken almost all of the afternoon for Talon to finish Nakor's bidding, and now he was ready to return to his quarters to take a quick bath before supper. But when he got there, he found Rondar and Demetrius picking up the wooden chest that held Talon's belongings. 'What's going on?' Talon asked.

'Moving,' said Rondar.

'We're moving?'

'*You're* moving,' said Demetrius. 'I don't know why, but we just got orders to take all your things down to that little cottage by the lake. You know the one.'

Talon grinned. The cottage was often used by students for assignations after hours. Then his grin faded. If he was being assigned that hut as quarters, any number of students would be less than thrilled.

As if reading his mind, Rondar said, 'They can use the stable.'

Demetrius laughed. 'He's right. There are plenty of other places to get friendly. I'm partial to the baths after dark, myself. Water's still very warm, it's quiet . . .' He grunted theatrically as he lifted the trunk, but Talon knew it wasn't heavy, just big.

He let them go past him and out through the door, then fell in behind them. 'My bed?'

'Moved an hour ago,' said Demetrius. 'Along with your painting gear. We just couldn't get this trunk into the wagon with the rest.'

'Why?' asked Talon. 'I don't have much, certainly not enough to fill a wagon.'

Demetrius again grinned. 'You'd be surprised.'

They moved down the hall to where the now-empty wagon waited, and loaded the trunk. In a few minutes they were bumping along down the track that led from the village, past the lake, to the small hut.

It might once have been a charcoal-burner's hut, or perhaps the hut of a gamekeeper, but it had for some reason fallen out of use and been uninhabited for years. When they got there, Demetrius reined in the horse and Talon jumped down from the back of the wagon. He and Rondar got the trunk down and manoeuvred it to where Demetrius stood, holding open the door.

As he stepped into the cottage, Talon stopped stock-still. Then he said softly, 'I'll be . . .'

'The girls were in here yesterday cleaning, and Rondar and I moved everything else,' Demetrius said.

'But where did all this come from?' asked Talon, indicating the room.

The cottage was spacious, larger than the hut he had shared with Magnus. A hearth complete with spit and an iron cauldron on a hook for stews and soups waited for a fire. A free-standing pantry had been placed near at hand, and a small table occupied the corner between the pantry and the fireplace. His bed rested against the opposite wall, near the door, and at the foot of it had placed a large wooden wardrobe. Talon and Rondar set the trunk down next to the wardrobe. Talon opened its door and exclaimed, 'Look at this!'

Fine garments, of various colours and cuts, hung neatly inside.

Rondar said, 'Gentleman.'

Demetrius nodded. 'Seems to be the case. But why here I have no idea.'

Looking at one doublet, with enough eyelets and fasteners to confound the eye, Talon said, 'To practise getting dressed, I suppose. Look at these things.'

Hose, leggings, trousers, singlets, doublets, waistcoats, all hung neatly from wooden rods and hangers. In the bottom of the wardrobe half a dozen different types of boots and shoes were neatly arranged.

Then Talon caught sight of the far corner. 'Books!' he exclaimed with pleasure. He crossed the room to examine the titles on the shelves there. 'All new to me,' he said quietly.

'Well,' said Demetrius, 'we're for supper. I've been told to tell you you're on your own for a while. Someone will bring you your supper tonight and some other provisions, and then you're to keep to yourself for a while.'

Talon knew better than to ask why. No one would have told Demetrius.

Rondar pointed to the easel. 'Practise.'

'Yes,' said Talon. 'I guess they want me to focus on that, and these other things.'

'We'll see you around, I'm sure,' said Demetrius. 'Come along, Rondar. Let's get the wagon back to the stable.'

The two friends left, and Talon sat down and drank in his new surroundings. It was strange to think that, at least for a short while, this would be his home, and it filled him with an odd melancholy. He had never lived alone, not since the day of his birth. The only significant time he had been by himself had been upon Shatana Higo, waiting for his vision.

He sat quietly, letting the mood sweep through him. He remembered what he had been taught and allowed the nostalgic longing for his childhood to pass through him; he would not engage that sorrow now. He would acknowledge it and renew his vow that some day his people would be avenged; and then he would let it go.

Twilight was upon him before he realized it. He was just lighting a lamp when he heard a wagon pull up outside the hut. It must be his supper, he thought.

He opened the door and almost fell over backwards to get out of the way of Alysandra, who marched purposely into the room carrying a steaming kettle of something wonderful. Behind her a voice called, 'I'll unload.'

'Thanks, Jom,' she said over her shoulder.

'What are you doing here?' Talon asked.

'I've brought you your supper,' she said. 'Didn't they tell you?'

'They told me someone was bringing it, but not who,' he answered, then felt foolish for having said it.

She smiled, then removed the light cloak she had around her shoulders. Underneath it she wore a simple dress, off the shoulders, and her hair fell around her face. Talon felt his chest tighten.

He stood there speechless for a long moment, then said, 'I'll help Jom.'

She smiled and turned to find plates and cups.

Jom handed down two large sacks to Talon and said, 'I've got more in that box, there.'

'What is it?'

'Food. You're supposed to cook for yourself, I was to tell you. Practise what Leo taught you. Whoever he was and whatever it was he taught you,' Jom added. He took up a third sack and jumped down from the wagon.

Talon picked up the food and carried it inside. 'Better dig a cold cellar out back,' said Jom as he put down the sack. 'Got some ham and a quarter of beef coming tomorrow, I was told to tell you. There's a shovel and some tools in a shed out there, if you didn't know.'

'Thanks,' said Talon as Jom went out of the door.

Talon turned, expecting to see Alysandra moving to follow Jom, but instead she stood at the table, ladling out portions of stew into a pair of bowls. 'Ah . . . you're staying?' asked Talon.

She waved for him to sit, and produced a bottle of wine. Then she poured two mugfuls, pulled out one of the two small stools that had been stored beneath the table and sat down. 'Yes, I'm going eat with you. Didn't they tell you?'

Talon sat down. 'Apparently everyone else got told except me.' He could hardly take his eyes off Alysandra, but each time she glanced at him, he looked away.

She laughed. 'It's like that sometimes around here, isn't it?'

'It's like that a lot around here,' he replied, and she laughed again.

They ate in silence for a few minutes, then Talon said, 'I'm pleased you're here, really, but . . . well . . . what *are* you doing here?'

'Oh, didn't Master Maceus tell you that, either?'

'No,' said Talon. 'As I said, no one has been telling me much of anything.'

'I'm going to be staying here with you. I'm your new model.'

Talon put down his mug. He could not believe what she had said. 'You're the model.'

'Yes, for the nude study you're doing.'

Talon felt his cheeks begin to burn, but he forced himself to calmness. Obviously, she had no problem posing for him, so he needn't feel uncomfortable, he decided. Despite this, however, he couldn't eat, so he put the contents of his plate back in the pot. 'I'm not really hungry,' he said weakly. 'I was in the kitchen all day and you know how it is, a bite here, a bit of a nibble there.'

She smiled and said nothing.

When she had finished her supper, she said, 'Fetch me some water from the lake, and I'll clear up.'

Glad for the excuse to be alone for a moment, Talon hurried to comply with her request, taking the large oak bucket from beside the door and hurried down to the lake. A small stream fed the lake and Talon filled the bucket there, where the water was freshest. He lugged it back and found that Alysandra had already cleared the table and put the plates and cups on the rack outside next to the door. When he appeared, she took the water from him without comment and quickly washed up.

Talon went inside, agonizing over what to say next to her. But before he had been able to think of anything, she stepped into the doorway and paused there, letting herself be framed in it. 'It's warm tonight,' she said.

'Yes,' said Talon, realizing that he was perspiring, but certain it had nothing to do with the weather. 'It's a bit warm.'

Suddenly she was undressing. 'Let's go for a swim.'

Talon sat in mute astonishment as she quickly removed her dress. Seeing his expression, she laughed. 'Get used to seeing me this way, Talon. You're going to be painting me for a while, remember.'

'I suppose so,' he said, watching as she turned and hurried down to the water.

'Come on!' she ordered, laughing at his obvious discomfort.

Talon stripped off his boots, tunic, and trousers, and ran after her. Alysandra was already splashing into the water by the time he reached the shore. He ran into the water and executed a shallow dive. Coming up, he wiped his hair back and said, 'This feels wonderful.'

She swam over to him. 'Yes, doesn't it?'

Talon ducked his head beneath the water and came up again. 'I missed bathing today, and I think I needed this.'

'You didn't smell any worse than usual,' she said.

'Huh?' he said, stunned by the remark. 'I smell bad?'

She laughed. 'It's a joke, you simpleton.' Then she began to splash him.

He splashed back, and quickly they were drenching one another as if they were children. Then they swam for nearly an hour, until the large moon rose in the east, and finally Alysandra said, 'Time to get out.'

'I didn't bring towelling or robes,' Talon said, as if he should have thought of such things.

'It's warm. We'll be half-dry by the time we get back to the hut.'

They left the water and walked along side by side. Talon couldn't take his eyes from the way her body was bathed in the moonlight. She was slender, as he had known she would be, but her breasts were larger than he had imagined, and her hips were narrower than he had expected, almost boyish from certain angles.

'You're staring.'

He flushed. 'Sorry, but I was thinking of how best to pose you.'

She glanced away. 'Oh. Of course.'

Embarrassed, Talon realized that his body had started to respond to the sight of her. He wished he could creep away and die, but luckily Alysandra ignored his embarrassment. When they reached the hut, Talon stopped at the door. 'I just realized . . .'

'What?' she said, turning to face him.

'There's only one bed.'

'Of course,' she said, stepping forward until she was pressed up against him. Arms snaked around his neck and suddenly her face was in front of him, and her mouth was upon his. Talon hesitated but only for an instant, then he pulled her into him and everything else in the world was forgotten.

'What is that you're whistling?' she asked.

'Hold still,' Talon commanded, with a grin. 'Some tune, I don't know. Something I made up.'

'I like it. Can you play it on the pipe?'

'I think so,' he said, stepping back to look at the painting he had begun that morning, the third since Alysandra had come to the hut. For the first time since taking up the brush he was confident, and the first sketch he had made required little correction. He was now applying paint in blocks and patches, giving colour to a black-on-white image, and before his eyes he could see it taking form.

He had spent the first night with her in a state of euphoria. He had never imagined he could feel for any woman the way he did for Alysandra. She was sweet, warm, passionate and giving, as well as insistent and demanding in a playful and arousing manner.

They had hardly slept, save for brief naps between bouts of lovemaking. Finally, she had announced that hunger was making it impossible to sleep and he cooked while she bathed in the lake. He took a quick swim while she ate, then returned and wolfed down bread and cheese, a gulp or two of wine, and then dragged her back to bed.

Somehow between lovemaking, eating and sleeping, he had contrived to dig the cellar in the rear of the property next to the abandoned shed. He had been delighted to discover that someone had started the same project years before, and most of the hole was already dug, so that he only had to clear away years of accumulated detritus and brush, and then trim the sides, dig out steps, and measure a door.

He finished the task on the second day. The meat, ale, wine and cheese, along with a basket of fruit now rested in the cool cellar. Since then, he had devoted himself to one thing only, Alysandra.

He stepped back from the painting and made a considering noise. 'Hmmm . . .'

She dropped her pose and came over to look. 'That's me?'

'Yes,' he said in mock seriousness. 'It'll start looking more like you as I refine the details.'

'If you say so.' She came around behind him and hugged him. Then she let her hands drop down along his stomach and with mock surprise said, 'My, what's that?'

He turned in the circle of her arms, kissed her, and said, 'Let me show you.'

For the entire summer, they lived an idyllic life. Occasionally Master Maceus would come to review Talon's work and would find ways to improve it; yet he never criticized. As autumn drew on, Talon was finishing his twelfth portrait, this one of Alysandra reclining on the bed.

'I've been thinking,' he said, applying further details he had just noticed. Now he was starting to seek perfection in the work.

'About what?' she asked with a smile.

'About what is to come next.'

'Another painting?' she said with a grin.

'No, I mean about us.'

Suddenly her smile vanished. She stood up and quickly moved to stand in front of him. Without the slightest hint of warmth she raised her right hand and put her index finger over his mouth. 'Shush,' she admonished. 'There is nothing to think about. We just are here, now, and that's all that matters.'

'But—'

She pressed her finger hard and there was a flash in her eyes he had never seen before. 'I said shush.' Then her smile returned, but there was a hardness to it that was new to Talon. She reached down and stroked him, saying, 'I know how to make you stop thinking about things best left ignored.'

He felt a twinge of concern, for he glimpsed something in her that was alien to him, and a little frightening. Yet as always, her touch inflamed him, and moments later all concerns had fled before his passion.

The next day the rain came. They awoke to the sound of it tattooing the roof of the cottage, and Talon soon found there were half a dozen leaks to plug. He made do with wadding cloth; the roof was daubed thatch, and he would have to wait until it dried before he could patch it properly.

After eating, Alysandra rose and began to dress. He said, 'Going somewhere?'

'Back to the estate,' she said in flat tones.

'Why?' he asked. 'Is something wrong?'

'No, I'm just doing as I was told.'

'By whom?'

'Master Maceus. He said I would stay through the summer until you finished a dozen different portraits of me, then I was to return to the estate for other duties.'

'What about me?' Talon asked.

'He said nothing about what you would do after I leave. I'll tell him you've finished the paintings and I'm certain he'll come and view the last two, then tell you what is next.'

Talon positioned himself by the door. 'Wait until the rain is over.'

'I can't,' she said, starting to move by him.

'Wait!' He seized her upper arm. 'A moment.'

She looked up at him with eyes devoid of any warmth. 'What?'

'What about us?'

'What about us?' she repeated.

'I mean, I love you.'

With a tone that could only be called impatient, Alysandra replied, 'Talon, you're a sweet boy and I had fun this summer, but love had nothing to do with what passed between us. I like men and enjoy the games of men and women. I think I've improved your education in that area quite a bit, but if you think it's because I love you, you're mistaken. Sadly mistaken.'

A tingling flush rose in Talon's cheeks and his eyes felt as if they were filling with tears, but no moisture gathered. It was as if someone had struck him a blow to his belly with a mace. He felt short of breath. His mind raced, and he fought to make sense of what he had just been told, but he could not find the words. 'Wait,' he repeated softly.

'For what?' she asked, opening the door and stepping into the rain. 'For you to grow up? I hardly think so, boy. You've a stallion's constitution, and you've learned to pleasure me, but when I wed it will be with someone of importance, a powerful man who will shower me with riches and protect me and my children.

'And love will never be even a remote consideration.'

With that she turned and disappeared down the path past the lake, while Talon stood gripping the door jamb so hard that finally he heard a crack of wood. He stared down at his palm and saw that there were splinters embedded in it, and then he gazed out into the deepening storm.

Not since awakening in Robert's wagon had he felt so bereft of anything joyful. For the second time in his life he felt as if every good thing he had cherished had been taken from him.

CHAPTER THIRTEEN

Recovery

*T*ALON GROANED.

He had lain on his bed for two days, getting up only to relieve himself and drink water. He felt weak and unfocused, as if suffering a fever. His thoughts wandered and he relived Alysandra's last words to him over and over in his mind.

A hand shook him again.

'What?' he said, forcing himself out of his numb doze, to find Magnus standing above him.

'It's time for you to stop feeling sorry for yourself.'

Talon sat up and his head swam. He tried to focus his eyes.

'When did you last eat?' Magnus asked.

'Yesterday, I think.'

'More like three days ago,' said the magician. He rummaged around near the hearth and returned with an apple. 'Here, eat this.'

Talon took a bite and felt the juices run down his chin. Wiping his mouth with the back of his hand, he swallowed. His stomach seemed to flip at the introduction of food after his short fast.

Magnus sat down on the bed next to him. 'You feel bad?'

Talon nodded, unable to find words.

'She broke your heart?'

Talon said nothing but tears gathered in his eyes. He nodded again.

'Good,' said Magnus, striking him on the knee with his staff.

'Ow!' Talon exclaimed, rubbing at the knee.

Magnus stood up and rapped the boy lightly on the side of the head, hard enough to make Talon's ears ring and his eyes water even more. Stepping away, Magnus shouted, 'Defend yourself!'

This time he unleashed a vicious swipe at the other side of Talon's head, and the young man barely avoided being brained. He fell to his knees and rolled away, gaining a moment as Magnus had to come around the foot of the bed to reach him. When he did, he found Talon standing beside the table, his sword drawn and ready. 'Master Magnus!' he shouted. 'What is this?'

Magnus didn't answer, but instead feigned a jab with the foot of the staff towards Talon's head, then swept the rod around in an overhead arc. Talon caught the staff on the forte of his blade with just enough angle to force it past his shoulders, but not enough force to break the sword. Then he stepped inside and grabbed his teacher by the front of his robe, yanking him off-balance. Placing his sword at Magnus's throat, he said, 'Am I supposed to kill you now?'

'No,' said Magnus with a grin. He gripped Talon's sword hand

and Talon felt his fingers go numb. As the sword fell from his unresponsive grasp, Talon heard Magnus say, 'That was very good.'

Talon stepped back, rubbing his hand. 'What is all this?'

'If your enemy comes upon you unexpectedly, do you think he's going to stop and say, "Oh, poor Talon. He's upset over his lost love. I think I will wait for another day to kill him"?'

Talon kept rubbing his sore fingers. 'No.'

'Precisely.' He motioned for Talon to sit on the bed once more. 'Our enemies will attack you in ways you have not even imagined, Talon. Caleb and others can teach you weapons and hone your natural talents. I can show you things about your mind and make it more difficult for your enemies to confuse you or beguile you. But the heart . . .' He tapped his own chest. 'That is where many men are the most vulnerable.'

'So this was a lesson?'

'Yes,' said Magnus, with a grim expression. 'As harsh a lesson as I've ever seen, but necessary.'

'She didn't love me?'

'Never,' said Magnus coldly. 'She is our creature, Talon, and we use her, just as we will use you and every other student here.

'Once this was a place for learning, education for its own sake. My father founded the Academy of Magicians down at Stardock. Did you know that?'

'No.'

'When politics overtook the Academy, he started another place of learning here, for students of special gifts. I was raised here.

'But when the Serpentwar raged, and Krondor was destroyed, my father realized that our enemies were relentless and could never be counted on to give us respite. So, this school became a place of training. Some students from other worlds attend, but there are fewer of them each year; father brings in some teachers from other realms, as well, but mostly he, Mother, Nakor, myself, and others – like Robert – teach.'

'I've not asked, for I assume I'll be told in time, but who is this enemy?'

'It is very hard to tell someone as young as you. I'll leave it for Father and Nakor to tell you when you're ready to understand.

'But you will be tried by the enemy's agents, and as you saw on the night the death-dancers came for me, they can strike in the most unexpected fashion in places you think quite safe.'

'So I must . . . ?'

'Learn, be wary and trust only a few people.' He paused, considering what to say next. 'If I were to tell Rondar or Demetrius to kill you, they would. They would assume my reasons were valid and that you were a threat to us here. If I were to tell Alysandra to kill you, she would. The difference is that Rondar and Demetrius would feel remorse. Alysandra would feel nothing.'

'You made her this way?' said Talon, his anger rising and his sense of order outraged.

'No,' Magnus answered. 'We found her that way. Alysandra is . . . flawed. Tragically and terribly. She doesn't think about people as you and I might. She thinks of them as we might a stick of wood or a . . .' he pointed to a chair '. . . a piece of furniture. Useful, to be cared for, perhaps, so it can continue to be useful, but with no intrinsic value beyond its use to her.

'We found this terribly damaged person and brought her here.

Nakor can tell you about that; I know only that one day this lovely young girl was among us and Nakor was explaining what we needed to do with her.'

'But why? Why bring her here?'

'To train her to work for us. To use that remorseless nature to our own ends. Otherwise she might have ended up on the gallows in Krondor. At least this way we can channel her and control who gets hurt.'

Talon sat silently, staring out of the open door. 'But it felt so . . .'

'Real?'

'Yes. I thought she was falling in love with me.'

'One of her talents is to be what she needs to be, Talon. It was a cruel lesson, but necessary. And I can't stress this enough: she would have cut your throat while you slept had Nakor ordered it. And then she would have got dressed, and whistled a happy tune as she walked back to the estate afterwards.'

'Why do this to me?'

'So that you can look hard inside yourself and understand how weak the human heart can be. So that you can steel yourself against anything of this sort ever happening again.'

'Does this mean I can never love another?'

Now it was Magnus's turn to fall silent, and he also stared out of the door for a moment. Then he said, 'Perhaps not. But certainly not with some young woman who simply happens to command your attention because of a shapely leg and a winning smile, and because she's in your bed. You can bed women who are willing to your heart's content, time and circumstances allowing. Just don't think you're in love with them, Talon.'

'I know so little.'

'Then you've taken the first step toward wisdom,' Magnus said, standing up. He moved to the door. 'Think about this for a while: remember the quiet times when your father and mother were caring for you and your family. That's love. Not the passion of the moment in the arms of a willing woman.'

Talon leaned back against the wall. 'I have much to think about.'

'Tomorrow we return to your training. Eat something and sleep, for we have a lot to do.'

Magnus left and Talon lay back on the bed, his arm behind his head. Staring at the ceiling, he thought about what the magician had said. It was as if Magnus had thrown icy water over him. He felt cold and discomforted. The image of Alysandra's face hung in the air above him, yet it was now a mocking, cruel visage. And he wondered if he could ever look at a woman again in the same way.

Talon spent a restless night, even though he was as tired as he could remember. It was even more profound a fatigue than those occasions when he had recovered from his wounds after almost dying. It was a weariness of the soul, a lethargy that came from a wounded heart.

Yet there was a fey energy within; a strange flashing of images, memories and imagination; phantasms and fantasies. He rejected Magnus's judgment of Alysandra. Talon *knew* he could not have imagined his feelings, but at the same time he *knew* he had. He was angry and his pain sought an outlet, yet there was no place to focus it. He blamed his teachers, yet he knew they had taught him a vital lesson that might some day save his life. He raged at Alysandra, yet from what Magnus had told him, she could no more be blamed for her nature than a viper could be blamed for being venomous.

The dawn rose and the sky turned rose and golden, a crisp and clear autumn morning. A knock roused Talon from his dark introspection and he opened the door.

Caleb stood there before him. 'Let's go hunting,' he said.

Talon nodded, not even wondering how Caleb had so suddenly appeared on the island. Magic was a foregone conclusion on Sorcerer's Isle.

Talon fetched his bow from inside the wardrobe, where he had lodged it in the corner and forgotten it. He had spent hours dressing and undressing in the fine robes there when he and Alysandra had spent the summer contriving games. He had thought them games of love, but now he thought of them as exercises in lust.

He held the bow, and it was solid and real in his grip and he knew that he had lost something in his days with the girl. He pulled out a quiver of arrows then turned to the older man. 'Let's go,' he said.

Caleb set a punishing pace, leading and not looking back, expecting Talon at all times to be a step behind him or at his side.

They ranged north, far away from the estate. Half the time they ran. At noon, Caleb stopped and pointed. They were standing on top of a ridge which offered a clear view of most of the island to the north. In the distance Talon could see the small hut where he had lived with Magnus when he had first come to the island. He said nothing.

Eventually Caleb said, 'I thought myself in love once.'

'Does everyone know about it?'

'Only those who need to know. It was a lesson.'

'So everyone keeps saying. I can't help but feel it was a cruel jest.'

'Cruel, no doubt. Jest, no. I doubt anyone has told you yet what is in store for you, and I do not know, though I have some sense of it. You are going to be sent places and see things no boy of the Orosini could ever have dreamed of, Talon. And in those places the wiles of a pretty woman may be as deadly as a poisoned blade.' He leaned on his bow. 'Alysandra is not the only girl with a deadly side to her. Our enemies have many such women in their ranks. Just as they will have agents like you.'

'Agents?'

'You are working on behalf of the Conclave; this you know.' He glanced over at the boy and Talon nodded. 'Nakor and my father will some day tell you more, but I can tell you this much, even if they don't think you're ready to know: we are agents of good. It is ironic that sometimes we must do things that appear evil so that eventually good can triumph.'

Talon said, 'I am not a learned man. I have read a certain amount, enough to know I know very little. But I have read enough to have some sense that all men think of themselves as heroes, at least heroes of their own lives, and that no man who did evil thought he was doing such.'

'In one sense, you are right.' Caleb stopped for a moment, as if to savour the brisk autumnal breeze. 'In another sense you must know you are wrong. There are men who knowingly serve evil, who embrace it and who seek to gain by its triumph. Some seek power. Others seek riches. Others still seek darker ends. But it's all the same. They bring suffering and agony to innocents.'

'What are you trying to tell me?'

'Only that you are about to begin the next phase of your education and you must be ready to accept many things that seem terrible and unwelcome. It is necessary.'

Talon nodded. 'When does this next phase begin?'

'Tomorrow, for we leave for Krondor. But for now, let's hunt.' Caleb picked up his bow and ran down a game trail, not looking back to see if the boy was following.

Talon paused and then started after Caleb, knowing that like all wounds the one he felt deep inside would heal. But he also suspected that like some wounds, this one would leave a scar that would last throughout his lifetime.

The ship raced westward, driven by a near gale-force wind, slamming through the waves like a living creature. Talon stood as far forward as he could, behind the bowsprit, still amazed and exhilarated by the voyage even after a week at sea. Sometime this afternoon or during the night they should be reaching their destination, Krondor, capital city of the Western Realm of the Kingdom of the Isles.

For reasons not clear to him, his masters had decided he would take ship to Krondor, and caravan to Salador, and from there to wherever else they wished him to go. He had expected Magnus to use his magic to take him to his next destination, but instead he was travelling by conventional means with Caleb.

Caleb was a calming presence and Talon was thankful for the choice. He could talk when Talon wished to discuss something, yet he was not bothered by silence. They shared a hunter's sense of things, and of all those he had met since the destruction of his village, Talon felt more kinship with Caleb than anyone else.

The sea was as alien to Talon as the coastline had been, yet he was drawn to it as he was to the mountains of his homeland. It was unending, ever changing, enduring, and mysterious. The air was as fresh, though of a different character, and even in the constant foul weather, somehow glorious to him.

The ship was named *Western Lady* and flew the banner of the Empire of Great Kesh. He had heard enough chatter among the crew to know it was a convenient registry, for the ship belonged to Pug. More than once Talon had wondered about Pug. He seemed to be a young man, or rather a man of early middle years, but he was still vigorous and in his prime. Miranda appeared to be roughly the same age, yet they were Magnus's parents, and Magnus looked to be around the same age as his parents.

Pug was a quiet man who spoke to the students on rare occasions, but when he did so he was affable and forthcoming. Yet there was something about him which made Talon uneasy. He had a power within him, that much was apparent even to a mountain boy from the east. Robert, Nakor, Magnus and Miranda all had magical abilities, Talon knew; but in Pug he sensed something greater. It was something his grandfather would have called being 'touched by the gods'.

Talon mused about what sort of childhood a man like Pug might have had. Who were his parents and what sort of education did a magician of great power undertake? Perhaps one day Talon might ask, but for the time being he was content to enjoy the voyage and let the questions lay waiting.

His bout of heartsickness had passed, and now he could look back on his days with Alysandra and feel only a bittersweet irony. On that last day he was thinking of marriage, or spending his life with her, and now he felt she was nothing more than an object of pity or contempt. Or both. A thing without a heart; but despite this, Talon knew that in some sense he must learn to be like her, for everything he had been told since that day led him to believe she was far more dangerous than he could yet imagine.

Caleb came up on deck, wearing an oil-soaked canvas cloak similar to the one Talon had on. Chilled sea spray washed over the bow, but Caleb paid it no attention. He came to stand beside Talon and said nothing, content to take in the view.

Roiling swells and spindrift vanished into the fading light of day, as dark grey clouds edged in black raced by above. In the distance they could see flashes of lightning. At last Caleb said, 'We should reach Krondor ahead of the storm, but only just.'

Talon nodded. 'I think I could be a sailor,' he said after a while.

'The sea calls many men,' Caleb observed.

They remained silent for the rest of the afternoon, until half an hour before darkness, when the lookout above called, 'Land ho!'

The captain of the ship came forward to greet them. 'Gentlemen, we shall reach Krondor after dark. We'll heave to in the lees of the breakwater and shelter against the storm, then at first light, I'll signal the harbourmaster and we'll enter the sound. It should be a noisy, but safe night.'

Talon nodded. He felt a strange anticipation at seeing this city. He had read about it in the history of Rupert Avery, and in other books.

Caleb put his hand on Talon's shoulder, and signalled that they should go below. Talon turned and led the way.

Reaching their cabin – which was barely big enough for the two bunks, one above the other – they doffed their wet cloaks and sat down, Talon on the upper bunk, Caleb on the lower.

'We have some time before supper,' said Caleb. 'I know you have rehearsed your story.'

'Yes.' Talon replied. He was to tell anyone who asked that he was a hunter from the woodlands near Crydee, which might explain his slight accent. As there was limited travel between Krondor and the Far Coast city, it was unlikely they'd encounter anyone who was familiar with that distant town. And if they did, Caleb would take the lead, since he knew that area.

'Caleb?'

'Yes, Talon?'

'Why are we travelling this way?' He had wanted to ask since they had left the island.

'To broaden your knowledge,' said Caleb. 'It is much like any other thing, travelling; being told this or that about a place is one thing, but doing it is another. You will see a thousand sights and many will be different to what I see.'

'Where are we going?'

'From Krondor we find a caravan and travel to Malac's Cross, the border between the Western and Eastern Realms of this Kingdom. From there we shall secure horses and travel to Salador. Both cities will offer you many opportunities for learning.'

'Fair enough, but what are we to do when we reach Salador?'

'Study,' said Caleb, lying down upon his bunk. 'Now, be still so I can take a nap until they call for supper.'

'Study,' Talon muttered. 'It seems to be my life.'

'And as such, it's a fair one. Now be quiet.'

The boat nestled alongside the quay as a dockhand fended it off the stonework then tied off the bowlines. Talon stepped ashore, followed by Caleb. A man wearing an armband bearing a crest depicting an eagle flying over a mountain peak approached, looked them up and down, and spoke in a bored manner. 'Where are you from?'

'Crydee,' said Caleb.

'You arrived on a Keshian ship.'

'It was the first one leaving the Far Coast when we decided to come this way,' Caleb replied in an affable manner.

'Well, if you're Kingdom citizens, that's fair enough.' The man walked on, leaving Caleb and Talon alone.

'That's it?' said Talon.

'It's an era of peace, so they say.' Caleb motioned for Talon to follow him. 'At least here in the west. King Ryan has pledged his daughter in marriage to the nephew of the Empress of Great Kesh, and the Emperor of Queg has a cousin who is wed to King Ryan's younger son. Trading with the Free Cities is brisk, and the Governor of Durbin is keeping his "privateers" on a short leash. Hasn't been a major conflict in seven years.'

As they climbed the stone steps from the quayside to the road above, Caleb added, 'It's in the east where things are balanced on a razor's edge, and that's where you'll find yourself subject to far more intense scrutiny than here.'

They walked down a street towards the centre of the city. When Talon craned his neck, he could see a castle to the south of the harbour. 'That's where the Prince lives?'

'Prince Matthew, son of King Ryan. King Patrick's been dead for less than two years and Matthew is still a youngster, less than fourteen years of age.' Caleb said, 'But he's not the power in the city, anyway.'

'Who is?'

'Two brothers, the Jamisons. James is Duke of Krondor, as his grandfather was before him, and they say he's nearly as wily as his legendary grandpa. His younger brother Dashel is a rich businessman. It's said whatever James doesn't control, Dashel does. They're dangerous men, by any measure.'

'I'll remember that,' said Talon.

'Well, it's unlikely that you'll ever make either man's acquaintance, but stranger things have been known to happen. Here we are.'

Talon looked up and saw that they were standing before an inn, a sign above it bearing the faded image of a grinning face, a man with a dark beard wearing a plumed hat. Below it was written, 'Admiral Trask'.

Caleb pushed open the door and they stepped into a smoky room, the air thick with the smell of roasting meat, tobacco smoke, spilled ale and wine. Talon's eyes began to water.

Caleb pushed his way past several dock men, sailors and travellers, until he reached the counter. The innkeeper looked up and grinned. 'Caleb! It's been too long, old friend!'

'Randolph,' answered Caleb, taking his hand. 'This is Talon. Do you have a room?'

'Yes,' said the innkeeper. 'You can have your pick. The one in the back?'

'Yes,' said Caleb, understanding the question.

'Are you hungry?'

Caleb smiled. 'Always.'

'Then sit down and I'll have the girl fetch you your supper. Any baggage?'

'You know I travel light.' Talon and Caleb both carried all their gear in light packs which they wore across their shoulders.

The innkeeper tossed a heavy iron key to Caleb, who caught it neatly. 'Sit,' he said, 'and then retire when you're of a mind to.'

They took their seats and in a moment a girl appeared from the kitchen, carrying a tray on which rested an abundant heap of steaming food: hot chicken, roasted duck, a slab of lamb, and steamed vegetables.

When she placed the tray on the table, Talon glanced up and his mouth fell open. He started to rise, but a firm hand from Caleb pushed him back into his chair. Lela looked down at him with a friendly smile, but there was no hint of recognition in her eyes. 'Can I bring you drinks, fellows?'

'Ale,' Caleb said, and she hurried off.

'What—?'

Caleb spoke in a low voice, 'She's not who you think she is.'

In less than a minute, the girl returned with two large pewter jacks filled with foaming ale. 'What's your name, girl?' asked Caleb.

'Roxanne,' she replied, 'sir. Is there anything else?'

'No,' said Caleb, and the girl left them.

Softly, Talon said, 'That was Lela.'

'No,' said Caleb. 'You're mistaken.'

Talon looked at his friend and then nodded curtly. 'Yes, I must be mistaken.'

They ate in silence.

They spent three days in Krondor, making arrangements to travel with a caravan. Caleb and Talon would serve as guards, in exchange for transportation and food. The caravan master was pleased not to have to pay the mercenary bonus, and counted himself fortunate.

The mystery of why Lela was working at the inn under the name of Roxanne was not discussed, and Talon assumed it was yet another of those things which might never be explained to him. Yet it was oddly reassuring to discover a familiar face in such strange surroundings, even if under circumstances that could only be called bizarre.

Krondor was a revelation to Talon, for while Latagore had seemed fabulous to his untutored eyes when he had visited it for the first time, it seemed a provincial village compared to the capital of the Western Realm of the Kingdom. The city was teeming with people, from distant lands as far away as the Keshian Confederacy, the captive nations in the Empire's southern reaches. Dialects and languages strange to the ear could be heard in every market and inn.

Caleb took him to see famous sights: the remaining portion of the sea wall, which had been destroyed during the Serpentwar when, according to legend, the armies of the Emerald Queen had invaded from across the sea and the entire city was virtually destroyed. Talon had to pause when Caleb told the story to remind himself that Caleb was speaking of his own grandmother, who had been enslaved by a demon. Talon judged that many of the tales told around the campfire in his boyhood might need to be re-evaluated, rather than merely dismissed as folk tales.

He visited Barrett's Coffee House, where finance, as complex and mysterious as magic, was conducted. He had a vague sense of what the place meant to the economy of the Kingdom from his reading of the life of Rupert Avery, who had been a businessman of some fame at Barrett's. They went to see the palace, though they observed it from a respectful distance, for while Caleb hinted at some past relationship between his family and the crown, there seemed no plausible reason to gain entrance. Nor any motive, for that matter, apart from curiosity. Talon felt a mild interest in these things, as he did with anything that was alien to his experience. Now when he reflected upon his childhood, he realized how little of the world he had known as a boy; but even so he remembered with clarity how much he thought he understood of it. Such had been the heritage of his people, who were content to live out their lives in the mountains as their ancestors had done before them. Generations passed with little change among the Orosini, and it seemed a good life. Talon looked around the city, taking in the crowds clogging the streets and wondered if perhaps that was one thing his people had correctly apprehended – the quality of a good life. Certainly, most of the people he viewed as they passed were evidencing little by way of joy. Most were intent upon the business at hand, or making their way somewhere in a great hurry. A few children played in the streets, but only the very young; the older children seemed to be banded together in groups of ten or more and often could be seen running with a constable of the law in pursuit.

They travelled with the caravan through the Western Realm, through rolling hills and into low mountains not unlike those of his homeland. But where those mountains had been populated by folk living in villages of wooden huts and stockades, these mountains boasted towns and castles. In Ravensburgh they had the finest wine Talon had tasted, and he asked many questions of the innkeeper. He stole an hour to seek out a winemaker and plied him with questions, too.

Demetrius had said at some point that their masters would be teaching Talon about wine, and he now thought this would be a good thing.

The journey continued to the town of Malac's Cross, and there they bade goodbye to the caravan master. After a night spent sleeping in a relatively clean room, Caleb secured two fine horses and they set off to the east.

As they rode towards the rising sun, Talon said, 'Caleb, am I to ever discover what it is we are doing?'

Caleb laughed. 'I suppose it matters little if I tell you now or tell you when we reach Salador.'

'Then tell me now, for I am afire with curiosity.'

Caleb said, 'In Salador we shall finish with your education in manners and breeding. For a year or more you will learn at least two musical instruments – the lute and another, perhaps a horn or pipe. You will learn even more about the culinary arts, though you are well on your way, having tutored under Leo. And you will learn more about manners of the court, costumes appropriate for all occasions, and how to comport yourself with persons of any rank. You will learn to judge wine and you will learn to sing, though I suspect this last matter may be a lost cause.'

Talon laughed. 'I can sing.'

'I've heard you, and I'd hardly call it singing.'

'But to what ends does all this training in the art of being a man gentle born lead?'

Caleb switched from the King's Tongue, which they had been speaking since arriving in Krondor, to Roldemish. 'Because in a year's time, my young friend, you shall journey to the island kingdom of Roldem, and there you shall enroll in the Masters'

Court. And if the fates are kind, we shall establish you there as a minor noble, a distant cousin of a noteworthy family, rich in heritage but poor in resources, and as such employable.'

'The Masters' Court? Kendrick told me a little about it. He said the finest swordsmen in the world trained there.'

'And that, my friend, is your task. For when you leave Roldem, you must be counted as the best of them all. You must be counted as the greatest swordsman in the world.'

Talon stared at his friend in stunned silence and rode on.

PART TWO

Mercenary

'Revenge is sweet but not nourishing'
Mason Cooley

• CHAPTER FOURTEEN •

Masters' Court

*T*AL BLINKED.

The blade that hovered for the briefest instant in front of his face flicked to the right, and he hesitated, then moved in the same direction. As he had anticipated, his opponent was feigning to the right and went left. He slipped past his guard so fast that the other swordsman couldn't react in time and Tal's blade struck home.

'Touch!' cried the Master of the Court.

Tal retreated a step, then came to attention and saluted his opponent, a young noble from the coastal city of Shalan. Duzan or Dusan, Tal couldn't quite recall his name. The spectators applauded politely as if the match had run to form, which it had.

The Master of the Court stepped forward and declared, 'Point and match to M'lord Hawkins.'

Talwin Hawkins, a minor noble from Ylith, distant cousin to Lord Seljan Hawkins, Baron of the Prince's Court in Krondor, bowed first to the Master of the Court, then to his opponent. The two men removed the protective mesh masks they wore, and crossed to shake hands. The young Roldemish nobleman smiled and said, 'Someday you're going to guess wrong, Tal, and then I'll have you.'

Tal smiled in return. 'You're probably right. But as my man, Pasko, says, "I'd rather be lucky than good." Right, Pasko?'

The burly servant, who had appeared at his elbow and was now taking his master's sword and mask, smiled and said, 'As my master says, given the choice, I'll take luck any time.'

The two combatants exchanged bows and retired to opposite corners of the huge duelling hall that was the heart of the Masters' Court in Roldem City. Large carved wooden columns surrounded a massive wooden floor which had been polished to a gleam like brushed copper. Intricate patterns had been laid into the floor and, once he had been introduced to the instructors, Tal had quickly seen they served a function beyond the aesthetic aspect. Each pattern defined a duelling area, from the very confined, long and narrow duelling path for rapier fencing, to a larger octagon for longer blades.

For blades were the reason for the existence of the Masters' Court. Over two hundred years ago the King of Roldem had commanded a tourney to name the greatest swordsman in the world. Nobles, commoners, soldiers and mercenaries had travelled from as far away as beyond the Girdle of Kesh – the mountains that separate the northern and southern halves of the Empire, the Far Coast of the Kingdom, and all points in between. The prize had been fabled: a broadsword fashioned from gold and studded with gems – an artefact worth a kingdom's taxes for years and years.

For two weeks the contest had continued until a local noble, a Count Versi Dango, had prevailed. To the King's astonished delight, he announced he would reject the prize, so that the King might make use of the value of the sword to pay for the construction of an academy dedicated to the blade, and there hold the contest on a regular basis: and thus the Masters' Court was born.

The King ordered the construction of the school which covered an entire city block in the heart of the island kingdom's capital, and over the years it had been rebuilt and refined, until now it resembled a palace as much as a school. Upon its completion, another tourney had been organized, and Count Dango had prevailed in defence of his rank as premier swordsman in the world.

Every fifth year the contest was held, until on his fourth defence, Count Dango was wounded in his match by the eventual winner and was forced to retire from the contest.

Since then thirty-one different men had won the championship. Talon of the Silver Hawk, now known as Tal Hawkins, planned to be the thirty-second such champion.

The duelling master approached and Tal bowed. 'Master Dubkov,' he said with respect.

'That was a fine display, but you took your opponent for granted. If you did that with a more experienced swordsman, you might have found yourself taken, my young friend.'

Tal inclined his head in acknowledgement of the duelling master's correct appraisal. Then he grinned and said, 'If I never offer the less skilled a slight chance to win, what motive do they have to spar with me?'

Master Dubkov laughed. 'And those with more experience – say, those anticipating a place in the tourney – will not spar with you lest they reveal too much and disadvantage themselves to you during the contest, eh?'

'Exactly,' said Tal.

'Well,' said the duelling master, lowering his voice, 'I don't know how much good you think you're doing yourself by these exercises, but the crowds enjoy them – especially the young ladies.' He inclined his head towards an area of the gallery where a dozen of Roldem's noble daughters sat observing the bouts.

Several smiled and nodded in Tal's direction. He smiled back and returned the nod in their general direction without making eye contact with any specific girl. Master Dubkov raised an eyebrow at this. Then he said, 'Well, I must be about my duties. Good day to you, young Talwin.'

'Good day to you, master.' Tal bowed like a lifetime courtier.

He removed the padded jacket with Pasko's assistance, and Pasko handed him a towel. Tal dried his neck and his damp hair, which was clinging to his head. Then he donned a fine brocade jacket, suitable for afternoon wear, and stood patiently while Pasko fastened the frogs and loops. 'Dinner invitations?' he asked.

'Four, m'lord. The Lady Sabrina wishes you to dine with her and her father. The Ladies Jessica and Mathilda each wish for you to dine with their entire families, and the Lady Melinda wishes for you to dine with her, and mentioned that her father is away on business.'

'Melinda it is, then,' said Tal with a grin.

'You seem unusually happy today,' Pasko observed. Robert's former servant had appeared during the first month Tal and

Caleb had taken up residence in Salador. He played the part of manservant with such conviction and ease that Tal could easily believe he had held such a post for a nobleman at some point in his obscure past. He had certainly inculcated Talon of the Silver Hawk with all the necessary nuances of noble manner and bearing to become Talwin Hawkins.

Tal nodded and smiled. 'Rumours, idle gossip and sources of impeccable unreliability lead me to believe that before the contest I shall be invited to the palace for an audience with the King, or at the very least, be listed as a guest for the next gala.'

'That's unsurprising, Master,' said Pasko. Dropping his voice so that he could be heard only by Tal as he put a cape around the young man's shoulders, he said, 'What's surprising is that it's taken so long.'

Tal smiled. 'Indeed.'

They departed from the practice hall, past the gallery, and as they entered the grand hall that led to the outer courtyard, more than one servant pressed a note into Pasko's hand. Portraits of past champions lined the walls of the grand hall and in the centre of the entrance, a heroically large bronze statue of Versi Dango welcomed visitors and students to the Masters' Court. They hurried down the steps to a waiting carriage, and the driver held the door open for them.

Once inside, Tal said, 'I am only the second swordsman in the history of the Masters' Court never to have lost a bout.'

'Hmmm,' said Pasko. 'I seem to remember you taking a drubbing from Master Dubkov one afternoon, m'lord.'

'That wasn't a bout,' said Tal. 'And it was instructional. And, mainly, it was because I let him.'

'You let him?'

'Yes, for two reasons,' said Tal as the carriage pulled out of the courtyard and entered the streets of Roldem. 'First, he is a Master of the Court and I need friends there, and second, I learned more in losing that match than I would have if I had pressed and won.'

'So that's why you've settled for draws in some bouts?'

'Yes,' said Tal. 'But only in practice, you'll note. I've never lost in competition and I don't intend to start doing so any time soon.'

'Swordsmen from all over the world are coming for this competition, I'd remind you, m'lord.'

'Yes, and I may lose, but that is not my intent.'

'Good,' said Pasko.

The carriage wended its way along the cobbles, and Tal sat back and enjoyed the passing view while Pasko quickly read and discarded the notes pressed into his hand. They were all the same, young women asking Tal why he had not called upon them recently.

Tal sat back and let the fresh ocean air that blew constantly from the west refresh him, while he drank in the sights. He had seen three great cities, Krondor, Salador and now Roldem, and by far he preferred his present location. Krondor seemed rough-hewn and almost primitive compared to the other two, perhaps as a result of having been largely rebuilt from rubble over the last thirty years. Caleb had told him the story of the Emerald Queen and the destruction of the city by her forces, and about the gallant stand by the Kingdom Army at Nightmare Ridge.

Salador, by contrast, was an ancient city, sprawling and metropolitan. The outer districts were dominated by small local markets and streets of businesses, and the inner city bore little resemblance to the ancient walled fortress it must once have been in the dim past. Tal remembered passing through an open gate from one precinct of the city to another, but otherwise there was little to indicate the great wall which must once have been the city's main defence.

Salador possessed some charms, and the two years Talon of the Silver Hawk had spent there becoming Talwin Hawkins had been two of the best years of his life until he had come to Roldem. He had learned to play the lute, the brass horn and a variety of percussion instruments. He had lost all accent when speaking the King's Tongue or Roldemish, and could pass as a gentleman from either nation. He had refined his painting, learned to tell a good wine from a poor one – discovering a passion for the former – and mastered the intricacies of court dances.

He had read books and scrolls and studied everything he could about the history of the nations of this continent of Triagia. He learned of the other nations he had not visited, and became an avid student of history.

He had met and known women. At first he had nursed his injury at Alysandra's hands, but Caleb had forced him one night to accompany him through the city, drinking at inn after inn until at last they had arrived at a particularly well-regarded brothel. There Caleb had entrusted Tal's care to a cadre of skilled and enthusiastic young courtesans who had found ways to revive his interest in women. After that, there had followed liaisons with serving girls, merchants' daughters, and the occasional daughter of the minor nobility.

By the time his twentieth birthday arrived – he had adopted the Kingdom custom of using Midsummer's Day to mark his birth – he was ready to make his entrance at the Masters' Court.

Robert had appeared one night with forged documents, naming him Talwin Hawkins, a distant cousin to a minor noble in Yabon Province in the Western Realm of the Kingdom of the Isles. So Talon of the Silver Hawk had become Talwin Hawkins, Squire of Morgan River and Bellcastle, Baronet of Silverlake, vassal to the Baron of Ylith, who had left his father's home to serve with the northern garrison for a while as a Bannerette Knight Lieutenant under the command of the Duke of Yabon, and had honourably left that service to seek his fortune: a young man of rank but no wealth.

Along the way, somehow, he had amassed enough resources to purchase a modest, but tasteful, apartment in the better quarter of the city, where he entertained small groups of young nobles; and had distinguished himself as the finest swordsman and the most eligible foreign bachelor to have arrived in the city in years.

Tal had been impressed with the amount of work that had gone into preparing his way into Roldem society. Letters of credit, introductions, and references had all been prepared in advance. Several locals presented themselves as old acquaintances, even going so far as to remind Tal of details of their past encounters.

To Pasko and Robert's delight, Tal turned out to be a skilled gambler, the result of the logic games forced upon him while he studied with Robert and Magnus. He resisted the temptation to win large stakes, preferring to consistently win small amounts. To ensure that he was invited back to games of cards and dice, he conspired to lose upon occasion, with grace and good humour.

He was judged by everyone who knew him an upstanding

young man. Direct, polite, and amusing, he was counted as a prize dinner guest, and rarely did he eat alone at home. His fluency in many languages, his grace as a dancer, his ability to sing and play many instruments, all made him one of the most popular young men around town. Only an invitation to one of the King's galas was lacking; and now rumour provided hope that might be imminent.

The only criticism levelled at Tal Hawkins was from the young ladies of Roldem. He was charming, handsome, witty and, at the right time, ardent. But more than one young woman had accused him of having no heart, for he would never speak to them of love. Desire and the pleasures of the body, yes, and his directness and bold approach had won more than one young flower of Roldem who had been determined to resist the noto-rious young man from the west. His bed was empty only when he wanted it to be, but often he found little joy in those who shared it with him. Release, pleasure, and amusement; but never joy. His mind turned to Alysandra from time to time, and he wondered if he was becoming like her, and then decided he was not for he still felt affection for his mentors and remembered the love he held in his heart for his family and those of his village; but when it came to young women, he found them a means to an end, either to satisfy his lust, to gain him social access, or merely providing diversion.

The carriage stopped in front of his apartment, a three-room, first-floor flat. The ground floor home was occupied by a moneylender and his family. The family had a daughter who was far from unattractive, but Pasko had commented and Tal had agreed to leave that one young lady alone; having an angry father with money as a neighbour could prove to be difficult.

For although the father might not be any threat with a blade, money could buy many blades. So Tal was polite to the father and mother, brotherly to the young son, and slightly flirtatious, but always mannerly, with the girl.

The driver opened the door and Tal and Pasko got out and Pasko went ahead to the door to the stairs leading to the apartment while the carriage rolled off to a public stable a street away where the driver lived in quarters and was available to Tal whenever he was needed.

Tal made his way upstairs and entered the apartment. Pasko said, 'Shall I draw a bath?'

'No,' said Tal. 'A cold wash doesn't appeal to me right now. I think I'll take a nap and in an hour go to Remarga's Bath House and dress there for supper with Melinda. While I sleep, please send a note to her that I will be more than pleased to dine with her this night, and send my regrets to the other ladies who invited me.'

'Yes, m'lord,' replied Pasko. Initially, to Tal's initial surprise, Pasko had treated him as if he had been born to the nobility, and never once referred to Talon's past history or forgot his place, even when they were alone. And in the entire time since they had arrived in Roldem, Talwin Hawkins had come to live the role of an adventuring nobleman of the Kingdom of the Isles so deeply and so well that his past before arriving in Salador was even starting to become to him a dim memory, as if it belonged to someone else.

When Pasko set off with the messages, Tal undressed himself. He removed his cloak, jacket, and tunic and boots, then threw himself across his bed wearing only his trousers. He was tired from the practice, yet sleep was elusive, for he was restless, tensed up in anticipation of news of an invitation to the palace. And, in addition to that, the tournament began in less than a month's time. He was beginning to feel the edge build. He must be careful; too much of an edge could make him overly anxious, make it difficult for him to keep his focus on the task at hand.

And he also knew that once the tournament was over, something else lay ahead for him, and he didn't know what. Adopting the role of a Kingdom gentleman appeared to be as Rondar had predicted, the ostensible reasons for his years of training, but as yet no one had explained to him why.

His personal agenda had not changed. Eventually he would hunt down and destroy those who had murdered his family and friends, but until this current role was completed, until such time as Master Pug and his companions decided that his duty to the Conclave was discharged, then he must wait.

Even so, over the last few months a growing concern had been gnawing at him; what if he was *never* considered discharged of his duty to the Conclave; what if he were to die before he could avenge his people? The second alternative could not be considered, for if fate decreed that the last of the Orosini died before vengeance was visited upon the guilty, then so be it. But the first possibility worried him, for which duty was paramount? A life-debt was not something that any Orosini would lightly discard, for to do so would not only shame the man, but also his family and his ancestors. But the blood-vengeance demanded by his culture was equally important. Perhaps the gods would turn a kind eye and show him a way to serve both debts honourably?

He rolled over onto his stomach, and then thought maybe they would not. Such things were out of his hands, so it was best not to worry.

He lay quietly for almost half an hour, but still sleep wouldn't come. At last he decided that his mood would be better served by a longer bath than he had anticipated. He stood and called out for Pasko, whom he had heard returning from his errands.

The servant appeared and Tal said, 'Bring clothes. I'm for Remarga's. Follow as soon as you have selected suitable attire for tonight's supper. Have the carriage pick us up at Remarga's an hour after sundown.'

'Yes, m'lord,' said Pasko.

Tal dressed and left his apartment, walking briskly down the streets of Roldem. He never tired of the experience of travelling by foot through the city. The hive of shops clustered along each street, the press of people of all stripes – young, old, men and women, merchants, sailors, nobles and commoners. The scent of the sea was everywhere, and that combined with the noise and confusion was intoxicating to a boy who had been raised in the isolation of the mountains.

Tal wondered if fate would provide him with an opportunity to return to his boyhood, and whether he would take that opportunity if it were offered. After barely a moment's reflection, he knew he would. For no matter how wondrous the things he had gained, the knowledge, experience and material wealth, they paled in comparison to what he had lost: home, family and an authentic way of life.

Had he a wish, he'd trade everything to have his mother, father, sister and the rest of his clan healthy and happy at home. It was a bitter thought that even the mightiest magician, or every one of them put together could never bring that wish into being.

He reached an intersection, turned right and wended his way through the late afternoon crowd. After just a few seconds he *knew* he was being followed. His hunter's instinct or his 'bump of trouble' as Nakor had called it, a casual glance to the rear, a reflection in the window of a shop, *something* had alerted him: somehow he knew there was a man about thirty feet behind him who had been tailing him since he had left his apartment.

Talon paused to look into a shop-window as if inspecting some item on display. The figure he saw out of the corner of his eye resolved itself as the man halted and appeared to be searching for something he had forgotten. With a feigned look of disgust, the man quickly turned and walked away, but not before Tal had marked him. He was a short, wiry man, but he walked quickly and with an economy of movement that alerted Tal: this man was dangerous.

Tal knew he would vanish into the crowd, so he did not pursue him. It would prove to be pointless and would also reveal to the man that Tal had discovered him. That man, or another, would soon be back. Someone was stalking Tal and he needed to find out who and why.

If it were an assassin employed by some angry young woman or her father, that was one thing, but if this had anything to do with the Conclave of Shadows, that was another. He might have to send Pasko to alert Robert and the others.

Talon took a leisurely stroll to the bathhouse, avoiding his usual route, and stopped several times to ensure he was no longer being followed.

At Remarga's he was greeted by one of the many attendants, this one well known to him. 'Good afternoon, m'lord,' the man said.

'Good afternoon, Sven,' Tal replied. 'Is Salmina free?'

'I shall see, sir. You wish to have her services?'

'Yes,' said Tal, and he went into the changing room.

Sven stood by to care for Tal's clothing and provide him with whatever he needed. To begin with, Tal was given a large cotton towel, in which he wrapped himself. As he left the changing room, Sven put his clothing and sword away. Tal found himself a small wooden stool next to a large bucket of warm water. Beside the bucket was a bar of scented soap and a brush. Placed next to the stool was a tray containing small, delicate, earthenware jars adorned with floral designs. Tal picked up the bucket and poured the contents over his head, and as soon as he set it down, a young boy appeared with a fresh bucket of warm water and took the empty one away.

First of all Tal treated his hair with a scented oil, and wondered not for the first time what his grandfather would have thought of all this. The old man's way of taking a bath had been plunging into the iciest streams and lakes and revelling in it. But given his grandfather's appreciation of comfort, Tal decided that the old man would have approved of the entire process. Just then a young woman appeared, wearing a brief robe of white linen, which clung to her in the damp heat of the bathhouse. Tal knew his grandfather would very much have approved of *this*, for the old man had never lost his eye for women, a fact he regularly commented on, to the ire of Tal's grandmother.

Feeling a moment of nostalgia, he said nothing but allowed her to begin soaping his back. Remarga trained his staff well: she would not speak unless spoken to first. Some customers wanted banter and flirtation, and a few desired more personal services, which could be arranged for a price which included a small private suite at the back of the building. Others preferred calm and quiet and wanted nothing more than to keep their thoughts to themselves while they bathed.

Tal stood up and the girl finished washing his back and shoulders, then started on his chest. Tal gently removed the bar of soap from her hand and dismissed her as he finished the task himself. He knew that had he remained motionless, she would have washed every inch of his body, but his mind was on other things besides playing with a bath-girl, and he ought to keep his mind focused on Melinda, who would be more than eager to meet his need for passion after supper.

Tal picked up another bucket and rinsed off the soap, and then moved to the next room, which was clouded with steam. The bath was very hot and Tal entered slowly, feeling the hair on his neck and arms rise as he forced himself into the deeper end of the pool, where he could sit on a underwater bench, lying back with his shoulders against the coping that ran around the edge of the pool.

A plump matron entered, handing her towel to the attendant and got into the water. Tal had travelled enough since being saved by Robert to have some sense of the various ways different between people regarded the showing of parts of the body and other personal practices, but Roldem seemed among the oddest. Female fashions tended to the conservative, except for grand occasions, at which time women wore clothing that was revealing to the point of being entirely scandalous. The Countess Amandi had arrived at Baron Gruder's gala the previous week in an ornate Keshian gown which left both breasts uncovered, which she had compensated for by wearing a complex choker of pearls which draped down her chest. The constantly-moving pearls had provided a provocative attraction, to say the least. Plunging backs, and deep décolletage at such events were common for women who during the day went about the city covered from neck to ankle. Even more strange, to Tal, was the way in which women and men changed in separate rooms, yet bathed together publicly. Talon assumed that at some time in Roldem's history someone in authority had decided that nudity was fine, but dressing and undressing in front of members of the other gender was a bad thing.

Talon found himself chuckling over that, which gained him a raised eyebrow from the matron. He smiled at her, and said, 'Remembering a jest, m'lady.'

She nodded, not quite convinced.

Talon felt himself relaxing and his thoughts began to drift. If he fell into a doze, the attendants would keep an eye on his property and, given the number of seriously intoxicated customers over the years, he knew they would also prevent him from falling face-first in the water and drowning himself.

Pasko would prevent him from staying overly long, and he would soon be here with the clothes he had selected for this evening. So Tal dozed in a warm haze of well-being, his momentary sadness passing quickly.

Sven appeared some time later and said, 'Salmina can take you now, m'lord.'

Tal rose and accepted the large towel provided for him by one of the boys in attendance. He followed Sven to a small room curtained off from the changing area. Salmina was a Rodezian woman who stood nearly as tall as Tal's six feet and an inch. She was strong, with powerful hands, but nature had conspired to keep her slender. Tal knew from personal exploration that she had a well muscled and supple body under the short tunic she wore.

As soon as Sven departed, pulling the curtain closed, she slipped out of the robe and started pouring scented oil upon her hands. 'The complete massage, today, m'lord?' she asked playfully.

Tal lay with his chin on his arms, and said, 'Not today, my dear. I must save my energy for another, tonight.'

She applied oil to his naked buttocks with a playful slap, just hard enough to let him know that she was slightly disappointed at his answer. Despite being past forty years of age, she was a striking woman and years of experience made her a prodigious lover. Tal had left with wobbly legs the first time he had consented to the 'complete' massage.

'A lion like you? You should be able to make me smile and be ready for half a dozen others in less than an hour.'

Talon had to laugh. 'I can barely remember my name or the way home when you've finished with me, Salmina.'

'I take pride in my work.'

'As well you should,' he said with genuine affection.

'Who's the lucky girl?' she asked as she set to, kneading his shoulders.

'Could I call myself a gentleman if I named the lady?'

'Many do, but I suspect you're a bit more discreet than most.'

'Thank you.'

As she always did, she clucked her tongue as she ran her fingers along the many scars on Tal's body. 'So young to have suffered so many wounds,' she observed, not for the first time. 'Do you think you're ready for the contest?'

He sighed as she started working at his neck. 'If I'm not, I'll find out as soon as it begins, won't I?'

'There is that,' she said with a chuckle.

They exchanged banter and then Salmina turned away to get another vial of oil from a table next to the wall.

Suddenly, a sense of danger shot through Talon and he lunged to his right.

Pain exploded in his left arm as a blade sliced through the skin from his shoulder to a point half-way to his elbow. He rolled off the table, and hit the floor in a crouch, ignoring the burning pain.

Salmina stood up, one hand pressed hard against the wall. There was confusion in her eyes as she reached up with her right hand, trying to somehow staunch the blood flowing from the side of her neck. For a grotesque moment she seemed concerned about the river of crimson that ran down between her breasts and onto her stomach, as if it was too unseemly for a woman of her beauty. Then her eyes rolled up in her head and she collapsed.

The man was the same one who had followed him and he held a lethal blade, slender and sharp as a razor. From his movements and his quick reaction to Tal's move, he was an expert in its use. In addition, he had not tried to follow Tal as he rolled, but had moved in the opposite direction, placing himself between his victim and the curtain.

Tal knew that the man had less than a minute in which to kill him, for he must expect Tal to cry out and someone to come quickly to investigate. This was already a botched assassination attempt. In just an instant, the man would have to make his move.

Tal moved first. The assassin might have expected him to retreat, perhaps gaining a bit of room to make a dash for the curtain, but instead Tal reached down with both hands and overturned the table. There was no real threat, but the man stepped back instinctively in order to prevent himself being struck, and that was just as Tal had planned.

Tal leapt over the falling table, ignoring the blade. He was already cut, and had many previous wounds so another wouldn't matter, but he wouldn't let this man kill him.

The assassin aimed a slicing blow for Tal's throat, and Tal ducked underneath the blade and drove his shoulder into the man's stomach. As he had known he would, Tal received a searing slice across his back, but not at the base of the neck which was where he was now most vulnerable.

He shoved hard and rolled, splattering his blood all over the floor. Customers entering the changing area started to shout and scream at the sight of all the blood and two men struggling on the tile floor.

Tal came up on his feet, naked and weaponless, in a crouch and bleeding from two serious wounds, but ready to defend himself as best he could. The assassin hesitated, unsure as to whether to attack one more time, or make a bid for escape.

The hesitation cost him his life. Suddenly his eyes widened, and the blade fell from his fingers. Tal saw Pasko stepping up behind the man, yanking hard at the dagger he had just plunged into the assassin's back.

He glanced down to make sure the man was no longer a threat, then quickly crossed to kneel next to Tal who had collapsed to the floor.

'You look a mess, m'lord.'

'No doubt,' Tal said as his head began to swim. 'I think you'd best send regrets to the Lady Melinda,' he added, before his eyes rolled up and he fainted.

CHAPTER FIFTEEN

Mystery

*T*AL AWOKE.

'That's the third time,' Pasko said.

Groaning a little from the pain and the effort of moving his body, Tal managed to asked, 'Third time what?' His eyelashes felt as if they were matted together and his mouth was dry. 'Water, please?'

Pasko helped him to raise his head and placed a cup of water to his lips. Talon sipped as another voice said, 'Third time we've had to struggle to keep you alive, Talon.'

Moving into Tal's line of vision, Robert de Lyis shook his head as he added, 'That's three lifetimes you owe us.'

Tal continued to drink until his throat was wet and he could speak without sounding like a frog. 'I'm sorry to admit, I have but one to give. And please called me "Tal" since my name is now "Talwin".'

'You almost gave your only life yesterday, *Tal*,' said Robert.

Tal glanced at his left arm and his eyes opened wide. His body ached and was stiff, but the wound to his arm was gone, as was the one across his chest. 'What—?'

'Magic,' said Robert.

Pasko said, 'You have a tournament in less than two weeks' time, m'lord, and from the depth of the wounds and the loss of blood, it was clear you would never be fit to compete.'

'One of the possible reasons you were assaulted,' added Robert, 'though I think it unlikely to have been the main one.'

'How . . . ?'

'There are some very gifted healing priests in Roldem,' said Robert. 'A few of them are very co-operative with the Conclave.'

'Is that what brought you here?' asked Tal. He started to move his arms and found that the stiffness was easing.

'I sent for him, m'lord,' said Pasko.

'Pasko noticed something that made it imperative someone from the Conclave with magician skills came at once. He reported that there was no way the assassin could have got inside the room you were being massaged in unless he had used magic.'

Tal thought about this. The table had been large enough for someone to hide under, but he would have been seen by anyone entering. There were no cupboards or other doors. Tal said, 'I should have realized that.'

'You were indisposed,' said Robert. 'Pasko has already reported to the appropriate gossips that most of the blood came from the unfortunate young woman who was killed and that you suffered only bruises and a small wound that will heal quickly. You will be fit for the tournament.'

Tal sat up and found the stiffness almost gone. 'I'm starving,' he announced.

'The result of the healing spell our priest friend used. You are thinner if you bother to note such things. The body needed energy from somewhere to heal the damaged flesh, so it burned off what little fat you possessed, Tal. You look positively gaunt.'

Tal stood up and his head swam. 'And I feel as weak as a day-old kitten.'

Pasko lent him a hand and helped him put on a robe, then escorted him to the table in the main room of the apartment. There was food waiting there and Tal set to eating vigorously. As he ate, his strength began to return.

'You'll need to rest for the rest of the day, Tal,' said Robert, 'but then you need to appear somewhere publicly to dispel any rumours about your injuries.'

'Why?' asked Tal. 'Why the rush?'

'Because people will already be speculating as to why you were attacked and how injured you are,' said Robert. 'The why we shall leave to conjecture, for as I understand it, there are any number of people who would like to see you not enter the tournament or see their daughters.'

Tal nodded without a blush.

'As to the injury, we must make it clear to whoever sent the assassin that they failed. So that they will try again, soon.'

'Ah, so I'm to be bait?'

Robert shrugged. 'Someone is trying to kill you. Liken it to a hunt. If you're being stalked by a predator, what do you do?'

Tal said, 'You don't run. You lay a trap.'

'As we will.'

Tal finished eating and said, 'What time is it?' He glanced out of the window and could tell it was afternoon.

'Two hours past noon,' supplied Pasko.

'Then my best course is to return to the Masters' Court, make some remarks about the poor girl who was murdered –' suddenly he thought of Salmina, and realized that he would never see her again or experience her enthusiastic lovemaking, and for a moment he felt a terrible regret '– and then back to Remarga's for another bath and massage.' He looked at Pasko. 'Any invitations?'

'Three.'

'Decline them all. If I need to be seen publicly, then I shall dine at Dawson's.'

Robert nodded. 'And after that?'

'Gaming at the Wheel of Fate.'

'Good, that will make it clear to all that you are fit.'

Tal stood up and stretched. 'I feel remarkably well for someone who was carved up like a side of venison yesterday.'

Robert's expression was wry. 'That spell didn't come cheaply.'

Tal smiled. 'It's well I've chosen to serve a master with resources.'

Robert's expression turned from wry to clouded. 'Hard-won resources, young Tal. It may appear easy to conjure up wealth if one knows nothing of the magic arts, but you've been around enough of our craft to have some sense of things. You've seen the island, and how many we clothe and feed, and you are just now gaining some sense of how many people we support in other places.' His hand described an arc taking in the apartment, clothing and other items. 'None of this came without expense and none of this was "wished" into existence.'

Tal wasn't sure of the point Robert was trying to make, so he said, 'I'm not unappreciative of what my masters have procured for me. But I am *painfully* aware of who is an assassin's target right now, so I appreciate having some power behind me at the right moments.' His expression turned deadly serious. 'But if you remember, you have yet to give me a hint as to why I've been trained, and exactly what my task is, beyond winning this deuced tournament.'

Robert was silent for a few moments. Then he said, 'True. We haven't told you much, and we shall continue to keep you unawares for as long as it suits our needs. If you were to fall into the wrong hands now . . . there are ways a skilled magician could peel your memories from inside your skull just as you'd core an apple, Tal. Those unconcerned with your well-being could do it in less than a day and leave you drooling outside an inn, and no one would think you other than a drunk with a damaged mind. But before they were done, they'd have extracted every secret from you.'

Pasko nodded. 'Very painful, too, I've been told.'

Robert agreed. 'They'd take him somewhere very remote, so the screaming wouldn't disturb anyone.'

Tal continued to stretch. 'Then I shall count upon my mentors to use their magical arts to keep me safe from such as you describe. But do you know who the assassin was?'

'Pasko was intent on getting you out of the bathhouse—' Robert nodded towards the other man in approval. 'He managed quite a feat, staunching your wounds with towels, and getting you to the carriage before anyone could see how much blood was your own and how much was the girl's.'

Pasko shrugged. 'You're generous in your praise, Robert. Most people were running the other way, or confused by the screams and shouts. The bathhouse is not well lit, and . . . well, I just knew it would not do well to have people see Tal lying like a piece of bloody meat on the floor.'

'You did well.' Robert looked at Tal. 'You will know your mission when it is time, my young friend. Rest assured we are happy with your progress so far, and right now your only concern is to win that tournament.'

'Why?'

'When you win, I will tell you why.'

'And if I don't win?'

'Then you'll never need to know what would come after, will you?'

Tal's expression turned to one of dark amusement. 'I suppose that is true, master.'

'Talon calls me "master" Squire Talwin Hawkins can call me Robert.'

'Yes, Robert,' said Tal. Falling back into his role, he said, 'Pasko, fetch clothing to Remarga's and have the carriage there at the appropriate time.' Turning to the other man, he asked, 'Robert, would you care to join me in the baths? They are quite refreshing.'

Robert inclined his head. 'I think it might be wise if I was with you. The assassin may not have been magically able, but someone got him into that room using a spell, either one of transport or one of invisibility. If something amiss occurs between now and the contest, especially involving the mystic arts, I need to be close at hand.'

Tal said, 'Do you have any idea as to who the assassin was?' Talon asked a second time.

'A man,' said Pasko. 'No one recognized him and the City Watch carried the body off.'

'Do we have anyone at the constabulary we know well enough who might inquire more about this malefactor?' Tal asked.

Pasko said, 'You've played cards with the Day Constable Captain, Drogan, to ask without anyone taking too much notice.'

'Then I will, tomorrow,' said Tal. Turning to Robert, he said, 'Let us take a stroll back to Remarga's and try to put yesterday's unpleasantness out of mind.'

'Let's make it *appear* we've done so,' said Robert, 'but I want you always to remember how close these people came to killing you.'

'Which people?'

Robert smiled slightly. 'We shall find that out soon enough, I think.'

The two men left, and Pasko began to gather up clothing for the evening.

The morning was overcast, which fit Tal's mood, as he made his way down the narrow streets to the Constable's office, which was located near the old market at the centre of the city. The night before had been uneventful, but he had spent the entire time on edge, anticipating another attack, and found he had not much enjoyed the little things which usually pleased him. The dinner at Dawson's, a former inn now exclusively serving meals to the nobility and the wealthy who did not wish to dine at home in upstairs rooms which had been converted into private dining salons, had provided its usual excellence, but while the meat was cooked to perfection – the glazes and sauces were equal to any Tal had ever known – and the sevice was flawless, he and Robert had dined in relative silence. Even the usually fine Kingdom wines imported from Ravensburgh scarcely warranted his comment.

Gambling at the Wheel of Fate club had provided little of note or interest. Tal played indifferently, his mind obviously elsewhere. Even Lady Thornhill remarked to Tal that he appeared distracted. He smiled and reassured her it had nothing to do with the unpleasantness at Remarga's the day before, and no he was not seriously injured, only looking that way because he was covered in the poor girl's blood and had struck his head hard upon the tile floor, and, yes, he was mainly lost in contemplation of the coming contest.

He excused himself from the game early, having suffered modest losses, and he and Robert returned to his apartment, where he went to bed early, while Robert and Pasko spoke quietly in the next room for hours.

Now he was seeking answers, to a number of difficult questions. He reached the office of the Constable, Dennis Drogan, nephew to a minor palace functionary, who had achieved his office through political connection, but who had nevertheless proven to be competent at it.

When he was ushered into Drogan's office, which consisted of little more than a desk and chair in the corner of the muster room with a wooden screen erected to give the Chief of Constables some privacy, he was greeted with a polite, but distant smile. 'Tal, I was going to visit you later today.' Drogan was a heavy-set man of middle years, with as round a head as Tal had ever seen, which was further emphasized by the way he kept his hair cropped close about his skull, and by shaving clean.

He had a blob of a nose which had been broken repeatedly over the years, and half of one ear had been bitten off in a brawl, but his eyes were always focused, never missing much.

'I assume you'd want to talk to me about the murder.'

The Constable's eyebrows lifted. 'Yes. Who'd want to kill you, Tal?'

'Me?' Tal said, feigning surprise. 'I assumed it was a jealous lover or someone who had it in for the girl, Salmina. She was the one he killed. I think he went after me to stop me from identifying him.'

Drogan reflected on this a moment, then said, 'Did you ever see the man before?'

'No. As a matter of fact, I was curious if he was someone known to you.'

'No, none of my lads has ever seen him before. We searched the body before we dumped it in the lime pit and found nothing that might tell us anything about him, save he must have been recently in from the Isles, since he had some Kingdom silver coins on him.'

Tal sat back as if pondering. 'Well, that's a puzzler, then, isn't it? Maybe it's a lover come back from a trip who was unhappy to find Salmina working at the baths?'

'She's been working there more than ten years, my friend. If it's a lover who finds that surprising news, he's a lad who's not been around for a bit.'

'Well, that was the first thought that sprang to my mind,' Tal replied.

'It's an obvious choice, and that usually proves to be the right choice. But I don't think so this time. If someone wanted to kill the girl, why not wait until she's on her way to her crib? No, it's more likely someone wanted to catch the best swordsman in Roldem on his stomach naked, a room away from his sword. That's my guess.'

'But who would want to send an assassin?'

'Who said the lad was an assassin?'

'I've never seen him before, Dennis. There may be one or two men who have a grievance against me, but certainly I'd know them by sight. If someone wants me dead, then it follows this man was hired to kill me. Although I don't think it likely.'

'Why not?' asked the Constable.

'Because there may be a father or two who would rather not have me see a daughter or two, or even a lady who might *wish* me dead, but there's no one I know who would seriously send someone to do the job.'

'You know what's oddest about this?'

'What?'

'No one saw the man enter the bathhouse. To get to where you were attacked, you have to enter past half a dozen attendants and porters. From the moment the baths open in the morning to the minute the doors are locked at night, there's no concealed entrance into that part of the building.'

'Yes, very odd, isn't it?'

'You have any idea how he could have appeared there, as if by magic?'

Tal leaned back, with a rueful smile. 'Magic? That would make things far more . . . odd, wouldn't it?'

'It would mean that if someone wanted you dead, they were willing to pay a great deal to have the deed done. Not only paying someone to wheel the blade, but also paying someone else with the magical ability to get him into the building unseen.'

'An invisibility spell?'

'Something like that. My uncle has a friend who knows a magician. I asked that fellow some questions and he says that's the most likely spell to have been used. To send the man into the room from another place . . . that's very difficult and only a few magicians could manage it.'

Tal thought it best not to mention he knew at least three or four who could achieve that result. Leave it for the Constable to discover such facts for himself.

'So, no one knows anything about this man?'

'No, sorry to say.'

'So, you can't even be certain which of us was the intended victim?'

'No, we can't. I just have a problem with all this bother over a woman who's little more than a common whore.'

Tal stiffened. 'Salmina was never common.'

'So I've heard,' said Dennis.

Tal stood. 'Well, I'll not keep you from your duties. If you find out anything else, please let me know.'

'Rest assured, I will.'

They shook hands and Tal left the office and headed back towards his quarters. He was frustrated that no information about the assassin was forthcoming, even though he had not really expected it to be.

Still, he had to turn his mind away from the imponderables of life, and turn his attention full on the tournament. It was less than two weeks away and if he was to win, he could not be distracted further.

* * *

The contest drew nearer, and Tal found his anxiety increasing. No matter how much he employed the mind-calming exercises Magnus, Nakor, and Robert had taught him, no matter how much he attempted to divert himself from thinking about the tournament with dice, cards, or lovely company, he found himself constantly haunted by thoughts of the coming contest.

Not even an invitation to the palace, two nights before the tournament was to commence, eased his fixation. He killed hours at a tailor, having the latest in court fashions cut and sewn to fit. It was a gaudy bit of foppery, consisting of a pair of tight trousers, tucked into polished black boots that were absolutely useless for anything practical. They were too low at the calf for riding – the top of the boot would grind the calf to blisters in an hour – and too tall to wear on the march. But they had lovely silver buckles and a red stripe of dyed leather down the side. The trousers were tight to the point of being constricting, but the tailor assured him this was the current fashion at court. He forwent the codpiece that was also said to be the rage. There were things he found too silly to bear, even for the sake of court fashion. The shirt was a work of frippery, being open at the neck, and gathered below the breastbone by a series of pearl buttons, with a lace collar and more lace at the sleeves. The jacket was completely decorative – a gold-thread-on-red-brocade monstrosity, designed to be worn on the left arm only, hanging by a golden cord across the right, with pearls sewn at the collar and cuffs. The crowning glory was a hat, a broad-brimmed thing of snow-white felted fur, with a hand-crafted silver-wire band, in which a dyed plume had been placed. Tal's plume was black, so the contrast was dramatic. The tailor assured him the outfit was as fine as any that would be worn in court, but Tal could not help but feel someone had put the man up to this, so that his arrival for his first appearance at court would be greeted with laughter and derision.

But, as his carriage arrived at the palace gate on the night of the gala, he could see other young men of the city dressed in equally absurd rigs. He remembered with nostalgia, the simple skins and fur jackets his family had worn in the mountains in the winter, and going almost naked during the summer heat. As he mounted the steps to the palace, Tal decided that fashion was a conspiracy created by tailors to bilk the nobility out of excess gold. He knew from what he had heard at various social gatherings he had attended, in Salador and Roldem that by this time next year everything he wore would be counted out of style, and new fashions would be all the rage.

Tal handed his invitation to the squire responsible for ensuring no uninvited guests appeared in the King's court. The squire was backed up by a squad of palace guardsmen, who despite being garbed in gaudy red-and-yellow livery, looked quite capable of repelling an invasion, let alone removing an unwanted guest. Then a page was assigned to escort him to the main hall. As they walked, the page said, 'Sir, tonight the King has decreed there to be no formal seating. Everyone will avail themselves of a buffet.'

Talon didn't know the word and had to search his memory for it. 'Boo-fay,' he said softly. The boy motioned to the long tables at the side of the hall, heavily burdened with food and servants moving rapidly through the hall with pitchers of ale and wine, filling cups at request. Everywhere he looked he saw people in colours of riotous hue engaged in conversation, some holding a plate with one hand and eating with the other.

Then it came to him, *buffet* was a Kingdom word, from the Bas-Tyran dialect. And it meant to eat from an open table without sitting. *Sometimes you only* think *you can speak a language*, Tal reminded himself silently.

He moved through the crowd, noticing half a dozen or so familiar faces and these he smiled and bowed to, as he made his way to the tables of food. Everything he could imagine dining on was laid out there, from smoked game-birds and seasoned eggs, to vegetables prepared in every conceivable fashion, from fresh out of the kettle to pickled and spiced, to cheeses and fruits – some expensively out of season – and sweets. He picked up a plate and found it to be lighter than he had expected, and a quick inspection showed him it was some sort of hard ceramic, rather than stone or metal. It had been hand-painted with the royal crest of Roldem, a dolphin leaping from a wave over a star. It was quite impressive.

A voice at his right said, 'Yes, it is impressive, isn't it?'

Tal turned and saw Quincy de Castle, a merchant from Bas-Tyra with whom he had gambled several times. 'Reading minds?' he asked with a smile.

'No,' answered the merchant. 'If I could, I wouldn't have lost as much money to you at cards as I have, Tal. No, I saw you admiring the plate and guessed your reaction.'

'It is quite impressive,' Tal repeated.

'Well, as they say, "it's good to be king". It allows one to indulge oneself in all manner of niceties.'

At this moment the Master of Ceremonies struck the floor with the iron-shod heel of his staff of office. 'My lords, ladies and gentlemen, the King!'

All eyes turned to the archway that led from the royal

apartments and there, sweeping into the hall, was King Carol the Sixth. A middle-aged man who still looked as fit as he had when twenty-five, the King escorted a plump, but pleasant-looking woman wearing a small crown, 'The Queen, and the Royal Family!' announced the Master of Ceremonies.

Everyone bowed and the King said, 'It is our pleasure that you return to the festivities. We are informal tonight!'

A light round of applause greeted this message and everyone attempted to return to their previous activities.

Tal said to Quincy, 'Have you attended one of these before?'

'Yes, but not this sort of informal gathering. I hear that so many are in attendance for the tournament that there aren't enough chairs in the palace to enable everyone to sit down, even if there was a table big enough to accommodate everyone. So, instead we have this buffet, and one in the next hall, and the hall beyond that.'

Tal nodded. 'I find myself feeling far less honoured by my invitation than I did a minute ago, friend Quincy.'

The man laughed. 'Don't feel slighted. For every one of us who has been invited, there are three outside the gates wishing they could be inside. I am here only because I've traded with the royal purchasing agent for twenty years and have come to the competition before. This will be my third tournament. You are among the favourites to win the golden sword, Tal, and as such, you would certainly be invited to attend. Expect a few words from the King himself before the night is out.'

'I don't know what to say,' Tal replied.

'Say little, laugh at his jokes, and agree to anything he proposes. That's the way to deal with kings.'

'Thank you for the advice.'

They parted company and Tal drifted through the three halls, saying hello to those he knew and nodding to anyone who nodded at him first. After two hours, a page sought him out asking, 'Sir, are you Squire Tal Hawkins?'

'Yes,' he answered.

'The King commands your attendance, sir. Follow me, please.'

The boy led him back to the centre of the three halls where the King was standing in the corner with Queen Gertrude and other family members, a boy of no more than thirteen who must be Prince Constantine, and two other boys and a girl. The younger children looked bored, but stood quietly, clearly on their best behaviour.

The page spoke quietly into the ear of a servant, who in turn spoke in the ear of the Master of Ceremonies. The Master of Ceremonies nodded curtly in Tal's direction, then said, 'Your Majesty, may I present Talwin Hawkins, Squire of Morgan River and Bellcastle, Baronet of Silverlake.'

Tal executed his most courtly bow and kept silent. He knew better than to speak before the King.

King Carol smiled. 'I've heard of you, young sir. They say the smart money is wagered on you to win our tournament.'

'Your majesty is kind,' said Tal. 'I would be fortunate indeed to prevail among all the master swordsmen who are coming to compete.'

'You're being modest,' said the King with a laugh. 'I hear things. There are no secrets in the Masters' Court.'

'Your majesty,' said Tal, 'that I can readily believe.'

The King's smile broadened. Then he said, 'Ah, here comes one now who will seek to prevent you from winning the golden blade.'

Tal turned and saw a party of men approaching. The smile on his face froze, as the King said, 'Squire Talwin, may I present to you our cousin, Kaspar, Duke of Olasko.'

The leading man was burly across the shoulders, but narrow in the waist, and Tal could see that he was both powerful and dangerous. His face was moon-round, but his chin jutted forward and his dark eyes were narrow and focused, as if he was stalking prey. His chin sported a still-dark beard, but his upper lip was shaved, and his mouth was curled into a smile that was almost a smirk. 'So, this is the young lad who is going to prevent my man from winning?' He turned to the man on his left, who was wearing a dress uniform, and said, 'Majesty, this is Lieutenant Campaneal, the finest swordsman in my duchy and, I wager, the man who will win the tourney.' With a laugh, he added, 'And when I say wager, I mean heavily.'

The King laughed. Tal nodded a greeting to the Duke and the Lieutenant. After a moment the Duke of Olasko said, 'Squire, you are staring. Do you know one another?'

'No,' Tal lied. 'For a moment, I thought perhaps I recognized the Lieutenant, but I was mistaken.' He turned and said, 'It is an honour to meet you, Duke Kaspar.'

Tal allowed the Duke to take over the conversation and faded into the background. It took all the control he could muster to keep his face a mask, for he *had* seen Lieutenant Campaneal once before. He had been the man taking orders from Captain Quentin Havrevulen, who was sitting on a horse beside the man called Raven. Lieutenant Campaneal was one of the men Tal had seen destroying his village. He was one of the men Tal had vowed to kill.

• CHAPTER SIXTEEN •

Tournament

*T*AL CHEERED.

The Tournament of Masters' was underway, at last, and to his delight, Tal discovered his prodigious success at the Masters' Court over the last year had earned him ranking. Over four hundred swordsmen had made their way to the city of Roldem to seek the golden sword and the title of the world's greatest swordsman. The finest thirty-two, either by reputation or accomplishment at the Masters' Court, were permitted to sit out the preliminary rounds of the contest. The thirty-two were not ranked by the Masters' Court, though book-makers who took wagers on the proceedings made their own ranking. In most cases, Tal was ranked no less than third. In several, he was the favourite to win the tourney. Only one man apart from Tal, the legendary Versi Dango, had gone undefeated in a year of bouts at the Masters' Court. Should Tal win the tournament three times, it was said that another statue might join the Count's in the atrium of the Masters' Court.

Tal was afforded special seating in the central gallery, a section on the upper level with seating for the thirty-two chosen fighters and their friends, attendants, and companions. At present over seventy people were sitting or standing in the gallery, where refreshments were provided by attentive servants.

Tal sat with Pasko. 'Isn't that Kendrick standing back in the shadows in the corner?' he asked.

'Yes, it is, m'lord.'

'Has he entered the contest?'

'No, he lacks the vanity to imagine he's the best there is,' said Pasko dryly, then added, 'm'lord.'

'What's he doing here?'

'Watching your back,' said Caleb, dropping into a chair next to Talon.

'Both of you?'

'And Magnus, whom you wouldn't catch dead here, but who is nearby,' added Pug's younger son.

Tal grinned. 'Caleb, I never thought I'd see you dressed so fashionably.'

Caleb returned the smile, though he seemed nowhere near as amused as Tal. 'Camouflage,' he replied. He looked like a wealthy merchant or minor noble of the Kingdom. The only thing on his person that Tal recognized was his sword, which was unchanged. Other than that, he was bedecked from head to toe in the latest fashion of the day, though he made choices considerably less flamboyant than most in Roldem for the festival, choosing a dark chocolate coloured overjacket, a pale yellow shirt and black trousers and boots. In place of the more colourful hats worn by the dandies in the city, Caleb had opted for a simple black beret with a golden clasp and a single hawk's feather.

Tal laughed. 'You look the part of a Kingdom noble, 'struth.'

Caleb said, 'Did you encounter the Duke of Olasko at the King's gala two nights ago?'

Tal's expression darkened and he leaned forward, his elbows on his knees. He dropped his voice so that only Caleb could hear him. 'Yes, with some family members. But I recognized one man: a lieutenant, named Campaneal. He led the Olasko soldiers who supported Raven and his murderers when they destroyed my people.'

'I know. He's in the tourney. He's one of the thirty-two, so there's a fair chance you'll meet him.'

'I'd rather meet him somewhere else, without witnesses,' said Tal.

'Accidents have been known to happen in the tourney. Fatal accidents.'

Tal looked at Caleb. 'Are you telling me I should kill the man in front of the King and a thousand witnesses?'

Caleb shook his head with a rueful smile. 'The vanity of youth. No, I was telling you to be careful, because if Campaneal has even a remote suspicion of who you are, you could be the accident victim.'

'How would he know?' asked Tal. 'I have no tattoos that market me as Orosini. I think I'm convincing in the role of a minor nobleman's son. Why would he think otherwise?'

'Because of the way you looked at him, no doubt. A man like that will have made many enemies over the years, and not even know them all by sight. Just be wary.'

'I will.'

'No, I was curious about anyone else in the party, someone who might not have looked . . . quite as if he belonged.'

'No,' said Tal. 'The Duke had some relatives with him, a son I gather, because of the resemblance, but he made no introductions; I doubt I rank high enough in his estimation to have taken the bother. Who are you looking for?'

'I don't know,' said Caleb. 'There's a man . . . a magician. He and my father crossed paths before, years ago. We have reports he might be back. We thought him dead, but perhaps we were wrong . . .' A distracted look crossed his face, then he said, 'From what I've been told, this man is harder to kill than a cockroach.'

'What is his name?'

'He's used several, so I doubt he'll be using any that we know.'

'What does he look like?'

'His appearance changes.'

Tal's eyes widened, and his tone became sardonic. 'A man who may look like anyone with a name no one knows. I'll be certain to keep an eye out for him, Caleb.'

'From what Father has told me, you'll probably sense something about him the moment you meet, if you do. He's a magician, a powerful one, and his heart is as black as pitch.'

Tal was quiet, watching the contests below: four bouts in different corners of the hall. Eventually he said, 'At some point I must kill the Duke of Olasko.'

'I know. He was behind the destruction of your people, Tal.'

'Why?'

'Because they were inconvenient to his plans, nothing more. He wanted a clear road to Farinda's northern frontier, and your people were in the way. It was easier to obliterate them than to attempt to negotiate a way through the mountains. He was concerned your people might tip his hand to the King of Farinda.'

'So he killed every man, woman and child in the High Fastness.'

'Yes.' Caleb leaned forward, onto the gallery rail. 'He's been working on the invasion of Farinda for five years now. He bullied Latagore into a treaty allowing him to garrison troops there. Word is he marches in the spring against the Orodon.'

'Why?' asked Tal. 'They're not remotely close to Farinda.'

'Because he wants something they have: gold mines. War is expensive, and the Orodon hardly mine the gold in their part of the mountains. He can finance ten years of war from what he can take from there in one year.'

Tal's mind turned over. The Orodon were distant cousins of his people, and as such were the only people left alive with whom he felt kinship.

'Spring?'

'Yes, that's the rumour.'

Tal stood up. 'Caleb, let's go back to my apartment. I must talk to Robert and Magnus.'

Caleb stood up as well. 'About what?'

'About what it is you think I'm going to be doing after I win this damned tournament.'

Without looking to see if Caleb was following him, Tal quickly left the gallery and hurried down the stairs to the main atrium.

Robert and Magnus sat at the table while Pasko brewed up a pot of Keshian coffee. Caleb leaned against the wall while Tal stood facing the two magicians. 'So, if I win this tournament, what next?'

Magnus looked at Robert, who nodded. 'We will have a task for you.'

'I anticipated that much, but what is it?'

Magnus leaned his elbow on the table. 'You'll be told when the time is right.'

Tal's frustration came to the surface. 'For years I have done as I was told. I owe you my life, several times, but at some point you have to trust me. This is too much of a distraction. It appears I have someone trying to kill me, and I don't know why. I don't know if it's because of you,' he pointed at the other four men in the room in turn, 'or because of something I've done, playing this role you've created.'

Robert said, '*You've* created, Tal. We told you what to become; *how* you became Talwin Hawkins was your choice. No one ordered you to become a gambler, womanizer, and libertine. You could have posed as a scholar, or a man of trade, but you picked this life.'

Magnus added, 'And by all appearances, it's a life that suits you, Tal.'

Tal couldn't rein in his frustration. 'It's about my life. That's *my life.* I owe Robert a debt. My education over the last five years has taught me much, and one thing I've learned is to look at my choices through different eyes. 'I'm Orosini, and I will honour my debt. No man will ever hear me renounce a pledge or break an oath. But that doesn't mean I will simply obey blindly, Robert. If I'm to serve well, don't I need to know things?'

Robert sighed. 'This much I'll tell you now, Tal. Events conspire to bring our goals closely in line. This man we warned you of, he will be close to the Duke, if not here in Roldem, then back in Opardum, his capital. Duke Kaspar has ambitions.'

'Obviously,' said Tal. 'I gathered as much when I saw his Captain Havrevulen in Latagore, conspiring to overthrow the Dominar. I know he means to have Farinda. What I don't know is why.'

Robert said, 'To Kaspar's south lie the lands controlled by the Lords of the Border, a group of duchies constantly at one another's throats: Miskalon, Ruskalon, the Duchy of Maladon and Simrick, Salmarter and Far Loren. The only successful conquest in the history of that sad region was when Maladon subdued Simrik two hundred years ago. All contend over the Disputed Lands, and Olasko ensures that no one quite gets the upper hand. It's to his advantage to keep them all weak and off-balance. To his west is the Principality of Aranor. The Prince of Aranor is Kaspar's cousin on the Prince's mother's side, and cousin to the King of Roldem on his father's side, so Kaspar and his ancestors have had to keep their hands off Aranor for many years; though this prince is a weak idiot and Kaspar might as well be ruling there given how much influence he has.

'Beyond Aranor is Far Loren and Opast. Both have close ties with the Kingdom of the Isles, though both have warred with the Isles in the past. The Isles would be quick to react if Olasko moved against them.

'To the north is Bardac's Holdfast, which is hardly a nation at all. The original ruler, King Bardac the First, was a pirate with delusions of grandeur and his descendants are hardly any more than that. Most of the "nobility" of that land are robber barons and King Haloren rules most effectively by leaving them alone. For Olasko to invade would be like marching into a swamp. County Conar is little better, but the tribal chieftains are honourable barbarians, as are the swamp people to their north.

'This is why Kaspar wanted Farinda, to put his army on the

frontier of the Kingdom of the Isles, without having to overly disturb his other neighbours.'

'Why? He means to go to war with the Isles?' Tal shrugged. 'My memory of geography may be a bit vague, but wouldn't that put his army several hundred miles away from the nearest Kingdom city of any size, down in Ran?'

'Yes, and we have no idea why he'd want an army up there, but several theories. We'll save the speculation for later, but this much we know for certain: Duke Kaspar of Olasko is perhaps the most dangerous man living today when it comes to the peace of the region. He means to have control over the Eastern Kingdoms, and we suspect he's looking for a way to pull Roldem into a war with the Isles.'

'Ah,' said Tal. 'And if Roldem goes to war with the Isles, then Kesh will take a hand.'

'And a regional conflict becomes a much broader conflict, with war in both the Eastern and Western Realms of the Kingdom,' supplied Magnus.

'I've read enough history to understand ambition a little,' Tal said, 'but it seems to me that Kaspar's overreaching himself.'

Robert said, 'He wouldn't be the first ruler to reap benefit from others' woes. He can gobble up the Lords of the Border at whim. He has little interest in ruling the chaotic peoples' to his north, unless he decides to bring them to heel sometime in the future.

'For now he must secure control over Farinda and complete his preparations for war with the Kingdom. So, first, he must subdue Farinda. To ensure his security in that undertaking, he must neutralize the Orodon and Latagore, and the High Reaches.'

Tal's eyebrows shot up. 'So now the pattern emerges. First he obliterates my people, securing a path to Farinda. Now he protects his right flank by ensuring that no aid can reach Farinda though High Reaches or Latagore.'

'Yes, if the Kingdom were to take a hand early and if King Ryan is as clever as they say he is, he'd react as soon as he recognized the risk. He can't attack Olasko directly without pulling Aranor and then Roldem into the war, but he can certainly hire companies of mercenaries and run them by ship to Coastal Watch, and from there either to Latagore or High Reaches. Kaspar can't risk an army at his back.'

'Why hasn't someone dealt with this problem before?' asked Tal.

Robert looked at Magnus, who said, 'I could toss a fireball into Kaspar's lap and after destroying the King, his family, and half the nobility of Roldem, Kaspar would still walk out of the ashes unscathed. The man we spoke of earlier is very powerful and Kaspar has more wards against attack by magic than any man in the world, I'm certain. His bodyguards are fanatical and he is never alone. Killing him will be no mean feat.'

'Is this where I come in?'

'Perhaps,' said Robert. 'We don't know yet. If you win the tournament, there's a fair chance Kaspar may take an interest in you. He likes having people of great talent around him, musicians, singers, painters, chefs, magicians, and great swordsmen.'

'Well, then,' said Tal. 'I can now see why you think it important for me to win this contest. It seems that both our aims are served if Kaspar of Olasko dies.'

Robert sat back and looked directly at his former student. 'Yes, it seems that way, doesn't it?'

'Then here's my one condition.' Tal said grimly. 'Kaspar dies last.'

'Why?' asked Magnus.

'Because from what you say, I stand the best chance of getting myself killed in reaching him, and if I am to fail to avenge my people, I'd rather die leaving one murderer alive than letting a dozen survive. Kaspar dies after Raven and his men, but first comes Lieutenant Campaneal.' Looking at Robert, Magnus, Caleb and Pasko, Tal said, 'He will not make it alive out of the tournament.'

The early rounds produced little by way of surprises, the most unexpected turn being the emergence of a young commoner from Kesh named Kakama, who had handily defeated every opponent. Those inclined to take risks in gambling bet heavily on him.

The fourth day saw Tal's first match as the final sixty-four contestants began the last three days of contest. Over four hundred swordsmen had fought in as many as three matches a day to winnow the field down to thirty-two who would be added to the thirty-two who had already been ranked. There would be matches in the morning then in the late afternoon, until the final bout on Sixthday afternoon, before the King and his court at the palace.

Tal's first opponent was a captain from the personal guard of a Roldemish baron. This was his third tournament and the first time he had made the final sixty-four places.

The matches were fought with naked steel to first blood, a yield, or a forfeiture. A contestant could yield at any time, and usually only did so for fear of injury or public humiliation. A man could forfeit by not appearing in time for a match, or by being disqualified by the judges, three Masters of the Court who supervised each bout. Ignoring the judges' instructions, intentionally trying to harm an opponent, or refusing to remain in the described combat area were all grounds for forfeiture.

Tal let the captain enjoy a few moments of accomplishment, and refused to shame him after twelve years spent in trying to better himself. But it was no contest. After exchanging blows, thrusts, and parries for three minutes, Tal could easily see many openings. Tal had noticed that the young captain had been wished good fortune by an adoring young woman, whom he assumed to be his wife or betrothed, so he decided to allow the man to lose with some dignity. He kept the match going for another two minutes, before lightly cutting the man on the arm, drawing first blood and the victory.

The young captain made a formal salute, which Tal returned, then he retired to the comforting embrace of the young woman.

Other matches were not so graceful. Several of the combatants were loud, boasting louts, who had one gift: skill with a blade. Three serious injuries occurred in the first morning's contests – one man undoubtedly maimed for life – and Tal watched as many as he could, to get some sense of who he might face in later matches.

His next opponent was a large, broad-shouldered swordmaster from the Kingdom City of Rodez, named Raimundo Velasquez. He was quiet and efficient, and was cat-quick to pounce on an opening. Tal saw he would have to be wary with this man during the afternoon's contest.

Tal retired to the cloaking room, where refreshments for the combatants were laid out in sumptuous fashion. He avoided those foods which would make him feel slow and sleepy, and ate lightly, avoiding wine or ale. He drank cold water and returned to watch the bouts.

He avoided talking to anyone, including Caleb, who kept close watch. Tal knew that Magnus and Robert were not too far away, against any magical threat, but he felt no need of idle chatter. He was now in the tourney and from everything he had seen, he must surely win.

When the last of the morning bouts was over, he retired to Remarga's for a bath and massage, so that he would be fresh when the afternoon combat began.

The next two rounds were challenging, but Tal took the measure of both men: the Rodezian swordmaster then a captain of the guard from the Royal household. The afternoon of the second day saw attendance swell to capacity as every noble and rich commoner who could gain entrance to the Masters' Court wedged themselves inside to watch the field of eight reduced to four.

Tal's first opponent was a mercenary soldier from the Kingdom, a man named Bartlet, from Hawk's Hallow. He enquired about Tal's relationship to the more famous Hawkins, and Tal told his tale, as if it were common knowledge. Bartlet remarked he had never heard of the Squire's holdings, and he had been born in the region.

Tal waved off the remark with the observation that his father held lands quite distant from the more famous branch of the Hawkins family and he avoided further conversation by saying that he had to ready himself for their coming duel.

Tal dispatched the mercenary in record time, within seconds after the judges called for combat. He took two steps forward, and rather than launching a feigned attack with a combination of blows, he lunged and struck the man in the upper left arm, drawing blood.

The gallery exploded in applause and the mercenary stood in stunned amazement, both because of the speed of the attack and the lack of guile, which had caught him by surprise. He looked angry, more at himself for being made to look the fool than at Tal, but he saluted and as they left the floor, he said, 'Be sure to win, will you, Squire? It makes me look far less of a buffoon if I'm disposed of by the champion.'

'I'll do my best,' said Tal with a smile.

When the other three contests were over, Tal found that his opponent would be the surprising Keshian youngster, Kakama; while Lieutenant Campaneal was to face Count Jango Vahardak, the man who had finished second the year before to the retired champion.

Tal spent a restless night worrying more that Vahardak would defeat Campaneal than about his own match. He had watched the young Keshian and knew his victories were due to speed – perhaps even superior to his own – audacity, and a willingness to leave himself open when making a bid for a winning touch. Tal had already anticipated how he would defeat the Keshian.

He awoke early and dressed quickly, then roused Pasko and the others. At the Masters' Court, he put himself through a vigorous set of stretching exercises. When he had finished, he ate a light meal of fruit and juices, then took a carriage to the baths.

The two bouts to determine the finalists would start at noon, with the winners fighting before the King and his court at the palace after dark. Tal kept his mind as focused as he could on the coming match, but all he could really think about was of facing Campaneal.

Two hours before noon, he returned to the Masters' Court and retired to the room set aside for contestants. He was not the first there, for the young swordsman from Kesh was already sitting in a corner. When the first day of the contest had commenced, the room had been crowded and loud with the chummy chatter of contestants and their servants. Today it was as silent as a tomb. Talon retired to the far corner and nodded once to Kakama. Pasko leaned over and said, 'I believe that lad is Isalani, like Nakor.'

'What of it?'

'Just that if he's anything like Nakor, you haven't seen half of what he has. Just remember that.'

'You think he's been thinking that far ahead?'

'I caught him watching you watching him, just before he won his third bout. I think if you saw an opening, he wanted you to see it.'

'Why me?'

'Because you were the favourite.'

'One of the favourites.'

'Not to anyone who knew what was going on. You're vain, Tal, and show everything you have when you win. You don't hold back. That boy has a complete inventory of your moves. You have no idea what he's capable of; be careful.'

Tal sat back and then said, 'Thank you. You may have saved me another time.'

'Well, at least this time I may have saved you from embarrassment, not from death.'

'No, I think not.'

'What?'

'Look at him.'

Pasko turned and regarded the young Keshian, who sat quietly watching Talon from under hooded eyes.

Talon said, 'Call it intuition or my bump of trouble, but unless I'm sadly mistaken, he means to kill me today.'

The semi-final round was conducted with more pomp and ceremony than the earlier rounds. Many members of the royal family were in attendance, as well as most of the important nobility.

When the combatants for the first match were announced, Tal felt his stomach flip. Campaneal and Vahardak would go first, and Tal and the Keshian afterwards. He realized that as the favourite, the Masters were saving his bout for last. Even so, he wished to get it over with.

Neither he nor the Keshian watched the first match, each of them content to sit in opposite corners of the room. Vahardak and Campaneal had done the same, each taking a corner with their retainers. The Count was accompanied by at least five servants, while Lieutenant Campaneal had a batsman and a sergeant of the Olasko Household Guard with him. Tal had Pasko, and the Keshian sat alone.

From the droning voices in the distance, Tal could tell that the Master who announced the final matches to take place in the court was indulging himself in as grand a presentation as he could muster and, from the accompanying cheers, the crowd seemed eager to savour every word.

Pasko said, 'I've been asking around. This lad came from nowhere, it's a fact. None of the other Keshians I've encountered have ever heard of him; seems odd that a youngster with his skills wouldn't have made some sort of name for himself down in Kesh.'

'Yes, it is odd, isn't it?'

'I don't know if he's going to try to kill you or not, m'lord, but there is something very strange about him. He hasn't moved in an hour.'

'Perhaps he's asleep.'

Pasko said, 'Then he has nerves of iron.'

A shout from the hall informed Tal that the bout was over and he watched the door to see who entered and how they carried themselves. A minute later the door flew open and in strode Count Vahardak, clutching his left arm. Blood ran through his fingers. One of his attendants was trying to console him. '—a close thing, my lord. It could have gone either way, I'm certain. It was . . . luck, nothing more.'

The Count appeared unwilling to be mollified and just barked, 'Stop talking and bind this damn thing.'

Into the room came Lieutenant Campaneal, a slight smile of satisfaction on his face. He glanced first at Tal then at the Keshian, as if saying silently, *I will see one of you in the palace tonight*, but he kept silent. He acknowledged each of them with a slight nod, then went to say something to Count Vahardak.

A Master of the Court entered and announced, 'Talwin Hawkins, Kakama of Kesh, places, please.'

The Keshian carried his sword wrapped in a long black cloth, rather than in a scabbard. He knelt and unrolled it, and Tal's eyes widened at the sight of it. 'That's not the longsword he's been using. What is it?'

Pasko swore. 'It's a *katana*; they're used either one-or-two-handed and they are sharper than a razor. You don't see many of them around, because the bad ones can't stand against armour, and the good ones are too expensive for any but the richest noble to buy. But for cutting flesh, they're wicked. He's about to show you a style of fighting you've never encountered.'

'Talk to me, Pasko. What must I do?'

As they rose to answer the call of the Master, Pasko said, 'Whatever you saw from Nakor in his open-handed fighting, think of that. Misdirection and sudden strikes. You'll probably only get one look and then he's going to be coming at you. If there was ever a time to chose luck over skill, this is it.'

Tal took a slow, deep breath, then let it out as they walked to the door leading to the main court.

They entered to loud applause and cheers, and each man was directed to an end of the room. Markers had been placed at the corners of the largest rectangle on the floor, so Tal knew he had a lot of room to work with.

When the din quieted, the Master in charge spoke. 'My lords, ladies and gentlemen. This is our final match of the Tournament of the Masters' Court. The winner of this bout will fight tonight in the palace for the Office of the Golden Sword and be acknowledged as the greatest swordsman in the world. 'On my left, I give you Kakama, from the village of Li-Pe, in the Empire of Great Kesh.'

The applause was thunderous, Kakama was the long shot who had earned his way in from the first round, and many who had no other cause to cheer him on did so for that reason alone.

'To my right, I give you Talwin Hawkins, Squire of Morgan River and Bellcastle, Baronet of Silverlake of the Kingdom of the Isles.'

He motioned for the two men to come to the marks on the floor which showed their starting positions. Then he said, 'My lord, master Kakama, this is a fight to first blood. Obey the instructions of the masters and defend yourself at all times. Upon my command . . . begin!'

Tal saw Kakama take a single step back, raising the sword with his right hand, his left hand outstretched, palm outward. Then suddenly he took a spinning step forward, much like a flying kick Nakor had shown him several times, his left hand coming up to join his right and the sword swirling around in an arc at incredible speed, aimed at Tal's head.

Tal ducked and rolled, a move not seen in the tournament before, but one common to ale-house brawls. Several men in the audience hooted and laughed, but most cheered, for it was clear that the Keshian had intended to take Tal's head from his shoulders.

'Kakama!' cried the Master of the Court. 'First blood only!'

The Keshian ignored the instruction and with three little steps made a running charge at Tal. Tal didn't retreat, but leapt forward himself, his own blade coming around as quickly as he could execute the blow.

Steel rang out against steel and the crowd gasped, for even the slowest among them realized that this was no exhibition match, but that they were watching two men attempting to kill one another.

'Halt!' came the command from the senior judge, but neither man listened. Kakama spun again and levelled a blow that would have gutted Tal had he paused to obey the command.

Tal shouted, 'Pasko, dirk!'

Pasko pulled his dirk from his belt and when Kakama lunged again and Tal leapt away, Pasko threw the dirk to him. Tal caught it in his left hand and spun away, as Kakama came at him again.

The type of fighting the Keshian employed was alien to Tal, but he hoped the use of the duelling dirk in his left hand, to block his opponent's blade or to use in close if he got inside his guard, would rebalance the contest.

The Masters were calling to the gallery for men to come and stop the contest, which was now clearly beyond the scope of the rules. No one came forth. The idea of trying to separate two of the deadliest fighters on the island didn't appeal to anyone.

Tal thought he heard someone call for crossbows, but couldn't spare the attention to be sure. Kakama was coming at him hard, again, and this time Tal had run out of room in which to dodge.

He barely saved his life with the dirk, for Kakama's overhead slash suddenly became a sideways blow to the neck with a twist of the wrists. Tal's hand came up in reflex and he caught the blade just enough to parry the blow. That gave him an opportunity and he lashed out with his own sword, catching the Keshian on the shoulder.

The Master cried out, 'First blood!' but Kakama ignored the judge and pressed home for the kill.

Tal backed up, as if trying to put some distance between them; then he suddenly planted both his feet and threw the dirk, underarm, as hard as he could at Kakama's stomach.

The Keshian turned his blade, using both hands, so that it pointed downward, and batted the blade aside, but as he did so, Tal came in fast and high with his own sword, and as Kakama attempted to raise his blade to block the second strike, Tal was already inside, his blade slicing deep across the side of the Keshian's neck.

Tal didn't pull back and risk a return blow from the dying man, but rather slammed into him, hitting him as hard as he could. The Keshian flew backwards, the sword knocked out of fingers which were quickly going limp. Blood fountained out of the gash in his neck.

Tal knelt beside the dying man and looked into his eyes. 'Who sent you?' he demanded, but the Keshian said nothing.

Pasko came to stand beside Tal, while the hall was deadly quiet. No one seemed ready to applaud the victory, for it was clear this had nothing to do with sport.

The judge walked across the floor and declared: 'Since you were clearly defending yourself Squire Talwin, you are not to be disqualified for failing to halt when commanded to do so.'

Tal looked up from where he knelt then rose and with a bitter laugh said, 'Can't ruin the King's party tonight.'

The judge looked at Tal but did not reply. At last, he said, 'Appear at the palace at sundown, Squire Talwin.'

People remained in the gallery, as if unwilling to leave until someone explained what had taken place. Finally, porters appeared and took away the body while other servants cleaned up the blood on the floor.

Tal turned to Pasko. 'I really need a bath.'

'And we need to have some questions answered,' Pasko said.

Tal nodded. Pasko placed a cloak over his shoulders and took Tal's sword from him. 'I know who I want dead, but now I've got to worry about who wants me dead.'

'And why,' added Pasko grimly.

• CHAPTER SEVENTEEN •

Target

TAL WAITED.

The Masters of the Court, the Master of Ceremonies for the Palace, and the Captain of the Royal Household Guard were gathered around Tal and Lieutenant Campaneal. Looking on were half a dozen officers of the royal court.

Master Dubkov of the Masters' Court paced up and down in an obvious state of agitation. 'We've never had a display such as that in the two hundred years of the tourney. There have been accidents, and two deaths as a result, but never has one contestant set out with cold blooded murder as his intent, knowing that there was no way in which the killer could succeed, escape the court.'

Tal had to admit that it appeared the Keshian must have been indifferent to his fate once he had succeeded in his task.

'What troubles us,' said the Captain of the Guard, a gaunt man named Talinko, 'is what the consequences might have been should the draw have been different and should that combat have taken place in the palace.'

Lieutenant Campaneal said, 'Gentlemen, I watched the contest, as did most of you; Squire Talwin was merely defending himself – and most ably I'll avow – from a man who clearly was intent on killing him. In his place I would have acted in the same fashion.'

'What we want is to ensure there are no repeats of today's events, in the presence of the King,' Captain Talinko stated firmly.

Lieutenant Campaneal spread his hands. 'Gentlemen, I serve my lord Kaspar and am certain that his endorsement of my good behaviour should be sufficient. Squire Talwin has resided here in Roldem for some time now, I have been told, and is a regular visitor to the Masters' Court. Given his rank and standing in the community, is there any question of his demeanour?' He looked at Master Dubkov who nodded in agreement. 'I think we can ensure there will be a fair contest and nothing will go amiss.'

Captain Talinko nodded. 'We believe so, but the safety of the royal family is paramount, as well as the safety of our honoured guests –' his nod in Campaneal's direction made it clear that he was speaking of the Duke and other visiting dignitaries '– hence we will take precautions. Archers will be placed in the gallery above the royal hall, with orders to shoot either contestant should one of three things occur: upon my order; if the judge cries halt and is not heeded; and if a contestant crosses a line we shall mark between the contest floor and the King's throne.

'And mark me, gentlemen, that last is a true deadline. If for any reason either man steps across that line before the contest is halted and the winner presented to the King, he shall die before a second step toward the crown can be taken. Is that clear?'

Both men nodded.

'Very well,' said the Captain. 'We shall put that shameful exhibition of this afternoon behind us. That will be all.' As everyone began to leave, the Captain said, 'Squire Talwin, a moment, please.'

Tal lingered and when he was alone with the Captain, Talinko asked, 'Have you any idea why the Keshian was trying to kill you?'

Tal let out his breath slowly, and shook his head. 'Honestly, I can't. I can imagine a lot of reasons, but nothing that makes sense.'

'Humour me with a few of them,' said a voice from the shadows.

Tal smiled, but there was not much humour in it. 'Ah, Constable, I was wondering when I'd see you again.'

'This is the second time you've been standing next to a bloody corpse, Squire, and this time you can't tell me you weren't the target. You may have noticed that we had a few witnesses to the deed this time.'

'Including myself and several members of the royal family,' added Captain Talinko.

'Talwin,' said Drogan, 'the reasons, if you please.'

'I've had my share of dalliances with some young women who take it poorly I'm not as interested in long-term alliances as they are.'

'They think you're going to marry them and react badly when you don't,' said Drogan. 'Continue.'

'I've done fairly well at the gaming tables.'

'I've already looked into that and from what I've heard from various owners of the halls in which you gamble, your winnings are steady, but modest enough that no one should be looking to kill you out of revenge, or for an unpaid debt.'

'I've never lost a bout in the Masters' Court.'

'Hardly a reason to pay the fee to the Guild of Death.'

'Guild of Death?'

Drogan looked at Tal as if he was speaking to a particularly slow student. Tal had seen that expression from Robert, Nakor and Magnus over the years. 'The man was prepared to die, expected to die. He could have put poison in your drink, stuck a knife in your back on a dark night, cut your throat while you slept, or killed you any of a dozen different ways, but instead he tried to kill you during a public tournament, in the one thing *you were recognized as being very good at*. In other words, he knowingly gave you a chance to survive while expecting to die himself.

'He was either crazy or a member of the Assassin's Guild. He was a Keshian Izmali, and he died because he was ordered to die.'

'It makes no sense,' said Tal.

'Agreed, and moreover, it's costly. I've asked around and a suicide contract like this is likely to cost in excess of ten thousand golden dolphins.' The dolphin was a slightly heavier coin than the Keshian imperial or the Kingdom sovereign, so he was talking about eleven thousand gold coins by common trade parlance. 'It makes less sense the more you think on it.'

'Someone paid ten years' wages to give me a chance to survive?'

'I hate it when things aren't simple,' said the Constable.

Captain Talinko frowned. 'I appreciate that you have a crime to explain to His Majesty, even if that explanation is less than complete, but I have duties I must see to. Gentlemen,' he said with a nod and left.

Constable Drogan said, 'Tal, I've seen you play cards and you're a good enough bluffer, but I've been a constable for the better part of twenty years, and I can tell when a man is lying. You really have no idea who's behind this, do you?'

'By the gods, Dennis, I do not. I'm barely twenty years old, and I've travelled a bit, so it's hard to imagine I've made an enemy in that time who would stage such an elaborate assassination.'

'I don't think that's what it was,' said Drogan. 'After thinking about it some more, I think it was more of a test.'

'A test?'

'Someone wanted to see just how good you were, and sent someone better than anyone you were likely to meet here at the tourney.'

'Better?' said Tal. 'The winner here is considered the best in the world.'

'Don't let that vanity sweep you away if you win, Tal.' Drogan put his hand on Tal's arm and started walking him towards the door. 'You need to get ready for tonight. We'll talk as we walk.

'Look, you may be the best of the bunch who chose to walk into that building and start whacking away at each other, but the Izmali are just one of a dozen different bunches who spend every day in their life learning how to kill people.' They moved aside as a pair of servants carried a long table back towards the Captain's conference room. 'There may be half a dozen soldiers scattered from here to the Sunset Isles who are better than anyone on this island but who couldn't gain leave of their lords and masters to come here to compete. There are probably men your equal who can't be bothered to travel here and waste their time, no matter the prize. I'm sure there are brilliant swordsmen the world over who have never heard of Roldem, let alone the Masters' Court, or this contest.

'If you win, don't take the title of "world's finest swordsman" seriously. It could get you killed.'

They reached the far end of the hall. 'You're through there,' Drogan said, indicating the door. 'You'll find a salon where you can rest, be massaged, eat, sleep, whatever you need until you're called.' He put out his hand and shook Tal's. 'Good luck, tonight.'

As the Constable turned to leave, Tal said, 'Dennis?'

'Yes?' The Constable paused.

'Am I under suspicion for anything?'

Dennis smiled. 'Unless you're paying a prince's ransom to have someone try to kill you, in order to impress the ladies, I can't see how you'd be under suspicion for this bloody nonsense.' Then the smile faded. 'As for anything else, I'm always suspicious, my friend. Of everybody.'

He turned and left Tal alone in the hall. Tal weighed the Constable's words and decided that at least for the next hour or so he needed to put all this nonsense out of his mind. For while there was nothing remotely whimsical about the situation, it made no sense whatsoever.

Tal waited to be summoned for the final match. The room assigned to him was sumptuous, with all types of refreshments from a light broth to a full ham, fresh fruit to cakes and other sweets. Wine, ale and fresh water had been placed in pitchers on the board, and two servants waited nearby for any other need he might have. There was a bed if he wanted a quick nap.

Tal sat on the bed while Pasko hovered over the refreshments, nibbling at this and that. Magnus appeared through a door from the servants' wing, took one look at the servants and said, 'Leave us, please, for a few minutes.'

The two servants looked to Tal who nodded, and then quickly departed. When they were gone, Tal said, 'How did you get into the palace?'

Magnus smiled, a hint of self-satisfaction on his lips. 'If I want to go somewhere, it takes a great deal more than a few guards at the door to keep me out.'

Tal shrugged, conceding the point. 'Then I suppose the appropriate question is, what brings you here so unexpectedly?'

'I've just spoken to our agents in Kesh. The assassin was a member of a particularly obscure sect of Izmali, but we're attempting to see what we can discover about them.'

Tal didn't ask how Magnus had spoken to agents thousands of miles away, assuming that the magician must have some far-speaking magic or just used his powers to take himself there and come back. 'What I'm trying to puzzle out is if they will try again, or if this was some sort of test which I passed.'

'We won't know unless they try to kill you again,' said Magnus.

'I think it's a test of some sort,' said Pasko. 'If they'd wanted you dead, m'lord, they'd have found a lot of easier ways, as I said before. I think someone out there is trying to take your measure.'

Tal sat back on the bed with his back against the wall. He picked up a pillow and put it behind himself to get more comfortable. 'So then the question becomes, who measures me and why?'

'Two possibilities spring to mind,' said Magnus. 'Whoever sent those death-dancers to kill me might have decided to take an interest in whoever foiled them.'

Tal said, 'But how would they know it was me? I mean, we were all on the island, and I was taken back to the estate at once. It could have been any number of people on the island who ruined their attack.'

'The fastest way to end up dead, m'lord, is to underestimate our enemies. They are devious beyond understanding and I'm certain they have as many agents out working as we do, if not more.'

'You think there are spies on Sorcerer's Isle?'

'Not there, but in other places where they can get intelligence about some of the things what transpires on the island,' answered Magnus. 'The farther removed from my parents we are, the less secure we are; that's a fact of life for those of us in service to them.

'You've been out from under their direct care for more than three years now, Tal, and over that time someone may have discovered just enough clues to determine that you were the one to foil the attempt on my life.'

'Revenge is unlikely if I understand anything about the nature of the conflict you've only hinted at Magnus.'

'True,' Magnus agreed. 'But removing a dangerous opponent does make sense. Tal, they are always seeking to weaken us, to thwart any attempt we might make to gain an advantage, much the same as we do, so if they can identify one of our agents they are likely to do whatever they can to remove him.'

'That still doesn't explain why they should try to kill me when I'm the least vulnerable, in front of hundreds of witnesses . . .' Tal waved his hand in frustration. 'It just doesn't make sense.'

'It makes sense if someone is trying to send my father a message.'

'What message?' Tal asked.

'That none of his agents is safe, anywhere, at any time.'

Tal pondered that and then said, 'You said there were two possibilities. What's the other?'

'Someone wants to recruit you.'

'Who?'

'We'll know if you're offered a position, won't we?'

'You think someone went to all that trouble to see if I'm worth hiring?'

'Some of the people you'll encounter along the way, m'lord,' said Pasko, as he finished eating a slice of pungent cheese, 'are capable of almost anything.' He sat back against the table, and picked up a slice of onion, which he daubed with mustard as he spoke. 'You're a dangerous man, all things being equal. Someone might want a great swordsman in his service, but only if he's both a fine duellist and a deadly fighter. That surprise this afternoon showed you were both.'

'True,' said Magnus. 'The Conclave and our enemies are not the only people with resources, wealth and a desire to bring talent into service.' Magnus glanced over to where Pasko was eating the mustard-covered onion and said, 'How can you stand that?'

'It's wonderful, after the cheese,' Pasko said around a full mouth. 'Wash it down with some good white wine . . .' He made a gesture with his thumb and fingers together, rolled his eyes, then closed them and said, 'Simply wonderful.'

Tal said, 'I appreciate food as well as the next man, Pasko, but I think I'm inclined to agree with Magnus on this one.'

'Try it, m'lord.' Pasko grabbed a plate, put on it a slice of onion and a slice of cheese next to each other, then spread mustard on the onion. He picked up a cup of wine and crossed to stand before Tal. 'First a bit of the cheese, then the onion, then the wine.'

Tal bit the cheese and found it a strong, hard cheese, and when he bit into the onion, discovered the mustard was especially hot. As his eyes began to water, he gulped the wine down. When he could speak he said, 'Not bad, but I think you need to get used to it.'

Magnus barked a short laugh. 'I must be off. I have to speak with Father. I'll be back to watch the contest.'

'It's less than an hour,' said Pasko.

'I'll be back.' Magnus gripped his staff and suddenly he was gone. There was a light inrush of air and a small popping sound and then nothing.

'That's very dramatic,' said Tal.

'That's one very dangerous young man,' said Pasko. 'No one talks about it, but he may be more powerful than his father, some day.'

'Some day someone will have to tell me all about that family,' said Tal. As Pasko started to say something, Tal held up his hand and said, 'But not today. Right now I want to rest for half an hour, and get focused. I've had enough distractions to last a lifetime, and in less than an hour I've got to face a man for the championship.'

As he settled back on the bed, his head propped up on a pillow, Tal added, 'And I've got to work out how I'm going to kill the bastard without getting myself shot full of arrows and crossbow bolts.'

Pasko paused in lifting another slice of cheese and onion to his mouth and watched Tal as he closed his eyes. Then he slowly put the food in his mouth and bit off a chunk. Nodding, he thought to himself that the mustard was indeed a bit on the hot side.

Tal stood before the King, his eyes fixed ahead. The Master of Ceremonies was droning on, obviously relishing the opportunity to bore the assembled nobility and influential commoners with the entire story of how the tournament of the Masters' Court had begun.

Tal resisted the urge to glance to his left and look at Campaneal. He expected the officer of the Duke of Olasko's guards would be standing still, eyes forward, as Tal's were.

Finally the history lesson was over, and the Master of Ceremonies said, 'Your majesty, before you stand the two finest combatants in the world, each eager to prove their worth before your august presence. May I present Lieutenant George Campaneal, in service to your cousin, the Duke of Olasko.'

The Lieutenant bowed to the King.

Then the official announced, 'May I present Talwin Hawkins, Squire of Morgan River and Bellcastle, Baronet of Silverlake, in service to his grace, the Duke of Yabon.'

Tal bowed to the King.

'Gentlemen,' said the Master of Ceremonies. 'You have acquitted yourself in admirable fashion, achieving success in the most demanding competition in skill-at-arms, and now one of you will be named the greatest swordsman in the world. You have been made aware of the rules, and should either of you wish to retire from this contest now, no fault will be laid at your feet.' He glanced at each man to see if either wished to withdraw; but neither man acknowledged the question.

'Very well, then, let the contest begin.'

The senior master from the Masters' Court, who had held the office nearly thirty years, walked slowly to the centre of the area designated for the contest. He motioned for the two men to approach, took Tal by the wrist and moved him slightly to his left, then did the same by moving Campaneal to the right. 'Turn and face me!' he barked, his voice still strong. 'Bring no dishonour upon yourself or this court,' he demanded of them.

Tal sneaked a glimpse up at the gallery above the court and saw that there were armed bowmen and crossbowmen at the ready.

The Master had the grace not to make mention of their presence. 'Upon my command, commence the contest, and may the gods grant you strength and honour.'

Tal turned to Campaneal, who bowed to him. Tal managed the slightest inclination of his head, not wishing to show any courtesy to this murderer.

Suddenly the command was given, and Campaneal moved straight at Tal, his broadsword held aloft, and then suddenly it was moving in a snap blow to the side of Tal's body. Tal flipped his wrist, bringing his blade point-down to his left to block the blow, then spun to his right. It was an unexpected move and for a brief instant his back was exposed, but by the time Campaneal could recover and turn, Tal was unleashing a blow of his own, one that should have taken Campaneal in the left shoulder.

But the seasoned swordsman from Olasko squatted slightly, and the blade passed harmlessly over his shoulder, missing it by a bare inch. Tal had to step back, for fear his momentum would turn him so his back was again exposed.

Now that the two opponents had exchanged their first blows, they circled one another, both moving to the left, away from the other's blade. Tal measured his opponent: Campaneal was nearly as fast as the Keshian assassin, but he more than made up for his slightly slower attack by being far more practised in the longsword. He carried a perfectly balanced weapon and knew how to execute a complex combination of blows, feints and ripostes.

Every attack Tal made was met and answered, and several times it was only Tal's almost supernatural reactions that saved him from losing. Within minutes, both men were panting for breath and drenched in sweat.

The cheering, the urging-on of the combatants, and all the shouted remarks faded, then died away off completely as the contest wore on. At last, the court sat silently, without even the softest murmur or whisper, as all those gathered watched every move the two combatants made. People held their breath and even tried to refrain from blinking, less they miss the sudden resolution that was sure to come.

Tal felt the pressure mount, for Campaneal was easily the finest swordsman he had ever faced. He was cunning and refused to fall into any pattern of moves Tal could discern and, as the moments wore on, he felt his chances of winning slipping away. Tal also felt the need to find the perfect attack, the one that could be slightly 'off' and deliver a killing blow that looked accidental. But as minutes slipped by and fatigue started to creep into arms and legs, Tal realized it would be very unlikely that he would have the opportunity to kill this man, and he might even be denied the pleasure of winning the bout.

Then Tal saw something. He watched the Lieutenant flip his sword as he swung at Tal's offside, then pull the blade around and try to come back from Tal's right side as Tal's blade was moving the other way. Tal had seen that move before.

Minutes dragged by, and for long periods the two opponents moved away from one another, circling and trying to catch their breath as they looked for an opening. Tal decided to take a risk before he was too tired to execute the difficult move.

He started a rather clumsy overhead blow, twisting his wrist so the blow came from over his own left shoulder in a downward arc aimed at Campaneal's right shoulder. Then he slowly turned his wrist, as if attempting a cut beneath Campaneal's elbow at the man's briefly-exposed ribs as he brought his own sword up to block the high attack.

Campaneal saw the opening, and instead of continuing to block high, he thrust his blade forward, attempting to take Tal in the right shoulder.

Tal let his momentum carry him forward, until he was bent over, legs spread wide, his body twisting to the left, the sword on the floor with the point now facing his own right boot. Rather than pull back, he kept going until his right knee touched the floor as Campaneal's sword point jabbed through empty air.

As the startled Lieutenant realized he had missed his mark and started to pull back his blade, Tal twisted his wrist and stabbed upward with the point of his own blade, taking the Lieutenant in the groin.

Campaneal let out a grunt of pain and collapsed to the floor, clutching his groin, as blood seeped through his fingers. Tal stood up and stepped back, while the crowd sat in stunned silence.

It had been a foolish, dangerous move; but it had worked. The crowd exploded into applause and cheering as Tal moved back another step away from his opponent.

The senior master approached and put his hand on Tal's shoulder, signifying that he had won. Tal made a display of crossing to stand over Campaneal and offering him a hand so that he could rise. The Lieutenant lay in agony, his face a contorted mask of pain, and Tal paused, then turned and said, 'Someone should send for a healer. I fear the wound is deeper than I intended.'

Two soldiers in the garb of the Duchy of Olasko hurried to Campaneal's side and attempted to render him aid. At last, the King's healer appeared. He examined the wound quickly, then ordered the Lieutenant carried to a nearby room to be tended.

Servants hurried to clean up the blood on the floor and within minutes everything in the chamber was restored to order.

Tal barely listened to the praise heaped upon him by the King and the Master of the Court. He nodded and smiled when appropriate and accepted their approbation. When the King finally handed him the golden sword, a small replica of the original prize presented to Count Versi Dango two hundred years previously, Tal bowed and spoke a few words of appreciation.

But the entire time he wondered how deep that cut had been.

Pasko escorted him back to the room he had used before. There he found a hot tub of water waiting and he allowed himself the luxury of falling across the bed and letting Pasko pull his boots off.

'I almost lost,' Tal said.

'Yes,' Pasko replied, 'but you didn't. He was wearing you down; you're a fit lad and a strong one, but he's a seasoned soldier and he's had years of campaigns and real wars to toughen him which you haven't. That was his edge. Your edge was your willingness to risk everything on a foolish move. But it worked.'

'Yes, it worked,' said Tal. 'I almost lost because I kept trying to find a way to kill him, and almost too late I realized I had barely enough left to have a chance to win.'

'Well, done is done.' Pasko put the boots down. 'Now, get cleaned up, for there's a gala already underway and you're the guest of honour.'

Tal got into the tub and felt the warmth seep into his muscles. 'To think as a boy I thought the cold lake a treat,' he muttered.

There came a knock at the door. Pasko crossed the room to answer it. He spoke briefly and then opened the door wide. Half a dozen pages entered, carrying clothing fit for a king. The most senior page said, 'His majesty sends you greetings, Squire, and wishes you to accept these garments as a humble token of his appreciation and delight at your victory. His majesty awaits your appearance in the main hall.'

'Thank you,' said Tal, rising and taking a towel from Pasko. 'Tell his majesty I am overwhelmed with gratitude, and I shall be along shortly.'

The pages bowed and departed, and Pasko helped Tal to dress quickly. The clothing was of the finest weave and fit as if Tal's measurements had been taken by a master tailor. 'I wonder if there's another suit somewhere cut to fit Campaneal,' Pasko mused.

'No doubt,' said Tal. 'Are those pearls?'

'Yes,' said Pasko. 'Your doublet is sewn with seed-pearls. This rig is worth almost as much as that dainty little golden sword you won.'

When he had finished dressing, the young victor stood before a rare and costly polished glass mirror and regarded himself. The yellow jacket and black breeches were complemented by a white shirt and red hat. Yet it was a stranger he saw. For a brief instant he didn't recognize his reflection. There was no hint of the mountain boy who had sat shivering upon a chilly peak waiting for his vision. Before him stood a stranger, replete in the costly and most fashionable garb in Roldem, an urbane, educated young man who spoke many languages, played several instruments, could cook, paint, compose verse, and woo ladies of rank. For a bitter moment, Tal wondered if the boy within was lost forever. Then he pushed this dark thought out of his mind, and turned to Pasko. 'Come, we must not keep the King waiting.'

They hurried to the main hall, where the Master of Ceremonies announced his arrival. Tal entered and walked across the hall to stand before the King while the on-lookers applauded enthusiastically.

Next to the Queen stood the Duke of Olasko and when the general compliments were finished, the Duke stepped forward with a slight smile on his lips and said, 'If I might have a moment, young sir.'

Tal allowed the Duke to steer him off a short distance away from the King. Duke Kaspar spoke evenly, his voice a deep and soothing tone, belying the dangerous nature Tal sensed within him. 'Do you have plans now that the contest is over, my young friend?'

Tal said, 'I have some family business I must attend to, but I haven't given much thought to what happens after that, your grace.'

'I'm always seeking men of special talent, young Hawkins, and you strike me as just that. The way you dispatched that Keshian Izmali put you far above most swordsmen, and your defeat of my champion today – well, let's say there may not be another man in Olasko who could stand up to Campaneal.'

'You flatter me, your grace.'

'No,' the Duke said softly. 'Empty flattery is a waste of time. Those who serve me win praise when it's deserved, just as they receive punishment when they fail. I'm pleased to say the rewards far outstrip the punishments in my court, for as I said, I seek exceptional men.' His smile broadened, and he said, 'And women as well.'

The Duke looked past Tal and when Tal turned, he saw a slender woman with golden tresses approach, a small smile upon her lips. Tal's expression remained neutral, as the Duke said, 'My dear, may I present Squire Talwin Hawkins, late of the Kingdom?' To Tal he said, 'Squire, this is my companion, the Lady Rowena of Talsin.'

'My lady,' said Tal with a bow.

'My pleasure, Squire. I was late arriving in the city, but managed to reach the palace in time for the duel. You were magnificent.'

'You praise me too much, Lady,' said Tal.

Turning to the Duke, she said, 'It's a pity about the Lieutenant.'

'Yes, isn't it?' said Kaspar. Then he turned to Tal. 'Ah, you won't have heard, will you? Your blow cut an artery in the groin. It's a tricky thing, which pulls back up into the body when severed. I'm afraid my lieutenant bled to death while they were sending for a healing priest.'

Tal felt his heart stop for a moment, then he said, 'That is indeed regrettable, your grace.'

'You know, it's only the fourth fatality in the history of the tournament, and you're responsible for two of them, in the same day. This afternoon's was certainly justifiable, given the circumstances, but tonight's . . . an unfortunate mishap. It's a murderous wound.'

Tal stiffened, but the Duke added, 'A poor choice of words, my young friend. I watched the bout closely, and your thrust was blind. I don't think you could see where the point was heading. It was clearly an accident.'

'I am very sorry to have cost you a fine officer.' Tal said.

'Well, then,' answered the Duke. 'Make it up to me by coming to Opardum, and take service with me.'

Tal's heart beat faster. 'I'll consider it, your grace. As I said, I have some family business that requires my attention, but once that's finished . . . perhaps.'

'Very good. Now if you'll excuse me,' the Duke said, extending his arm and escorting the Lady Rowena away.

Tal made his way back to where Pasko was waiting, acknowledging a dozen congratulatory remarks on the way. When Pasko saw Tal's face, he said, 'What's wrong?'

'We must leave at and once and find out where Magnus is lurking.' Tal looked around the great hall. 'I'm certain he's out there somewhere.'

'And then?'

'I will tell him I know who sent the assassins to kill me. It was the Duke of Olasko.'

'How do you know?'

'He knew the assassin was an Izmali. Only Magnus knew that for certain, because he had been to Kesh. The only way Olasko could know is if he had hired the man's clan to send him.'

Pasko's expression changed. Then he said, 'I'll find him.'

As he started to step past Tal, he felt the young swordsman's restraining hand on his arm. 'One other thing,' Tal said.

'What?'

'That woman with Olasko.'

'Yes, what about her?'

'It's Alysandra.'

- CHAPTER EIGHTEEN -

Choices

*M*AGNUS PACED.

'I sent word to my father about Alysandra. I'm awaiting a reply.'

'You didn't know she was with the Duke?' asked Talon.

'No,' said Magnus. 'I'm not privy to every detail of every plan my father has in place. All I know is she left the island less than a year after you did.'

'Nobody told me.'

Caleb sat quietly in the corner of Tal's apartment. 'Seemed no reason to, Tal. You'd been given a harsh lesson, but we assumed you'd got over it; besides, many of those who were with you on the island come and go on different missions for Father.'

'So do I assume she's working for . . .' He was about to say

325

'the Conclave', but had been cautioned against referring to it anywhere he might be overheard, and the business with the Duke of Olasko was making him especially cautious. Instead, he said, '. . . for us?'

'If she wasn't,' said Magnus, 'you'd already be dead. Kaspar doesn't know specifics about us, but he knows there is someone out there working against his interests and the interests of those he's allied himself with. If he had a hint you were part of that opposition . . .' He shrugged, leaving the sentence unfinished.

Tal said, 'I could have said something to her without thinking.'

'If you were that untutored,' said Caleb, 'you would never have been permitted to come this far, Tal.' He stood up and walked over to his brother. 'Who's supervising the girl?'

'Mother.'

Caleb shook his head and gave a rueful smile. 'Then anything is possible, and that's why no one told any of us Alysandra was here in the east.' He said to Tal, 'Mother is the least likely to share information. It has a lot to do with her past, but whatever the cause, this isn't the first time she's taken it upon herself to conduct business without even bothering to tell Father.'

Magnus rolled his eyes. 'The fights . . .' Then he said, 'Caleb is right. I'll speak with Mother tonight and see if she'll let me know what Alysandra is doing with the Duke.'

There came a knock at the door downstairs. Pasko indicated that he would see to it, and the others fell quiet. 'Probably an invitation,' Pasko said as he walked out of the room and down the stairs.

'Celebrity brings many new friends,' Tal's tone was dry and he made a face. 'I've had a dozen invitations to supper in the last four hours.'

Pasko returned and handed Tal a note. It bore a seal he had not seen before and Pasko said, 'From the Lady Rowena of Talsin.'

Tal broke the seal and read the note. 'She says that she will depart with the Duke in two days' time and may not have the opportunity to see me, so she sends word. Olasko moves against the High Reaches before the end of summer.'

'He's cutting off the eastern approaches to his army when he invades Farinda,' said Caleb.

'Which means next spring he'll be invading the land of the Orodon,' said Tal. He looked at the message again, then said to the brothers, 'At least this appears to mean Alysandra is still working for your mother.'

Caleb said, 'Apparently.'

'What do you want to do next, Tal?' Magnus asked.

'I thought you'd tell me.'

Magnus leaned on his staff. 'We can't supervise every step of every day for those we put out in the world to work for us. You've been placed here in Roldem to create a name for yourself, to gain access to places of power and influence. We have many such in the Kingdom and almost as many down in Kesh, but we are just now placing our agents in the Eastern Kingdoms.

'But when we decide an agent is ready, we let him start deciding how best to serve our cause.'

'I'd know better how to serve if I understood the cause, Magnus.'

Magnus raised his hands and his lips moved, and for a moment, Tal thought the room went slightly darker. 'No one can see us inside this spell for a minute or two.' He moved to the table and sat down. 'Tal, we are agents for good. I know

327

you've heard that before, and much of what we've visited on you seems to give lie to that, but it is true. There is a lot I still cannot tell you, but now that you have come to this place in our service, here is what you must know.

'The Duke of Olasko has a man serving with him. That man did not come with him to Roldem, which doesn't surprise me. He rarely leaves Opardum these days. It may be that Mother has placed Alysandra in Olasko to influence Kaspar, but more likely she has her there to keep an eye on this man.

'He uses the name Leso Varen, but that is no more his name than any of a dozen others he has used over the years. My father has faced this man before. He is as close to my father's counterpart as the enemy has, for he is a magician of terrible power and subtle craft. He is mad, but he is no man's fool. He's dangerous beyond contemplation and is the true heart of evil behind Kaspar's ambitions.'

Caleb added, 'This is no exaggeration, Tal. The man is evil incarnate.'

Magnus said, 'This much you should also know. We who serve my parents and the others who lead us will see no victory over our enemies in our lifetime or the lifetime of our grand-children's grandchildren.

'We struggle because me must. Evil has an advantage, for it is served by chaos and confusion. It can destroy and ravage, while we must preserve and build. Ours is the more difficult task.'

Caleb said, 'Nakor once told Magnus and me that by its nature, evil is madness, and if you think back to the destruction of your village, you must agree.'

Tal nodded. 'That Kaspar could destroy my people just because of his evil ambitions . . . you're right, it's madness.'

'So, to the point,' said Magnus. 'We will never defeat evil entirely, but we work to stem it, to protect as many innocents from the forces that destroyed everything you knew as a child. To that end, we agreed in council what must be done, but each of us has a different role to play in how we achieve the goals we've established.'

'So the goal is to kill Kaspar?' asked Tal.

'Perhaps,' said Caleb. 'Almost certainly, eventually, but right now we must bide our time and see if we can isolate Leso Varen. If we can somehow, finally, destroy him, we will have set our enemies' cause back . . . centuries.'

Tal said, 'You're now speaking about things that I can't imagine, Caleb. I won't be here centuries from now.'

Magnus said, 'It's a habit learned from those who have far longer lifespans. No, we don't expect you to understand everything, Tal, but if you can imagine some day being a father, what you do now will help secure a safer future for your children.'

Tal was silent for a moment. He had become so estranged from his own history, from who he had been, and become so lost in the role of Tal Hawkins that thinking of any sort of personal life in which he might some day wed and father children had almost no meaning for him. Then he remembered those heady weeks with Alysandra when he had ached to imagine they would be together forever; the girl might have played him false – for whatever reason – and he might hate her for that, but his feelings had been real: he had wanted to wed and be a father. At last he said, 'I understand the point.'

'Good,' said Magnus. 'Now, have you given any thought to Kaspar's offer?'

Tal said, 'I'm wrestling with it. I will almost certainly go to

Opardum and hear him out, listen to what he proposes, but I can't imagine taking service with him.'

'It would put you close, Tal,' said Caleb. 'You could help our cause a great deal if you were to ingratiate yourself with Kaspar, and if you could gain access to Leso Varen.'

'I'm Orosini,' said Tal. 'I may look like a gentleman of Roldem or a Kingdom nobleman, but I am still Orosini.' He touched his cheeks. 'I may not have my clan tattoos, but I am Orosini.'

Caleb said nothing, just looked at Tal and waited for him to continue. Magnus raised an eyebrow, but also kept silent.

'If I give my oath to Kaspar, I will keep it. I cannot give false oath. It is impossible. I cannot serve the Conclave and serve Kaspar at the same time. I understand how Alysandra or others can, but I cannot.' His voice dropped. 'I may be the last of my people, but that is our way, and I will not abandon it.'

'Then you must not,' said Caleb.

'Besides,' said Magnus. 'Kaspar will have the means to determine if someone has a false heart when he swears an oath. Leso Varen might not actually be able to read your mind, as such, but I suspect he'll be able to tell if you're lying.'

'So, then,' Caleb asked Tal. 'What do you propose to do?'

'I told Kaspar I'd come to Opardum after I took care of some family business.'

'What is this family business?' asked Magnus.

With a deep sigh, as if something tormented and angry was being allowed to escape, Tal said, 'Vengeance.'

The man fell backwards, knocking over a table. People nearby scattered, for no one wanted to deal with the obviously enraged young man standing over the moaning form which had just slammed into the table.

He was a broad-shouldered youth, in his early twenties by his appearance, clean shaven and clear-eyed. His hair was long, tied back and pushed under a black cloth, knotted at the back like those worn by Quegan pirates. He was clearly no pirate, for his boots were a horseman's, and his sword was a fine long blade, not a heavy cutlass, but he looked as fearsome as any buccaneer boarding a ship: his anger was obvious for anyone to see.

He looked down at the fallen man, who rubbed his mouth with the back of his hand, and said, 'Where's Raven?'

The man tried to move as if to stand, and Tal kicked his hand away, causing him to fall backwards. 'Where's Raven?' he repeated.

Tal had stayed in Roldem until the Midwinter Festival, then he had travelled to Kendrick's. He had stayed there and relived some of the pleasures he had known before, mostly spending time in the kitchen with Leo concocting new delights. Leo was impressed with the progress the young Talon had made in matters of dining and wine, but he still treated him as if he were an ignorant child in the kitchen.

Except for Leo and his wife, Gibbs and Kendrick, the inn was populated by people unknown to Tal. Meggie was gone, no one knew where, and Gibbs had been surprised when Tal told him Lela was in Krondor. Tal was saddened to hear that Lars had died in a lake, drowned after falling through the ice, earlier that winter.

After this, Tal had come to Latagore, and had found the place much the same as when he and Caleb had visited years before, despite the installation of a new Dominar who was one of Kaspar's lackeys. There seemed to be more city guards, but otherwise people went about their business and the sun shone, and nothing indicated that dark forces were in play.

Tal had asked around discreetly for information on the coming conflicts. There was already fighting in the High Reaches, for Olasko had made his move there, but the mercenary bands who normally flocked to such conflicts were conspicuously absent.

The man on the floor was named Zemos, and he had been willing to talk to Tal for a price, assuming that he was a mercenary looking for employment. Zemos was, according to several barkeepers, a broker of sorts who could find a man a billet with a mercenary band for the right price. But as soon as Raven's name had come up, Zemos had appeared to forget everything he had ever known about the mercenary trade.

Tal had decided to stimulate his memory.

'Still assaulting people, I see,' said a voice from the end of the bar.

Tal glanced over and saw a face which looked vaguely familiar to him, and it took a moment for him to recognize it. 'John Creed,' he said with a nod at last. 'Only when they suddenly forget information I've paid for.'

Zemos said, 'I'll give you back your gold. I thought you were just looking for a billet.'

Creed came to stand beside Tal. 'Forgive me, but I can't say as I recall the name.'

'Tal Hawkins.'

For an instant, there was a flicker of recognition, then he nodded. 'You're getting nowhere fast with this fool.' He gave Zemos a nudge with his boot and said, 'Get up, man.'

When Zemos was upright, Creed said, 'Give the lad back his gold, and don't make promises you can't keep.'

The gold was returned and Zemos hurried from the inn, nursing his split lip. Creed looked around the room. 'Why don't we go for a walk and find a better inn?' Tal nodded and followed him outside. 'What happened to that fellow you were travelling with, the one who tripped you with a chair to prevent me from killing you?' Creed asked, grinning.

'Why?'

'Because I should thank him. I didn't make the connection until just now, but you're the lad who won at the Masters' Court last summer ago, aren't you?'

Tal nodded. 'I didn't realize that sort of news travelled this far.'

'Oh, it does, my young champion.' Creed said, 'So I think maybe your friend deserves my thanks, because if you're that good, you might have done a fair job of carving me up.'

Tal grinned. 'I had a lot of practice between our first meeting and winning that contest. You probably would have skewered me in the first minute.'

'Would have tried, anyway, and that would have been a shame. Anyway, what are you doing looking for that swine Raven?'

'We have business,' said Tal.

'The killing kind, no doubt.'

'Yes.'

They walked down the street and Creed said, 'Rumour is he's got a camp outside of Coastal Watch and is getting ready to move north in a few weeks.'

'He's going to start burning Orodon villages,' said Tal. 'The same business he did years ago with the Orosini.'

'Nasty stuff, that,' said Creed. 'I don't mind fighting for my pay, and I certainly have no problems gutting a man who's holding a sword, but killing women and children is not something I'll be party to. Lot of lads feel the same way, so Raven's paying top price for swords. But there's something strange going on.'

'What?'

'Zemos and the others who usually are eager to get you to a mercenary captain to claim their bounty, well, they're not doing business as usual.'

'What do you mean by that?' They reached another inn and gesturing with his chin, Creed indicated they should enter.

It was quiet inside with barely half a dozen seated at the tables, engaged in low conversation. One nodded at Creed who returned the greeting. He and Tal pulled out chairs and sat down. 'What I mean is that suddenly no one knows where Raven's camp is, or the camps of a couple of other companies who are probably working for Olasko.'

'People know Kaspar is behind this?'

'If you kill people for a living, you sort of want to know who's paying you,' said Creed. 'Raven's not going to get good swords on promises of bounty. Those hill-people and fishermen don't have a lot of valuables to loot. Raven's got to make guarantees, and the men have to know where the gold is coming from, so that they know they won't find promises unmet at the end of a campaign.' He paused and scanned the place for a moment.

'Fact is,' Creel continued after a while, 'some of the lads are hoping the other side shows up and starts recruiting.'

'Other side?'

'The Orodon. They aren't a rich people, but they've got some gold and other goods to trade.'

Tal signalled to the barman to bring them two ales. 'Why would you want to face an invading army?'

'Won't be an army,' said Creed. He leaned forward and put his elbows on the table. His shaggy light brown hair hung down over his eyes, giving him a hooded look. 'It'll be two, maybe three, mercenary companies. They'll be hitting villages all up and down the coast, and counting on surprise and getting in and doing their dirty work before word spreads.'

Tal nodded. That was exactly how they had done it when they wiped out the Orosini villages. He said, 'So if one village is ready for Raven and his men, and can hold them, the entire campaign could fall apart?'

'Exactly. One good fight, and if you win, Kaspar's got to rethink his entire approach to the Orodon. Maybe negotiate with them so they leave his flank alone as he conquers High Reaches. I know he doesn't want to fight on two fronts – no general does.'

Talon nodded. 'What do you need in order to put together a company?'

'Me?' Creed smiled. 'I'm no captain. I can recruit lads, have fifty for you in a week, but I can't lead. Why?'

'I'm thinking that it might be a smart move to put together a company and ride up to the Orodon border and see if we can make a deal.'

'We?'

'Sure. I'm looking for Raven because I mean to have his guts on a stick, and I'd just as soon do it in a stand-up fight as stalk him through the woods, avoiding his mercenaries.'

'You're talking about cracking a very tough nut, boy.'

'I know, but it's a personal matter.'

'Then here's what you need,' said Creed as the barman

brought over two ales. Tal paid him and Creed continued. 'You need enough gold to pay fifty men for three months, against whatever bonuses you offer.'

'I can do that.'

'Then you need supplies, wagons – at least two – and mules. If you can get some engineers, they'll cost you more, but they'll save lives and make it that much more difficult for Raven or the other companies to just ride through.'

'Keep going,' said Tal.

Creed continued to talk and Tal drank in every word, and they continued making plans as the afternoon wore on. At sundown, the innkeeper brought them supper, and the two men continued talking late into the night.

As dawn broke, a column of riders moved slowly down the pass. Creed huddled under the heavy wool cloak he wore and said, 'We're being watched, Tal.'

'I know. For about the last half an hour, since we crested the ridge.'

They had left Latagore a week earlier, forty swordsmen and archers, a company of a dozen engineers, half a dozen porters, and two wagons. They moved slowly, and Tal kept his point and outriders in close, since he did not wish to appear too menacing as they reached the land of the Orodon.

At the frontier between Latagore and Orodon, they had bedded down outside a small inn, and there Tal got as much information as he could on the land on the other side of the mountains. It had taken them three days to reach the meadow where they had slept the night before, then they had broken camp an hour before sunrise.

'If that innkeeper knows what he's talking about,' said Creed, 'the first village should be about five miles ahead.'

'Closer, I think,' said Tal. 'They wouldn't have sentries posted that far from home.'

'Unless they were expecting trouble,' answered Creed.

They continued to ride as the sun rose, and as they reached the foothills Tal felt a stab of familiarity. In the distance he could see the haze that he knew hung over the ocean, but between there and where he now sat, the land reminded him achingly of his home mountains. In the distance he saw a haze. 'Cooking fires,' he murmured. Turning to the men, he said, 'Rest here until I get back, but don't get too comfortable.'

The men muttered and a few made jokes, but as he was their captain and was paying them well, they obeyed. Creed had convinced Tal that he had to take the role of captain, otherwise disruption would ensue. Men who had fought alongside one another, or at other times against each other, didn't feel comfortable taking orders from each other, but from a young captain, obviously a gentleman – that was different, especially when he paid good gold up front.

Talon rode on, moving slowly, not wishing to appear rushed or anxious. He sensed that he was being watched, and as he got closer to the Orodon village he knew there would be more eyes, bows and swords close by.

He saw the stockade. The gate was closed. Although he could see no figures on the wall, he knew they were there, just as there would be many warriors in the woods behind him as he rode into the clearing.

He came within a bowshot of the gate and dismounted. Rather

than speak, he squatted down with most of his weight on his right foot, his left foot extended a little in front for balance, in the fashion of his people. He waited.

Nearly an hour went by before the gate opened and a single man walked out. He appeared to be in his late fifties, for his hair was mainly silver-grey, but his bearing showed he was still a fit and powerful man. He came to stand before Tal and knelt in a similar fashion, saying nothing.

Slowly, in his native language, Tal said, 'I seek a parley with the Orodon.'

'You speak the tongue of the Orosini,' said the man with a heavy accent. 'It is a speech I have not heard since I was a boy.'

'I am Orosini.'

The man smiled. 'You are not. You have no markings.'

'I am Talon of the Silver Hawk, of Village Kulaam, called Kielianapuna, as a boy. My village was destroyed on my naming day, as I waited on Shatana Higo for my name vision. I was left for dead by those who slew my people. I am the last of the Orosini.'

'Who are your people?'

'I am son to Elk's Call at Dawn and Whisper of the Night Wind, grandson to Laughter in his Eyes. My brother was Hand of the Sun, and my sister was called Miliana. All were slain and I am here for vengeance.'

'Why do you come here for vengeance, Talon of the Silver Hawk?'

'Men are coming to burn you out of your villages, to slaughter your people and scatter your ashes to the winds. They are the same men who destroyed the Orosini.'

'I am called Jasquenel,' the old chieftain said. 'In our tongue it means Rock Breaker. If you have cause against our enemy, then you are a friend and welcome. What of the others you've left in the hills?'

'They are my men,' said Tal. 'They obey me and will fight alongside your warriors. I have weapons in the wagon, and I have brought engineers, for if we can turn the invaders away while you warn the other villages, then can you save your people.'

The old man nodded, then stood up. 'You may enter the village. I will send a man who speaks the Common Tongue to summon your men. We shall feast tonight and discuss what is to be done when the invaders come.'

Tal stood up as well. He extended his hand, and the Orodon chieftain gripped his forearm, in the same fashion as the Orosini used to greet one another. Jasquenel said, 'You are welcome, Talon of the Silver Hawk.'

Tal smiled. 'Among my men I am known as Tal Hawkins. They do not know me to be Orosini, and think me a gentleman from the Kingdom of the Isles.'

'Then we shall also call you Tal Hawkins. Come. Let us go inside and talk to the other men of the village.'

Leading his horse, Tal followed the old man. As he entered the stockade, he felt a stab of emotion. It was all so much like his own home, yet there was enough that was different that he knew it wasn't home.

Home would never exist for him again.

• CHAPTER NINETEEN •

Defence

TAL WAITED.

Jasquenel stood beside him on the stockade, watching for the first sign of the invaders. For a countless time Tal reviewed all the things they had done in the last ten days. Runners had been dispatched to all the nearby villages, who in turn sent more runners to villages farther north. If Raven and his company managed to fight their way past this village – Queala – they would be resisted at every other village until they were turned south.

In the ten days since Tal had come here with his company, he had felt sudden bouts of sorrow and yearning, for no place since his boyhood reminded him of his home as Queala did. The Orodon were not the Orosini, but it was clear that at one time they had been close cousins, for many of their ways were Orosini ways. There was a familiar long house where the men gathered in council, and a round house where the women worked. Their dress and customs were much like his own people's, too. But there were differences too, and often it was these differences as much as the similarities that reminded him of how much he had lost.

Queala was larger than his home had been, for it had thirty families living within its walls, compared to the dozen or so in Village Kulaam. There were four common buildings, the men's long house, the women's round house, a community kitchen, and a bathhouse. Smaller homes filled the stockade, with only a central clearing left empty.

He looked back over the wall and down at the clearing in front of the stockade now. The engineers had dug traps and covered them with canvas; then added light coats of earth for camouflage, and wind and a light dusting of snow two nights before had completely hidden them. There was an inconspicuous-looking twig stuck in the ground a hundred yards to the right and fifty yards away from the wall, and a large rock at the edge of the clearing. From the rock to the twig, then the twig to the gate was the safe route to the gate; otherwise one risked being impaled upon a nasty set of stakes.

Tal thought about the defence of the village and realized that he had been fortunate; the village had only two walls that could readily be attacked – the south and the west, where the main gate was. The north wall overlooked a very steep hillside which should be impossible for a significant number of men to climb; two bowmen could easily sit up on the wall there and pick off any attackers foolish enough to try to come at the village that way. The east wall overlooked a gorge that fell away sixty feet below the base of the wall.

Two massive catapults had been assembled by the engineers. These men had fascinated Tal by their ability to walk into the woods with a set of simple tools, some ropes, a few nails and some spikes and emerge three days later with these impressive engines. The leader of the engineers, a man named Gaskle, had said that if they had a good smithy, some iron ore and a forge to work with, they could build him a proper trebuchet in a week, but Tal had observed that he thought the catapults would be sufficient, as they would probably get only one chance to rain rocky death on the attackers before Raven and his men beat a retreat.

Glancing down at the walls, Tal saw where the engineers had reinforced the stockade, against the possibility of the attackers using a ram. It was unlikely they would bring a heavy, covered ram; but they might think to try a large tree bole fitted with wooden wheels, which they could roll down the hill towards the gate. It should bounce off, if it didn't get fouled up in the pits that had been dug along the way. Tal was satisfied that all had been done that could be done.

And so they waited. Sentries two days before had sent word of bands of armed men riding through the southern passes and marshalling in a meadow half a day's ride to the south. Tal glanced skyward. It was now mid-morning, so the attack could come at any time. He looked across to the southern wall. John Creed met his glance and nodded. Nothing in the woods there to see.

Tal pondered. He was no expert on tactics or strategy, having read only a few books on the subject while studying in Salador, and having no practical experience of warfare. The skill he had with a sword was as a duellist, and he did not know if it would serve him on the field of battle. Which was why he had come to rely on John Creed and his experience. There was no rank in the company, but it was clear to all the other men that Creed was the unofficial second-in-command.

At the moment, the thirty men of the company were lounging in doorways or under the overhang at the wall, saving their energy for the coming battle. Tal had sent ten men each to the next two villages up the line, with the engineers, to bolster their defences.

By all rumour more than one company was moving north, probably two; perhaps three. Tal was occasionally visited by the fear that Raven and his gang would raid another village, leaving Queala to a different band and robbing him of the chance for revenge. He tried to put that out of his mind and be content to let fate bring him what it would. Either way, he would save the Orodon from the fate of the Orosini. Eventually, he would find Raven and those others who had wronged his people – if not in this next battle, then the next, or one after that.

'The signal,' said Jasquenel suddenly.

Tal looked where Jasquenel indicated and saw sunlight flash from a mirror. He waited and counted, and when the signal started to repeat, he said, 'Two hundred horsemen coming through the southern pass.' He calculated quickly. 'Less than an hour. Creed!' he shouted.

'Yes, Captain?'

'Two hundred riders coming from the south!'

Creed nodded, knowing that every man in the village had heard that. 'We're ready.'

Tal nodded. They were ready. Orodon warriors were even now making their way along the palisades, holding both their own weapons and the new swords and bows which Tal had brought in one of his two wagons. As Tal had guessed, like his own people, the Orodon harboured a collection of weaponry that ranged from the merely serviceable to the downright useless. Many swords were family treasures which had been handed down from father to son, with an accompanying story as to how each nick and crack had been earned. Heavy with honour, they would fail as soon as the first blow was struck.

And while the Orodon might have good hunting bows; war bows were better. The men of Queala were not stupid; they tossed aside their own short bows for the new composite recurved bows Tal had purchased in Roldem from a trader from Kesh. The first time he had seen one of these was when Rondar had used one, for it was the favourite weapon of the Ashunta when on horseback. Made from laminated bone and wood, cured to curve one way, then curved back on itself, it was a short bow with stunning power. In the hands of a strong bowman, it could punch an arrow through light armour like a crossbow. And Tal had brought crossbows, too. A dozen Orodon women stood in doors in the village, armed with them. Should the gate fail and the riders enter the stockade, they would be ambushed from every building they passed.

The older children were also armed. Any child over the age of ten carried a short blade and the older girls and boys also had been shown how to crank, load and fire the crossbows. Tal had only to explain once, around the first campfire the first night, what had happened to the women and children of his village to convince the men to put aside their tradition of hiding their families in the round house. The Orodon men were loving husbands and fathers: swiftly they helped their wives and children prepare to fight.

Creed left the south wall, crossed the compound, and climbed the ladder to stand next to Tal. 'I wish you'd let me take half a dozen lads into the woods, Captain.'

'I know, and if I hadn't sent twenty men to the other villages, I'd gladly let you.'

'It will break them if we hit 'em in the arse when they're on the verge of being repulsed. I know mercenaries, and while Raven may be a murdering loon, some of his boys will quit if it looks like they're going to be slaughtered. Not all of them think they're invincible.'

'We can harry them from here.'

'Well, I'll say it one more time,' said Creed. 'Those pits that keep them out, they keep us in.' He pointed to where the twig marked the safe route. 'We've got to go there and then over to the rock to get out, and if they've dropped some lads into the pits, they'll see that. Raven can put three bowmen over there –' he indicated a place of relative safety in the trees '– to keep us bottled up while he regroups. If we don't kill at least half his men, it'll be a siege, and it won't take that murderous bastard long to realize it.' Suddenly he paused and sniffed the air. 'Smoke!'

Jasquenel also said, 'Yes! Pitch smoke.'

'They mean to burn us out,' Tal said grimly. 'They fired my village as they came in.' He turned and shouted in Orodon, 'Bowmen! Target the riders with torches first!' Then he repeated the order in the Common Tongue. A general acknowledgement came from the bowmen on the wall. Tal turned to John Creed. 'You'd better get back to the south wall. They're going to hit us here and there, I'm certain.'

Creed nodded and returned to his post. Moments later a

sentry at the southwest corner of the stockade shouted, 'Movement in the trees!' and suddenly horsemen erupted from the woods, racing into the clearing.

'Mark your targets and don't waste arrows!' Creed shouted.

Tal watched in fascination as the riders galloped toward the first line of traps. He searched faces to see if he could spy Raven or any other man who might look like those who had killed his family. But these were just men, and his chest constricted at the thought that some of those responsible for the death of his people might go unpunished. Then the first rider reached the line of traps. For the briefest of moments, Tal wondered if the canvas-and-earth coverings were too sturdy, for the horse's front hooves struck it, and for an instant it held. Then the canvas and twig frame under it collapsed, and the horse went down. A man's scream echoed the horse's as both animal and rider were impaled on sharpened stakes. The riders' momentum was too great for those in the second or third ranks to rein in before they also plunged into the traps. A few lucky ones managed to get their horses to leap over the ditches, landing on solid ground a yard or two beyond the ditch, only to find two strides later that another line of traps had been dug.

As the fourth rank of riders reined in, Tal shouted, 'Catapults!'

The two boys who had been given the responsibility for firing the war engines yanked hard on the lanyards that released the big arms, launching huge baskets of fist-sized rocks into the air. The missiles came crashing down onto a dozen riders, unhorsing many of them, and killing or injuring them all. Tal made a quick count and reckoned that thirty or more riders were down, either too injured to fight, or dead. His men had yet to suffer an injury. He knew that would change. Then he saw Raven. The leader of the marauders emerged from the treeline, calling for his men to regroup. Those nearest the wall were being cut down by archers, and any man with a torch was struck with half a dozen arrows before he could throw his flaming brand. Even with his exceptional sight, Talon couldn't make out Raven's features, but he could imagine that the mercenary captain's face would be set in an enraged mask as he shouted orders to his panic-stricken men. What they had expected to be an easy raid – the burning and destruction of a sleepy village, executed with few casualties – had turned out to be something of a rout in the first five minutes, with nearly a quarter of Raven's men dead or too injured to continue the fight.

Suddenly Tal understood he had been too cautious. Had he let Creed take half a dozen bowmen into the trees behind Raven's position, a flight of arrows at this moment would have broken them. They would be in full flight now instead of regrouping for another assault. Instead, he realized Raven was not going to let the defenders sit comfortably, but was hatching some other plan. He watched men dismounting and disappearing into the woods. Within minutes they could hear the sound of axes, as trees were being felled.

'What now?' Tal called to Creed.

'I think he means to deal with the pits,' said Creed, waving his hand to indicate the pocked ground where the network of pits stood revealed.

Tal glanced around and saw that everyone was still holding their place. He hurried down a ladder, crossed the yard, and climbed up next to Creed. 'You were right about the archers in the woods, so I'll be far more willing to listen to anything you have to say now.'

'I could still get some men over the north wall,' said Creed, 'but surprise is no longer possible. I think we should just sit tight until we see what he's got up his sleeve.'

'What would you do if you were Raven?'

'I'd turn tail and trek back over those mountains to the south, but then I'm not a murderous lunatic who dare not show his master failure. No, I'd be building turtles for my men to use to get close to the wall, and I'd be building ramps to drop over those trenches, and then I'd get some men in close enough to fire the logs of the stockade. Either the gates burn off and I rush the place, or I wait until the defenders come out and take them as they do.'

'How do we deal with these turtles?'

Creed swore. 'If this was a conventional siege, they'd have been made in an engineer's shop; they'd be big things, on wheels, with a ram hidden under a roof, or room for men inside to shelter from arrows. Then they'd have to get close to the gate or down to the wall so they could start excavating at the plinth and collapse it. So we'd pour burning oil over it, or drop hooks on ropes and hike it up with a winch so that it turned over . . .'

'But this isn't a castle and they're not building anything that fancy. What do you think they'll do?'

'They'll construct a shell of sorts in which half a dozen or so men can run along while we bounce arrows off their heads until they can get close enough to the wall to throw something. If they've got the right kind of oil, they can fire a section of the stockade and make a breach.'

Tal glanced back to the boys standing next to the catapults. 'Can you rewind those things?' he called down.

One of the older boys nodded enthusiastically, and shouted, 'I watched them load it!' He grabbed up a long pole and fitted it into a notch in a gear and yelled to the other boys, 'Come on, give me your weight!'

The boys piled on and levered the simple arm of the catapult back to its original position. One of the women in a building nearby ran over to help. Suddenly all the women and children were there, rewinding and setting the catapults, locking down the throwing arm.

'Put anything you can find in there that can do some damage!' shouted Tal. To Creed he said, 'I wished we'd known we'd get a second round off. I'd have ordered more rocks brought inside.'

'No sense worrying about what we might have done,' said Creed. 'Better to worry about what Raven is going to do next.'

'So, when will he make his next move?'

Creed looked around and seemed to be thinking for a long time. Eventually, he said, 'I think he'll wait until nightfall. If he comes at us in darkness we lose some of the advantages we have now. He can get his ramps down and maybe our archers won't be as accurate while he's doing that. Maybe he'll slip a small company over to the east wall and get a few men over while most of his boys are pounding on the west gate.'

Creed's prediction turned out to be apt; throughout the afternoon, the defenders could hear the sound of axes and hammers echoing through the woods, but no attack came. Then at sundown, as the last rays of light were reflected off clouds high above the western horizon, the sounds of building ceased. For long minutes the villagers seemed to be holding their breath. The breeze rustled the branches, and birds chirped their evening song but otherwise all was silent. Then a low rumbling sound, the sound of boots cracking twigs, and the snort of horses could be heard. A moment later a long wooden bridge emerged from the trees, and after that came the turtle. It looked like a flat boat with square ends, about twenty feet long, and the men who carried it walked in a line, each man with his hands above his head lifting it overhead. Tal grabbed his bow, though he judged the distance too far for a decent shot in this fading light. Then the men carrying the turtle turned beneath the wooden shell to face the wall and started walking forward, those with the wooden bridge falling in behind.

'Will arrows have any effect?' Tal asked Creed.

'That's fresh-cut wood; damn close to green. If we had some naphtha or oil that would stick and burn, maybe, but . . .' Creed shrugged. 'We might get it to char in places, but it won't catch fire.'

An arrow whistled off the wall on the other side of the gate, striking the ground a few yards in front of the advancing turtle. Tal cried, 'Save the arrows!' Then he turned back to Creed. 'I have a plan,' he said.

'Good,' said Creed. 'I always like it when a captain has a plan; makes getting killed a lot less random.'

'Take some men and pull down the bracing on the gate.'

Creed's forehead furrowed. 'You want the gate to fail?'

'At the right time.'

Creed nodded. He turned and shouted to a group of men nearby, 'Follow me!'

They quickly set to dismantling a series of braces and rein-forcing timbers that had been put in place to make the gate that much harder to breech. Talon looked from the men frantically pulling away the supports to the turtle advancing across the ground outside. It reached the first line of pits and halted, the men underneath waiting as those behind brought forward the bridge.

'Arrows!' Tal shouted.

Bowmen along the ramparts arced arrows high into the darkening sky, most landing harmlessly, though a shout and a scream suggested that some damage had been done. Tal didn't think he was going to have any success with his archers, but he knew Raven would think it suspicious if the defenders didn't harass the attackers while they bridged the first trench.

Raven's men grunted with the exertion as they quickly ran the bridge out over the trench. The men in the turtle backed up, then moved in file until they were end-on to the bridge and quickly hurried across the first trench. When they reached the edge of the second, they turned again, providing as much cover as they could, and a second bridge emerged from the woods.

Tal could see Raven exhorting his men in the failing light, though he couldn't hear exactly what he said. Torches were lit within the stockade, and Tal refined his idea. He turned and shouted down to Jasquenel's son, a youth named Tansa, 'Pile as much flammable material as you can around the catapults, and be ready to fire them when I give you the signal.' The young man didn't hesitate, but ran off to pass the word. Within moments, women, children, and a few older men were carrying personal items from the various log buildings and piling them around the catapult.

Creed shouted up, 'We've finished!'

'Stay there,' Tal said. He hurried down the ladder. 'Here's what I want you to do. Take a dozen of your men and horses and hold them back at the east wall. Be ready to ride. I want your other men behind that building there –' he pointed to the first building on the right, as one entered the gate '– out of sight when the gates come down. I want Raven to think he's got a rout in progress, and I pray he comes riding in mad as hell and doesn't realize it's not just a bunch of Orodon hillmen he's facing.'

'What are you going to do?'

'I'm going to be on the wall with as many of the Orodon who will go up there with me.'

'Man, you're going to burn.'

'Not if I get off in time.'

Creed shrugged. 'Well, what's the signal?'

'No chance of a signal from me. It's going to be too noisy. Tell whoever you think is best able to lead to just start shooting from up on the south wall when most of Raven's company is inside the compound, then yell down to the men you've got behind that building to rush them from the rear. When you think it's right, come riding hard and we'll roll them up.'

'Captain, it's crazy. We've only got a dozen men and Raven's got a hundred and twenty or more.'

'The odds will be less by the time you hit them. And he won't know how many riders you've got. Try to make as much noise as you can: he won't be able to see much with all the smoke.'

'Smoke?'

Tal pointed to where the villagers were busy putting everything that could burn around the catapults.

Creed shook his head. 'Man comes to burn this place to the ground and you're going to do it for him?'

Tal laughed. 'These people can always rebuild, but they've got to be alive to do it.' He thought for a moment. He had thirty mercenary fighters and another twenty-five adult Orodon warriors, as well as some boys who could be pressed into service, as well as about thirty fit women who would fight if it came down to it. 'If I can knock Raven's force down below seventy by the time you come riding out, we can throw equal numbers at them.'

'It'll be a slaughter,' said Creed.

'These people are fighting for their lives, John. What are Raven's men fighting for?'

'Gold, but they're hard, practised men, and . . .' Creed shook his head in resignation. 'You're the captain, and I'm damned if I have a better plan, so we'll do it your way.'

A shout from the wall told Tal the second bridge was across the second trench. He said, 'Pick your best dozen horsemen, John, and may the gods be with us all.' Then he turned and ran to the ladder, climbed quickly to the wall, and started passing the word to the men as to what he wanted next.

The mercenaries all left, some going to the south wall, others moving behind the building as ordered. To Jasquenel, Tal said, 'I need brave men who will stay here with me and shoot arrows at Raven's men once they're inside the compound.'

'All of our men will stay if you wish.'

'I need just ten,' said Tal. 'Five on this side of the gate with me, and five more on the other side. Make it your best hunters. But they must make the invaders think there are many more of us on the walls, so tell them to yell, and move back and forth.'

'It will be done.'

'Tell the others to go to that building below us –' he pointed to the building opposite the one where Creed was placing the eighteen mercenaries '– and wait behind it. When you see the men I brought attack from behind that building over there, attack the enemy with everyone who can fight.' He paused. 'And tell the women to start screaming, as if they are watching their children being murdered, when I set the fire over there.' He pointed to the catapults. 'Make it sound as if all is lost, but I want them all armed, and ready to defend the children.'

'They will be, Talon of the Silver Hawk,' said Jasquenel with a bow of his head. 'No matter what occurs this night, the Orodon will sing your name, Last of the Orosini.'

Tal gripped his arm and said, 'May our ancestors watch us and smile upon us tonight.'

'May it be so,' replied the old chieftain, and he started passing orders.

Looking down from his vantage, Tal saw the turtle was now almost up to the wall. Arrows stuck out of the wood like quills on a porcupine, while others bounced off harmlessly. He shouted, 'Save your arrows!'

The turtle remained below the gate for nearly half an hour. Tal wondered what they were doing, and then the men below started to withdraw. Glancing down, he saw something nestled against the gate, though in the darkness, he couldn't make out what it was. He hurried down and made his way through the village to where Creed waited, and described what he had seen.

'Skins full of something nasty, something that burns,' Creed said. 'Watch out for their bowmen lighting arrows to fire it off.'

Tal nodded. 'Thanks. Good luck.' He ran back and reached the wall just as the archers standing in front of Raven and his captains started to light their arrows. Tal drew his own bow and sighted. If they were close enough to strike the gate, they were close enough to be targets. As soon as the first fire-arrow was loosed, Tal shot his own arrow. An archer screamed, then Tal was drawing arrows and nocking them as quickly as possible. Five of Raven's archers were wounded or killed – he didn't know which – before enough arrows struck the bags of oil at the base of the gate to ignite them.

As Creed had predicted, it was something nasty, a foul-smelling oil that burned with a very intense heat. Black smoke rose up and threatened to choke Tal and the others on the wall, but they held their places. Blinking away tears from the smoke, Tal waited.

For ten minutes the gate burned, and Tal crouched low behind the upper part of the stockade wall. He heard timbers creaking as the heat washed over him in waves, and knew that the binding which held the logs together would soon part, and then the gate would disintegrate.

Moments later, the logs fell and the gate lay open. In the distance, Tal heard a voice shout and then the pounding of horses' hooves preceded a hundred men charging in file towards the first bridge.

Tal raised his bow. 'Get ready!' he commanded, and he waited for the first rider to get close enough for him to fire.

• CHAPTER TWENTY •

Battle

*T*AL AIMED.

The first rider within range flew backwards from his saddle as another archer got in a lucky shot. Tal followed an instant later and one of Raven's mercenaries screamed as he was also lifted out of his saddle.

Tal turned and shouted down to the boys by the catapults, 'Fire!'

The lads holding the lanyards pulled hard, and rocks, pottery, broken furniture, and even cooking utensils were hurled at the enemy.

'Burn it!'

Torches were thrust into rags soaked in oil so that black smoke rose from the catapults as the boys ran to their designated locations. The older ones picked up the bows that had been left for them and got ready to attempt to take out any rider who might get within range.

Tal turned his attention back to the attackers and started firing. He struck at least two more before the column raced into the open grounds in the centre of the village. Smoke from the gate choked the night air, and the fire from the catapults suddenly illuminated the enemy.

Tal shouted to a woman down below, 'Tell the others to start the screaming!'

She complied and instantly the air was filled with the sounds of terror, the women screeching and wailing as if their babies were being butchered before their very eyes.

The riders who cleared the gate looked around in confusion, momentarily disorientated. They could hear the screaming, but there were no women in sight, and no men on the ground attacking them. Instead they were being peppered with arrows by the men on the wall. Soon, raiders were falling on all sides.

'Dismount!' shouted one man, leaping from his horse to crouch behind its neck. 'They're up on the walls!' He pointed.

Tal and the others loosed their arrows as fast as they could, keeping the riders pinned down. In the Orodon language Tal cried, 'Stay here and keep shooting!'

Ignoring the ladder, he jumped onto the roof of a nearby building. Then with another leap, he moved onto the eaves of the building and threw himself at the nearest raider who remained in the saddle, pulling the man down and drawing his sword as he rolled to his feet. The raider already had his sword out, having managed to hang on to it, but he died before he realized where his opponent stood.

Tal was now in the middle of a milling band of more than a hundred men, all attempting to hold onto horses made frantic by the smoke, the cries of dying men, and the constant sound of arrows speeding past them. Occasionally an arrow would strike a horse, causing it to rear or kick, and then the animals nearby would panic and try to pull away. More than one raider was suddenly yanked off his feet, or dragged a dozen yards by a maddened horse.

Tal dodged under the necks of horses, killing any man he came within a sword's length of. Six men were on the ground dead or dying before the raiders realized that an enemy was in their midst. Just as men started shouting orders, John Creed unleashed his attack.

Creed's men raced out from behind the building where they had been hiding, and a moment later Jasquenel and his warriors attacked from the other side. The raiders still had superior numbers but they were in turmoil while Tal's forces had both a purpose and goal.

For a moment there seemed to be a balance, as the outnumbered defenders held the attackers at bay, while Tal moved among the raiders like death incarnate, killing with bloody efficiency. His opponents would see him for a moment, then he would vanish behind a rearing horse only to be seen a moment later leaping over the body of a fallen comrade.

But the enemy began to organize themselves, and soon the Orodon and mercenary ambush was repulsed. Tal shouted, 'Keep attacking!' in the Orodon language, then repeated the command in the Common Tongue.

Horses were running through the smoke, between the buildings and back out of the gate, and the conflict began to resolve itself. Tal found himself suddenly surrounded by six men, and at that moment he felt fated to die.

Then the man directly in front of him was struck by an arrow through the neck, and the one beside him went wide-eyed as he was struck from behind by John Creed's blade. Tal spun and slashed out with all his strength, taking a man's head completely off his shoulders, then carrying the blow through to strike the shoulder of the man next to him.

Then the dozen riders at the rear of the village attacked.

Raiders turned to see horsemen emerging from the smoke, shouting and bearing down on them, and a number of the enemy turned to run. More followed, and suddenly it was a rout.

Those raiders who could, mounted horses and sped back across the clearing towards the trees, while others fled on foot. Many were slain by the archers who had stayed up on the wall despite the dangerous proximity of the burning gate and the choking smoke.

Tal shouted, 'Hold!'

The Orodon and mercenary riders reined in and Tal cried, 'We don't want to get scattered out there in the dark! We could lose everything we've won.'

The Orodon began to cheer. Then people started to deal with the fires, fetching water from the village well, and attacking smaller fires with blankets or kicking earth onto them.

For a full minute the people celebrated with backslapping, congratulations, and a great sense of triumph, although soon chance-fallen comrades would be discovered in other parts of the village, or beneath the wall. Tal was about to tell the men to search for wounded and the dead who might be out of sight when a shout came from the wall above. 'They've stopped!'

Tal hurried to the gate, which was now a smoking pile of embers on either side of a gap in the wall, and looked into the distance. The fire behind him had blinded him to the night, so it took a full minute for his vision to adjust so that he could properly see what was taking place across the clearing.

Raven was rallying his forces!

Tal could not afford to hesitate. 'Everyone fights!' he shouted. 'They're coming back.' To the few remaining bowmen he shouted, 'Up on the walls! Pick your targets carefully.' Placing his left hand on Jasquenel's shoulder, he said, 'Tell the older children to get the little ones out into the woods now, but the women stay and fight if they're able.'

Creed said, 'Your eyes are better than mine. All I see is some movement.'

The fire behind them illuminated half the distance between the gate and the edge of the clearing, and most of the men near Tal could see only a confused blur. 'They're coming,' he observed. 'Most are on foot, but I think he's got a dozen horses moving out there somewhere.' Then he yelled, 'We stand here!'

'Well, I always prefer a stand-up fight to a running battle or a siege,' Creed said. Lowering his voice, he asked, 'How many?'

'More than us,' Tal replied.

'Well, wouldn't be the first time.'

Tal hurried to what was left of the gate, blinking away tears from the acrid smoke, and stared into the gloom once more.

As shapes began to loom up out of the darkness, Tal saw that Raven had bullied his men back into some semblance of order. They advanced in three lines, about twenty men abreast, with the first rank holding shields in front of them. The second rank had every pole arm weapon they possessed – halberds to pull riders from horses, spears; even two lances had been pressed into service. The third line was composed of archers.

To the men on the wall, Tal shouted: 'Ignore the men in front. Kill their archers if you can!'

Creed squinted. 'He's ready for the cavalry to charge.'

Tal nodded. 'Too bad we can't oblige him. He doesn't know our cavalry consisted of a dozen men who are now standing here.'

Two dozen children, the oldest carrying the very youngest, ran past, darting to the left at the gate, hugging the wall and heading south into the woods.

The women came out, many bearing weapons which had once belonged to Raven's men. Tal directed them into the buildings on the right and left, telling them to fall on the attackers from behind once the archers came into the stockade.

Tal moved his forces back as close to the burning catapults as they could go. The flames had diminished, but there was still enough heat to discourage anyone from approaching any closer. They would be silhouettes against the flames, while Raven's men would be revealed by the light once they entered the compound.

As the attackers advanced to the first bridge, those in the first rank started racing across in pairs, holding their shields high to protect themselves from archers. The expected fusillade of arrows didn't materialize as those on the walls waited for Raven's archers to come into range.

'Get ready!' Tal shouted, and suddenly the first line of raiders charged. 'Hold your ground!'

Bellowing their war-cries, the twenty men in the first rank ran into the compound, and battle was joined. Tal wished he had spent more time practising against an opponent with a shield when he had trained in Salador, for while he could quickly best most swordsmen on the duelling floor of the Masters' Court, a man with a shield was a rather more difficult proposition.

The sound of bow strings snapping told Tal that the archers on both sides were busy. He heard shouts and screams of pain nearby, and guessed that Raven's archers were shooting at the enemy on the ground, ignoring the half a dozen bowmen who were firing at them. He hoped his own archers could diminish the number out there quickly.

Tal slashed and thrust as frantically as he had ever done in his life, trying to protect those on either side of him as well as to defend himself. Raiders fell, only to be replaced by other raiders.

Time seemed to slow as Tal laid about him, striking blows and blocking them with almost no thought, letting his swordsman's instincts take over. Part of his mind tried to apprehend the chaos around him, but he just didn't seem able to make sense of what was happening.

A big mercenary with a scar shouted in rage and leapt at him, bashing him in the face with his shield. Tal reeled backwards and fell, feeling sudden pain in his back. He rolled to his right as he realized he had fallen upon a smouldering hunk of wood, still red hot, and had been burned on his left shoulder blade. He flipped up onto his feet, his sword at the ready, and saw the scar-faced mercenary lying on his stomach, John Creed pulling his sword from the man's side. 'John!' shouted Tal, and the mercenary ducked and turned just in time to avoid another raider's blade.

Tal pushed forward between Creed and an Orodon warrior

and killed the man who had almost taken Creed by surprise.

Then he was once more assailed by the sounds of battle – metal clanging, grunts of exertion, cries of pain and frustration, curses and inarticulate shouts of anger. The air was thick with the reek of blood, faeces, urine, smoke, and sweat.

Then the madness seemed to double as the Orodon women ran out of their hiding-places, falling onto the enemy archers as they entered the compound. The archers were forced to drop their bows and draw their swords, and in that moment the women seized the advantage. Ignoring their lack in weapons skill, they hurled themselves at the archers, swarming down a half dozen of them who died from the thrusts of daggers, kitchen knives, pokers or whatever else came to hand. One woman dispatched a raider with a bone knitting needle driven into his eye. She clawed his belt-knife from his fingers, and turned to leap upon another raider.

The balance turned. Tal stepped back and for a moment saw everything as if it were a still painting, and he were studying it in detail. Four Orodon bowmen still survived and they were firing down from the battlements, taking care to pick off raiders who were at the edges of the conflict. The core of Raven's men wavered, held at bay by Tal's line while those behind were being swarmed by the women. The villagers had the advantage in numbers for the first time. Behind all of this, Tal saw something that made his eyes widen. Two of the boys sent with the younger children into the woods had returned, calmly picked up bows dropped by the archers and were now shooting arrows into the backs of the men engaged in grappling with the women.

Tal sensed that this was the moment he had been waiting for. 'Charge them!' he shouted, and leapt into the fray.

He killed two men with a side-to-side attack, and suddenly the raiders were attempting to flee. 'Kill them all!' he shouted, as much to frighten the invaders as to release all the anger harboured against these men since the death of his own people.

Hacking downward, he severed the hand from a man about to strike out at a woman who was on top of another enemy. The raider stared in disbelief for an instant as blood fountained from his severed forearm, then shock and pain struck him and he fell to his knees, clutching his wounded arm. Tal cut him across the base of his neck with a quick flick of his blade, and the man collapsed like a wet rag-doll, all the life drained out of him in a moment.

Tal kicked hard against the back of the leg of a man who turned away from him, causing him to stumble, throwing him off-balance and forcing him to drop his shield, which allowed an Orodon warrior an opening in which to kill him.

For a moment, Tal was almost overwhelmed by three raiders who all turned to confront him at once so that he had to furiously parry three blows in blinding succession; but then the man on his left was struck from behind, the man on his right took an arrow in the shoulder, and once he faced the man in the centre, Tal quickly dispatched him.

Dodging through the mêlée, he struck at two more men, missing one and turning himself around for an instant. He started to move to his left, for he had overbalanced and had an enemy behind him.

Detecting movement out of the corner of his left eye, he turned. Something exploded in his face and the world turned a brilliant flash of yellow, then red. Then everything went dark.

*　*　*

Tal came back to consciousness as water was poured over his face. He blinked and found John Creed kneeling over him, a ladle of water in his hand. The sounds of battle were absent. There was shouting, and some other noise, but no clash of arms, screams, or swearing.

'What happened?' he asked, trying to sit up. His head swam from the exertion.

'Easy,' said Creed as an Orodon woman helped Tal to sit up. 'You got knocked out by the backswing of a sword. The bloke who brained you was rearing back to hit me. Caught you with the flat, else you'd be sitting up in Lims Kragma's hall.'

At mention of the ill-fated deity, the Orodon woman said a word of prayer to appease the dark goddess.

'How long was I out?'

'Only a few minutes,' said Creed, helping Tal to his feet. 'Steady.'

Tal nodded and put his hand to his forehead. He could feel the bump rising and the tenderness told him he was indeed lucky to be alive. 'I'd rather be lucky than good,' he said, thinking of Pasko for the first time in months. He glanced around, 'It's over?'

'This time they broke for real. Most of the ones here threw down their weapons and begged for quarter. The rest broke outside the gate and were shot down by archers. A few made it to the trees and got away.'

'Raven?'

'He's riding south, I suspect, as fast as his horse can carry him.'

Tal looked around and details began to resolve themselves. A dozen enemies were on their knees, their hands tied behind their backs. The raiders' dead were being carried to a place near the gate and stacked like cordwood.

Several women were in tears, having found their husbands dead, and more than one man wept for a dead wife.

Jasquenel approached reverently. 'You have saved my people, Talon of the Silver Hawk.'

He spoke the Orodon language, so that John Creed didn't understand it, but he could sense the gratitude in the man's voice.

'I helped to avenge my people,' Tal answered in the Orosini language. Then in the Common Tongue he said, 'I need a horse.'

'It will be done,' said Jasquenel. He shouted to a boy to fetch Tal a mount.

'What are you doing?' asked Creed.

'Going after Raven,' said Tal.

'You've been addled by that blow to the head. It's night, he'll have half an hour's start on you by the time you get out of here, and he's probably got some men riding with him.'

Tal nodded. 'I know, but I can track him.'

'Track him? At night in these mountains?'

Jasquenel looked at Creed. 'If he says he can track him, he can.'

'Should I go with you?' John Creed asked.

'No. You'll only slow me down.' Tal placed his hand on Creed's shoulder. 'Thank you for everything, John. I would not have been able to help these people without your guidance.'

'You're welcome, Tal. You have the makings of a fair captain. If you decide you'd like to run a company again, let me know. I'll always be willing to serve with a man who's not afraid to be in the van.'

'My mercenary days are over. This was a one-time thing. In the baggage wagon you'll find a small bag of gold coins. Divide it among the men as you see fit and keep some for yourself. Play captain long enough to get the lads back to Latagore, OK?'

'I can do that.' Creed motioned to the dozen prisoners. 'What do we do with them?'

'What do you normally do when opposing mercenaries surrender?'

'If it's up to us, we cut them loose with a parole they won't fight against us, but usually it's up to our employers.'

Tal turned to Jasquenel. 'These are the men who slew my people. They would have burned your homes and murdered your women and children without mercy. You decide.'

Jasquenel didn't hesitate. He simply looked at the warriors who guarded the prisoners and said, 'Kill them.'

Before the prisoners could attempt to stand, each man had his head yanked back and his throat cut.

Jasquenel looked at Creed and Tal and declared, 'It is just. They get mercy as they gave it.'

Creed looked uncomfortable, but he nodded. 'Not a lot of sentiment for Raven's crew out there, but some of the boys won't like it. We'd best be for the south come first light.'

The horse arrived and Tal said, 'I need a full waterskin.'

A woman ran to her hut and returned a moment later with a full skin. She also held up a bundle. 'Food, for the chase.'

Tal nodded. He gathered up his weapons – his sword and bow – and retrieved a full quiver of arrows. He waved, then put his heels to his horse's flanks, and headed out of the gate and into the night.

• CHAPTER TWENTY-ONE •

Hunt

*T*AL HALTED.

He had pushed his horse through the night and let the animal have a short break. Since leaving the village of Queala he had dismounted three times to ensure that he wasn't losing Raven's trail.

As he had suspected, Raven chose speed over stealth and kept to the main trail south, the most direct route to the city of Coastal Watch. Tal looked to the east, where the rapidly approaching sun had turned the sky steel-grey, and knew that dawn was less than minutes away. He guessed that Raven would make camp and set up a sentry and rest before moving on, probably at mid-day. At least that's what Tal would do if he thought no one was following him.

He decided to take a short rest himself; then he would start down the trail slowly, looking for sentries or ambushes. He found a small, grassy clearing, less than two hundred yards across and perhaps twice that long, unsaddled the horse and staked her out with enough room to graze. Then he used the saddle for a pillow and lay down under a tree.

He monitored the position of the sun, then closed his eyes and fell into an exhausted sleep.

Two hours later, as he had planned, he awoke. The sun beat down with unexpected intensity for this time of the year. Tal could feel the air suck the moisture out of his skin even before perspiration could form. It would be hot and dry for days, if these mountains were anything like his homeland.

He saddled his horse and set off down the trail. After a while, he found a small brook and let the horse drink at it while he refilled his waterskin. Then he continued on. Half an hour later, he smelled campfire smoke.

Tal dismounted, tethered his horse, and set off on foot. Moving through the trees just a few yards off the trail, the going was slow, but he knew he would be far less likely to be seen as he overtook his quarry.

Quickly and quietly, he wended his way through the trees, stopping to listen every few hundred feet. The fourth time he paused, he smelled horse dung and could just make out the faint sounds of horses moving around and cropping grass.

Slowly, he made his way through the trees, each cautious step bringing him closer to his enemies. In the distance he saw that the tree-cover was thinning and he anticipated a small meadow or clearing ahead where Raven and his surviving riders would most likely be resting.

He moved cautiously from one tree to the next, his bow

clutched in his left hand, an arrow held alongside the bow, so that he could draw and shoot in an instant. Every nerve was drawn taut as he expected the raiders to sound an alarm at any moment. At last he could see the horses, staked out in a picket line a short distance from the trees, near a small brook that bubbled down a narrow dale. The horses lifted their heads as he neared, so he paused and waited until they returned to their grazing.

A fire had been allowed to burn out, but the smoky smell still hung over the area. Five figures lay near the cold campfire site, while six horses grazed. Tal glanced around, trying to find the sentry.

He crept along just inside the trees, the thick boles hiding him from view. He saw a flicker of motion near the point at which the path entered the little dale, and he froze.

Someone was standing so close to a tree that he was all but invisible in the dark shadows cast by the branches overhead. Tal knew that he must be tired, for otherwise he would surely have spotted the man critical seconds earlier. He took a deep breath, and crept forward.

The sentry was watching the trail, his back to Tal. Tal glanced back towards the camp and saw that the other five figures remained still.

He considered his options. He could kill the sentry, but could he do it silently? Slowly, he nocked his arrow and drew the bowstring. The sentry leaned against the tree, but Tal waited.

Then the sentry stretched, flexing his shoulders, and Tal let fly the arrow. The shaft struck the man at the base of the neck, and he went down without uttering a sound. But he hit the ground with enough of a thud that one of the horses shied, whinnying. As soon as the scent of blood reached them, the other horses also looked to where the body had fallen.

Two of the mercenaries were light sleepers: they were up with weapons drawn in seconds. 'Garth!' one shouted. 'What is it?'

Tal assumed that was the name of the man he killed, so he retreated deeper into the woods. As he lost sight of the camp, he heard a man shout, 'Raven!'

Tal hurried, dodging through the woods as he heard Raven's voice clearly for the first time. 'Fan out! Find him!'

Tal knew he couldn't stand and fight. He was too fatigued and not thinking clearly. He had missed an opportunity to kill the two men who were awake, and perhaps finish off the other three before they could have got to cover. He had made a mistake and it could cost him his life.

He heard movement behind him and knew that at least one of the raiders was able to track. He saw an outcropping of rock, a ridge that ran for a hundred yards before it rose to be too high to climb, and he leapt up onto it. As if walking a tightrope, he hurried along it as fast as he could, then where the rock became impassable, he jumped down and took cover.

He drew another arrow and waited.

Whoever was tracking him was good, he was forced to admit after a few minutes of waiting. He heard nothing and saw nothing.

He continued to wait.

After a few more minutes had passed, something changed. It was difficult to assess exactly what it was, but one moment the noises in the woods – the air rustling through the branches barely more audible than a whisper, the fall of leaves and needles – changed.

Tal knew it wasn't important to understand what the change

was, only that it meant he was not alone. He hunkered down behind the outcropping of rock and sniffed the air, looked for shadows that didn't belong, listened for anything that would reveal the whereabouts of his pursuer.

Time seemed to drag past, but Tal knew that whoever was behind him was playing the same game, waiting for him to make a mistake.

There came the faintest noise, the tiny grinding of a boot sole against rock, and Tal sprang up and whirled about. For a brief moment, his enemy's face was in his sights. Time stood still while Tal ordered his fingers to release his arrow, and as he did so, he was able to take in details he would not have been able to imagine before this moment. The man's hair was black, dusty from having rolled on the ground at one point, perhaps fearing another arrow shot after Tal had killed the sentry. He was dark-skinned, and was perhaps Keshian in ancestry, for his eyes were almost black. There was a slight flicker of recognition in those eyes: a mix of fear and resignation, as the arrow left Tal's bow. The man's muscles began to tense, as if he was about to cry out or try to move, but before whatever act he had begun could complete itself, the arrow struck him through the throat.

The man's eyes widened in shock, and then the light in them went out before he crumpled and fell away out of Tal's sight.

Tal scrambled over the rocks and quickly examined the man. He carried only his weapons. Tal kept his own bow, but added the tracker's arrows to his supply.

He glanced around to see if any of the other raiders might be close by, but he saw and heard nothing.

Leaving the dead man for the carrion-eaters, Tal hurried away.

Now there were only four left.

*   *   *

Tal slept. He had found a small notch cut by a stream and there he had left his horse tied. It would take horrible luck or an excellent tracker to find him. Tal trusted to luck: he had killed their best tracker, he was certain.

Besides, he suspected Raven would wait only for an hour or two before gathering up his remaining three companions and fleeing south. For all the raiders' captain knew, Tal had been an advanced scout and two dozen Orodon warriors might be riding fast to overtake him.

He had rummaged through the bag of food given him the night before and found hard cheese, bread almost as hard as the cheese, and some dried fruit. Nourishing if lacking flavour. He ate it all, knowing that saving food now would be a mistake. He could pass out from hunger after he had killed Raven.

He had rolled up as best he could under an overhanging rock, ignoring the damp and cold, determined for rest for a few hours. In his sleep he dreamed, and in that dream he was on top of the mountain peak of Shatana Higo again, waiting for his vision, filled with anticipation for his coming manhood ceremony. When he awoke, he rose and made ready to begin the chase again, even though he was still tired to his bones. The cold had got into his joints and he had to move around to force some warmth back into his body. He gauged it was less than two hours to sunset, and knew he must have slept for almost three hours.

He had given Raven a lead, but he was sure he could make it up. It would take the raiders three more days of hard riding to reach the flatlands on the road to Coastal Watch. Tal knew if he could find forage along the way and keep his strength up, he would have them before they reached the city.

And if it was necessary for him to enter the city and search them out there, he would.

Tal saddled his tired horse and moved off down the edge of the stream, until he could ride up the bank and head across a clearing for the trail. He turned south on the trail and set off at a slow walk. He knew where Raven's last camp was, and he was almost certain Raven wouldn't still be there, so there was no need to hurry at present. He let the horse warm up at a walk for a few minutes, then urged her into a comfortable canter.

As he neared Raven's camp, he took the horse inside the trees and dismounted. Although he would be shocked if Raven had stayed there, he decided he'd rather be shocked than dead.

He quickly covered the ground to where he had killed the sentry and found the man still lying where he had fallen. Tal knelt over him but could see nothing to provide a hint as to his identity. Another nameless soldier of fortune hired to kill for pay. Tal checked to see what he might be carrying with him and found that only a dagger in his belt remained. His purse had been cut from his belt – what use would gold be to the dead?

Tal walked to the clearing and looked around. The campfire remained where he remembered, but nothing else had been left behind. They had taken the extra horses, which was logical. Raven wouldn't risk being hunted down just because a steed had gone lame.

Tal looked at their tracks and saw they had not even bothered to disguise their choice: back on the trail to the south.

Tal hurried back to his own horse and mounted, then set off again in pursuit.

The day was ending, and the sounds were changing, as they always did when the diurnal denizens of the mountains gave way to the nocturnal. Tal knew this was when both worlds overlapped, when hunters of the night stirred early and occasionally preyed on day's creatures who were slow to find safe haven.

Tal looked down the trail and tried to anticipate what Raven would do next. After the surprise and losing two men, Tal doubted he would be careless enough to camp out in the open and post only a single watch. He would be holed up somewhere – a cave or under an overhang of rock – keeping a cold camp, and he'd have two men awake at all times.

At sundown, Tal picked up their trail again, and he followed it until darkness fell completely. He found as hospitable a place as he could in which to wait out the night, knowing that Raven was at least as uncomfortable as he was.

He awoke a little before sunrise, and tried to warm up by moving his arms and legs. His neck and back were stiff, and his nose ran. He knew he was becoming sick from fatigue and hunger. He had seen nothing to eat since leaving the village. Knowing that lack of water was an even bigger threat than going hungry for a few days, Tal drank what was left in the waterskin, then set out looking to replenish it.

He studied the contours of the land and followed a downslope until he reached one of the plentiful streams that existed in these mountains. To his relief, a stand of blackberry bushes lined the banks, and he set to with a will. Most of the berries were not yet ripe, but the few that were provided him with enough of a repast to boost his spirits and hold off hunger fatigue for a while longer. He spent an hour filling his empty food pack with ripe berries.

Still hungry, but feeling much better for the food and water, Tal set off after his quarry.

By mid-morning, Tal felt something was wrong. From the distance between hoof-prints, he could tell Raven and his men were not in a hurry. Something gnawed at him as he looked down at the tracks.

He had passed a pile of horse dung half an hour back and it was not yet dry; so he must be a very short time behind Raven. But something about the tracks bothered him.

He stopped and dismounted. Raven and his three remaining companions had taken the extra horses with him. Then it struck Tal. One of the horses was missing! He moved quickly to make sure he was correct. Yes, he was looking at four horses' prints, not five. And only three sets of hoofmarks were deep enough to show they carried riders.

Someone had slipped off along the way.

Tal leapt back onto his horse just as an arrow skimmed past him. He lay himself along the neck of his mount and shouted, startling the animal forward. He let her run into the trees; then he turned and waited.

Whoever had shot at him hadn't followed. Tal sat quietly with his hand upon the horse's neck, trying to keep the tired and cranky mare calm. He waited.

Time slowed. It might be that whoever had shot at him hadn't stayed around to see if any real damage had been done, but had instead fled back down the trail to alert Raven. Or he might be in the trees on the other side of the road waiting to see if Tal emerged.

At last, Tal grew tired of waiting, so he slipped off his horse, tied her to a bush and headed off on a course which ran parallel to the road. He moved south and at the narrowest point he could find, dashed across the road, then turned north. If Raven's ambusher had fled south, he'd see signs of it; but if he was still waiting for Tal to show himself, he'd be ahead.

Tal dodged silently through the trees. He kept his ears and eyes open for any hint of an attacker's whereabouts.

Then the man coughed. Tal froze: the sound came from not more than a dozen yards ahead. Tal knew that a sneeze or cough had killed more than one man. He waited, listening for any other sound to betray the man's location.

Tal moved slowly, one foot lightly placed on the ground, shifting his weight before picking up the other foot. He wanted no disturbed leaves or cracked twigs to give away his presence.

Then a smell assailed his senses. The breeze blew from the northwest, coming through a pass in the mountains, and suddenly Tal could smell the man's stench. He hadn't bathed in weeks, and he must have been in the middle of all the smoke yesterday, for his scent was acrid.

Tal strove harder to listen and to look, and then he saw the man.

He was pressed up against a tree, keeping his body close to the bole, holding another arrow ready and his eyes scanning the trail anxiously for any sign of Tal. Tal assumed the man had been told not to return unless he brought Tal's head.

Tal targeted the man and moved in an arc, until he had a certain killing shot. Then he said softly, 'Put down your bow.'

The man froze. He didn't turn his body, but his head moved so that he could see Tal out of the corner of his eyes. He opened his hand and let the bow fall to the ground.

'Turn around, slowly,' said Tal.

He did so, until he was standing with his back to the tree. Tal aimed his arrow at the man's chest.

'Where's Raven?'

'South, maybe two miles, waiting for me to bring you in or for you to come riding into his next trap.'

'What's your name?'

'Killgore.'

'How long have you been with Raven?'

'Ten years.'

The bowstring twanged and suddenly the man named Killgore found himself pinned to the tree. His eyes went wide and he looked down a moment, then his head fell forward as his body went limp.

'Ten years means you were at my village, murderer,' Tal said quietly.

He left Killgore pinned to the tree and hurried back across the road to fetch his horse.

Now there were only three left, and Tal knew they were waiting for him two miles down the road.

Tal swore. It was a big meadow, and he understood instantly why Raven had chosen it. It was too large for Tal to hide in the trees and pick off anyone from cover.

Raven and his two remaining raiders sat their horses in the centre of the field, hands casually resting on the horns of their saddles, waiting.

Either their own man would ride into view, and they'd continue on south, or Tal would appear, and they'd have an end to the chase, one way or the other. Tal weighed his options. He could hide in the trees, until Raven gave up the wait and continued south, or went back north to see what had happened to Killgore. But he had only a bag full of berries and a skin of water, and he was extremely tired. He would only get weaker by waiting.

Raven was tired, too, no doubt, but he had two other swords with him.

Tal held the title of the world's finest swordsman, at least until the next tourney at the Masters' Court, but there were three of them, and they would be fighting from horseback. Tal had no illusions that they'd consent to dismount and meet him one at a time.

He took a deep breath. It was time to end this.

He picked up his short bow, put an arrow between his teeth and another in his bow-hand. Urging his mount forward with his legs and with one hand on the reins, Tal rode into view.

The three mercenaries saw him and without fuss drew their weapons. Tal felt a sudden rush of hope. None of them appeared to have a bow.

Thanking the gods that Rondar had been a good riding instructor, Tal shouted and brought his mount to a gallop. He rode straight at the three men, keeping his eye on Raven, who sat in the centre.

Raven didn't move, but his two companions did, spurring their mounts in a circling move, so that Tal would have to turn his back on someone. Tal released the reins, letting them fall across his horse's neck as he stood up in the saddle, gripping the horse hard with his knees.

He drew the first arrow and let fly. The rider on Tal's right ducked, as he had expected, so he had aimed low. The arrow struck him in the thigh, up near the hip joint. The man screamed as he fell from the saddle. It was not a killing wound, but he wouldn't be up fighting any time soon.

Tal used his leg pressure to veer away from Raven and the other man, while he nocked his second arrow. The rider who had circled to Tal's left was now right behind him, riding straight at his back.

Still standing high in the saddle, Tal twisted to his right and brought his mount around in a circle. He turned his body as far as he could until he was almost facing backwards. He could see the surprise in the second man's eyes as he let loose his arrow.

The man took the arrow right in the joint between his neck and shoulder, which was unprotected by his chainmail shirt. He came out of his saddle, rolling over backwards and dropping behind his horse. He was obviously dead before he struck the ground.

Raven charged.

He could not afford to give Tal the chance to reach around behind and draw another arrow, having seen what he was capable of and having no doubt he would die if he didn't close instantly.

Tal threw away his bow and drew his sword, turning to meet the charge at the last moment. Raven's horse slammed into Tal's and the mare almost fell. As it was, she stumbled sideways from the blow.

Tal reined her around hard, his sword slashing through the air at the point where he hoped Raven's head would be. He realized his error and tried to pull up. The effort was a moment too late; pain ripped across his left shoulder, as Raven's sword-point sliced through the skin, scraping across the shoulder bone.

Tal grimaced in pain but kept his wits about him. He urged his horse on, resisting the urge to clutch at his left shoulder with his right hand, instead bringing his sword overhead to block another blow from Raven.

Tal blinked away tears and forced the pain in his shoulder to fade, for it was clear that on horseback, Raven was the more practised swordsman. Still, bladework was bladework, and Tal knew he had never been in a more important fight.

Rondar had drilled into him how to control his horse with one or no hands, relying on his legs to instruct the animal, so he tried to make the horse an extension of his own body, and tried to think as if the horse's legs were his own.

He blocked out the pain in his left shoulder, although he knew that had Raven's blow been inches lower, he'd be a dead man. The wound would have severed tendons or even cut off the arm entirely, and the blood loss would have doomed him. As it was, the superficial cut was soaking his shirt with blood at the shoulder, but he would live if he could end this fight quickly.

Tal worked his horse around to keep Raven on his right, lest he risk further injury to his damaged arm. Raven attempted to use his horse to bully Tal's and perhaps throw its rider. He moved right in next to Tal and for the first time Tal saw his enemy up close for the first time since he had sacked Village Kulaam.

The once neatly-trimmed beard was now ragged and

unkempt, and the man's angular face was haggard and worn. Raven's skin had a grey complexion, and his dark, deep-set eyes were rimmed with red, with deep circles of darkness below.

Yet there was an iron will in his face that told Tal that Raven was as dangerous a man as he would ever meet. A man didn't rise to run as ruthless a company as Raven did without such a will. Tal knew he had to match that will with his own. It didn't matter if he stayed alive; Raven must die. He must atone for the wrong visited on Tal's people.

They circled and traded blows, steel ringing on steel, but neither man gained the advantage. Raven was more deft at moving his horse, but within striking range, Tal was the better swordsman.

For long minutes they rode around one another thus, trading blows and parries, with neither man gaining the upper hand. Raven tried three times to charge Tal, but both horses were on the verge of exhaustion and the third time, Raven retreated with a slash across his cheek. Blood flowed down the right side of his face, and now Tal saw something else. The determination in Raven's face was gone! He seemed suddenly to be a man fearful of dying.

Tal charged. He shouted at the top of his lungs, and rose up in his stirrups, slashing downward with all his strength. Raven's years of mounted swordplay served him well, for what Tal didn't expect was that instead of turning away, sword raised to take Tal's blow, Raven leaned forward, hanging by his left hand from the saddle, to slash at Tal's right leg.

Tal felt the pain as Raven's blade cut deep into his calf muscle, and the leg collapsed. His own momentum from the downward slash carried him headfirst off his horse.

Tal tucked his shoulder and tried to roll, but the impact

stunned him. His fatigued and frantic mount trotted away, leaving Tal lying unprotected on the ground. The mercenary captain turned his animal and urged it on for one more attack, intending to trample Tal underfoot.

Tal rolled, barely avoiding the animal's hooves, and felt Raven's sword pass over him, missing him by bare inches, for the mercenary captain had not leaned over far enough in order to deliver the death blow.

Tal levered himself upright, placing his weight on his uninjured left leg, and got ready to fight again. But instead of the expected attack, he saw Raven riding to the south.

The murderer had had enough, and was running away, his exhausted mount barely able to sustain a trot. Tal shouted for his mare; but she took no notice. She was too far away for him to get to with his injured leg. He needed to tend his injuries or he would faint from blood loss. He was already dizzy from the blow to his head sustained when falling from his horse.

Black frustration rose up and swept over him when he spied his bow and quiver only a few yards away. As fast as he could he hobbled over to where they lay and picked up the bow. He drew one arrow from the quiver, nocked the string, and pulled back. He judged the wind and elevation, and let fly.

He knew he would have just this one shot.

Raven never heard the arrow. He rode along, slightly hunched over the animal's neck.

Then the arrow struck. It slammed into Raven's back, between the shoulder blades, punching through the leather armour he wore.

Tal saw him go limp and drop from the horse. It was such a boneless fall that Tal had no need to walk over to the body to know that Raven was, at last, dead.

Tal's leg collapsed. He felt as if all will and strength had been drained out of him. His horse was unconcernedly cropping the grass a hundred yards away. In a minute, he would try to get her. First, he must rest a little. Just sit and catch his breath. Then he'd deal with his leg and shoulder.

His last thought before he fainted was that was the best shot he'd ever made.

He awoke to the smell of food and coffee. He was lying under blankets next to a wagon. Someone had bound his shoulder and leg. It was night.

'Coffee?'

Tal turned his head to see John Creed sitting next to a fire, while half a dozen men from his company were gathered around a larger campfire a few yards away.

Tal used his uninjured arm to lever himself up. He leaned back against the wagon's wheel. 'Thanks,' he said.

Creed handed him an earthenware cup and while Tal sipped the bitter brew, said, 'Good thing we happened along. You damn near bled to death.'

'How'd you find me?'

Creed laughed. 'It wasn't hard.' He handed Tal a still-warm cut of meat wrapped in trail bread and Tal discovered that he was ravenous. He bolted the food down, while Creed continued. 'You littered your trail with corpses.' He pointed north. 'We left the village at daybreak, maybe seven hours after you took out after Raven.' He scratched his chin. 'Fact is, I figured you for a corpse yourself, but you did well, Tal Hawkins. When I saw the first body, me and a couple of the lads hurried on ahead, to see if you needed a hand. You didn't.' He chuckled again. 'You most certainly didn't.

'Too bad you couldn't see the expression on Raven's face when I rolled him over. He died very surprised.' Creed chuckled. 'Your arrow was sticking through him, and he had his chin down like he was looking to see what just popped through his chest. Bastard never had enough of a sense of humour, if you ask me.' He stood up and pointed some distance away. 'We found you over there, just about done in. I patched you up and the wagon and the rest of the boys got here two hours ago. You can ride in the wagon until we get to Coastal Watch. That leg is nasty, but if you can keep it from getting infected you'll be fine.'

Tal chewed his last mouthful of food and asked, 'Where's the other wagon?'

'I left it at the village. We didn't need two, and I didn't think you'd mind giving it to the Orodon.'

'No, I don't.'

'They're singing some songs about you around the fires, Tal. You're a damned hero to those folks.'

Tal didn't know what to say. He thought about his own people and wondered what his life would be like had a band of men like his mercenaries ridden to Village Kulaam ten days before Raven's band and the men of Olasko had turned up. He sat back and closed his eyes. 'I'm no hero. I just had to take care of some business.'

'Well, that you did,' said Creed.

'Thanks for taking care of me, John.'

'You've the makings of a fine captain, Tal. If you need men, you'll have no trouble getting them. You're fair, take care of things, and you pay better than most.'

'If I ever need a strong right hand, John Creed, you'll be the first I call.' Tal put down the cup and settled back. Sleep was coming again, he knew: his body needed rest to heal.

'You call, and I'll come,' said the mercenary with a grin. Then, looking off into the night, he asked, 'What next?'

Tal gazed at the stars above. 'Some rest. Then more business.'

'Well,' said Creed. 'Business can wait at least for a few days. Rest while you can, I always say.'

Tal settled back in the blankets and felt sleep rising up to claim him. He thought about his family and hoped they knew some peace now.

Then he thought about the Duke of Olasko and his Captain, Quentin Havrevulen. Those two must also join Raven in death before Talon's family could truly rest. And it was with those unpleasant thoughts that Talon of the Silver Hawk fell into a deep, exhausted sleep.

• EPILOGUE •

Scorpion

*T*AL SIPPED HIS WINE.

Nakor said, 'What you did was effective, but limited.'

'Not for the Orodon,' said Tal.

He was sitting in Pug's study on Sorcerer's Isle. Magnus, Caleb and Robert sat around a table. A merry fire burned in the hearth. Pug and Miranda were absent, away on some mysterious errand, according to Nakor.

Tal had made his way to Coastal Watch, where he had purchased passage on a ship to Salador. There he had located some old acquaintances from his time there with Caleb, and had sent word to Magnus that he had finished his business in the north.

Magnus had appeared and taken Tal to the island, using his arts as he had the first time he had transported the young boy from Kendrick's to Pug's estates. Tal had wished more than once for that knack: he was sick of horses, ships and coaches.

He had been back on the island for a day and already the events of the previous month seemed a distant memory. His wounds had healed, though there was stiffness in his shoulder and leg, but the healers on the island assured him there would be no permanent damage, just two impressive scars to add to his collection.

Nakor said, 'You acquitted yourself well, Talon.'

'Tal, please,' he replied. 'I've grown used to thinking of myself as Tal Hawkins.'

'Tal, then,' said Nakor.

'Your defence of the Orodon village was pretty effective, for someone with no formal military training,' said Magnus. 'You made do with the best at hand, though I admit I wasn't entirely certain why you burned those catapults.'

Tal sat up. 'I never mentioned that.'

Magnus smiled slightly. 'No, you didn't. I watched you.'

'Where?'

'At Village Queala, from a nearby hillside.'

'You were there!' Tal leaned forward in his chair. 'You were there and did nothing to help?' His tone was accusatory.

Caleb said, 'He couldn't, Tal.'

'There is much you still do not know,' Nakor added. 'But this much you should be able to understand. The magician we spoke of – Leso Varen – must remain ignorant of our part in the things you are doing. If a magician of Magnus's power had appeared and destroyed Raven, it would come to his attention immediately. You would never have been free of that connection in Leso Varen's mind.'

Tal nodded. 'I don't like it, but I understand.'

'Which brings us back to the question, now, what next?' Nakor said.

'Unless you have something else you require of me, I must decide what to do about Kaspar of Olasko.'

'There is no decision to be made,' Nakor declared. 'You must take service with him.'

Tal's eyes opened wide. 'I cannot!'

'Why not?' asked Caleb. 'Mother already has her "Lady Rowena" in his service. More than one agent is good.'

'I cannot be false to an oath, so I cannot take any oath I will be unable to embrace.'

Nakor said, 'That is as it must be.'

'I cannot serve a man like Kaspar, even if you have some plan you think would keep me from being detected by his magician when I lie. For I will not lie and make false oath,' Tal continued angrily.

'No,' said Nakor. 'You misunderstand me. When I said it is as it must be, I mean you must not make a false oath. You must make an oath with all your heart, and serve Kaspar as needed, even at the risk of your life. If you are ordered to hunt one of us down and kill us, you must endeavour to do so with all your heart and if needs be, to kill one of us.'

Tal frowned. 'You want me to take wholehearted service with our enemies?' He was utterly bemused.

'Yes,' said Nakor, 'for only that way can you get close enough to Kaspar to kill him when the time is right.'

Tal sat back. 'I don't understand. How can I serve him without foreswearing my oath and still plan to kill him?'

'Your oath holds just so long as Kaspar holds his oath sacred,' Nakor said.

'Ah,' said Tal, smiling a little now. '"It is the responsibility of the master to honour his part in fealty as much as it is the servant's."'

Nakor said, 'Have you heard the parable of the scorpion?'

'No.'

'Once a scorpion sat upon the bank of a river which was too deep and swift for him to traverse. A frog swam by and the scorpion called out, "Frog, carry me upon your back to the other shore!"

'The frog replied, "I will not, for you will sting me and I will die."

'The scorpion said to the frog, "But why would I do that? For if I were to do that, I would drown."

'The frog considered this argument, and at last said, "Very well. I shall carry you across the river."

'So the frog came to the shore and took the scorpion upon his back and halfway across the river, the scorpion stung the frog.

'With his dying breath, the frog cried out, "Why have you done this? For now we will both die!"

'And with his dying breath, the scorpion said, "Because it is my nature."'

Nakor looked at Talon. 'Eventually, should you live long enough, Kaspar of Olasko will betray you, Tal. It is his nature. And when he does, you will be free of your oath and then you may kill him.'

Tal sat back, uncertain of what to say. For a long, long time he reflected on what Nakor had said. Then, he took a deep breath and nodded.

'I will go to Opardum. I will serve the Duke of Olasko.'